Melancholy Experience in Literature of the Long Eighteenth Century

Melancholy Experience in Literature of the Long Eighteenth Century

Before Depression, 1660–1800

By Allan Ingram, Stuart Sim, Clark Lawlor,
Richard Terry, John Baker, Leigh Wetherall-Dickson

First published 2011 by
PALGRAVE MACMILLAN

Palgrave Macmillan in the UK is an imprint of Macmillan Publishers Limited,
registered in England, company number 785998, of Houndmills, Basingstoke,
Hampshire RG21 6XS.

Palgrave Macmillan in the US is a division of St Martin's Press LLC,
175 Fifth Avenue, New York, NY 10010.

Palgrave Macmillan is the global academic imprint of the above companies
and has companies and representatives throughout the world.

Palgrave® and Macmillan® are registered trademarks in the United States,
the United Kingdom, Europe and other countries.

ISBN 978–0–230–24631–7 hardback

This book is printed on paper suitable for recycling and made from fully
managed and sustained forest sources. Logging, pulping and manufacturing
processes are expected to conform to the environmental regulations of the
country of origin.

A catalogue record for this book is available from the British Library.

Library of Congress Cataloging-in-Publication Data
Melancholy experience in literature of the long eighteenth century :
    before depression, 1660–1800 / by Allan Ingram ... [et al.].
        p. cm.
Includes index.
ISBN 978–0–230–24631–7 (hardback)
    1. English literature—18th century—History and criticism.
    2. English literature—Early modern, 1500–1700—History and criticism.
    3. Melancholy in literature. 4. Depression, Mental, in literature.
    5. Mental illness in literature. 6. Depression, Mental—History—18th
century. 7. Depression, Mental—History—17th century. I. Ingram,
Allan. II. Title.
PR448.M44M45 2011
820.9'005—dc22   2011004139

10   9   8   7   6   5   4   3   2   1
20 19 18 17 16 15 14 13 12 11

Printed and bound in Great Britain by
CPI Antony Rowe, Chippenham and Eastbourne

Contents

Acknowledgements

We gratefully acknowledge the support of the Leverhulme Trust for its funding of the research project, 'Before Depression, 1660–1800', between 2006 and 2009. This enabled us to mount an ambitious programme of activities and to prepare a series of academic publications, of which this is one. Our website, <www.beforedepression.com>, gives further details.

We are also grateful to the School of Arts & Social Sciences at the University of Northumbria for resources and encouragement in many aspects of the project. In addition, we should like to thank all those who participated in the various 'Before Depression' events, including lecturers, conference participants and members of the public, and who thereby made it a richer and more rewarding experience for all of us. Several individuals gave generously of their help with the present volume: Diane Buie, Hélène Dachez, Michelle Faubert, Charlotte Holden, Pauline Morris and Palgrave's unnamed reader, who provided detailed and positive suggestions: to all, our thanks and appreciation.

All authors' royalties for this volume are being donated to MIND.

Authors' Biographies

John Baker is Maître de conférences (Senior Lecturer) in English at the Université Paris 1 Panthéon-Sorbonne. He has published in French and English on themes associated with the writings of Edward Young and the *Night Thoughts*, and more generally on poetry of the eighteenth century. His interests include eighteenth-century critical theory and the history of ideas, and he is currently working on a study of 'philosophical' poems of the early eighteenth century. He has also written on twentieth-century French literature, in particular on Georges Bataille.

Allan Ingram is Professor of English at the University of Northumbria. He has published widely in the field of eighteenth-century studies and particularly on literature and madness. His main works include monographs on James Boswell, on Swift and Pope, and on madness and writing, as well as two edited collections of source material, *Voices of Madness* (Sutton, 1997) and *Patterns of Madness in the Eighteenth Century* (Liverpool University Press, 1998). His most recent book is *Cultural Constructions of Madness in Eighteenth-Century Writing* (Palgrave, now Palgrave Macmillan, 2005, with Michelle Faubert). He was Director of the Leverhulme Trust 'Before Depression' project. He is co-general editor and volume co-editor for the forthcoming *Depression and Melancholy 1660–1800* set (Pickering and Chatto, 2012).

Clark Lawlor is Reader in English Literature at the University of Northumbria, and has published many works on literature and medicine – including *Consumption and Literature: The Making of the Romantic Disease* (Palgrave, now Palgrave Macmillan, 2006), which was shortlisted for the European Society for the Study of English book prize 2006–08. At present he is writing *Depression: The Biography* (Oxford University Press, 2011).

Stuart Sim retired as Professor of Critical Theory at the University of Sunderland in 2008, and is now Visiting Professor of Critical Theory and Long Eighteenth-Century English Literature in the Department of Humanities, University of Northumbria. He has published widely in his two main subject areas, and among his recent books are *The Eighteenth-Century Novel and Contemporary Social Issues* (Edinburgh University Press, 2008) and *The End of Modernity: What the Financial and Environmental Crisis Is Really Telling Us* (Edinburgh University Press, 2010). A co-editor and founder-member of the journal *Bunyan Studies* (1988–), he was elected a Fellow of the English Association in 2002.

Richard Terry is Professor of Eighteenth-Century English Literature at Northumbria University, having worked for many years at the University of Sunderland. He has published extensively on eighteenth-century poetry and on mock-heroic as a literary device and form, and is the author of *Poetry and the Making of the English Literary Past 1660–1781* (Oxford University Press, 2001). His most recent book is *The Plagiarism Allegation in English Literature from Butler to Sterne* (Palgrave Macmillan, 2010).

Leigh Wetherall-Dickson is Senior Lecturer in Eighteenth- and Nineteenth-Century English Literature at Northumbria University, and began her career there as a post-doctoral Research Associate on the Leverhulme-funded 'Before Depression 1660–1800' project. She has previously published on the life of Lady Caroline Lamb, with particular focus upon Lamb's historical reputation for madness, and was the co-editor of *The Works of Lady Caroline Lamb* (Pickering and Chatto, 2009). She is currently involved as co-general editor and volume editor for the forthcoming *Depression and Melancholy 1660–1800* set (Pickering and Chatto, 2012).

Introduction: Depression before Depression

Allan Ingram and Stuart Sim

'Before Depression 1660–1800'

There are many definitions of depression, from the simple statement of lowness of spirits of the standard dictionary to the clinical symptoms of the medical compendium and the changes in linguistic emphasis and usage of the historical dictionary. Perhaps the most telling definition, though, is actually a description, a bald account (and all the more powerful because of its baldness) of what it is like to experience depression. This is Kay Redfield Jamison, from her book *An Unquiet Mind*:

> Depression is awful beyond words or sounds or images...It bleeds relationships through suspicion, lack of confidence and self-respect, the inability to enjoy life, to walk or talk or think normally, the exhaustion, the night terrors, the day terrors. There is nothing good to be said for it except that it gives you the experience of how it must be to be old, to be old and sick, to be dying; to be slow of mind; to be lacking in grace, polish, and co-ordination; to be ugly; to have no belief in the possibilities of life, the pleasures of sex, the exquisiteness of music, or the ability to make yourself or others laugh...
>
> Depression...is flat, hollow, and unendurable. It is also tiresome. People cannot abide being around you when you are depressed. They might think that they ought to, and they might even try, but you know and they know that you are tedious beyond belief: you're irritable and paranoid and humorless and lifeless and critical and demanding and no reassurance is ever enough. You're frightened, and you're frightening, and you're "not at all like yourself but will be soon," but you know you won't.[1]

Jamison is not concerned with definitions (though in her professional role as a professor of psychiatry she undoubtedly is). Definitions pale to irrelevance when confronted with the actuality of what it is like to be depressed. Nor is she interested in its pre-history, how modern depression, for example, maps onto the understanding and experience of its equivalent, or roughly equivalent, states in previous periods. Other writers, Jennifer Radden for one,[2] explore that overlap, and the present volume is partly focused on that question of continuity and discontinuity. More emphatically, though, we share Jamison's implied view that the experience of depression is what counts, and therefore those conditions, social, cultural, religious and scientific, that encroach on the experience in different periods of our history, and for us most notably the long eighteenth century, are demanding of attention insofar as they help to shape how depression is suffered and survived, how it is treated, or engaged with, or indeed stigmatized, and how people's views of it are expressed.

Depression, of course, is a universally recognized phenomenon in our day and a range of treatments have been devised for it, from counselling and psychoanalysis through to medication of various types. Studies suggest that most people experience periods of depression at least some time in their lives, and that a significant number of the population qualify as clinically depressed. The more severe cases of clinical depression, often thought to be the product of a chemical imbalance in the brain, can involve taking medication for very long periods, sometimes indefinitely. Debates still rage about the causes of depression, and dealing with it as a cultural phenomenon has turned into something of an industry in recent times (the antidepressant market is large, highly profitable and very influential among the medical profession), but it was not until the nineteenth century that it was classified as a condition in its own right. This generates the question: what was depression like before depression existed as a standardized medical concept with a recognizable cluster of symptoms? It was just such a question that prompted the formation of the three-year research project entitled 'Before Depression: The English Malady, 1660–1800' by an academic team drawn from the universities of Northumbria and Sunderland, funded by a grant from the Leverhulme Trust. The team took it as their brief to investigate what the experience of depression was over this period, and how it was represented in both the arts and society at large in an era when the medical profession was only just beginning to emerge in its modern form. The book that follows is a record of their collective researches into the topic, designed to outline the world of depression before depression, and to discover what we can learn from our predecessors in coping with its various manifestations.

It was not as if the period had no understanding of the condition at all, just that they described it, and explained it, in different ways to our modern conception – sometimes as spleen, melancholy or the vapours, for example. Perhaps the closest they came to us was in their recognition of the widespread existence of the state of melancholy, which becomes a recurrent figure in the arts of the time. Painters such as George Romney evoked a sense of melancholy in their pictures; the 'Graveyard Poets', such as Edward Young, caught the same atmosphere in their work; Laurence Sterne communicated a powerful sense of melancholy through the adventures and misadventures of his hero Tristram Shandy in one of the eighteenth century's most celebrated novels. Melancholy becomes one of the primary ways of defining what to us would usually count as depression. It is not a perfect match, however, since melancholy can range from being a relatively pleasing state – as when responding to sunsets, the passage of the seasons or the transience of individual exis-tence (sensations so well captured in the novels of Ann Radcliffe) – to something far more debilitating, and even personally incapacitating, as with Samuel Johnson's 'black dog'.[3] When it is the last experience then we are in the presence of what we would now call clinical depression, and we would know how to go about treating it – although it has to be acknowledged that treatment is not always entirely successful. In the eighteenth century, however, treatment, where it was available at all, was much more hit and miss (and in the early part of the period more religiously than medically based), and the individual was all too often thrown back on his or her own devices in learning how to live with the condition. How these varying states were talked and written about, how they were portrayed in the realm of the arts, how medical practi-tioners dealt with a spectrum of responses running from mild sadness to crushing existential despair, all of these set the agenda for the Before Depression project team.

Cultural inheritance

No age comes to its illnesses, either physical or psychological, with a clean sheet, and both the medical and cultural inheritances for eighteenth-century melancholy were dauntingly large and perplexingly varied. While physicians, medical theorists and mad-doctors disagreed with regard to understanding and practice, the cultural predecessors were less obviously in open disagreement but far more conspicuously interested in different sets of aspects of the condition, both the condi-tion as it was felt and experienced and the concept as it was fashioned and cultivated as a set of significations, and as a pose.

Among the most significant writers were Shakespeare, Milton and Cervantes, with inherited models like Hamlet, Jacques from *As You Like It*, Don Quixote and Il Penseroso remaining popular and persuasive forces throughout the period. Burton's *Anatomy of Melancholy*, while a key text for Samuel Johnson, had lost much of its popularity by the eighteenth century, and, among visual representations, Albrecht Dürer's enigmatic key to melancholy, *Melencolia I*, was also less well known than during the previous period. Many of these works still clarify for us just what it might have meant to have been an eighteenth-century melancholiac and help to bring out some of the associations and forms that by then had attached themselves to the condition.

One text, to begin with, less often thought of as a repository of melancholy, was Ben Jonson's *Every Man In His Humour*, particularly the revised and 'anglicized' version of 1601, which moves the plot from Florence to London and renames all of the characters. (This, in fact, was one of the most performed comedies during the middle years, at least, of the eighteenth century at the patent theatres in London.)[4] The significance of Jonson's play, with regard to melancholy, is its portrayal of the two 'gulls', Stephen, the country gull, and Matthew, the town gull. 'My name is master Stephen, sir,' declares the former on being first introduced to the latter:

I am this gentleman's own cousin, sir; his father is mine uncle, sir: I am somewhat melancholy, but you shall command me, sir, in whatsoever is incident to a gentleman.

To which Matthew replies in kind:

Oh it's your only fine humour, sir: your true melancholy breeds your perfect fine wit, sir. I am melancholy myself, divers times, sir, and then do I no more but take pen and paper, presently, and overflow you half a score, or a dozen of sonnets at a sitting.

'[M]ake use of my study', invites Matthew, 'it's at your service': 'I thank you sir,' says Stephen, 'I shall be bold I warrant you; have you a stool there to be melancholy upon?' Jonson has Matthew reply:

That I have, sir, and some papers there of mine own doing, at idle hours, that you'll say there's some sparks of wit in 'em, when you see them.[5]

Here, shared between the country gull and the city gull, are several of the leading characteristics of Renaissance, and what was to become eighteenth-century, melancholy: it seeks solitude; it betokens refinement; it has a natural affinity with poetic form, especially of the personal, contained and reflective kind; and it is associated with a certain kind of 'wit', not, of course, with comic or satiric wit, but with the wit that finds satisfaction in the coming together of thought, mood and language. It is a humour, moreover, that, while essentially solitary, nevertheless takes itself with a degree of pride, even of complacency, so much so that even while alone it would rather like to be on view, in consequence of which it has a tendency to become itself the viewer, applauding in secret the supposed incapacity that keeps it apart: 'it's your only fine humour'. It follows that when two 'melancholiacs' come together the mutual admiration is intolerable. On top of this, though, melancholy, apparently, is the sole preserve of neither city nor country: Boswell and Johnson, independently, might have associated gloomy moods with country living ('a Hypochondriac proprietor is sick and sick again with ennui,' writes Boswell of plantations, 'and is tempted with wild wishes to hang himself on one of his own trees long before they are able to bear his weight'),[6] and the city with life, culture and enjoyment, but for Ben Jonson Matthew and Stephen are not in opposition but are strictly complementary. Folly and the capacity to ape what is considered fashionable do not stop at the city limits.

For Jonson, then, at least in this instance, melancholy is highly capable of being an affectation, its characteristics genuine enough, but of a kind that makes the condition in many ways seem a desirable one. Not least among these is the appeal of a dignified, gloomy aloofness, a stance that was to come into its own with the creation of the Byronic hero two centuries later, and also of melancholy's supposed association with creativity: 'half a score, or a dozen sonnets at a sitting'. Jonson's attitude to this affected creativity is made clear by having Stephen ask for 'a stool', with its secondary meaning of a privy or commode, 'to be melancholy upon', and Matthew's offering him the use of the 'papers' there, the product of his own 'idle hours'. The line that goes to Swift and Pope and their inheritors in which false wit and faeces are inseparably linked also, at this stage, has the affectation of melancholy as an essential ingredient in the mix.

Above all, melancholy and would-be melancholiacs emerge from Jonson's play as fit subjects for mockery. We are not, in *Every Man In His Humour*, asked to take melancholy seriously, still less to sympathise or engage with it. What is serious in the analysis offered by the play is the abiding gullibility of folly and the damage done to selves and society, decency and taste, by foolish aspirants to what they see as the appeal of the melancholy humour. Melancholy, especially false melancholy, equals mockery, and this line, too, comes through to the eighteenth century, not least in Pope's 'Cave of Spleen' canto in *Rape of the Lock*, where 'Spleen' is discovered sighing 'for ever on her pensive Bed, Pain at her Side, and Megrim at her Head', along with 'Affectation', who 'sinks with becoming Woe' on her 'rich Quilt', 'Wrapt in a Gown, for Sickness, and for Show'.[7] Mockery remains a powerful response to melancholy, or to would-be melancholics, throughout the period, with Swift, Gay, Hogarth, Fielding, Sheridan and Gillray, among others, ready to adapt the tradition to their own needs.

Every Man gives a clear set of signals: there are some very specific characteristics of melancholy that are seen as fashionable and are therefore liable to be aped by foolish people. Like all folly, such affectation must be laughed out of court and that is the job of comedy. *Hamlet*, however, as a tragedy, albeit with comic elements, not least within the character of Hamlet himself, sets a very different agenda and presents yet another series of faces of melancholy, and these too are of major influence when we reach the eighteenth century. Whatever Hamlet is or is not (and he is capable of being many things to most people), he is above all preoccupied, and his preoccupations define a very clear cycle of issues to be melancholy about: the self, especially the adolescent self, family, sex and love, death, the nature of the universe and universal justice, friendship, betrayal, religion and suicide. When Boswell, already in his fifties, writes in his journal, 'Afternoon read a good part of *Hamlet,* to interest me in a melancholy character',[8] he is not only giving testimony to the enduring appeal of Shakespeare's portrayal of young male angst but also making clear the extent to which Hamlet's circles of self-absorption had helped to define the critical issues of eighteenth-century melancholy. If *Every Man In His Humour* gave the surfaces of the melancholic state, and found them to be comic, then *Hamlet* is a dramatization of the melancholy mind from within, and it is potentially tragic.

'Seems madam? Nay, it is. I know not "seems" ', declares Hamlet to Gertrude's apparently innocent question in Act I scene ii:

'Tis not alone my inky cloak, good mother,
Nor customary suits of solemn black,
Nor windy suspiration of forc'd breath,
No, nor the fruitful river in the eye,
Nor the dejected haviour of the visage,

> Together with all forms, moods, shapes of grief,
> That can denote me truly. These indeed seem,
> For they are actions that a man might play;
> But I have that within which passes show,
> These but the trappings and the suits of woe.[9]

Surfaces, in *Hamlet*, are nothing to go by: they lie and mislead and stand in for hidden truths. In order to 'denote . . . truly' one must give voice to 'that within' and specifically, here, to the 'grief' within. But giving voice to that which is beyond 'seems' is far from straightforward, for denoting what truly 'is', especially when what 'is' is scarcely accessible to the mind that 'is' it, in fact constitutes almost the whole play, certainly that large portion of it that is occupied by the voice of Hamlet himself. So much, indeed, of the drama is to do with bringing out the inner voice, whether Hamlet is in riddling conversation with those about him or, more eloquently, in soliloquy concerning life, its meanings and its endings, that, paradoxically, the play also becomes an extended expression of inarticulacy. It becomes an exploration of the insuperable inadequacy of language, even language in its most engagedly poetic form, to bring out the truth of what 'is'. Some things simply cannot be stated, but are, rather, condemned to be restated time after time in a perpetual spiral of irresolution.

One of *Hamlet*'s major preoccupations is, in fact, human life, its potentials and capacities, and at the same time its crippling limitations – cause both for celebration and, here, for despair.

> What a piece of work is a man, how noble in reason, how infinite in faculties, in form and moving how express and admirable, in action how like an angel, in apprehension how like a god: the beauty of the world, the paragon of animals—and yet to me, what is this quintessence of dust?[10]

Man, with all his advantages, is crippled – by time, by flesh, by motivation, by death, and by uncertainty. The human mind would be capable of anything were it not for thinking. Even suicide, in Hamlet's analysis, would constitute an achievement within man's grasp were it not for the imagined consequences, those 'dreams' that 'may come' after the irrevocable deed. So we 'rather bear those ills we have / Than fly to others that we know not of'.[11] We compromise, and in so doing we sum up, over and over again, the pitiful shortcomings of our condition.

Here is mankind, and it is the dominant tragic condition that is inherited by the eighteenth century. We are as trapped by our possibilities as by our limitations, by our articulacy as by our lack of expression. We see the stars and have a sense of where we belong, as Pope so strongly asserts in the *Essay on Man*, but insist on remaining preoccupied with self, with meaning, with guilt. We spend for ever talking and thinking around the same cycles of worry and self-doubt without really saying anything, and certainly never reaching conclusion or capturing in words the essence of what is in perpetual motion within us. Even the act of ending it all, which might represent some resolution and therefore some meaning, is hampered by fear and uncertainty, and we therefore go on thinking, fretting, dreaming. Even language itself proves a false friend, offering explanation and analysis, delivering instead grammatical evasion and circumlocution. There is no way out, the very essence of the Shakespearean tragic situation. Or, as Pope was to put it in quite another context, 'On ev'ry side you look, behold the Wall!'[12]

Bernard Mandeville published his A *Treatise of the Hypochondriack and Hysterick Diseases* in 1730, with many of the details of Misomedon, his 'hypochondriack' speaker (the work is in the form of three dialogues), based upon his own case. At one point, in the first dialogue, Misomedon enlarges upon some of the characteristics of his mental state, especially as he advances, after some years, into the fullness of his condition. In doing so, he also indicates the extent to which another aspect of Hamlet's character finds its way into the eighteenth-century perception of melancholy, albeit with the extra physical edge that hypochondria brings: his paranoia. 'When I am at the best,' says Misomedon,

> I can feel that the long habit of my Illness has chang'd my very Humour: Formerly I fear'd nothing, and had the Constancy of a Man ... but now I am full of Doubts and fears ... I am grown peevish and fretful, irresolute, suspicious, every thing offends me, and a Trifle puts me in a Passion ... I can excruciate my self for all manner of Evils, past, present, and to come.[13]

And he gives an 'Instance' of 'how unaccountably I am afflicted by mere Thoughts, and sometimes work'd upon even by non entia (Things that have no existence)':

> I believe my Wife is a very honest Woman, nor have I ever had the least Reason to think the Contrary; and as to my self, I never lay

with any other besides her self since I had her. I have been married almost Thirty Years... Yet it is no longer ago than last Winter, that I could not be persuaded, but that I was Pox'd to all intents and purposes, and... for a considerable time I was all Day long examining my Shins, and Forehead, and feeling for Nodes and Tophi (Swellings on the Shins occasioned by the Pox).

This unshakeable conviction, produced, as he says, by something that has no existence, leads to a spiral of thought, apprehension and despair every bit as anguishing and disabling as Hamlet's, and as liable to endless repetition without hope of resolution:

The losing of my Nose, my Palate, my Eyes, and all the frightful and shameful Consequences of that Disease possess'd my Fancy for hours together, till the Horror of them entring deeper into my Soul, sometimes struck me with such unspeakable Pangs of Grief, as no Torture, or Death could ever be able to give the like.

And finally he draws the general conclusion: 'I have', he says,

read and heard of Hundreds of Melancholy People, that had as many several Whimsies, and imagining themselves to be what they were not, stuck close to the Absurdities of their Fancies, when they were well in every thing else, or at least in tolerable Health. But I was never so bad as that... I have always short Moments, in which, when my Soul exerts her self to the utmost of her power, I can judge of things as they really are.[14]

Mandeville, of course, is writing within a medical tradition before a literary and cultural one, and Hamlet is unlikely to be in his mind here. The inheritance, of which Hamlet is a supreme example, is clear, however. Among the features of the melancholy mind is the tendency to imagine the worst in any given situation, to build, perhaps, upon trifles – fancies, the merest suggestions, or even, we could say, ghosts – and to become so obsessed that only an 'utmost' exertion of the 'Soul' can return the mind to 'things as they really are'.

   Error, in the obsessive sense in which Mandeville is describing it, is not so obviously a feature of Hamlet's state of mind – there has, after all, been a murder, and Hamlet is, in fact, himself the intended victim of an assassination plot. Nevertheless, Hamlet is manifestly subject to the fears, frets and despairs that Misomedon experiences with all their implications for the state of mankind and his position within a meaningful, or meaningless, universe. One further influential text, however, in which error is the supreme characteristic of a melancholy character, is *Don Quixote*. And here again, we encounter melancholy with a difference, another set of pieces to fit into the eighteenth-century inheritance. Translated by Thomas Shelton shortly after its publication in 1605 (part two appeared in 1615), and then by Charles Jervas in 1742 and by Smollett in 1755, the book remained immensely popular throughout the period, and the Don himself a figure treated with affection and taken by a series of writers and artists as an archetype of the melancholy man.

If, in *Hamlet*, surfaces are scorned as a sequence of seemings, while the depths that Hamlet would inhabit turn out themselves to be equally incapable of truthful articulation, indeed, as themselves yet more surfaces, in *Don Quixote* surfaces are accepted at their face value. The Don, however, perpetually misreads those surfaces, interpreting them through the prism of his delusion, and so writes in the wrong depths, the wrong meanings, to everything he encounters. It is Foucault who says of the madman that 'he imprisons himself in the circle of an erroneous consciousness',[15] and for eighteenth-century readers Don Quixote was the exemplification of error, yet one that brought out not so much mockery or censure but rather the poignancy of human endeavour engaged in the furtherance of a hopeless cause, and striving not to know it: 'the malicious wretch who persecutes me, envying the glory I should have gained in this battle, hath doubtless metamorphosed the squadrons of the foe, into flocks of sheep'.[16] At the height of his madness, with the Don convinced not only that he is a knight-errant but also that he is still being held under a spell by an enchanter, Cervantes has the canon, 'moved by compassion', question him:

Is it possible, good sir, that the idle and unlucky reading of books of chivalry, can have so far impaired your judgment, as that you should now believe yourself inchanted, and give credit to other illusions of the same kind, which are as far from being true as truth is distant from falsehood? Is it possible that the human understanding can suppose that ever this world produced that infinite number of Amadises, with the whole crowd of famous knights, so many Emperors of Trebisond? ... Go to, Signor Don Quixote, have pity upon yourself; return into the bosom of discretion, and put those happy talents which Heaven hath been pleased to bestow upon you, to a better use; employing your genius in other studies, which may redound to the increase of your honour, as well as to the good of your soul.

To which Don Quixote replies:

> Why, then … in my opinion, the person impaired in his judgment, and inchanted, is no other than your worship, who have presumed to utter such blasphemies against an order so well received in the world, and established as truth, that he who like you denies it, deserves the same punishment you inflicted upon those books that gave you disgust; for, to say that there never was such a person as Amadis, or any other of those adventurous knights, with whom history abounds, is like an endeavour to persuade people, that frost is not cold, that the sun yields no light, and the earth no sustenance.[17]

Two characters holding incompatible world-views, both resolute in their conviction, each certain that the other must be insane, but one of them moved not by the urge to condemn but by compassion.

When James Boswell, in *The Hypochondriack* paper for December 1780, writes, of the hypochondriac, 'Though his reason be entire enough, and he knows that his mind is sick, his gloomy imagination is so powerful that he cannot disentangle himself from its influence, and he is in effect persuaded that its hideous representations of life are true',[18] he is pointing to the distressing presence within the individual mind of the debate that is played out in the conversation between Don Quixote and the canon. There are two incompatible world-views, and it is the fate of the hypochondriac, or the melancholy man, or indeed the manic depressive or the bipolar individual, to spend his days veering between one and the other, never able to predict or control when the sunny uplands will suddenly be transformed into the slough of despond. When Don Quixote surrenders himself at the beginning of the novel to the vision that has so captivated his imagination, that he is a knight errant destined to renew the age of chivalry, he enters actual madness, as the canon says, as much as if the Boswellian hypochondriac were to embrace for ever the persuasion 'that its hideous representations of life are true', even to the final desperate logic of taking his own life, seeing no other way out. When Don Quixote proudly adopts the name that Sancho Panza has wryly given him, 'The Knight of the rueful Countenance',[19] he is sealing that madness with the stamp of melancholy.

Ironically, it is at the most poignant episode of the novel, the death of the Don, that the issues of madness and sanity, melancholy and despondency, come into clearest relation. Feeling himself to be dying after a severe fever, Don Quixote, now back at home, calls his household and his friends, the local officials, about him to make his will:

> I feel myself... at the point of death; and I would not undergo that great change, in such a manner, as to entail the imputation of madness on my memory; for, though I have acted as a madman, I should not wish to confirm the character, by my behaviour in the last moments of my life... Good gentlemen... congratulate and rejoice with me, upon my being no longer Don Quixote de la Mancha, but plain Alonso Quixano, surnamed the Good, on account of the innocence of my life and conversation... now, are all the profane histories of knight-errantry odious to my reflection; now, I am sensible of my own madness, and the danger into which I have been precipitated by reading such absurdities, which I, from dear-bought experience, abominate and abhor.

The irony is that the priest, the Bachelor and the barber take his words as a new form of delusion:

> Now, signor Don Quixote, when we have received the news of my Lady Dulcinea's being disenchanted, do you talk at this rate? when we are on the point of becoming shepherds, that we may pass away our time happily in singing, like so many princes, has your worship taken the resolution to turn hermit? no more of that, I beseech you; recollect your spirits, and leave off talking such idle stories.

Taking the line of humouring their melancholy mad friend, they misinterpret his regained sanity, and call upon him to return to the deranged senses that they have conspired to call normal. It is Don Quixote who demonstrates, at last, his grip on reality by taking control of the situation: 'Gentlemen, I feel myself hastening to the goal of life; and therefore, jesting apart, let me have the benefit of a ghostly confessor, and send for a notary to write my will; for, in such extremities, a man must not trifle with his own soul.'[20] The madman has gone back into his wits, leaving the accommodating sane world gasping in his wake. The melancholy man has snapped out of the endless cycles of sadness and taken firm hold of what is real and of the issue that is now imperative. Surfaces will no longer do, for Don Quixote, finally, sees into the heart of things, and it is on his very deathbed that he does so.

The compassion that various characters, and many readers, feel and felt for the Don, especially at his poignant recovery of his wits at the time of his death – in which aspect he resembles, of course, his famous tragic counterpart, King Lear – became an increasingly significant feature of the eighteenth-century response to melancholy as the period wore on. Boswell and others might have been wary of speaking of their sufferings, fearing to become a butt for unfeeling mockery, while the herbalist, writer and quack John Hill might have written in 1766 of certain features of melancholy being made 'a jest to the common herd',[21] but the cultural tide was nevertheless in their favour. Laurence Sterne, perhaps, sums it up when he writes in *A Sentimental Journey*:

'Tis going, I own, like the Knight of the Woeful Countenance, in quest of melancholy adventures – but I know not how it is, but I am never so perfectly conscious of the existence of a soul within me, as when I am entangled in them.[22]

In Sterne, we no longer look askance or in contempt at the melancholy man, but rather we measure ourselves alongside him, even identify with him. Where Pope in *The Dunciad* and Swift in *Tale of a Tub* were ready to employ the figure of the madman, whether maniac or melancholiac, for satirical purposes, Sterne, and especially Henry Mackenzie in his novel *The Man of Feeling*, published in 1771, make it their business to recommend the melancholy, and therefore sensitive, individual as a repository of the best of human values, and therefore to be most emulated. The novel of sensibility, from the middle years of the century onwards, not only picks up on the cultural legacy of compassion, as opposed to the legacy of mockery, and of fellow-feeling and the exercise of pity, but also turns emotional engagement into one of the most sacred obligations of a fully developed human consciousness. As Sterne puts it, again, in *A Sentimental Journey*, having wept in tandem with the melancholy mad Maria: 'I am positive I have a soul; nor can all the books with which materialists have pestered the world ever convince me of the contrary.'[23]

Compassion, rather than cruelty, in looking at mental affliction has deep roots. It is easy with regard to a century that is notorious for images of brutality in Bethlem and of madness as a public spectacle to forget that a variety of attitudes and responses always co-existed, though their cultural presence was capable of being over or under emphasized. In the case of sympathetic attitudes towards those in low spirits, one major and enduring influence was that of the nonconformist ministry and the writings of individual ministers.

If poets, and particularly lyric and love poets, had always made a specialism of lamenting in verse for the misery of their lot, be it specific woes or general despondency in the face of the world as it seemed to them, it was nevertheless in the field of religious work, both preaching and writing, that awareness of 'trouble of mind' was transformed into a practical obligation. In the hands of people like Richard Baxter, John Bolton and Timothy Rogers, all of them members of the nonconformist ministry, key features of 'trouble of mind' were certain to be doubts over the Lord's intentions and consequent loss of a sense of personal spiritual worthiness. It became, therefore, a solemn Christian duty for other members of the family, the circle, the wider church, to sympathise with, engage with and offer comfort and practical help to those brothers and sisters unfortunate enough to be being tried in this particular way, for whatever purpose God had decreed. So, when Hannah Allen, as a young widowed mother in the 1660s, suffers a breakdown, bringing despair, self-loathing and attempted suicide – 'I would write in several places on the walls with the point of my Sizars, Woe, Woe, Woe and alas to all Eternity; I am undone, undone for ever, so as never any was before me'[24] – leaving her mother, aunt, brother, cousin and local minister helpless as to dealing with her, it is 'a good Friend of mine, a Minister, Mr. John Shorthose, who was related to me by Marriage' who eventually enables her recovery. Her account details something of the process whereby this is achieved. When Shorthose first enters the house with his wife unexpectedly, after Allen has refused to see them, she runs in terror to the chimney and takes up the tongs:

> Mr. Shorthose took me by the hand and said, Come, come, lay down those Tongs and go with us into the Parlour, which I did, and there they discoursed with me, till they had brought me to so calm and friendly a temper, that when they went I accompanied them to the door and said; Methinks I am loth to part with them . . .

The next day, he comes again and they walk

> into an Arbour in the Orchard, where he had much discourse with me, and amongst the rest he entreated me to go home with him; which after long persuasions both from him and my Aunt, I consented to, upon this condition, that he promised me, he would not compel me to any thing of the Worship of God, but what he could do by persuasion; and that week I went with them, where I spent that

Summer; in which time it pleased God by Mr. Shorthose's means to
do me much good both in Soul and Body.

From here she progresses to full recovery, to her status, in due time, as
'That Choice Christian', and to a second marriage, to 'Mr. Charles Hatt,
a Widdower living in Warwickshire; with whom I live very comfortably,
both as to my inward and outward man; my husband being one that
truly fears God'.[25]

Shorthose's readiness to spend time and to give time, his patience and
his sympathy, in spite of the initial rebuff, are what come across in this
account, and they are characteristic of nonconformist teaching at the
time. 'Look upon those that are under this woful Disease of Melancholly
with great pity and compassion', advises Timothy Rogers to 'the Relations and Friends of Melancholly People' in his 1691 work *A Discourse
Concerning Trouble of Mind and the Disease of Melancholly*. 'And pity them
the more,' he continues,

> by considering that you your selves are in the body, and liable to
> the very same trouble...Melancholly is a complication of violent
> and sore Distresses; 'tis full of miseries; 'tis it self a severe Affliction,
> and brings to our Thoughts and to our Bodies one Evil fast upon
> another.[26]

Richard Baxter, too, in giving 'Directions to the Melancholy', takes for
granted a company of friends and fellow believers who will regard it as
their Christian duty to aid their melancholy brother or sister:

> Avoid all unnecessary Solitariness, and be as much as possible in
> honest cheerful Company. You have need of others, and are not suf-
> ficient for your selves: And God will use and honour others as his
> hands, to deliver us his Blessings...But keep Company with the more
> cheerful Sort of the Godly. There is no Mirth like the Mirth of Believ-
> ers...Converse with Men of strongest Faith, that have this heavenly
> Mirth, and can speak experimentally of the Joy of the Holy Ghost;
> and these will be a great Help to the reviving of your Spirits, and
> changing your Melancholy Habit so far as without a Physician it may
> be expected.[27]

We cannot, the message is, be melancholy alone, though everything
about it would make us wish to be. We need our fellows if melancholy

is to be successfully dealt with, and our fellows owe it to us, to our immediate society, and to God, to welcome us among them.

One feature of medicine during the course of the eighteenth century, especially in its dealings with trouble of mind in all its manifestations, is the extent to which it slowly moves to an understanding, and a therapy, that can be seen as following in the wake of both literary culture and nonconformist religion. In medicine, the real flowering of compassion, or at least of humane treatment and of taking the disturbed seriously as individuals, deserving our attention as much as Hamlet or Don Quixote, comes as late as 1796. In 1796 Bethlem Hospital in London was still administering vomits according to the time of year: 'They are ordered to be bled about the latter end of May', as the physician Thomas Monro stated in his evidence to the Parliamentary Committee,

> or the beginning of May, according to the weather; and after they have been bled they take vomits once a week for a certain number of weeks, after that we purge the patients; that has been the practice invariably for years, long before my time; it was handed down to me by my father, and I do not know any better practice.[28]

In 1796 there were still nineteen years to the reporting of that committee, a report that brought out some of the worst abuses up and down the country; there were two years to go before the first edition of *Lyrical Ballads* and it was only two years after the first combined publication of *Songs of Innocence and of Experience*. In 1796, too, The Retreat opened near York for the reception of Quaker insane.

It is difficult to overstate the significance of The Retreat. Certainly the 1815 Parliamentary Report found itself constantly using its principles and practice as yardsticks for the treatment of the mentally ill. Measuring itself specifically against traditional mad hospitals like Bethlem, it set out, as Samuel Tuke describes in his 1813 work, *Description of The Retreat*, to espouse and uphold 'moral' principles in its treatment of its inmates. In fact, Tuke actually quotes John Haslam, apothecary at Bethlem until 1815, in support of what is meant by 'moral treatment' at The Retreat: 'I can truly declare, that by gentleness of manner, and kindness of treatment, I have seldom failed to obtain the confidence, and conciliate the esteem, of insane persons; and have succeeded by these means in procuring from them respect and obedience.'[29] In basing an institution on such intentions, the Tukes enshrined key cultural movements and a long-standing religious imperative as fundamental to society's valuation of and attitude towards its insane members, including those suffering from depression, who by the very nature of their condition would seem to question the worth of that society. As Boswell puts it in *The Hypochondriack*: 'All that is illustrious in publick life, all that is amiable and endearing in society, all that is elegant in science and in arts, affect him just with the same indifference, and even contempt, as the pursuits of children affect rational men.'[30] Boswell concludes this paper having found that the distraction of writing it, or 'some gracious influence',[31] has relieved the melancholy with which he began it. The same therapy, with the same concentration on the individual, is the basis of treatment at The Retreat:

> In regard to melancholics, conversation on the subject of their despondency, is found to be highly injudicious. The very opposite method is pursued. Every means is taken to seduce the mind from its favourite but unhappy musings, by bodily exercise, walks, conversation, reading, and other innocent recreations.[32]

What John Shorthose practised in the 1660s, at last, by the closing decade of the eighteenth century, and what is implicit in a text like *Don Quixote*, has become standard in at least one significant mental establishment.

The very notion of an asylum, in fact, itself encapsulates one major feature of the age, an age which saw enormous expansion of Britain's wealth and prestige, its trade routes and possessions, its naval and military dominance across Europe and beyond. These things come at a cost, and if the Hoxton madhouses, near London, specialized in contracts from the Admiralty for housing and treating (sometimes very badly) the naval insane during the Napoleonic wars, other forms of cost had been visible and assessable throughout the period. Several of the inmates that John Haslam describes in the Bethlem case histories that form a large part of his 1798 work *Observations on Insanity* are failed businessmen, driven into despair, apparently, by stress and debt.

> J.C. a man aged fifty, was admitted into the hospital August 6, 1796. It was stated that he had been disordered about three weeks, and that the disease had been induced by too great attention to business, and the want of sufficient rest...In April 1797, he was permitted to have a month's leave of absence, as he appeared tolerably well, and wished to maintain his family by his industry. For above three weeks of this time, he conducted himself in a very rational and orderly manner.

The day preceding that, on which he was to have returned thanks, he appeared gloomy and suspicious, and felt a disinclination for work. The night was passed in a restless manner, but in the morning he seemed better, and proposed coming to the hospital to obtain his discharge. His wife having been absent for a few minutes from the room, found him, on her return, with his throat cut.

He is readmitted, expresses 'great sorrow and penitence for what he had done', saying it was 'committed in a moment of rashness and despair', sinks into dispiritedness and silence, and finally dies after some ten days.[33]

Here, as much as with the naval insane, is one cost of the times, the dark side of an age of energy, just as Pope's 'Cave of Spleen' in *Rape of the Lock* is the dark side of the world of fashion. Equally, some of the leading figures of the age, politicians such as William Pitt the Elder and Edmund Burke, as well as financial and military men, like the Duke of Marlborough, suffered from acute melancholy, which in some cases actually led to insanity or even suicide. These included Robert Clive (Clive of India), who killed himself in 1774 after a lifetime of depression, and the politician Samuel Whitbread, who developed depression later in his life and committed suicide in 1815. Even physicians, some of the most energetic individuals of an expanding century, themselves succumbed to melancholy and despair, like Richard Lower, who had worked on transfusion of the blood while running his practice in London and who died in 1691. As Anne Finch writes of him in her landmark melancholy poem, 'The Spleen':

> Not skilful Lower thy Source cou'd find,
> Or thro' the well-dissected Body trace
>   The secret, the mysterious ways,
> By which thou dost surprise, and prey upon the Mind.
>   Tho' in the Search, too deep for Humane Thought,
>   With unsuccessful Toil he wrought,
>   'Till thinking Thee to've catch'd, Himself by thee was caught,
>   Retain'd thy Pris'ner, thy acknowleg'd Slave,
> And sunk beneath thy Chain to a lamented Grave.[34]

The individual figure of the melancholy physician, perhaps, is the most telling of all as a warning of the cost of progress as Britain, in 1691, stood poised at the edge of an age of energy and expansion.

Structure and topics

There are six main chapters in this book, approaching melancholy from a range of perspectives running from the medical through to the philosophical, literary and autobiographical. In Chapter 1, 'Fashionable Melancholy', Clark Lawlor analyses the phenomenon of 'fashionable' melancholy, posing the question of why it was that depressive states were generally viewed in a positive light over the course of the long eighteenth century, to the point of being seen to be a desirable attribute to possess. Literature, Lawlor emphasizes, provides templates for individual expression of health and disease, a point which will be picked up on throughout all the chapters of the book, where a wide range of writings from a variety of sources will be considered.

Lawlor's major concern is to explore how melancholy functioned in socio-cultural terms: what audience did it appeal to, and for what reasons? Melancholy is revealed to be a very flexible and adaptable disease, capable of being interpreted in a variety of ways, from psychologically crippling through to pleasurable. The response of two poets indicates the breadth of this range: for Anne Finch it feels like being trapped on 'a Dead Sea', whereas for Thomas Gray it can be 'a good easy sort of state' to find oneself in, and writers of the period move between these poles in their description of the condition's effects.[35]

Melancholy had a long-standing association with genius (to some extent it has retained this through into our own day), which could be traced back to such an illustrious intellectual authority as Aristotle. From the Renaissance onwards it also took on a class bias, becoming seen as a mark of both superior social and intellectual status and accomplishments, as it was for Richard Burton in *Anatomy of Melancholy* and George Cheyne in *The English Malady*. In consequence, melancholy subsequently became for the eighteenth century a sign of refinement, a fashionable condition to be afflicted by, and was thus embraced by the middle and upper classes, often drawing on the representations offered by literary models. Melancholy soon blended with sensibility, and in the case of a literary heroine like Samuel Richardson's Clarissa Harlowe it signalled moral discrimination, therefore yet more evidence of class refinement. For Lawlor, an investigation into the impact of medical theory on literary practice can help us to understand how this popularisation of melancholy occurred.

In Chapter 2, 'Philosophical Melancholy', Richard Terry's concern is to explore the link between unhappiness and philosophical pessimism, in particular the complex dialogue that many eighteenth-century thinkers conducted with classical stoicism, a philosophy that held it was possible to become largely immune to the experience of grief and misfortune. For those who espoused philosophical pessimism, melancholy was a perfectly reasonable and defensible response to the trials and tribulations of our life. There was not the expectation, so common in our own day, that happiness should be the overriding objective of all humanity, and that unhappiness was something we should be striving to banish from our lives. For those of a stoic disposition unhappiness was something to be borne as best as one could, whereas now it is more usual to regard it as an aberrant state that prevents us from enjoying life to the full, as is assumed to be our right.

There is a disinclination in our time, as Terry points out, to accept that unhappiness is simply part of the natural order of things, a quite understandable reaction to bereavement, illness, failed relationships, or any of the other emotionally testing experiences with which everyone's life is regularly punctuated. Instead, we tend to view depression, or any of its cognate states such as stress, low spirits, or general disillusionment with one's prospects, as forms of disorder that should be addressed professionally. But as Terry emphasizes, while medical treatment can mask the symptoms of such reactions, and the degree of misery they can induce, it cannot ultimately reconcile one to the emotional pain that events like bereavement leave in their wake; there is an inevitability to pain and suffering that each of us has to face up to and deal with at an individual level. In this connection, Terry is particularly concerned to draw our attention to the difficulties and problems that can arise when feelings of sadness are equated with depression. What most divides us from the eighteenth-century conception of melancholy, he believes, is precisely that assumption we now make that unhappiness is an abnormal state of mind demanding correction, that it is to be classified as ill-health. The eighteenth-century's cultivation of stoicism still has much to teach us in this respect. In the colloquial sense of the term, all of us have to learn to become much more 'philosophical' about life's downturns, to accept that misery is also part of the human lot.

Chapter 3, '"Strange Contrarys": Figures of Melancholy in Eighteenth-century Poetry', by John Baker, considers the impact of melancholy on eighteenth-century poetic discourse and how it was represented and developed there by figures such as John Pomfret, Anne Finch, Edward Young and William Cowper. For poets such as these and many of their contemporaries, as Baker goes on to demonstrate, melancholy was to become a rich source of inspiration, something to be invoked rather than kept at bay for its depressing connotations. Giving expression to the feeling of melancholy and summoning up the appropriate imagery of night, graveyards and generally gloomy scenes (as the so-called 'Graveyard School' so insistently did), could have a consolatory and even therapeutic effect on the poet, enabling him or her better to cope with what was often a personally devastating set of emotional experiences. Thus Edward Young's *Night Thoughts* sequence, which is explored in some detail, follows on from a series of bereavements in the poet's circle, eventually to confront a world in which death is an ever-present factor from which we cannot hide and must strive to come to terms with somehow or other, emotionally wrenching though the effort can be.

As Baker points out, the sheer prevalence of melancholy in eighteenth-century poetry argues that this was, depending on one's perception, either a historical high or low point for the condition. What is so fascinating about the poetry is how it manages to span the spectrum of melancholy states, from the apparently pleasurable to the deeply distressing. There is an intriguing mix of opposites to be noted, as poets indulge themselves in melancholy while also being aware that it is a condition that can take over their lives and leave them feeling bereft of all hope. What does come through in a survey of the poetry of the period is how effectively melancholy could act as a stimulus to creativity, providing an emotional context in which poets could reflect on the deeper mysteries of human existence – not least their own psychology.

Melancholy and despair are prominently represented in the prose fiction of the period, as Stuart Sim goes on to investigate in Chapter 4, 'Despair, Melancholy and the Novel'. The influence of spiritual autobiography on the development of the early novel is well documented, particularly in terms of the appropriation of the former's narrative structure by such authors as Daniel Defoe and Samuel Richardson. The structure involves cycles of sin to repentance and back again in the protagonist's life, until an epiphany yields evidence of divine grace being extended. Along with the structural pattern, therefore, comes a psychological landscape in which despair plays a critical role in reminding the individual of the necessity of amending their lifestyle. John Bunyan left us a fascinating record of his own experience of despair in his spiritual autobiography *Grace Abounding to the Chief of Sinners*, which carries over into his fictionalized spiritual autobiography *The Pilgrim's Progress* (Giant Despair, for example),[36] from where it is adapted by Daniel Defoe for *Robinson Crusoe* (the hero shipwrecked on what he dubs his 'Island Despair').[37] Defoe's handling of the topic puts religious despair firmly on the agenda of the new literary form, and the interplay between the spiritual and the secular, the individual and the society within which they live, becomes a fascinating phenomenon to observe in long eighteenth-century fiction.

Melancholy is perhaps best represented in a literary sense in this period in the work of Laurence Sterne, whose novel *Tristram Shandy* is underpinned by a consistent sense of melancholy about the human condition. Sterne was one of the main sources of the sentimental tradition that became increasingly influential in novel-writing in the later eighteenth century. There is a philosophical undercurrent to Sterne's melancholy which invites serious metaphysical analysis for all its sentimentalism, whereas in Ann Radcliffe's Gothic novels melancholy is generally a comforting experience, often tied up with nostalgic memories of one's past. Establishing the nature of the relationship between the individual and the narrative framework derived from spiritual autobiography can tell us a great deal about changing attitudes towards despair over the period, and might enable us to see the melancholy sentimentalism of someone like Sterne in a different light – perhaps as part of a secularization of despair.

One of the most characteristic aspects of depression is the loss of a sense of a coherent self, which can be very destabilizing indeed. Leigh Wetherall-Dickson goes on to analyse various attempts made to come to terms with this phenomenon through the act of writing in Chapter 5, 'Melancholy, Medicine, Mad Moon and Marriage: Autobiographical Expressions of Depression'. Wetherall-Dickson views depression as an act of turning in on oneself (as famously exemplified by the figure of the angel in Albrecht Dürer's *Melencolia I*, seemingly weighed down by its sense of woe), bringing with it a corresponding sense of alienation from the world and one's fellow human beings. Autobiographical accounts of the experience give us an insight into what this state of mind feels like, as well as how it can provide afflicted individuals with an outlet to express themselves and thus reaffirm their own sense of identity and humanity despite their often acute mental suffering. 'Writing the self' becomes a therapeutic activity.

The spiritual autobiographical tradition that was still so influential at the beginning of the period encouraged individuals to force their experience to fit into a pre-established pattern (as Bunyan for one did), thus promoting identification with other believers as well as the not-inconsiderable comfort of being a part of a like-minded community that shared a similar narrative line to their lives. Despair could thus be contained, and the individual enabled to overcome its more debilitating effects. As the period progressed, however, and religious fervour gradually abated (as has been already noted, spiritual autobiography was particularly identified with nonconformist enthusiasm), this template began to lose its authority in a general sense, and many individuals found themselves in consequence searching for new ways to validate their experiences. The various kinds of narrative this reorientation gave rise to, and the changing nature of the relationship between the individual and the wider social framework that they record, is outlined by Wetherall-Dickson through selected key texts, demonstrating the crucial importance of the written word in the process of adjusting to life with depression.

In the last chapter of the book, 'Deciphering Difference: A Study in Medical Literacy', Allan Ingram investigates what we have to learn from the eighteenth century about what is now called depression, recognizing that the latter is something of a blanket term which in many ways stifles discrimination between its various forms (as happened to some extent with melancholy in the earlier period too). As he points out, the emergence of a highly profitable antidepressant market has tended to homogenize depression and to discourage treating it on an individual basis: the sheer variety of the condition and the many kinds of dejection it can involve tend to be minimized in the face of the readily available, and seductively simple, antidepressant 'solution'. In the eighteenth century, however, it was treated on just such an individual basis and, as Ingram proceeds to demonstrate, physicians paid very close attention to the narratives of those suffering from melancholy and despair – something that has been lost in recent times with the turn towards antidepressants.

Ingram charts a shift from religious explanations of depressive states, by an ecclesiastical priesthood trained to view these from a spiritual perspective, through to physical and psychological explanations from a newly developing medical profession, arguing that the latter were in many ways more attentive to their patients than their modern counterparts often are (even if it has to be admitted that their treatments were not always successful). He regards the eclipse of this independently minded approach to the various forms that melancholy and despair could take as one of the great missed opportunities in the history of modern medicine. Antidepressants alone will not eradicate depression, which remains a more complex phenomenon than many medical professionals, with the considerable pressure of the pharmaceutical industry behind them, might care to admit. Recent studies are, however, beginning to raise doubts as to the overall effectiveness of antidepressants, so it may well be that the time has come for much more attentive listening to patients' personal narratives on the eighteenth-century model.

Melancholy assumes a variety of forms over the course of the eighteenth century, and we need to be very attentive to their character if we are to bring out their cultural significance. By delving into that variety across a range of discourses, from medicine and philosophy through the arts and personal reminiscence, this volume aims to deepen our understanding of what melancholy involves and make us aware of just how much suffering and personal torment it can bring to those caught up in its toils – whether in the eighteenth century or our own more medically sophisticated day. Neither is this just a case of asking us to be more sympathetic to the plight of some unfortunate others: there is a personal dimension too. Depressive experiences are something we shall all go through at some point in our lives, and the past can be a very useful guide as to how we can set about negotiating our way through something which we can now recognize is far more than just an 'English malady'.

1
Fashionable Melancholy

Clark Lawlor

The core problem – the paradox of fashionable disease

We know that melancholy could be a murderous condition for the sufferer in the eighteenth century, much as depression can be in our own time – a large part of this volume attests to the profound misery that melancholy and its cognates caused to people rich and poor, male and female, young and old. Nevertheless, the student of eighteenth-century melancholy is faced with a problem: for much of the period, melancholy was frothily fashionable, a condition that often seemed less of an illness and more of a blessing for the budding poet, wilting lady wishing to show off her latest nightdress, or anyone who desired to seem in the slightest bit sensitive or clever. This chapter tackles the thorny issue of melancholy's fashionability head-on, suggests reasons why the apparent paradox of such a phenomenon existed in the period, and clears the way for an understanding of how a positive interpretation of melancholy might live alongside the negative ones that seem to be a more logical response to the woes of the mind – at least intuitively.

It is not only melancholy that can be fashionable. In fact, James Mackittrick Adair, a Bath doctor of fashionable society, writes an essay on just this subject – 'On Fashionable Diseases' – in 1786. He details the progress of the fashionable diseases in polite society from spleen to vapours to nerves to bilious disorders(!).[1] How on earth have humans reached the point where they can regard diseases as fashionable? Disease is a negative thing, degrading body and mind, causing pain and suffering, disrupting the normal flow of life – or sometimes entirely destroying it. Disease brings woe and misery to all nations, creeds and colours: we are left, therefore, with a central paradox: how can disease be positive, fashionable, desirable, sexy?

Clearly the answer to this question is complicated, and I will be writing on this at length elsewhere, but for the moment we must confine ourselves to fashionable melancholy and its cognates like hypochondria, spleen and vapours. We need to give these terms greater specificity in our quest to open out the question of what depression was like before it was labelled as such in the modern era (during the later nineteenth century). The question of whether depression can be equated with melancholy has been much discussed, and I continue this debate myself later in this chapter, but for the moment we will assume that the core symptoms of causeless sadness and fear, around which were a variety of other symptoms that are less compatible with any equation of depression with melancholy, will ground our discussion.[2] I follow Arthur Kleinman in assuming a cultural relativist view that core biological states are altered, sometimes so radically as to be almost unrecognizable, by their insertion into the very different social worlds that we inhabit, either synchronically between cultures in our own time or diachronically between the depression of our day and the melancholy of previous centuries.

We also concern ourselves here with the importance of the representation of melancholy. If a disease is fashionable, it is more than ready for representation in the popular media of its day: in our own time televisual media (including the internet) are probably a more powerful template for our lay understanding of disease than the printed word, but in early modern times print and the printed image were clearly competing with oral forms of transmission for primacy in their impact on the popular imagination and the way it constructed its experience of illness. A fashionable disease, one might expect, would feature more heavily in literary and artistic representations than one that brought embarrassment rather than kudos. This raises another problem, however: our definition of 'fashionable disease'. Some diseases can be fashionable without having a positive connotation: AIDS has been regarded as a fashionable disease for attracting research funding without anyone feeling it to be a desirable condition to have personally; the Black Death similarly accumulated massive representational stature without being in any way lauded as accruing cultural capital (although the religious might see it as a scourge of society rightfully administered by an angry God). For the purposes of this analysis of melancholy as fashionable disease, we will focus on the discourse of melancholy that stresses the benefits of the condition, while fully aware that there existed a counter-tradition across the centuries that remained sceptical of any false flattery from such a debilitating condition.

Despite objections, melancholy has been a fashionable condition across a number of centuries, if not millennia. Why is this so and how did this fashionability play itself out in our period: 1660–1800? To think about this question we need to begin with a consideration of the symptoms of the various disease labels that were applied to melancholy and its cognates in the various historical contexts and then relate these symptoms to the possible social gain that might accrue from possessing these symptoms. The question of social advantage – cultural capital if you like – gained from melancholy cannot be disentangled from the discursive constitution of the social group being examined.[3] So: religion, gender, race, class and so on all play their part in determining whether a disease can achieve fashionability within that society. We will also need to consider – at the risk of being ahistorical – whether there are core symptoms or features of melancholy/depression that lend themselves to fashionability cross-culturally, or at least through time within a changing culture like Britain from the sixteenth through to the nineteenth centuries, not to mention the classical popularity of melancholy which gives form to later definitions of melancholy.

Definitions of melancholy

To begin with definitions, it is good to recognize the physiological and psychological complexity and symptomatological range of the object before us. John F. Sena wisely points out that we need to think of 'a plurality of melancholies'.[4] In the classical system of the humours, in which one of the four humours would predispose a person towards a certain personality and linked humoral type, a 'natural melancholy' would result from the predominance of the melancholy humour; an 'unnatural melancholy' might arise from excess melancholic humours being burned by heating processes such as overexcitement of the passions, poor diet or a fever. The burnt remainder was an ash of sorts called melancholy adust or atrabilious melancholy.[5] Because the variety of mixtures of the four humours within the human body was potentially infinite, each individual's constitution varied in subtle or indeed not-so-subtle ways. Each person's melancholy was in a sense unique to them: it was not a single disease entity like a bacterium or virus in the way we now understand it.

Melancholy could also be caused by problems in the hypochodriacal organs – those in the abdomen like the spleen and liver, which were known as the hypochondria or hypochondries (Gk, 'under the breastbone). This form of melancholy was known as hypochondriacal melancholy or 'hyp/hypo'.[6] Hypochondria tended to be gendered male, but not always, and was also known as 'flatulent' or 'windy melancholy' because of its origin in the disordered hypochondrias. Melancholy could ensue from the failure of the spleen to remove black bile from the blood: hence the cognate term for melancholy, 'the Spleen' (used for both sexes).[7] The spleen's malfunction might result in 'Vapours': undigested black bile that heated up and produced vapours which rose to the brain and caused melancholy. These vapours disordered the 'animal spirits', the supposed medium connecting the mind and the senses and, so the metaphor went, clouding the thoughts and images passing through the brain. This disorder of the Vapours inevitably affected the imagination, notoriously (as we will see) leading to hallucinations and visions as one component of its symptomatology. The particular vogue of the Vapours gained prominence in the Renaissance and was usually used to describe women: but again, it must be stressed, not always.[8] The definitions of these various forms of melancholy varied between doctors and different periods: even the nomenclature is unstable, as we have been tracing.

Hysteria was a further cognate term for melancholy that, for the most part and certainly in origin, was gendered female. *Hystera* was the Greek word for womb and hysteria was thought to be a problem – bizarrely to (post)modern readers – of the 'wandering womb', an entity that was supposed by the Egyptians to move around the body, causing damage to health as it went. Later incarnations of the disease dropped the idea of the errant womb in literal terms but the identification of hysteria with the female reproductive system persisted into the nineteenth century and beyond.[9] Sena points out that by the seventeenth century hysteric fits were regarded as attacks of melancholy and that by the eighteenth hysteria was another name for melancholy.[10] This slight deviation from the focus on the hypochondries to the womb gave hysteria a different inflection representationally, but still the focus was on the approximate area of the body where the digestive system operated: digestion was constantly stated to be a driving force behind melancholia in humoral, iatrochemical [*iatro* is the Greek word for doctor] and iatromechanical traditions of medicine. According to one's medical philosophy of choice (although humoralism was outmoded at the philosophical level in the eighteenth century), digestive disorder could unbalance one's humours, cause unfortunate heating of substances within the body, or even degrade the blood and result in blockages in the pipework of the body.[11] As Angus Gowland has argued, 'in terms of medical theory, the history of melancholy from antiquity to early modernity is predominantly one of continuity rather than change'.[12] Although the Galenic basis of the humoral definition of melancholy became passé in the later seventeenth century, the New Science's various physiological explanations 'were more or less straightforwardly grafted onto the traditional Galenic external aetiology, symptomatology and therapeutics'.[13] Thomas Willis replaced black bile with a more modern conception – the nervous system – yet the 'raving without a Feavour or fury' and core symptoms of fear, sadness and hallucinations remained as usual.[14]

Contemporaries recognized the confusion in this medley of terms: each jostled for their own definition. In an article entitled 'Of the Hypp' in the *Gentleman's Magazine* (1732), Nicholas Robinson stated that 'the old distemper call'd *Melancholy* was exchang'd for *Vapours*, and afterwards for the *Hypp*, and at last took up the now current appellation of the *Spleen*, which it still retains'.[15] He then goes on to say how melancholy has been divided in Spleen and Vapours, but then one contracts the Hypp, Hyppos, the Hyppocons, which then divide into the markambles, moonpalls, strong fiacs, hockogrogles. The slang for the various states of melancholy, some involving un-depression-like hallucinations and delusions, was also rich and varied. Robinson describes the case of a young scholar in Oxford who thinks he has swallowed a cobbler and – to defeat the disease by its own logic – has the cobbler pretend to have been expelled in a vomit. At the start of his attack of the melancholy the scholar is 'deep in the Shaggs, – Hypp'd to a violent degree, – full of the Glooms and Dismals'.[16]

Robinson firmly marked melancholy and its derivatives as fashionable: he describes the progress of the Spleen from 'Court Ladies' to 'a fine Gentleman [who] was pleased to catch it, purely in Compliance to them'. Then it goes down the classes and genders in a trickle-down effect – at least to an extent. The spleen is taken up, as it were, by an ironmonger's wife of the city, and thence to a Cambridge academic. It even moves from the city to the country, ending up in Northumberland. He himself has two patients – one a gentleman of a competent fortune and the other a clergyman's eldest daughter.

What was true in terms of other fashions such as clothing and other material effects was also true of disease apparently. Robinson had his class limits, however: 'the industrious Farmer, Shepherd, Plowman and Day-Labourer, are indeed safe from this evil; respect for their Betters not suffering them to pretend to it'.[17] Here Robinson was reflecting the common opinion, echoed by philosophers of disease from Robert

Burton to George Cheyne, that the rude labourer was not subject to the disease of melancholy because his lifestyle and intrinsically cruder nervous system would lack the necessary refinement to render him a prey to the paradoxically elevated and elevating condition of melancholy. Ironically, fashionable amusements might render the disease of fashionable lifestyle a cure: 'a person in the Spleen may be flung into a course of Diversions and Amusements; and a Mixture of Wakes, Fairs, Revels, Horse-Races, Assemblies, Operas, Masquerades and Puppet-Shewes, may be made up for him in a Prescription'.[18] Clearly Robinson's amused treatment of fashionable melancholy has its satiric edge, and the carnivalesque list of fashionable activities drives home the irony of fashion curing fashionable disease. Yet there was a serious body of medical work on the power of laughter to cure melancholy: Robinson was not entirely joking.[19]

Bernard Mandeville similarly complained in his *Treatise of Hypochondriack and Hysterick Passions* (1711) that

> I never dare speak of Vapours, the very Name is become a Joke; and the general Notion the Men have of them, is, that they are nothing but a malicious Mood, and contriv'd Sullenness of wilful extravagant and imperious Women, when they are denied, or thwarted in their unreasonable Desires.[20]

Despite this pernicious fashionability, Mandeville asserts – as many of his medical contemporaries did – the reality of the symptoms.[21]

We must return to the vexed question of intentionality and outright deception when it comes to melancholy and depression, but for the moment it is necessary to examine symptoms in a little more detail, although the sheer variety of symptoms attributed to melancholy across the centuries is nothing short of bewildering. Nevertheless, some broad contrasts can be made with physical diseases and indeed with other psychological disorders, contrasts which start to help explain the utility of melancholy as a fashionable disease. One core distinction in ancient Greek medicine was the tripartite division of madness into phrenitis (frenzy), mania (raving) and melancholy: a division that persisted into the eighteenth century, although sometimes with a different rationale. Melancholy was chronic, not acute like phrenitis, and not feverish; there was no violent raving as in mania. Causeless fear and sorrow were the basis of melancholy, sometimes accompanied by hallucinations. In our modern, popular picture of depression we have almost no room for this hallucinatory or visionary aspect of melancholy, yet it is fundamental to the Ancient Greek conceptualization of the disease because of the humoral theory of black bile (μέλαωα χολή) from which the word melancholy proceeds. μέλαωα χολή or *melaina chole* was translated into Latin as *atra bilis* and into English as *black bile*.[22]

Indeed, it is this hallucinatory aspect that appears to be the basis of the famous association of genius with melancholy, the core quality that drove the fashionability of melancholy and its cognates. To explain this association, we must briefly examine the well-known and extraordinarily influential statement in Aristotle (or his follower's) *Problemata* [*Problems*]:

> Why is it that all men who have become outstanding in philosophy, statesmanship, poetry or the arts are melancholic, and some to such an extent as they are infected by the diseases arising from black bile, as the story of Heracles among the heroes tells? For Heracles seems to have been of this character, so that the ancients called the disease of epilepsy the 'Sacred disease' after him. This is proved by his frenzy towards his children and the eruption of sores which occurred before his disappearance on Mount Oeta; for this is a common affection among those who suffer from black bile.[23]

Aristotle, in apparent contradiction of our classical model of madness outlined earlier, does see more extreme forms of melancholy as involving frenzy, including the introduction of epilepsy in an allusion to the Platonic idea of divine inspiration flowing through the epileptic. Klibansky, Panofsky and Saxl's study of melancholy and genius argues that Aristotle's move to describe epilepsy as a severe consequence of malfunction of the black bile is a secularization of the Platonic theory of the frenzied, visionary, creative personality.[24]

We will have more to say on epilepsy elsewhere, but for the moment it suffices to see Aristotle's point that black bile is in danger of becoming too hot or too cold, and that excess in either direction can result in a range of effects. Some people have a naturally melancholic temperament which is cold and therefore sluggish; some,

> with whom it is excessive and hot become mad, clever or amorous and easily moved to passion and desire, and some become more talkative. But many, because this heat is near to the seat of the mind, are affected by the diseases of madness and frenzy, which accounts for the Sibyls, soothsayers, and all inspired persons. Maracus, the

Syracusan, was an even better poet when he was mad. But those with whom the excessive heat has sunk to a moderate amount are melancholic, though more intelligent and less eccentric, but they are superior to the rest of the world in many ways, some in education, some in the arts and others again in statesmanship.[25]

So, moderation in temperament and temperature (the two terms are clearly related in humoral philosophy) inclines the melancholic to genius: overheating can result in the frenzy of prophecy, at least as the classical world understood it.[26]

Later versions of melancholy would jettison the pagan element like the Sibyls and soothsayers, but would instead incorporate religious Christian enthusiasm (although not without contention from the 'mainstream' churches). At this juncture it is difficult to see how modern depression can be equated with the classical understanding of melancholy as a range of temperamental possibilities based on a continuum of susceptibility to the effects of heat on one of the four humours. Even the later religious melancholy of the guilty Christian is foreign to our Western secularized mindset (we are conveniently ignoring other cultures in this discussion of British melancholy and depression). In his cross-cultural studies of depression in our own time, Arthur Kleinman has argued that

> because the cultural worlds in which people live are so dramatically different, translation of terms for emotion involves much more than the identification of semantic equivalents. Describing how it feels to grieve or be melancholy in another society leads straightaway into analysis of different ways of being a person in radically different worlds.[27]

Here we walk a tightrope, however, between the cultural relativism of this statement and Kleinman's further assertion that

> studies now offer overwhelming evidence of universal *and* culture-specific aspects of depressive disorder. Hence the depressive disorder category does appear to map an authentic phenomenon of human distress found cross-culturally, but one for which beliefs, norms, and experiences differ.[28]

Radden points out that Kleinman's position on the idea of a core depressive disorder that lies, as it were, beyond cultural construction, is ambiguous.[29] Nevertheless, Kleinman's model helps us to understand the way that melancholy might relate to modern-day depression, while not being reducible to our modern definitions. The interplay and indeed tension between the objective 'scientific' mapping of a disease is less obvious in 'soft' diseases, especially those of the mind where the diagnosis and interpretation of psychological processes and the way they interact with the body are far more complicated than, say, smallpox, cholera or bubonic plague.

Symptoms and narratives

In my previous work on the construction of the Romantic image of consumption (tuberculosis as we now know it), I argued – following David Morris's *Illness and Culture in the Postmodern Age* – that 'we are biologically grounded in bodies with certain inescapable material processes and that we express such biology through language and narrative'.[30] I also showed that

> we need to acknowledge, not merely that consumption has been constructed or fabulated in some kind of mythical language, but that consumption has certain biological patterns that impose themselves on, and give rise to, cultural meanings of the disease. As it happens, consumption has symptoms – we might say genres or given plots of physical events – which came to be constructed through various discourses as beneficial to the recipient of the illness.[31]

This dialectic (if that word is not overdetermined by now) between body and culture also plays itself out, as we see in Kleinman's work on depression in China and the West, in the more contentious field of mental illness. In the context of fashionable melancholy, we need to examine how the symptoms of melancholy (and later depression), as defined in their particular social worlds, served to construct a cultural narrative that fulfilled certain social functions and, in particular, created cultural capital or primary and secondary 'gain' for the individuals and groups within those social worlds.

We are indebted to the work of a number of scholars, primarily Klibansky, Panofsky and Saxl's foundational study, for tracing the development of melancholy from the classical form as outlined by Aristotle to the Renaissance form as it was fashioned by Marsilio Ficino in Italy and thence disseminated across Europe, ultimately arriving in England in time for Shakespeare to utilize its by-then known features in the character of Hamlet. To summarize a large body of work very crudely, Ficino's Neoplatonic astrology placed all melancholics under the star sign of Saturn (also famously typified in Dürer's *Melencolia*) and, following Aristotle, pronounced all men of genius and learning to be melancholic to some degree. It must be stressed that there were counter-traditions to this positive reading of melancholy, as indeed we have in our own time regarding 'creative' depression, for example, Kay Redfield Jamison's book *Touched with Fire: Manic-Depressive Illness and the Artistic Temperament*.[32] Nevertheless, we focus here on the positive representations of melancholy so common in this period, representations that could not have been so valorized with the intellectual foundations provided by the ideas of Aristotle and Ficino.

Melancholy had a strong literary association from the time of Aristotle: he asserts that many famous figures were melancholic, including Lysander, Ajax, Bellerophontes, Empedocles, Plato, Socrates, and

> the same is true of most of those who have handled poetry. For many such men have suffered from diseases which arise from this mixture in the body, and in others their nature evidently inclines to troubles of this sort. In any case they are all, as has been said, naturally of this character.[33]

The introspection required by the artistic and poetic temperament, the intense focus upon the self, was a prime component in the formation of depression, especially in its Renaissance emphasis on the nature of subjectivity as exemplified by the character of Hamlet. This introspection, like the condition of melancholy itself, was a double-edged sword, providing both the materials for literary creativity and the seeds of mental illness. As Robert Burton, the most famous 'anatomist' of Renaissance depression, put it in his *Anatomy of Melancholy*:

> most pleasant it is at first, to such as are melancholy given...to walk alone in some solitary grove, betwixt wood and water, by a brooke side, to meditate upon some delightsome and pleasant subject...A most incomparable delight, it is so to melancholize, and build castles in the ayre, to goe smiling to themselves, acting a infinite variety of parts...they could spend whole days and nights without sleepe, even whole yeares alone in such contemplations, and phantasticall meditations.[34]

But a time comes when 'this infernal plague of Melancholy seizeth on them, and terrifies their souls'.[35] Burton's poetic 'Abstract of Melancholy' highlights the paradoxical nature of the disease; he begins:

> When I goe musing all alone
>> Thinking of divers things fore-knowne.
>> When I build Castles in the aire,
>> Void of sorrow and void of feare,
>> Pleasing myselfe with phantasmes sweet,
>> Methinkes the time runnes very fleet.
>> All my joyes to this are folly,
>> Naught so sweet as melancholy.[36]

But later the core symptoms of depression take hold:

> 'Tis my sole plague to be alone,
>> I am a beast, a monster growne,
>> I will no light nor company,
>> I finde it now my misery.
>> The sceane is turn'd, my joys are gone,
>> Feare, discontent, and sorrowes come.[37]

What once was pleasurable solitude becomes a hellish isolation consisting of anxiety and depression.

At the heart of this matter there is the basic issue of the condition's severity: we have 'melancholy-lite', 'Leucocholy' as Thomas Gray would later term it, where the melancholic individual can wallow in a relatively symptomless isolation from society. Gray defined a sort of 'white melancholy, or rather Leucocholy for the most part . . . is a good easy sort of state, and ca ne laisse que de s'amuser'.[38] This, to all intents, is a form of self-indulgence, a freeing oneself from social obligations in order to engage in creative (or possibly entirely unproductive) use of the imagination. Sufferers from consumption often had a similar disease process where at first they rather enjoyed the almost symptomless early stages of consumption and later, when symptoms of greater severity emerged, the realization that they were condemned to suffering for the rest of their possibly brief life brought on psychological depression or at least a more negative view of their supposedly glamorous condition.[39]

Here we veer again toward the complicated question of symptoms and their functionality. At one level, following Burton's encyclopaedic volume, symptoms (and causes) are often dizzyingly complex and include many physical manifestations. As Burton's 'Contents' page reveals, the general symptoms of the body include: 'ill digestion, crudity, wind, dry brains, hard belly, thick blood, much waking, heaviness, and palpitation of heart, leaping in many places, &c.'[40] A 'Head Melancholy' might involve: 'Headache, binding and heaviness, vertigo, lightness, singing of the ears, much waking, fixed eyes, high colour, red eyes, hard belly, dry body; no great sign of melancholy in the other parts'.[41] For an 'Hypochondriacal, or windy melancholy', bodily symptoms are equally irksome: 'Wind, rumbling in the guts, bellyache, heat in the bowels, convulsions, crudities, short wind, sour and sharp belchings, cold sweat, pain in the left side, suffocation, palpitation, heaviness of the heart, singing in the ears, much spittle, and moist, &c.'.[42]

Psychological symptoms can be similarly varied in Burton and the early modern period: Head Melancholy might mean 'Continual fear, sorrow, suspicion, discontent, superfluous cares, solicitude, anxiety, perpetual cogitation of such toys they are possessed with, thoughts like dreams, &c.'.[43] 'Hypochondriacal, or windy melancholy' also varies from the core features of fear and sadness: 'Fearful, sad, suspicious, discontent, anxiety, &c. Lascivious by reason of much wind, troublesome dreams, affected by fits, &c.'.[44] All this is ignoring the 'Symptoms of nuns, maids, and widows melancholy, in body and mind, &c', in which section Burton invokes the old chestnut of the womb's role in female physiology and psychology and the idea of hysteria.[45]

At another level, however, we might argue that depression/melancholy is primarily a mental state characterized by causeless fear and sadness and therefore capable of social functions above and beyond those of physical disease. Burton seeks to identify and explain those symptoms of 'General Melancholy' (there are many other types) 'Common to all or most': 'Fear and sorrow without a just cause, suspicion, jealousy, discontent, solitariness, irksomeness, continual cogitations, restless thoughts, vain imaginations' ('Synopsis of the First Partition').[46] It is this second level of mental symptoms to which the positive representation of melancholy appears most related: arguably the less severe the symptoms, the more positively a disease can be regarded, constructed and represented. This is partly why the disease of consumption could be transformed into the Romantic disease: because its physical 'narrative', its progress and developing symptoms, was relatively benign in comparison to other diseases. Consumption did not usually kill one quickly (good news for the devout Christian who wanted to be prepared for death); it did not scar one's body; it was relatively painless because the lungs have less nerves than other areas of the body; it did not tend to result in mental illness. In fact, consumption had a number of symptomatological features that could be – and were – regarded in a positive light: the wasting of the body could be seen as a holy rejection of the world and the flesh or a sign of refined nerves and female beauty; the alternating hectic flush and pallor of the cheeks could also be seen in terms of classical female beauty; because sufferers were often unaware of the severity of their condition the term 'spes phthisica' or 'hope of the consumptive' was coined to describe the continuing creativity or feverish inspiration of the consumptive up until the point of death.

If we look at melancholy-depression in this light, we can start to see similarities in these two complex conditions: indeed, historically the two were related, consumption being a common result of love and religious melancholy according to the medics and popular representations in literature and art. In the Romantic period poets made a full-time occupation of being both consumptive and melancholic, as the examples of Henry Kirke White and Keats demonstrate. As described by Burton, melancholy could begin, like consumption, in a 'gentle' manner with less-than grievous symptoms; it could end, however, in ruination – like consumption. What was the symptom-complex of melancholy that could be positively construed? We have seen that melancholy could leave the body unscathed and free from pain, much like consumption.

We have also seen that the imagination is a key component in melancholy: initially explained by medical theory in terms of humoral disorder (vapours, which arose from the malprocessing/indigestion and burning of black bile in the spleen and hypochondries, ascending to the brain); and later in terms of mechanical-hydraulic or chemical dysfunctions relating to the digestion which in turn affected the supply of 'animal spirits' to the brain; and later still in terms of disordered nerves (again stemming from digestive malfunctions) that impacted on the physical operation of the brain. Other variations on this theme – such as the astrological influence of Saturn on the humoral constitution – might be elaborated, but the central status of the imagination in the popular and medical understanding of melancholy was certain. Although the medical theory changed in its rationale, its implications for the imagination had a certain amount of continuity, much like the way in which treatments for disease both physical and mental did not radically change until the advent of 'modern' developments (like the rise of bacteriology) in the nineteenth century. The disorderly imagination could be highly productive for artists and writers, and not just in the Romantic period where the idea of originality was beginning to be highly prized. Even before that the imagination put to the service of God in works of art, for example, could be aided by the happy derangement of the imaginative process.

Melancholy, like consumption, was and is typically chronic. For the literary and studious person, this quality had distinct advantages: if one contracted some acute and deadly condition like cholera, possibly all one might have time for would be a quick heroic couplet before Death put an end to one's earthly ambitions. Chronic diseases favour the development of thought and writing: dying of consumption or suffering from melancholy (especially of the love variety) might inspire a poet to compose a sonnet sequence (and did in many cases, both in the Renaissance and in the Romantic period and beyond). Melancholy's chronicity and the tendency to introspection and imaginative inspiration were a happy combination for the creative person. The 'story' of melancholy's progress as a disease process has its own characters or symptoms, if one can put it like that, but the time taken for melancholy to develop is a core element in the connection between literary-artistic people and this condition.

Whether one can strictly say that this story of melancholy's progress is a biological characteristic in the way one can of consumption, cholera, smallpox or the Black Death (however those disease structures might vary in their outcomes in themselves) is a point which is still being debated today.[47] The early modern period took its cue from the Classical writers in regarding mind and body to be fundamentally interrelated and that what affected one would affect the other, and such a view continued (despite the intervention of Descartes et al. and the decline of humoralism) until the rise of positivist science in the nineteenth century. Depression appears today to be as complex a phenomenon as melancholy did in Burton's time, with causes both social and physical, although – as today – both could interact in beneficial or deleterious ways.

When we are talking of fashionable melancholy, we are narrowing our focus towards the form of melancholy described by both Burton and Gray, in which the symptoms are chronic and the 'story' of the disease follows an arc that allows an initial pleasurable melancholy. Burton offers a tragic denouement, with the progressive worsening of the melancholy state (unless some intervention occurs) and ultimately death through disease or suicide occurs. The suicide option itself became fashionable in the Romantic period, from the fictional young Werther of Goethe to the spectacular alleged suicide of Chatterton, the archetypal poet of sensibility spurned and ultimately driven into suicidal depression by a cruel world (at least as represented by Victorian artists like Henry Wallis, who painted *The Death of Chatterton* (1856), a notoriously melodramatic rendition of the event). The fate of Keats and his consumption – allegedly brought on by a harsh review – echoes that of Chatterton in the correlation of disease and biography. Consumption suited a certain cultural construction of the role of a lower-class poet, and was closely related to melancholy, which also dovetailed with that same discourse of the poet of sensibility being nervously maladapted to the harsh circumstances of literary production prevalent at the end of the eighteenth and start of the nineteenth centuries.

Melancholy's core characteristics of sadness and fear were not inimical to its popularity because these emotions varied in severity and, as part of the characteristic of the disease, could go into remission, thus allowing at least some lucid intervals necessary for creative activity. Of course, it is possible to write even when one is suffering more severe states of emotion, and, in certain cases, writers can be motivated by these very states to express and even contain melancholy's agonies, as we see throughout this volume in various individuals, both male and female. Moreover, melancholy was not thought to disengage the individual from reality completely, as would occur in a 'raving' and psychotic lunatic of the kind represented in Caius Cibber's statue on the gates of Bedlam. Incarceration as a result of melancholy was not usually necessary as melancholics were perfectly capable of functioning in society most of the time: indeed, a cure for melancholy was to seek out company and occupation: 'If you are idle, be not solitary; if you are solitary, be not idle', said Dr Johnson, modifying Burton.[48] Melancholics were, if anything, likely to flee society rather than make trouble in it, like the doomed hero and poet in William Cowper's eponymous poem 'The Castaway' (1803). True, the visions and hallucinations part of the early modern complex of melancholy do not easily sit well with this neurotic rather than psychotic picture of the disease, but even these were largely benign, in the sense that they were not a permanent event: the individual might have a vision, but they would return to reality. Complete and total disengagement from reality was not normally a defining feature of melancholia. We have also already seen that visions were part of the potentially beneficial imaginative disorder that characterized the creative melancholy mind.

Melancholy detached one from society just enough to liberate the imagination, and indeed body, from social constraints that might be inconvenient to the creative process (in whatever direction that took the individual). Love-lorn poets, Renaissance or Romantic, could take advantage of such (motivated) melancholy; ladies too could retire into the quiet shades and groves (like an Anne Finch, for example) in order to nurse both their melancholy and their poetic imagination, preserved from the interruptions of domestic management. Because of depression's psychological core, because of its potential to be both mild and severe, because it was so difficult to diagnose the precise motivation and authenticity of the condition, it was a disease (or cluster of diseases) that lent itself to greater self-determination and self-expression: an ideal disease, one might assume, for the creative type.

Diane Buie has argued that religious melancholy, for example, could be a fashionable phenomenon because the sufferer could blame the mental illness on God rather than on her or his own particular faults. According to Buie, William Cowper deliberately portrays his melancholy in *Adeplhi* as religious melancholy 'in order to avoid the pressures placed upon him to earn a living'. Such a choice meant that, unlike other factors like idleness or bad lifestyle, the sufferer of religious melancholy could benefit from 'the greater degree of tolerance shown towards the idleness of those suffering from religious melancholy'.[49] How could it be a sin to love God to excess? There were concerns, of course, that it was not God that was being loved, but man's deluded concept of God, as in the case of the 'Enthusiasts' so vigorously pilloried by Jonathan Swift, to name but one satirist of alleged religious excess.

Leigh Wetherall-Dickson's fascinating example later in this book of Anne Dutton's quasi-erotic fascination with the spiritual love of Christ in her melancholic episodes nicely illustrates the way in which the culture of religious melancholy could lend itself to the legitimation of female desires both sexual and textual. Dutton exploits the very fact of her religious melancholy to give herself a voice in published form, and in a genre – spiritual autobiography, as Wetherall-Dickson explains – acceptable to her own community. Her illness buys her, metaphorically speaking, a room of her own to narrate her own identity.

Dutton's authenticity, however, is not in question, and it is a debatable point as to how many people were seriously tempted to put on the airs of melancholy and its cognates in the manner so often mentioned in the eighteenth century. No doubt some people did use 'the *Hyppo* [as] a fashionable Term of Art, and Preten[d] to it', as did another of Wetherall-Dickson's melancholics, the anonymous 'Private Gentleman' whose tendencies to masturbation were responsible for religious guilt and melancholy that he claimed to be authentic.[50] Much literary representation centred on the inauthenticity of claims to the spleen and vapours, and often smacked of an anti-feminist discourse now that the progress of melancholy had become a much more feminized affair. Pope's notorious lines from *The Rape of the Lock* in the melancholic Cave of Spleen characterize the ladies of the fashionable world as paradoxically subject to the vagaries of their wombs ('Hail wayward Queen! / Who rule the sex to fifty from fifteen') and yet wilfully manipulating the symptoms of melancholy: 'The fair ones feel such maladies as these, / When each new nightdress gives a new disease'.[51] Here, the better-known world of female fashion blends seamlessly with the fashionability of disease, even if negatively framed by Pope's profoundly ambiguous misogyny, both attracted and repelled as he was by the women of the upper orders, Catholic or otherwise.

Myths and realities of melancholy for Johnson and Boswell: masculine melancholies

Literary men might also find melancholy fashionable, but this was by no means a universal attitude, and by no means unambiguously expressed. The great Samuel Johnson had a clear sense of himself as more grievously affected than the majority of depressives. As Boswell relates,

> The hypochondriack disorder being mentioned, Dr. Johnson did not think it so common as I supposed. 'Dr. Taylor (said he) is the same one day as another. Burke and Reynolds are the same; Beauclerk, except when in pain, is the same. I am not so myself; but this I do not mention commonly'.[52]

Hypochondria meant depression in this case: in Johnson's time it largely lacked the exclusively negative connotations of inauthenticity it was to acquire in later centuries. Johnson had many episodes in his life when his depression was so severe as to make him think he was falling over the brink of an acceptable, what we might now call 'neurotic', melancholy into one that entirely broke with reason. In this pre-Freudian era, terms such as 'neurotic' and 'psychotic' had no meaning, but the boundary between a form of melancholy that had contact with reality and one that did *not* was of the utmost importance. As Johnson put it in his poem 'Know Yourself':

> I view myself, while reason's feeble light
> Shoots a pale glimmer through the gloom of night,

While passions, error, phantoms of the brain,
And vain opinions, fill the dark domain;
A dreary void, where fears with grief combin'd
Waste all within, and desolate the mind. (lines 29–34)[53]

This, after he had just revised and enlarged his gigantic work of Enlightenment, the *Dictionary*.

To Boswell, however, Johnson's malady was not a threat to his overall sanity, and possibly part of his genius. When relating the tale of Dr. Swinfen's 'exposure' of Johnson's complaint, Boswell leaps to a robust defence of his friend:

> But let not little men triumph upon knowing that Johnson was an HYPOCHONDRIACK, was subject to what the learned, philosophical, and pious Dr. Cheyne has so well treated under the title of 'The English Malady.' Though he suffered severely from it, he was not therefore degraded. The powers of his great mind might be troubled, and their full exercise suspended at times; but the mind itself was ever entire…Johnson, in his writings, and in his conversation, never failed to display all the varieties of intellectual excellence. In his march through this world to a better, his mind still appeared grand and brilliant.[54]

Boswell's mention of George Cheyne's famous treatise on what were called 'disorders of the nerves' is calculated to remind the reader that there were other great – not 'little' – men suffering from what Cheyne had characterized as 'The English Malady', and that hypochondria or melancholia might not mark a person out as being a dysfunctional member of society. On the contrary, Boswell trumpets that Johnson and Cheyne were highly productive, even heroic, in their resistance to constitutional disease.

Depressives are often credited with extraordinary abilities, especially creative genius. Johnson's case both confirms and denies this long-standing myth, as Boswell's praise of Johnson's efforts to keep on composing his *Rambler* essays demonstrates: 'notwithstanding his constitutional indolence, his depression of spirits, and his labour in carrying on his *Dictionary*, he answered the stated calls of the press twice a week from the stores of his mind, during all that time'.[55] Johnson was driven to write, partly by guilt about his idleness, even when dragged down by his melancholy: the fact that he could produce work at all shows that his depression was not at the severe end of the spectrum in these instances, and that work for him was a form of cure. Patently, melancholy cannot exist with creativity when at the worst stages of life-crushing misery. Johnson's highly masculine vision of successfully battling with melancholy in a literal war of 'nerves' was only possible because of this latitude in the impact of symptoms. His macho statement that 'a man may write at any time, if he will set himself doggedly to it,' is hardly an option for those more seriously affected, including himself at times.[56]

Johnson's attitude to the alleged genius associated with melancholy is rather brutally expressed in one of his letters to Boswell:

> you are always complaining of your own melancholy, and I conclude from those complaints that you are fond of it. No man talks of that which he is desirous to conceal, and every man desires to conceal that of which he is ashamed. Do not pretend to deny it … make it an invariable and obligatory law to yourself, never to mention your own mental diseases.[57]

This is hardly the talking cure of our own era. Johnson certainly had psychological insight into Boswell's partial pride in his position, but Boswell himself knew what it was to suffer. What Johnson lacked was any sense that talking through one's problems might alleviate them – 'if you are never to speak of them, you will think on them but little, and if you think little of them, they will molest you rarely … speak no more, think no more, about them'.[58] Push away your problems and the pain will go away: a laudable and Stoical attitude in one way, but in another one can see that Johnson, without the aid of post-Freudian insight, was storing up his problems so that the repressed could return with greater vengeance later on.

To do Boswell justice, he had warned his readers in his 'Hypochondriack' column not to believe Aristotle's famous dictum that melancholics were more intelligent and brave than other men and that 'their suffering marked their superiority',

> because I am certain that many who might have prevented the disease from coming to any height, had they checked its first appearances, have not only resisted it, but have truly cherished it, form the erroneous flattering notion that they were making sure of the undoubted though painful characterstick of excellence, as young ladies submit without complaint to have their ears pierced that they may be decorated with brilliant ornaments.[59]

Boswell's metaphor of fashionable decoration is clearly associating feminine susceptibility to shiny trinkets with the use of disease as display as well – we return to this issue later in Pope, but Boswell's serious point remains that this condition is not one confined to the fair sex: 'Melancholy, or Hypochondria, like the fever or the gout, or any other disease, is incident to all sorts of men, from the wisest to the most foolish.'[60] The caveat here, however, is that as 'men are miserable in a greater or lesser degree in proportion to their understanding and sensibility', so the more refined, like Boswell and Johnson, suffer more.[61] It seems strange that one could 'cherish' a disease, but this aspect of mental illness, in contrast to physical, has always had a degree of suspicion attached to it because of the comparative ease with which the symptoms can be imitated.

At a time when there was a cult of nervous suffering and fashionable melancholy, both seen as diseases of an advanced civilization and the price to pay for superior social rank, Johnson refused to admit that his malady could be anything other than God's scourge of the sinner. Boswell insightfully comments that 'Johnson, who was blest with all the powers of genius and understanding in a degree far above the ordinary state of human nature, was at the same time visited with a disorder so afflictive, that they who know it by dire experience, will not envy his exalted endowments'.[62] All the genius in the world does not compensate for the misery caused by depression, even though the genius might be aided by the malady.

Women and melancholy genius

Although it has been argued that women have been traditionally excluded from the masculine model of melancholy genius, more recent investigations by critics such as Katherine Hodgkin (in relation to the early modern period) and Heather Meek (in the context of eighteenth-century hysteria and the bluestockings) have shown that women actively sought to appropriate the possibilities of melancholy as a means of authenticating creative abilities and, indeed, the act of creation in itself.[63] We need look no further than Anne Finch's rightly much-anthologized poem 'A Pindaric Ode on the Spleen' (originally written around 1694) to see a female poet carefully teasing out different types of authentic and inauthentic melancholy, and finally placing her own particular form of genuine suffering as a marker of her identity as a poet.[64] Finch lambasts those fools who assume the mantle of the fashionable Spleen, but with a twist of the plot:

The fool to imitate the wits
Complains of thy pretended fits
And dullness born with him would lay
Upon thy accidental sway;
Because sometime thou do'st presume
Into the ablest heads to come.
      That often men of thought refin'd,
      Impatient of unequal sense,
Such slow returns, where they so much dispense,
Retiring form the croud, are to thy shades inclin'd.
      O'er me, alas, thou do'st too much prevail,
      I feel thy force, whilst I against thee rail.[65]

Yes, melancholy is a fashionable malady to which people of dullness resort, but it is also a condition that, in its true form, afflicts 'men of thought' (gender seems to be in the traditional mode here) who flee from the cloddish and pretentious mob who chase around in the whirl of city fashions. The solitary person of sense finds solace (and yet probably exacerbates the melancholic condition in the process) in the 'shades' of rural peace – a move that invokes the clear morality of the country/city dichotomy. Finch places herself as a solitary melancholic person of sense in a slick and quick shift from the 'men of sense' hastily retiring into country shades to her own suffering ('O'er me, alas') and retreat:

Whilst in the Muses paths I stray,
Whilst in their groves and by their secret springs
My hand delights to trace unusual things,
And deviates from the known and common rules.[66]

Finch invokes Longinus', and later Pope's, notion of the great poet as being able to deviate from accepted conventions and maps it onto her own poetic wanderings in the country retreat of male genius. By a metaphorical sleight of hand the splenetic woman becomes a melancholic poet of the most genuine kind. Finch's melancholy is fashionable but concurrently entails real suffering. Her conscious manipulation of poetic form (the Pindaric form of the ode mirrors the protean nature of the condition), tradition and medical discourse results in a legitimation of her art – no mean feat and elegantly achieved. In her rejection of false melancholy, she represents her own as genuine, even as she is framing her own representation, or rather constructing her own narrative of self as diseased and poetic simultaneously. Again, it must be stressed, this does not negate her own, very real, suffering.

We now move from the peculiar 'narrative' of depression itself and return to the way it was inserted into fashionable eighteenth-century culture and society. In order to achieve this, we look to a crucial theorist and diagnostician of social maladies after mid-century: Samuel Tissot.

Tissot: class, gender and fashionable melancholy in the Enlightenment

In his essay *On the disorders of the people of fashion* (1766) Samuel Auguste Tissot, the influential Swiss physician, argued that fashionable people are subject to fashionable diseases because of their modern, 'civilized' lifestyle.[67] The 'best citizens' (this seems to include all persons of the upper classes) have 'an aversion to simplicity' that causes them to develop 'many diseases unknown to the fields, and which are triumphant in high life'.[68] In contrast to 'the labourer' (although even this category of worker is 'unhappily inferior to the labourers of former times' because they are 'infected' 'with the customs of the city'),[69] with his robust nerves, fibres and balanced perspiration, people of fashion are weak in body and mind.[70] Their 'course of life' has 'nothing useful to support it' because they are divorced from productive and directed work, so these 'sons of idleness' rely on 'continuous dissipation' for the substance – or lack of it – of their lives. They attempt 'to defeat the insupportable tediousness of an inactive life' and 'kill time by pleasure'.[71] The problem is that 'real enjoyment is relaxation' from useful activity. The consequence is fashionable hypochondria:

> Undoubtedly the origin of luxury, which is only the combination of a multitude of superfluities, was invented by man to mingle variety with his being, or perhaps to distinguish himself. This is the perfect situation of the whimsically hippish, who require a great number of remedies to cure them of nothing. The healthy infant is amused with any thing, while the sickly child plays with every toy without being pleased.[72]

Inevitably 'this false taste is contagious' and 'hath past as a fashion to such as it detriments very much' rather than merely 'those who invented it through necessity'.[73] The guilty recipients of idle fashionability and hypochondria tend to be 'the well educated, who seem to propose it as the principal object of their pursuit; they are so careless with regard to health, that the greatest part of their diseases are scarcely known in the country'.[74]

Tissot's argument is not unusual in this part of the eighteenth century, but it does spell out the problems of civilization starkly for a European audience. He goes through the six 'non-naturals' – those factors regarding health that are not innate to a person's constitution such as food and drink, sleep and waking, the air they breathe, perspiration and excretion, and the passions – in order to show how people in 'high life' (as opposed to the labourer) affect their health.[75] The instance of dietary regimen is instructive: labourers eat simple foods that are flavoured just enough to inspire appetite without excess and so do not suffer the disastrous effects of continuous over-repletion.[76] In contrast, 'a person in high life gratifies appetite, and dilutes thirst with the sharpest things, or things which have so pleasing an impression on the palate as to excite a desire to indulge with more than is needful, which is less than what a working labourer requires'.[77] The tables of the great have

> the most juicy meats, the highest flavoured game, the most delicate fishes stewed in the richest wines, and rendered still more inflammatory by the addition of aromatic spices; poultry, crawfish, and their sauce; meat gravies, variously extracted; eggs, truffles; the most savoury vegetables, the sharpest aromatics lavishly used; sweet-meats of all kinds, brought from all parts of the world; candies infinitely various; pastry, fries, creams, the strongest flavoured cheeses, or the only viands introduced by taste.
>
> The strongest wines brought from every place which produces them; brandy, in the most attractive and dangerous forms; coffee, tea, and chocolate, are found upon their tables.[78]

The obvious consequence of such high living is the destruction (by indigestion and blockage) of the physical body, which itself leads to psychological disorders. People of fashion become 'delicate' and then 'valetudinary': 'They are hardly ever well; one day of health is bought by months of anxiety, and the irregularity is sometimes universal throughout the faculties, without being peculiarly distinguishable in any. They suffer a general depression without being able to point out their complaint.'[79] It is worth noting here that this use of the word 'depression' refers to the body quite as much as the mind: Tissot assumes that mind and body are mutually interactive, and that disorders in one lead to disorders in the other.

Indeed, a key plank in Tissot's analysis of fashionable disorders is his section on the role 'of the passions'. 'Strong passions, though the most agreeable, always exhaust, and sometimes kill upon the spot; the sorrowful passions absolutely destroy the animal oeconomy, and, doubtless, are the general causes of languishing diseases'.[80] Again, unlike the simple labourer in the field who has very few stimuli and can operate 'like an automaton without reflection', the person of fashion 'has continually before his eyes, and in his imagination, a variety of objects that keep him in continual agitation'.[81] The discussion at this point is very much gendered male, as it can only be a man who is subject to 'the ambition of honour, the love of titles, the desire of possessing such a fortune as luxury renders necessary'.[82] These are 'three principles that incessantly animate the man in high life, keeping his soul in continual agitation, which alone would be enough to destroy his health; frequently exposed to a reverse of fortune, to mortifications, to sorrows, to humiliations, to rage, to vexations, which continually embitter his moments'.[83] How happy is the labourer, who 'has no ambition but to have a plentiful crop, and does not place his happiness in a multitude of objects'. Worse still for the man of fashion, the competition for advancement means that he is constantly subjected to destructive emotions: 'fear, diffidence, jealousy, and aversion, reside in his heart and disorder his several functions'.[84] Courtiers cannot be healthy because 'they take no exercise, and their minds [are] being continually agitated between hope and fear' and 'never have a moment's repose; it is therefore not at all surprising if their weakness exposes them to hypochondriac complaints or diseases of the head'.[85] Cities are especially dangerous places, as they are where 'a number of people of condition are assembled' and therefore 'present every moment some cause of discontent. When the soul is in such a situation it necessarily influences the health'.[86] With a move that looks forward to the Wordsworthian and Romantic concept of the city as a location that assaults both body and soul, Tissot focuses on the peculiar threat to the upper classes more than the middling sort, a situation that would change as nervous disorders trickled down the social classes as the eighteenth century wore on, a point noted by Dr Thomas Trotter in his well-known treatise on nervous disorders.[87]

As Cheyne had before him, Tissot argues that the labourer has less sensibility than the man of rank, to the extent that 'the loss of person to him the most dear, scarce touches him; that of his effects, not much more, because poverty itself would hardly alter his manner of living'.[88] More than this, class divides the perception of time: the labourer 'is never sensible but to the present, while the affluent dreads the future,—his imagination, disordered by the agitation of his nerves, fills him every moment, with the vapours'.[89] This heightened awareness of time and the pressures such an awareness brings is a recipe for depression and anxiety, a generalized gloom about a future to be feared and shunned rather than embraced; the man of fashion cannot live in the moment, 'smell the coffee' as popular psychologists are so fond of saying in our own time.

Perhaps not accidentally at this mention of the vapours, a term more usually associated with women, Tissot turns his attention to the fair sex:

> Numbers of ladies are under an impossibility of being well, without mentioning other causes, by the continual succession of their fears, which every instant throws them into a violent situation, absolutely disorder the whole animal oeconomy; they scream out, if the least irregularity of the ground causes their coach to lean more on the one side than the other; while the labourer, preceding the brilliant equipage, will almost suffer it to run over him before he turns his head, or thinks of stepping aside to avoid it.[90]

As one might gather from Tissot's rather insulting depiction of the cloddish country bumpkin, people of fashion are not exactly objects of satire in his treatise. Perhaps mindful – again like Cheyne – of his paying customers, Tissot ends his section on the function of the passions with a panegyric to the moral consequences of the finer sensibility of the upper orders:

> This great sensibility occasions people of rank to be the victims of their most laudable feelings; all that afflicts or threatens others, all the evils incident to mankind in general, or merit in particular, are to them real grievances, afflicting them very frequently, more than their own private complaints, and essentially destroy their health; in a word, infinitely more sensible of tender impressions, and exposed to a much greater number than the peasant, of necessity they must suffer much more.[91]

The paradox of the excessive sensibility brought on by the modern civilized lifestyle is that collision between the suffering induced by the nervous hyperstimulation of the feeling individual and the moral superiority that such 'tender impressions' and 'laudable feelings' prove. The cult of the sentimental, in which the upper orders gain an apparently perverse pleasure from their own suffering at the sight of (and sympathy with) 'all the evils incident to mankind in general' – from a poverty-stricken family at the side of the public highway to a puppy with a thorn in its paw – is not far removed from Tissot's medical analysis of nervous sensibility and its concomitant disorders. More precisely, the fashionable cult of the sentimental is a consequence of the developments in nerve medicine from the late seventeenth century, as G. S. Rousseau and G. J. Barker-Benfield have shown.[92]

Tissot's analysis of fashionable ills is not confined to the passions, however. Other factors in a high-living lifestyle are important; sleep for the 'rich and brilliant inhabitants of the cities' is nothing short of disastrous:

> The man of fashion, disturbed by business, projects, pleasures, disappointments, and the regrets of the day, heated by food and drinks, goes to bed with trembled nerves, agitated pulse, a stomach labouring with the load and acrimony of his food, the vessels full, or juices which inflame them, indisposition, anxiety, the fever accompanies him to bed, and for a long time keeps him waking; if he closes his eyes, his slumbers are short, uneasy, agitating, troubled with frightful dreams, and sudden startings ... every night reduces his health, and fortifies the seed of some disease.[93]

One is tempted to digress into a discussion about the marvellous translation of Tissot's French here: the broken rhythms of the prose brilliantly enact the turbulent nights of the fashionable man apparently condemned by consumerist modernity to physical and psychological torture in wakefulness, and even in sleep with his 'frightful dreams'. In stark contrast – and predictably by now given Tissot's stated aim to make a continuous contrast between low and high livers –

> the peasant whose nerves are not agitated by any affection of the soul, or blood inflamed, or stomach labouring with the effects of an erroneous regimen, lays himself down and sleeps; his slumbers are tranquil and profound; it is difficult to wake him, but the moment his spirits are recruited, he awakes, he is perfectly easy, fresh strong and light.[94]

Tissot does not quite say 'How happy is the moron', but the implication is there and obviously informs the constantly double-edged critique of his investigation into both the fashionable and unfashionable parts of eighteenth-century society.

Even sexual activity – 'the pleasures of love' – comes under scrutiny under the rubric of 'secretions and excretions', a balance of these being necessary to the regular functioning of the body.[95] Too great a retention of bodily fluids could mean a build-up of harmful humours in the body; too great an excretion of bodily matter could mean a loss of vital spirits and lead to wasting disorders, among others. The simple rustic is 'accustomed to continual action unknown to the anxiety of idleness, sheltered from dangerous discourses, far from alluring objects, he knows not the business till his union is determined'.[96] Consequently 'the pleasure with him goes no farther than what nature requires, and he increases his health even while he exhausts it'.[97] Such a happy golden mean is not easily acquired in the life of a city-slicker: 'but with the youth of the town, who finds himself in circumstances absolutely different, debauchery, advancing age by force, is the general cause of his diseases, and of his perishing in the flower of his age'.[98] Tissot, of course, is the author of the famous *Onanania* or *On Onanism; or, A Treatise upon the disorders produced by Masturbation: or, the effects of secret and excessive venery* (originally published in 1760 and included as the third essay in the *Three Essays* which are begun by the present one on the disorders of people of fashion). Masturbation, for Tissot, wasted vital force contained in semen and, if continued excessively, could result in all kinds of disorders, not least melancholy. Again we are reminded that the causes of depression in this period were various, and concerned with the operation of the whole system, not reducible to an individual virus, bacterium, gene or hormone as in periods after the late nineteenth century.

From fashionable sensibility to Romantic vitalism – melancholy medicine and literature

Tissot's works coincided with the fashionable sensibility that drove the popularity of melancholy and which became increasingly popular as the century entered its final phase, one that we now call Romanticism. As George Rousseau has put it: 'Tissot's approach to nerves was anthropological: to classify medical conditions by nations and regions. But its symptomology was culturally identical with his British colleagues', and, while Tissot was being translated into English the 1760s, 'Robert Whytt, the Scottish physician and professor of medicine in Edinburgh, was lecturing to medical students in Britain's now most forward-looking university about the crucial significance of nerves, as well as training a generation of physicians who would invade Bath after Cheyne.'[99] The importance of the link between the theory of the nerves and the culture of sensibility and the sentimental is difficult to overstate: medical developments fed into literary and cultural trends in a feedback loop that Tissot and Cheyne's work exemplifies.

Albrecht von Haller (1708–77) had defined the quality of sensibility as something that resided in the centre of the nerve and that allowed the perception of exterior impulses or stimuli. Physical tissues containing nerves now could be said to possess sensibility, and the property of 'irritability' rested in the muscles and worked separately from the nervous system. Hence Haller enabled medical theory to recognize the importance of the solid parts of the body and the independence of sensibility and irritability from an allegedly separate and inviolable soul.[100] Nerves and fibres now took on a dominant role in medical theory, and allowed the progression towards Romantic concepts of the unconscious operation of the body and the erosion of the power of reason. Crucially for the study of representations of melancholy and depression, sensibility became an integral aspect of the novel, poetry and drama, from *Tristram Shandy*'s sometimes ironic transports to Henry Mackenzie's archetypal *Man of Feeling*. Heroines now fainted at the sight of distress compulsorily.[101] Such representations of the fashionable melancholy of sensibility and the sentimental could vary in degree. Laurence Sterne's melancholy sensibility, as discussed by Stuart Sim later in this book, is expressed increasingly in terms of the physical mechanism of the nerves.[102]

At the end of our period, then, fashionable melancholy was profoundly linked with the medical theory of the nerves, and this did not cease with the advent of Romanticism and the 'Brunonian' vitalist medicine that was so influential in the representations of the period. The boom in Scottish medicine furthered the cause of 'nerve theory'.[103] William Cullen had stated that a certain quantity of 'excitement' or tension in the nerves was needed to keep the body healthy: inadequate stimulation, both internal and external, meant 'depression' of the body's systems, and required exercise, air, food and drugs to return them to a suitable level of activity.[104] Overstimulation caused spasms and needed a depleting regimen that included blood-letting, a 'low' vegetarian diet, rest and calming medicines. Cullen's scheme fed smoothly into John Brown's (1735–88) 'Brunonian' theory of excitability: a quality that dominated all life, not just the muscles and nerves. Brown theorized that a fixed quantity of life-giving excitability, the body's 'fuel', was given to each person. Regular and orderly stimulation of that fixed quantity through internal and external impulses was vital to health. If the stimuli were too weak, the body would be 'aesthenic'; too strong, it would be 'sthenic'. The physician's had to raise or lower levels of excitement to a happy medium. Melancholy was one possible result of a 'depression' of the body's activity. Unfortunately for Brown, his ideas and the related systems proved a failure in practice and did not persist long in medicine, although vitalism itself was influential in the artistic sphere.[105]

By the late eighteenth century, melancholy had entered into a new phase of fashionability, partly informed by the literary and philosophical trends outlined in other areas of this book, such as the Graveyard School in poetry, and by a new emphasis on individual Genius, both of which resulted in the emergence of the figure of the 'gloomy egoist' so well described by Sickels's classical description of melancholic poets and poetry of the same name.[106] The role of medical theory of the nerves was also crucial in this continued fashionability, as it continued to mark out the sensitive individual (even if not a poet) as a person prone to melancholy, and enabled the mythology of melancholy genius to be reactivated, although via a different physiological rationale. This was in some ways an advantage for women, who were thought to be finer-nerved than men; the disadvantage was that they might also be considered weaker-brained. When Charlotte Smith states that 'I am so nervous I can hardly hold a pen', and when Keats talks repeatedly about the state of his nerves in his letters, they must be understood in a literal as well as metaphorical sense.[107]

Both Smith and Keats were undertaking a certain amount of melancholic self-fashioning, as many poets and writers did, and as has been well documented by critics from Sickels onwards, and by John Baker in this book. This is not to say that poets who invested their image into melancholic fashionability did not suffer – any cursory reading of Smith or Keats will confirm to even the most sceptical that they certainly did – but the discourse of melancholic genius was a conscious option for writers both male and female, and, by this period, of different social ranks. Much of the rest of this book documents the realities of depression and melancholy in the most severe forms, but we are left with the paradox that, from the start of the period and before to the end of the period and after, melancholy remained a resolutely fashionable disease.

2
Philosophical Melancholy

Richard Terry

Languages of mood

Wordsworth's 'Daffodils' was composed at some point between 1804 and 1807 after the poet had reread the entry for 15 April 1802 in his sister Dorothy's journal. The poem recalls a shared walk with Dorothy near Ullswater, during which the pair had happened on a swaying field of daffodils, a spectacle recorded by Dorothy through a vivid description of how the flowers 'tossed & reeled & danced & seemed as if they verily laughed with the wind that blew upon them over the Lake'.[1] The imagery captures her original impression, not only of rippling movement but also of how the flowers seemed to her animated by their own gaiety and high spirits. William's subsequent poem incorporates the same impression, but also adds to it:

> The waves beside them danced; but they
> Out-did the sparkling waves in glee:
> A poet could not but be gay,
> In such a jocund company.

William, unlike Dorothy, paints into the scene the way that the observing poet is himself stirred into gaiety by the infectious glee displayed by the flowers. Moreover, at the poem's close he records how he has been able to recall to his 'inward eye' this transport of intense pleasure as a means of dissipating subsequent spells of melancholy that left him languishing 'In vacant or in pensive mood'.[2]

William reshapes Dorothy's journal entry by turning her naturalistic observations into an inner colloquium between the poet's past and present selves, but he also introduces the idea that moments of such gaiety or charged happiness need to be hoarded as a defence against the future onset of melancholy.[3] What his poem understands is that gaiety and melancholy comprise reverse faces of the same coin, a recognition also shared by Sterne's Tristram:

> In mentioning the word *gay* (as in the close of the last chapter) it puts one (*i.e.* an author) in mind of the word *spleen*—especially if he has any thing to say upon it: not that by any analysis—or that from any table of interest or genealogy, there appears much more ground of alliance betwixt them, than betwixt light and darkness, or any two of the most unfriendly opposites in nature.[4]

Tristram justifies his mentioning of spleen or melancholy in the same vicinity as 'gay' as part of the authorial propriety of always maintaining a 'good understanding among words', of knowing which words consort harmoniously with each other and which stand in 'unfriendly' opposition.

Wordsworth's 'Daffodils' and the extract from *Tristram Shandy* testify to how the nomenclature surrounding both gaiety and misery has mutated over time. Not just 'spleen' but also the clustered terms 'glee', 'gay' and 'jocund' in the Wordsworth stanza have long passed from common parlance. We are now more likely to register a sudden access of high spirits by describing ourselves as 'euphoric', 'ecstatic' or 'over the moon' rather than 'blithe' or 'gay' or 'jocund' as our eighteenth-century predecessors might have done. Yet these marked changes of vocabulary do more than register alterations of verbal fashion, for the emotional state recorded by Wordsworth in 'Daffodils' seems in a more radical way no longer linguistically authorized, no longer identified by a functioning terminology in the language of today. One cause has, of course, been the way that the verbal rendering of heightened states of pleasure has been contaminated by the contemporary drug culture with its argot of sensation, stimulation, of taking a 'trip' or being on a 'high'. It is hard now not to associate the sort of emotional raptures that figure frequently in Wordsworth's poetry, those he connotes with words like 'bliss' and 'joy', with pleasures nowadays induced by intoxicants.

Yet a deeper reason exists for our sense of estrangement from the intense forms of gladness we sometimes encounter in earlier writers such as Wordsworth, which has to do with the relation between emotional states and personal identity. The words making up the terminology of gaiety in the eighteenth century had mostly, in their original acceptation, denoted forms of character disposition. 'Glad' (*Oxford English*

Dictionary 2), for example, had in its archaic sense meant 'Cheerful, joyous, or merry in disposition'; meanwhile 'gay' itself had been used to mean 'Full of or disposed to joy and mirth', as in Chaucer's merry Absalom who 'jolif was and gay'.[5] This habit of seeing happiness as an ingredient of personality gradually gets replaced by a view that such positive, rewarding feelings are essentially impermanent, needing to be provoked by a particular context, and not inherently constitutive of personality. We can see this direction of semantic travel in several related terms. Whereas *Oxford English Dictionary* 2 records the eighteenth-century meaning of 'glee' (3. a) as 'Mirth, joy, rejoicing', it gives its modern usage as 'a lively feeling of delight caused by special circumstances': in other words, 'glee' for us relates to an extraordinary surge of exuberant feeling, relating to a precise cause. Similarly, words like 'mirth' and 'merry', which formerly referred to a general state of cheerfulness or mental wellbeing, now refer almost exclusively to exceptional events of revelry. We can track this general process with the word 'joy' which has largely dropped out of usage as naming a radiant state of inner contentment, and yet 'overjoyed' has never been in so much verbal demand. The idea of being 'overjoyed' (unlike 'joy' itself) agrees with our peculiarly modern view that any state of enhanced positive feeling must result from a direct cause and should be seen as essentially transient and volatile.

The same mutations that have impacted on the language of gaiety have also affected that of glumness. As well as a broad spectrum of terms equating roughly to our modern concept of depression, including 'melancholy', 'hypochondria' and the 'spleen', the eighteenth century had a rich lexicon of terms to consider general mental anguish, such as 'sadness', 'sorrow' and 'dolour'. Of these, 'sorrow' is perhaps the most widely current, in the sense recorded by *Oxford English Dictionary* 2 as 'Distress of mind caused by loss, suffering, disappointment, etc.; grief, deep sadness or regret' (1. a). Sorrow has nowadays largely disappeared from our nomenclature concerning unhappiness, except in the specialized rhetoric of condolence in which we might express 'deep sorrow' for, or emotional regret at, the death of an acquaintance, not for one's own sake, however, but for the sake of the impact of that loss on another or others. Sorrow has become for us a confined and reactive emotion, no longer a generic term for 'Distress of mind' as understood by eighteenth-century moralists such as Dr. Johnson.[6]

One aspect of this semantic drift, not commented on so far, is that emotion, rather than being seen as a stable and integral element of human character, has come to be seen as essentially performative, or as something that acquires meaning through being received as a specta-cle for others. There are a number of related terms that begin to change meaning during the eighteenth century in a very specific way – where the shift is from originally denoting an attribute of character to coming instead to refer to a spectatorial judgement passed on another person. 'Risible' and 'ludicrous', words of similar meaning, are two such; origi-nally used to describe someone of a 'witty' or 'humorous' disposition, they have since come to refer to qualities inherent within a person or spectacle that provoke laughter, generally of an aggressive kind, in others.[7] We can see the same semantic flexing occurring in our own time with the word 'sad', commonly used (especially by the young) not to denote an emotional state as such so much as a spectacle likely to prompt that state, as in 'sad case'. The same looping around occurs with modern usages of 'sorrow' as suggested above: sorrow no longer means 'Distress of mind' so much as an empathetic regret caused by the mental distress of another person.

I have dwelt on these semantic instabilities in order to underscore a general point about the radical discontinuity between the eighteenth-century nomenclature concerning gaiety and misery and that of our own day. Yet the most pronounced of those disjunctions has so far gone unstated. It seems to me that what mostly separates us today from the mentality of our forebears is the tendency to see misery (and the same could be proposed about its opposite, joyfulness) as aberrant, in a con-text in which normal mental health is associated with the absence of strong negative feelings. Recently a rash of cautionary books has broken out, counselling against the way that modern western society has tried to expel unhappiness from the spectrum of tolerable mental states. Eric G. Wilson's *Against Happiness* (2008), for example, laments the addiction of contemporary American culture to positive thinking, an addiction that has exiled modern Americans from melancholy, from a deeper engagement with the complexity of what it is to be human. He exhorts Americans to reject the anodyne cushioning of their lives and instead to reclaim 'the sorrowful joy'.[8]

Wilson not only attacks the 'smoothness' and the endless sense of amenity of the American lifestyle but also identifies the medical treat-ment of depression as a particular way by which some western societies have tried to cleanse themselves of misery. The diagnosis of depres-sion has become the critical means by which we nowadays ward off the threat of unhappiness. The percentage of the United States popula-tion in treatment for the condition, for example, grew from 2.1 per cent in the early 1980s to 3.7 per cent in the early 2000s, a rate of increase of 76 per cent over two decades.[9] The role of the pharmaceutical industry in 'sponsoring' depression, or at least in encouraging the increased diagnosis and treatment of the condition, has been criticized by several recent commentators, including Gary Greenberg in his *Manufacturing Depression* (2010). While pharmaceutical firms may have actively promoted 'depression' as a diagnostic outcome, it remains equally the case that modern diagnostic methods, especially those codified in the third edition of the American *Diagnostic and Statistical Manual of Mental Disorders* (*DSM-III*), published in 1980, have also led to a significant increase in the apparent prevalence of the condition. Allan V. Horwitz and Jerome C. Wakefield have argued persuasively in their 2007 study *The Loss of Sadness: How Psychiatry Transformed Normal Sorrow into Depressive Disorder* that misguided diagnostic methods have led to thousands of people suffering from normal unhappiness to receive treatment as if afflicted by a mental disorder. Allan Ingram discusses these issues in more detail in the final chapter of the present volume.

The relation of depression to unhappiness is obviously close but complex. Andrew Solomon, in his intense study of his own personal depression, *The Noonday Demon*, for example, suggests that the opposite of depression has less to do with happiness than with 'vitality'.[10] However, modern clinicians mainly distinguish depression from normal sadness on the basis that the former comprises dejection ostensibly 'without cause'. The symptoms do not appear to have been triggered by any event or circumstance, or the emotional effect is wholly disproportionate to the cause, or the symptoms persist once the apparent cause of them has gone away. It is the absence of the cause, or the unpredictable link between cause and effect, that makes for the abnormality. The American diagnostic tool *DSM-IV* defines a 'Major Depressive Disorder' (MDD) in terms of the persistence of at least five out of a range of nine symptoms over a two-week period. Most of these symptoms, as Horwitz and Wakefield point out, do not diverge significantly from those common to normal unhappiness, such as dejected mood, loss of pleasure, disrupted sleeping patterns, reduced energy and loss of concentration; and the effect of cataloguing them in this way has clearly led to many patients who are merely evidencing a standard sadness response being misguidedly diagnosed as depressive.[11]

However, it is not merely the broad definition of symptoms given in *DSM-IV* that has been prone to exaggerate the number of identified cases of depression. Just as inflationary has been the manual's specification of potential causes of non-depressive unhappiness: confined alone to bereavement. While the manual accepts that emotional ill-health connected with the recent death of a loved one should not be labelled as depressive, no such diagnostic ruling is given to emotional discomfort caused by a range of other forms of loss, such as the break up of a relationship, loss of personal face, the frustration of a career aspiration or the subversion of financial wellbeing. Instead, even where the degree of unhappiness seems entirely proportionate to the personal calamity undergone, the manual still insists on a diagnosis of depressive disorder. Of course, it might be argued, with some validity, that sadness itself can amount to a debilitating condition, and its symptoms do not simply dissolve as a result of identifying an underlying cause. Sadness itself, it might be argued, requires appropriate medication, just as much as full-blown depression. While not dismissing that case, Horwitz and Wakefield argue instead that sadness, whatever its disabling effects, is a normal evolved human response, naturally selected for its evolutionary benefits; depression, in contrast, confers no individual or species benefits, indicating instead 'that something has gone wrong with mechanisms that were designed to respond to loss'. Their view is that it is not the pain of depression, so much as its biological disutility, that turns it into a mental disorder.[12]

What I hope to have established thus far is the practical difficulty of differentiating between normal sadness and abnormal depression. The two conditions share a common set of symptoms, and the label of 'depression' should not necessarily be taken to imply a more acute experiencing of these. Nowadays, patients have an opportunity to self-select as depressed by presenting their symptoms to a medical practitioner, whereas in the eighteenth century only the well-to-do enjoyed the privilege of a medical response to their unhappiness. There seems little doubt that, in our own time, depression has eaten into the territory formerly occupied by more quotidian kinds of sadness, both in the sense that people who are 'merely' unhappy get routinely treated as depressive and also in the general way that the discourse of depression dominates our sense of what it is to be miserable. In the eighteenth century, medicalized categories of unhappiness, such as melancholy and the spleen, certainly attracted devotees, but the medical discourse never established the pre-eminence that it enjoys in our own time. Instead, it found itself competing with a range of alternative discourses within which periodic unhappiness was accepted unflinchingly as a staple ingredient of human existence. No cure presented itself, but instead the sufferer could be tutored in moral remedies such as fortitude or forbearance or in more philosophical ones such as stoic indifference. This chapter will be about the larger environs of eighteenth-century melancholy, the broad emotional hinterland that stretches away from it, encompassing all those non-medicalized and unexceptional forms of human sadness and sorrow.

Coping with sorrow

It is probably during the eighteenth century that the close ties between sadness and melancholy first begin to dissolve. Earlier influential works on melancholy had generally distinguished that condition from sadness on the basis of the absence of any clear underlying cause. Timothie Bright, for example, in his *Treatise of Melancholie* (1586) takes the example of 'certaine persons which enjoy all the comfortes of this life' who in spite of such blessings become

> overwhelmed with heavines, and dismaide with such feare, as they can neither receive consolation, nor hope of assurance, notwithstanding ther be neither matter of feare, or discontentment, nor yet cause of daunger, but contrarily of great comfort, and gratulation. This passion being not moved by any adversity present or imminent, is attributed to melancholie.[13]

The fact that the sufferer's alarm and distress seems not to be 'moved by', or accountable to, any outward circumstance is what prompts the diagnosis of melancholy. Similarly, Felix Platter, in his *Praxeos Medicae* (1602) defines melancholy as a condition in which 'imagination and judgment are so perverted that without any cause the victims become very sad and fearful'.[14] The same elementary distinction passes into Robert Burton's influential *Anatomy of Melancholy* (1621), which draws a line between a melancholy 'disposition', by which everyone is afflicted on occasions of 'sorrow' or 'perturbation of the mind' and which might be seen as the inescapable 'character of mortality', and a melancholy 'habit', in which the sufferer lapses into a state of self-absorbed 'fear and sadness, *without any apparent occasion*'.[15]

It might be worth emphasizing that the taxonomy being advanced by Burton and others does not relate to the greater malignancy of melancholy compared to run-of-the-mill sadness, for the symptoms ascribed to both conditions are broadly the same, with the exception that the true melancholic could also be seen as labouring under a form of delusion about the non-existent cause of their condition. While the segregation of melancholy from normal sadness begins to occur during the eighteenth century, with physicians becoming more ready to classify acute melancholy as a form of madness, the older distinction still lingers on. As Horwitz and Wakefield point out, Johnson's three definitions of 'melancholy' in his great *Dictionary* (1755) consist of two that refer to it as a medical condition and one that responds to it as an ordinary human emotion.[16]

It is almost impossible now to imagine the persistent, background sadness that must have afflicted many lives in the eighteenth century, an era in which premature mortality was so commonplace. Many parents died in middle rather than old age, and children passed away in their infancy. Many marriages must have been broken by the death of a spouse in early adulthood. The accounts given of these tragedies are often exquisitely anguished. Elizabeth Rowe was distraught after the death of her husband in 1715 at the age of twenty-eight. In her elegy 'On the Death of Mr. Thomas Rowe', she paints her 'endless sorrow', and confesses to being 'Lost in despair, distracted, and forlorn'.[17] On the anniversary of his death the following May, she records that there can be 'no future chearful spring for me'.[18] A similar personal devastation was felt by George, Lord Lyttelton, on the 'fatal, fatal stroke' that separated him from his wife, Lucy, in 1747. Abandoned in a world that had become a 'desart', he captured his wife's memory and his own uncontrollable distress at her death in a monody 'To the Memory of a Lady':

> For my distracted mind
> What succour can I find?
> On whom for consolation shall I call?
> Support me, ev'ry friend,
> Your kind assistance lend
> To bear the weight of this oppressive woe.
> Alas! each friend of mine,
> My dear, departed love, so much was thine,
> That none has any comfort to bestow.
> My books, the best relief
> In ev'ry other grief,
> Are now with your idea sadden'd all:
> Each fav'rite author we together read
> My tortur'd mem'ry wounds, and speaks of LUCY dead.[19]

While the stanza tries to envisage possibilities for solace, it keeps collapsing under the weight of its own grief, as the metrical line flattens out (as in lines 6 and 14 above) with the addition of extra syllables.

Lyttelton's grief is exacerbated by the fact that the sources of relief or distraction available to him are tainted by association with his dead wife. He cannot turn to his books because of old memories of 'Each fav'rite author we together read'. The pleasure of surveying his magnificent gardens at Hagley is now lost to him because the garden's presiding deity has departed. The feeling of being haunted by associations with the loved one is a common reality for widows and widowers and also a standard form of poetic complaint. However, what seems unusual in Lyttelton's lines is his acknowledgement that his deep sorrow constitutes a sort of infirmity: 'an oppressive woe'. It should be seen as no insult to his wife's memory that he does not actually wish to grieve for her, but rather to have his grief abated or distracted so as to cure himself of the pain of 'tortur'd mem'ry'. He is not a mourner who wishes to indulge in his own grief but instead to liberate himself from it.

Both Rowe and Lyttelton found their lives overtaken by an incalculable sorrow. As Johnson points out in his celebrated *Rambler* 47 (28 August 1750), most human passions tend towards their own dissolution, in the sense that fear, for example, lends itself to flight, to the securing of one's safety, and so to the extinction of the original emotion that brought about the flight in the first place, but sorrow comprises perhaps the only human affliction that lacks an inherent impulse to self-limit, to bring about its own end. In Johnson's words,

> Sorrow is properly that state of mind in which our desires are fixed upon the past, without looking forward to the future, an incessant wish that something were otherwise than it has been, a tormenting and harrassing want of some enjoyment or possession which we have lost, and which no endeavours can possibly regain.[20]

What defines sorrow is partly its powerlessness, in that the sufferer wishes to change something that can never be changed, and hence the emotion always risks becoming interminable. In these cases, sorrow becomes a 'habit', a term that Johnson borrows from Burton, as the 'faculties are chained to a single object, which can never be contemplated but with hopeless uneasiness'. When sorrow curdles in this way, it becomes a 'putrefaction of stagnant life' or, in a very different metaphor, a creeping 'kind of rust of the soul'.[21]

Rambler 47 nowhere acknowledges that a rival nomenclature through which to discuss such inveterate forms of human unhappiness might be that of 'melancholy' or 'hypochondria' or 'the spleen'. He approaches the alleviation of sorrow as a task for the moralist not the physician, and he views sorrow as a disability but not a disorder, since personal tragedies and their attendant misery remain unavoidable aspects of human existence. Johnson would have been aware of a range of different moralistic or religious discourses that spoke to the problem of human unhappiness and that vied for prominence with the growing body of medically oriented literature on melancholy. Representative of one type of more scripturally based writings might be, for example, the sermons of the famous mathematician and divine Issac Barrow, published after his death under the title *Of Contentment, Patience and Resignation to the Will of God* (1685), and reprinted several times in the eighteenth century. Barrow understood 'contentment' to mean a due reconciliation with the ways of God's providence, so that people would accept, rather than exclaim against, or be downcast by, their personal lot. As Barrow says, 'We should believe our condition, whatever it be, to be determined by God; and that all events befalling us do proceed from him; at least that he permitteth and ordereth them, according to his judgment and pleasure.'[22] To practise Christian contentment, in Barrow's view, is to accept that human beings are essentially undeserving; that adversities afflicting us are the 'natural fruits of our sins'; and that true happiness should be seen as independent of any 'present enjoyments or possessions'. The perfection of such a state would be the ability to bear all our misfortunes with a steady calmness, and to quell any strong passions towards 'immoderate grief, fierce anger, irksome despair, and the like'.[23]

Christian apologists were also keen to resist those claims to the ownership of 'contentment' that were seen as being pressed by a range of secular philosophies. Addison's *Spectator* 574, for example, begins with an ironic description of the author's 'Discourse' with a Rosicrucian, in which the enthusiast hints at a great panacea in his possession. Its incalculable properties enable it, among many other things, to convert 'Smoke into Flame, Flame into Light, and Light into Glory'. More to the point, the great adept reveals 'that a single Ray of it dissipates Pain, and Care, and Melancholy from the Person on whom it falls'. Yet when the philosopher finally comes to the announcement of his great secret, it is revealed as 'nothing else but *Content*': the philosopher's recondite secret turns out to be no more than an everyday tenet of Christian morality. Moreover, while the contentedness espoused by the pagan philosophers might instruct sufferers not to despair, so Addison argues, it can never *justify* their not despairing, for what alone justifies the suffering incident to this world is the promise of everlasting bliss in the next one.[24]

'Content' sits alongside a range of related Christian virtues, such as 'forbearance', 'fortitude' and 'resignation', all of which had the design of counselling Christians how to bear up under the sorrows that they would inevitably face during their lives. Another term of the same sort, combining both the properties of a '*natural* State' and a '*Moral* Habit', was cheerfulness, a quality that Addison writes about in *Spectator* 387 as providing an antidote against depressive feelings. Cheerfulness, he claims, 'banishes all anxious Care and Discontent, sooths and composes the Passions, and keeps the Soul in a perpetual Calm'. Moreover, the possibility of our being cheerful is something that God has expressly given to us through his providence: the fact that God opted for green as the colour in which to clothe the natural world owes everything, for example, to his understanding that it 'comforts and strengthens the Eye instead of weakning or grieving it'.[25] Green is intrinsically a cheerful hue. However, while Addison recognizes that, scattering as he has done such incitements to cheerfulness, God did not intend that 'the Heart of Man should be involved in Gloom and Melancholy', to his embarrassment he is still forced to admit that Englishmen are especially prone to such moods: 'Melancholy is a kind of Demon that haunts our Island', he confesses. People in England accordingly have particular need to see to their own good cheer and always to 'consider the World in its most agreeable Lights'. Resisting melancholy in effect becomes raised to the level of a moral duty.[26]

The previous paragraphs should have indicated something of the range of non-medical discourses that offered moral or spiritual counselling against melancholy. In addition to general exhortations to contentment or cheerfulness, readers could also find advice on how to deal with the more baneful of personal tragedies. A whole genre of consolatory advice, for example, relates to 'loss of friends'. The genre tended to consist of an itemizing of the various grounds on which it might be possible to draw consolation following the death of a friend or loved one. The section devoted to the subject in *The Art of Patience and Balm of Gilead* (1694), probably written by Richard Allestree, author of the highly popular *Whole Duty of Man*, consists of eleven numbered paragraphs, each disclosing its own small pearl of solace. Consolations consist of arguments along the lines that expected tragedies should be seen as less painful than unexpected ones; that sometimes we mourn not for what our friends were in themselves but for what they did for us, thus succumbing not to genuine sorrow but to selfishness; that we should celebrate, not grieve at, the ascent of our good friends into 'the Beatifical Presence of the *King* of Glory'; and that all mortal separations are merely a prologue to the blissful reunions to be anticipated in the world hereafter.[27]

The 'loss of friends' genre, in which 'friends' were understood to include family, preserved its vigour into the eighteenth century. Shortly after the death of his daughter Charlotte at the age of five in March 1742, Henry Fielding drafted his own essay 'Of the Remedy of Affliction for the Loss of our Friends'. The essay includes what appears to be the desperate consolation extracted by his own wife Charlotte from the untimely loss of their child:

> I remember the most excellent of Women, and tenderest of Mothers, when, after a painful and dangerous Delivery, she was told she had a Daughter, answering; *Good God! have I produced a Creature who is to undergo what I have suffered!* Some Years afterwards, I heard the same Woman, on the Death of that very Child, then one of the loveliest Creatures ever seen, comforting herself with reflecting, that *her Child could never know what it was to feel such a Loss as she then lamented.*[28]

Fielding's 'Remedy' is an amalgam of philosophical and religious teachings on how to cope with the pain of losing loved ones, a separation that he sees as tantamount to 'tearing…the Soul from the Body; not by a momentary Operation…but by a continued, tedious, though violent Agitation'.[29] The palliatives he lists include ones to be called upon in advance of the loss (as always keeping in mind that separations must eventually happen) and those to be enlisted in the aftermath of the tragedy. His main prompting is that sufferers should resist merely abandoning themselves to their emotions and instead try to hearken to the voice of reason. We need to convince ourselves that friendship does not actually *require* from us exorbitant mourning just to discharge our duties to the dead, nor that anything can be gained from excessive grieving. We should try to avoid all places or objects that are strongly associated with the dead friend, and stiffen our fortitude by meditating on the inevitability of death and the relief that it offers from all the heartaches of life. However, the most 'ravishing' of all sources of consolation is the hope held out to the Christian of reunion with the loved one in 'Bliss everlasting'.[30]

Melancholy philosophy

Who, then, could best be entrusted with ministering to the everyday sorrows of the world? Fielding's 'Remedy' starts by citing a remark in the *Tusculan Disputations* in which Cicero notes how strange it would be if, while numerous treatments have been invented for diseases of the body, 'the Mind should be left without any Assistance to alleviate and repel the Disorders which befal it'. He claims the contrary in fact to be true, and that the 'infallible Method' to 'asswage' disorders of the mind comes from an application, not to medicine, but to philosophy.[31] Mental wellbeing is the province not of the physician but the sage. Throughout his 'Remedy', Fielding has in view the stern teachings of the Stoics (to whom I shall return later), as the school of classical philosophers most associated with the transcendence of physical or mental anguish. Yet, simply because of their discipline's intrinsic interest in the operations of the mind, philosophers have always been drawn towards trying to rationalize the occurrence of mental infirmities of one sort or another.

So much is true of John Locke, who we find, in his shorthand *Journal* for 1676, grappling with and trying to classify the different categories of mental comfort and discomfort. His starting assumption is that the mind should be considered as made for 'feeling' rather than, in Cartesian terms, for thinking, and further that '*voluptas* and *dolor*, pleasure and pain' comprise the 'two roots out of which all passions spring'. Emotions agreeable to the mind include 'mirth' (pleasure arising from 'light causes'), 'delight' (arising from 'agreeable sensible objects'), 'joy' (from the apprehension of some 'great and solid good') and 'comfort' (from the removal of some 'precedent sorrow'). Happiness, itself, is not so much an emotion as a synoptic mental state, based on the pleasurable forms of emotion welling up from below. Just as Locke categorizes the modes of happiness, so he also presents a schema isolating all those passions that make up human misery. These comprise 'weariness' (pain arising from 'the long continuance of anything'), 'vexation' (arising from some small cause but of which 'the mind is very sensible'), 'sorrow' (stemming from some past event), 'grief' (from the death of a friend), 'melancholy' (defined in terms of social withdrawal as 'when it hinders discourse and conversation'), 'anxiety' (defined in terms of reduced vitality) and 'anguish' (marked by the 'very violent' nature of the mental pain). It should be noted that Locke does not differentiate between ordinary forms of unhappiness and medically treatable ones: melancholy, for example, figures simply as part of a general continuum of mental unease, though, unlike most of the other passions, defined in terms of its symptoms not its underlying cause.[32]

The manner of Locke's inclusion of melancholy contrasts with its treatment in David Hartley's *Observations on Man, his Frame, his Duty, and his Expectations* (1749). Hartley's work expounds how complex mental and physical acts are built up from rudimentary sensations and associations, and he was keen to test his ideas against the counter-evidence that could be seen as being constituted by what he called 'Imperfections' in the 'rational Faculty'. These imperfections occur when the mind is alienated from itself for a variety of reasons, such as drunkenness, senility in old people, madness, or melancholy. His short discussion of the latter topic is decidedly eccentric and unsympathetic. Its proximate cause he attributes to an 'Irritability of the medullary Substance of the Brain', but he ascribes its root causes to overeating, drunkenness and excessive studying. Hartley's belief that thoughts and passions are generated from physical vibrations occurring in bodily organs (chiefly the brain) seems to have conspired with a general tendency for eighteenth-century depressives to somatize their condition: that is, to represent it through a range of physical, rather than psychological, symptoms. Accordingly, Hartley suggests that melancholy comes about in women through the 'uneasy' state of the uterus being transmitted upwards to the brain, while also adversely affecting the stomach on the way there. Similarly, male melancholy hatches out of the 'Organs of Digestion'. In addition to acknowledging these immediate vibratory causes of melancholy, Hartley also accepts that the condition might owe something to inheritance, in the transmission of 'an undue Make of the Brain'.[33]

Hartley, unlike Locke, does not place melancholy among other forms of unhappiness: rather it illustrates a particular reason why the rational faculty might fail to operate properly. Like many others in his time and earlier, he thinks of melancholy as being characterized by mental responses that are out of proportion to what triggers them. People naturally form desires, fears and anxieties, but the brains of melancholic people, affected by the negative vibrations emanating from the wombs of women and the stomachs of men, have the effect of exaggerating these emotions so that they swell far beyond 'their natural Magnitude'. In this condition, people can respond irrationally to the faintest emotional provocation.

For Hartley, then, melancholy is less a particular brand of sadness than a mental susceptibility to overreact to negative stimuli in a way that alienates the sufferer from his true reason. The condition has to do with how someone conceives and responds to the world around them. We can find a not dissimilar construction of melancholy in the Scottish philosopher James Beattie's *Dissertations Moral and Critical . . . on Memory and Imagination* (1783), in which melancholy figures as a category of imagination, specifically '*gloomy* Imagination'. People are seen as having fallen into melancholy when, not only suffering from 'anxiety and fear', they falsely believe that circumstances are entirely arrayed against them. People in this state, so Beattie alleges, mistake their own frenzied ideas for reality; moreover, so strong is the fixation as to be proof against any '[r]ational remonstrance'. Beattie argues that the cure for this 'distemper' belongs equally 'to the physician and to the moralist'. To prevent the condition afflicting us, we should maintain a sociable but sober lifestyle; we should keep up a general cheerfulness and a goodly, benevolent disposition; and we should take care over the books that we choose to read or study. In this latter connection, Beattie counsels against exposure to the misanthropic writings of the likes of Hobbes and Swift, and to tragic novels, like Richardson's *Clarissa,* that 'wear out the spirits with a succession of horrors and sorrows'.[34]

Both Hartley and Beattie, as scholars themselves, are all too aware of the status of melancholy as a scholar's malady. Hartley isolates one specialized cause of the condition, for example, as 'too much Application of the Mind'.[35] Meanwhile, Beattie warns scholars to choose their courses of study with care, with an emphasis on the pleasurable and useful, given that 'literary men' (meaning scholars in general) are especially 'liable to be haunted with this disease'.[36] Yet of all eighteenth-century philosophers, the one who best appreciated the depressive perils of scholarship, of philosophy specifically, and furthermore of philosophical scepticism in particular, was Beattie's compatriot, David Hume. Hume seems to have been afflicted with depression at least from his early manhood. In his early twenties, with his philosophical studies becalmed, he took a position with a Bristol merchant. As he travelled down to take up his post, he wrote a long letter to an unnamed physician, usually identified as John Arbuthnot, soliciting help in dealing with his depression. Though we do not know whether the letter was ever sent, or replied to, or indeed whether its recipient was, or was intended to be, Arbuthnot, we know from the letter itself that Hume selected his addressee with considerable care, knowing that only a unique individual would be qualified to minister to 'the Disease of the Learned'. Such an individual 'must be a skilful Physician, a man of Letters, of Wit, of Good Sense, & of great Humanity'. The qualifications supplementary to those purely of the doctor are the ones that matter most, for, as Hume observes, 'All the Physicians, I have consulted, tho' very able, cou'd never enter into my Distemper; because not being Persons of great Learning beyond their own Profession, they were unacquainted with these Motions of the Mind.'[37] The idea seems to be that only a scholar can fully appreciate the sort of melancholy that stems from excessive book-learning, but also that the treatment of depression requires not just narrowly specialized medical knowledge but also a more expansive wisdom and human sympathy. If the assumptions about the letter's intended recipient are correct, then Hume was turning to a man of catholic tastes and abilities. Arbuthnot, in his sixties when Hume penned his letter, had been a distinguished doctor, scientist, man of letters and member of the Scriblerian satiric club.

Hume recounts in his letter the process by which he descended into melancholy. He had formed a determination in his late teens to pursue a career as a 'Scholar & Philosopher', and for several months remained happy in this occupation. In September 1729, however, he felt all his enthusiasm and vigour begin to dwindle. It became easier to set his books aside than to take them up. Moreover, a particular aspect of the gloom that engulfed him was that, having pored over 'many Books of Morality', his mind became engrossed with thoughts about 'Death, & Poverty, & Shame, & Pain, & all the other Calamities of Life'. This malady remained with him for several months, yet seems to have dispersed of its own accord the following winter. The next part of Hume's letter details the renewal of the condition during the summer of 1732, manifesting itself in the first instance in his digestive system and resulting in 'a good deal of Wind in my Stomach'. At the same time, he began to grapple with the relation between his melancholy feelings and the content and aims of his philosophizing. He became cynical about the schemes of virtue and happiness promulgated by the classical philosophers (probably the Stoics), which seemed to him to be divorced from any genuine understanding of 'human Nature'.[38]

Hume explores the relation between philosophy and melancholy further in his first great philosophical work, *A Treatise of Human Nature* (1739–40), especially in the autobiographical 'Conclusion' to the first book. It begins with a vivid and remarkable formulation of the 'forlorn solitude' and apprehension that goes with the station of philosopher:

> But before I launch out into those immense depths of philosophy, which lie before me, I find myself inclin'd to stop a moment in my present station, and to ponder that voyage, which I have undertaken, and which undoubtedly requires the utmost art and industry to be brought to a happy conclusion. Methinks I am like a man, who having struck on many shoals, and having narrowly escap'd shipwreck in passing a small frith, has yet the temerity to put to sea in the same leaky weather-beaten vessel, and even carries his ambition so far as to think of compassing the globe under these disadvantageous circumstances. My memory of past errors and perplexities,

makes me diffident for the future. The wretched condition, weakness, and disorder of the faculties, I must employ in my enquiries, encrease my apprehensions. And the impossibility of amending or correcting these faculties, reduces me almost to despair, and makes me resolve to perish on the barren rock, on which I am at present, rather than venture myself upon that boundless ocean, which runs out into immensity. This sudden view of my danger strikes me with melancholy.[39]

He despairs of the inadequacy of his own puny intellectual faculties, and shrinks at the immensity of the ocean of intellectual speculation on which he has set out. In the next paragraph, he depicts himself recoiling in apprehension from the blows inevitably to be delivered on him by the legions of rival philosophers, exposed as he has now made himself to 'the enmity of all metaphysicians, logicians, mathematicians, and even theologians'.

The perils that Hume confronts are not, however, ones necessarily incident to any philosopher who knows that his published ideas will be fiercely contested. Some of the emotional toll relates specifically to the sceptical character of Hume's thought. The passage on his own melancholy comes at the very end of Book 1 ('Of the Understanding'), as the final section of Part IV: 'Of the Sceptical and Other Systems of Philosophy'. Hume's argument has been that our understanding relentlessly 'subverts itself' in that we construct our knowledge of the world on the basis of suppositions that can never be proven. We act on the assumption, for example, that one event causes another, but all that our senses can ever permit us truly to know is that events occur successively in time. In all circumstances, people should preserve their scepticism, their appreciation of the distinction between what is known and what is surmised: 'If we believe, that fire warms, or water refreshes, 'tis only because it costs us too much pains to think otherwise.'[40]

Yet the attrition of spirits that scepticism brings about does not just derive from the alienation of living in a world that we can never truly know, for it also stems from the uncertainty that the sceptical philosopher must feel about the rectitude of his own ideas. True scepticism can only but mean scepticism about everything, including about scepticism itself. How can Hume himself ever be sure that 'in leaving all establish'd opinions I am following truth'? Confounded by such radical uncertainties, he fancies himself in 'the most deplorable condition imaginable, inviron'd with the deepest darkness'. For such a depth of 'philosophical melancholy' (as Hume himself terms it), philosophy itself can provide neither cure nor solace. What alone can dispel it are the distractions of the world: 'I dine, I play a game of back-gammon, I converse, and am merry with my friends.'[41]

The complex relations of philosophy to melancholy in the period were not confined, however, to the philosophical analysis of melancholy as a disease of the mental faculty or to a sombre recognition of the depressive consequences of following sceptical lines of reasoning to their utmost conclusions. For added to such views was the notion that melancholy comprised a mental state almost uniquely congenial to philosophizing. Indeed, rather than melancholy being seen as a condition that sufferers might naturally spend their time trying to evade or alleviate, in the mid-eighteenth century it became viewed by certain poets as an auspicious mental state that could be actively pursued or artificially stimulated. In her classic study of melancholy poetry, *The Gloomy Egoist* (1932), Eleanor Sickels highlights the vogue for 'deliberate melancholizing', in which the brooding poet withdraws from the busy world to commune with his own most sombre musings. Sometimes these are attended with a decidedly gothic frisson as in the charnel house meditations of Thomas Parnell and Robert Blair, but on other occasions, as in Gray's famous *Elegy*, they consist of a more serenely understated contemplation of the conquering power of time and the inevitability of death.[42]

John Baker develops these poetic traditions more extensively in the next chapter. However, one particular melancholy *mise-en-scène* worthy of note here involves the poet searching out by night some remote forest glade or grotto, in order to conjure up visions and to indulge in what James Thomson calls 'prophetic Glooms'. In 'Autumn' of his *The Seasons*, for example, the poet takes just such a twilight pilgrimage, launching into a near-ecstatic hymn as he thrills at the dark solemnity of the scene:

> HE comes! he comes! in every Breeze the POWER
> Of PHILOSOPHIC MELANCHOLY comes!
> His near Approach the sudden-starting Tear,
> The glowing Cheek, the mild dejected Air,
> The soften'd Feature, and the beating Heart,
> Pierc'd deep with many a virtuous Pang, declare.
> O'er all the Soul his sacred Influence breathes;
> Inflames Imagination; thro' the Breast
> Infuses every Tenderness; and far
> Beyond dim Earth exalts the swelling Thought. (1004–1013)[43]

Though 'PHILOSOPHIC MELANCHOLY' arrives on the scene, he appears here only as an emotion in the poet's own breast rather than as a realized personage, the welling tear and the 'glowing Cheek' belonging not to Melancholy but to the poet himself. What his presence vouchsafes to the rapt poet is a moment of high humanitarian fervour: he finds himself suffused with a general love for humankind, with a zeal to act for the larger social good, and with a swelling indignation at social injustice and iniquity.

It is evident that Thomson envisaged all along that moods of rapturous melancholy or ecstatic pensiveness would form an integral part of the poem. In a letter of 1725 to his friend William Cranstoun, requesting financial assistance during the poet's uncertain early days in London, Thomson imagines Cranstoun as occupying the same role of the wandering melancholy poet that was to become a feature of *The Seasons*:

> Now, I imagine you seized w^t a fine romantic kind of melancholy, on the fading of the Year. Now I figure you wandering, philosophical, and pensive, amidst the brown, wither'd groves... while, deep, divine Contemplation, the genius of the place, prompts each swelling awfull thought.[44]

Here the gloom gets thickened by intimations of winter ('the fading of the Year'), denuding the trees of their foliage and inviting contemplation, at the year's end, of another kind of decay and ending that awaits us all.

The Seasons is one of numerous poems during the course of the eighteenth century to wax effusive about the pleasures of 'melancholy', or 'contemplation' or 'solitude'. Numbered among poems on the latter abstraction, for example, are Thomson's own 'Hymn on Solitude' and Joseph Warton's 'Ode to Solitude'.[45] Where the terms appear, they can often be found in close collocation with each other. In Joseph Warton's poem, *The Enthusiast: or the Lover of Nature*, composed when its author was merely sixteen, the poet-narrator imagines himself starting out on a moonlit night to 'seek some level Mead, and there invoke / Old Midnight's Sister Contemplation sage'. As he wanders musing, he finds himself confronted by a band of ghostly personifications, including 'sharp-eyed *Philosophy*', 'Virgin *Solitude*', hoary-headed Wisdom and the lady Virtue.[46] Though the word does not appear, melancholy was recognized as a concept closely kindred with these others, and inevitably attendant on acts of lonely contemplation. Interestingly,

Thomas Warton's *The Pleasures of Melancholy* sets out with an invocation not to its eponymous abstraction but instead to 'Mother of Musings, *Contemplation* sage'.[47] Contemplation needs to be invoked first as the necessary guide to convey the poet to the haunts of melancholy.

The close linkage between melancholy and philosophizing is incarnated in a particular class of beings appearing perennially in mid-eighteenth-century poetry: the druids. 'Summer' (lines 516–63) finds Thomson's poet-narrator once more setting out 'into the midnight Depth' in order to fulfil his nightly appointment with his own melancholy musings. Here he experiences a 'sacred Terror' as he becomes conscious of shapes in the air around him, and imagines, or thinks he imagines, a voice 'than Human more' inviting him to sing of nature and 'Nature's GOD'.[48] Invocations of druids, or of ancient bards or sages (implicitly referring to druids), are a staple of melancholy verse. The druids formed the priestly caste within Celtic society, and had supposedly led the military opposition to Roman occupation. They reputedly lived in trees, or at least deep in forests, and were venerated both for their magical powers and their sagacity. The vogue for crepuscular, woodland philosophizing, especially of a kind that leads to rapturous exaltation of nature, owes everything to their shadowy precedent.[49] Thomas Warton's *Pleasures of Melancholy* concludes, for example, with a poetical anecdote about the upbringing of the goddess Contemplation. Discovered by a Welsh druid on his evening walk, the foundling infant is brought up in the 'close shelter of his oaken bow'r'. Here the druid watches the dawning of 'solemn Musing' in the 'pensive thought' of the young child, this being taken to represent the first moment at which humans become aware of the pleasurable potential of melancholy.[50]

Of course, what we are observing is a rather fey literary conceit of a kind that one could only find in a poetry intoxicated by its own poeticality. People in real life did not as a rule avidly pursue melancholy as a state to be welcomed, let alone stumble out of bed on moon-lit nights and into the depths of forbidding forests in order to experience it all the more atmospherically. Yet these poems do appreciate a general truth that has a wider application than merely to the works themselves: namely, that some relation exists between thinking and sadness. Hamlet complains famously of his 'native hue of resolution' being 'sicklied o'er with the pale cast of thought', implying that thought itself comprises a sort of enfeebling sickness of the mind.[51] The word 'pensive', often invoked in melancholy poetry, and which we use nowadays to mean 'Full of thought; plunged in thought; thoughtful, meditative, musing' (*Oxford English Dictionary* 2), is defined in Johnson's *Dictionary* as 'Sorrowfully thoughtful; sorrowful; mournfully serious; melancholy'. In other words, 'pensive', in eighteenth-century currency, had a much more central place in the lexicon of misery than it does now, when it tends to mean little more than being mentally engrossed or preoccupied. No wonder, then, that melancholy could seem like an occupational hazard for philosophers – that category of individuals fated uniquely to be pensive by profession.

The rewards of indifference

The school of ancient philosophy most often associated with teaching ways of enduring or counteracting human unhappiness was stoicism, described by Dryden as 'the most noble, most generous, most beneficial to human kind' and as calculated in particular to 'raise in us an undaunted courage against the assaults of fortune', and championed by Thomas Cooke in the eighteenth century as 'the wisest Sect that ever was on Earth'.[52] Stoic philosophy had flourished in ancient Greece from the days of Zeno of Citium (*c.*335–262 BC), and had transplanted itself to Rome in the first century BC. Cicero was not a Stoic so much as a sympathetic observer of the movement, but his writings in translation, especially the *Tusculan Disputations*, became widely influential in the English neo-classical period, as were those of the later Greek Stoic Epictetus, translated in Elizabeth Carter's celebrated edition of 1758. A wide range of eighteenth-century authors, including Addison, Gray, Fielding and Johnson, were either cautiously attracted by Stoic tenets, sufficiently alarmed as to engage in fierce rebuttals, or at least involved in some kind of moderate dialogue with them.[53]

The Stoic tenets most recognized and debated in the eighteenth century were those relating to apathy and suspense. These positions (as others) tended to be illustrated by application to the sage, the ideal and unvarying embodiment of all Stoic principles.[54] Being a sage was partly defined by a serenity of mental wellbeing, ensured by the fact that the sage always followed the edicts of 'nature' and prized virtue as the unique good and true source of happiness. Stoics (unlike Epicureans) rejected the notion that pleasure itself constitutes a positive good, or that life-attributes of any kind, such as good health, prosperity, freedom and reputation, ones that could be seen as valuable precisely in terms of their capacity to yield satisfaction or pleasure, could have any material bearing on true human happiness, which alone arose from an adherence to virtue. The tranquility of the sage was seen as being borne out of a pronounced 'indifference' to all potential attributes, including freedom from pain, other than virtue itself, though Stoic philosophers did draw a distinction between ostensibly attractive 'indifferents', such as health or wealth, and unappealing ones, such as sickness or bereavement. However, though a sage, in the practice of his life might favour certain 'indifferents' over others, the removal of them would never be sufficient to disturb his inner tranquility.

The extent to which it might be possible to anaesthetize ourselves to mental anguish or depression, to the common grievances of life, by practising Stoic indifference or apathy was a common topic among eighteenth-century moralists, and one to which I shall return later. But another doctrine, equally salient in the popular perception of Stoicism, one moreover at which much of the hostility surrounding stoical beliefs was directed, was that of suspense. 'Suspense' meant the ability to withhold mental assent, to refuse to adopt a conviction relating to the world around oneself (such as on the existence of an afterlife). Knowing anything consisted in stoical doctrine of strongly assenting to a mental impression, but only the sage could be attuned to nature at such a level to be able to assent categorically to any construction of the world. This doctrine of non-assent tended to drive a wedge between stoicism and orthodox Christian faith based on allegiance to the cardinal religious truths. The famous scene at the start of Act V of Addison's *Cato*, for example, when Cato, entering with Plato's treatise on the imperishability of the soul clasped in his hand, articulates his new-found conviction of the soul's immortality, seems to have been expressly written to show the hero's renunciation of suspense in the moments immediately prefacing his death. The concept is also condemned, again for its spiritual emptiness, by other pious commentators. Swift, for example, remarks that it 'is a miserable Thing to live in Suspence; it is the Life of a Spider', and the concept is decried in a famous passage of Johnson's 'Vanity of Human Wishes': 'Must dull Suspence corrupt the stagnant Mind?'.[55]

The doctrines of suspense and apathy belong together in both supposing the ability of the mind to elevate itself above sensory existence in general, and above the everyday vicissitudes of life, including our susceptibility to both mental and physical pain. A favourite exemplum of the Stoics, recorded by Cicero, Seneca and others, and attributed often to the philosopher Anaxagoras, tells of a sage who had so long meditated on, and conditioned himself to, the certainty of mortality that on hearing of the sudden death of his son, he could respond with the level and dispassionate comment that 'I KNEW I *had begot a Mortal*'.[56] This resistance to bereavement, echoed in Addison's play by Cato's emotionally sterile response to the death of his son Marcus, lent itself to both positive and negative constructions. It was possible to consider such behaviour as closely aligned with Christian values such as forbearance or fortitude, where the sufferer struggled to overcome their dark feelings by reflecting on the happier place to which the deceased person had gone or on the example of Christ's own passion and sacrifice. At the same time, such conduct could be seen as almost a dereliction or denial of full emotional life. Richard Fenton, for example, laments the 'unfeeling stoic's heart of stone'; and Pope, in his *Essay on Man*, refers to 'lazy Apathy', implying that stoic self-restraint might emanate more from a lack of capacity to generate strong emotions than from any great powers of self-control over them.[57]

A conventional rhetorical *divisio* exists in a number of eighteenth-century texts in which Christian and philosophical (these latter being essentially Stoic) schemes of consolation are held up for comparative inspection. A letter 'Against immoderate Grief for the Death of Friends' published in *Mist's Journal*, for example, advises that sufferers 'ought to set Bounds to extravagant Sorrows' and should be influenced not just by 'Considerations of Wisdom and Morality' but also by the enduring 'Sentiments of Religion'.[58] Henry Fielding's *Tom Jones* is perhaps the most famous eighteenth-century work to explore the competing claims of Stoic and Christian consolation to tranquillize mental suffering. On the death of his friend and brother-in-law Mr Blifil, for example, Squire Allworthy finds himself beset by 'those Emotions of Grief', to which all men 'whose Hearts are not composed of Flint' would be susceptible in similar circumstances. Yet the passage of time inevitably blunts Allworthy's grief, as the least worldly reader could have foreseen:

> what Reader doth not know that Philosophy and Religion, in time, moderated, and at last extinguished this Grief? The former of these, teaching the Folly and Vanity of it, and the latter, correcting it, as unlawful, and at the same time assuaging it by raising future Hopes and Assurances which enable a strong and religious Mind to take leave of a Friend on his Death-bed with less [sic] indifference than if he was preparing for a long Journey.[59]

Here the sternly rationalist hectoring over the 'Folly and Vanity' of human grief comes from the Stoic philosopher, and adherent to the moral rule of rectitude, Mr. Square, while the other-worldly presentiments are poured into Allworthy's ears by the rigidly ortho-dox clergyman, Mr. Thwackum. To Fielding's mind, both alternatives arrogate too much to themselves, both alike favouring the claims of an impersonal, systematizing doctrine over the human interest of the stricken individual.

Though Fielding curses both their houses in equal measure, other commentators entering into the comparison of secular and Christian forms of consolation do so specifically to demonstrate the greater effi-cacy of the latter. One case in point is Oliver Goldsmith's *The Vicar of Wakefield* (1766), in which the Reverend Primrose orates *de profundis* on the comparative apportionment of happiness and misery in the great scheme of providence. What he notes is how cruelly mismatched the pleasures and miseries of life are, such that no pleasures exist that ever prove fully satisfying, whereas the opportunities for misery seem boundless. Moreover, whereas all of our felicities fall short of ultimate fulfilment, we can be so fulfiled in our miseries as to have nothing left for which to hope, and so be driven to suicide, occurrences of which, as Primrose reports, 'we daily see thousands'. No reasons for such an inher-ent bias in our moral world seem to have been divulged to us, and what providence has alone provided are a number of 'motives to consolation': chiefly those of philosophy and religion. Yet, though he places philo-sophical consolations alongside those of Christianity, Primrose is quick to denigrate them as 'very amusing, but often fallacious'. Such consola-tions consist of contradictory platitudes telling us that life exists for us to enjoy, but if we can't enjoy it we can be blessed at least by its brevity. Religion, in contrast, 'comforts in an higher strain' by holding out to everyone the prospect of perpetual happiness in another world, a con-solation that Primrose sees as imbued with a principle of equality and fairness.[60]

The idea that stoic consolations were less efficacious than those of religion, or less true, morally satisfying or internally coherent, dove-tailed with a suspicion about their underlying fraudulence. Nowhere could the fallibility of such claims be better demonstrated than in the case of stoics themselves. The hypocritical stoic, who either declines to take his own medicine or who certainly fails to feel the benefit of it, is a stock figure in a range of eighteenth-century fictional or moralis-tic texts. Fielding's Abraham Adams, for example, berates the despairing Joseph, distraught at the loss of Fanny, with Christian apothegms on the folly of immoderate grief combined with several passages of Stoic consolation recited from Seneca. Yet neither Christian nor 'heathen' consolations stand Adams in any stead at all when in a later chapter he receives news of the death of his son Dick.[61] A similar stoic figure, incapable of absorbing the wisdom of his own teaching, is the 'wise and happy man' in Johnson's *Rasselas* (1759). Encountering this 'superiour being', who professes to have fully mastered his own passions so as no longer to be 'depressed by grief' or agitated by any of the normal upheavals of emotional life, Rasselas is reduced to awestruck emulation. Yet, in his next visit, he finds the philosopher strangely altered, weighed down with sorrow at the death of his daughter. When Rasselas tries to restore his spirits by invoking the traditional stoic consolation advising of the inevitability of death, the philosopher cuts him off with the retort that 'you speak like one that has never felt the pangs of separation'.[62] As Fielding points out in *Tom Jones*, 'Philosophers are composed of Flesh and Blood as well as other human Creatures', and faced with the normal vicissitudes of life will invariably end up behaving like everyone else.[63]

The passages excerpted above will have suggested something of the tone of anti-stoical sentiment during the eighteenth century.[64] Yet it would be misleading to suggest that this comprises the full picture. It is certainly not difficult to find other commentators for whom stoical tenets did apparently enable them better to withstand their conditions of grief or melancholy; furthermore the very distinction between Christian and philosophical sources of consolation in practice often breaks down, with the effect that exhortations to practise religious consolation take on a distinctively stoical hue. We can see this mingling of different consolatory discourses in Lady Mary Chudleigh's fascinating essay 'Of Grief', written in the aftermath of watching over her mother during her painful final illness, and then losing her daughter shortly after. In such traumatic circumstances, Chudleigh clings rapaciously to her 'Equality of Temper' by force of reason:

> If when we have lost any of those dear Relatives, we find our selves discomposed, if the natural Tenderness of our Souls inclines us to melancholy Reflections, let us resist the first Beginnings of Sorrow, and reason our selves into a calm Resignation.[65]

She believes absolutely that force of mind alone can release us from all categories of mental or physical distress, allowing ill-health to be experienced as something less concerning than a 'real Evil'. Sorrow itself, she suggests, can be wiped away by the mere exertion of the human mind, for which reason no justification exists for us to 'trouble the world' with 'tedious Accounts of our Sufferings, nor indulge our selves in making dismal Reflections on the disagreeable Circumstances of our Lives'.[66]

Yet around the time of her double bereavement, there appears to have been a climactic moment of grief and despair against which even her rational mind could provide no defence. She fell to exclaiming against the unfairness of her lot, and her thoughts turned to suicide as the only way of taking 'an everlasting Leave of all my Misfortunes'. At this point of utter extremity, her reason no longer being capable of assisting her, she feels a force of divine support without which, as she says, 'I'd still be groveling in my melancholy Shades'. From this point on she sees her troubles in better proportion and realizes that she had created 'Phantoms of Grief' which had had the effect of clouding her reason. The most interesting aspect of Chudleigh's essay is its wavering between endorsement of Christian and Stoic forms of consolation. She ends by describing her advancement towards 'Tranquillity', seen as conditional upon her strong faith, and by explicitly renouncing the rival claims of Stoicism: 'I would not have it thought that 'tis a Stoical Apathy I've been recommending'. Yet in fact much of her emotional counseling seems indistinguishable from classical Stoic indifference, including her rejection of the inherent evil of pain and refusal to acknowledge good health as constituting a fundamental good.[67]

One of the issues inevitably raised by Chudleigh's essay, as well as other consolatory writings that touch on Stoicism, is the extent to which sensibility itself should be considered as a human blessing or a burden. Would we want to give up all the positives of an emotionally sensible existence if we could release ourselves from the negatives? Would we want to sacrifice our capacity for joy if by doing so we could also rid ourselves of the potential for melancholy? Chudleigh's view is positively not, and she disclaims having any design on making 'Persons insensible'. Rather, she encourages her readers both to pursue and enjoy the very same attributes (health, riches, reputation and so on) whose loss would actually be most traumatic for their mental wellbeing. However, not everyone would necessarily have endorsed such a conclusion, with a particularly striking statement of the counter-case being Frances Greville's celebrated poem 'A Prayer for Indifference'. It appeared first in the *Edinburgh Chronicle* in 1759 having previously circulated in manuscript; much reprinted in magazines and miscellanies of the time, it has been hailed by Roger Lonsdale as 'the most celebrated poem by a woman in the period'.[68]

Greville's 'Prayer' refuses to accept the wager by which we undertake to live a 'sensible' life on the expectation that the pleasures reaped from doing so will outweigh the emotional pain to which we also expose ourselves. Her view is rather that sensibility comes at too high a price, that of constant emotional agitation:

> Nor ease nor peace that heart can know,
>   That, like the needle true,
> Turns at the touch of joy or woe,
>   But, turning, trembles too.
>
> Far as distress the soul can wound,
>   'Tis pain in each degree:
> Bliss goes but to a certain bound,
>   Beyond is agony.
>
> Take then this treacherous sense of mine,
>   Which dooms me still to smart;
> Which pleasure can to pain refine,
>   To pain new pangs impart.
>
> Oh! Haste to shed the sovereign balm,
>   My shattered nerves new-string;
> And for my guest, serenely calm,
>   The nymph Indifference bring.

Greville's condition is more akin to nervous disorder than melancholy as such. Her poem contains a keen sense that all of our affective responses, even those consistent with pleasure, contain some degree of unwanted emotional upheaval or smart, and that moreover the wager of sensibility is always loaded, in as much as our happiness will always be circumscribed whereas our miseries are potentially unbounded. At the end of the poem, she elects to reduce her exposure to emotional risk by practising a sort of emotional neutrality, charting a serene middle way between happiness and misery. This she terms her 'sober ease' or half-pleasure.[69]

The opposition between sensibility and stoical indifference as ways of navigating the emotional travails of life is nowhere better illustrated than in Gray's famous *Elegy Written in a Country Churchyard* (1751).[70] We associate the poem nowadays with the 128-line edition, concluding with an elaborately crafted sentimental set-piece. The poet conjectures about his own death, and imagines how 'some hoary headed swain' might relate it to visitors to the churchyard. The cause of it is closely associated with melancholy, with the swain describing the poet's last days spent 'drooping, woeful wan, like one forlorn', before directing the traveller to the epithet engraved on the nearby headstone which memorializes the poet as one that *'Melancholy marked ... for her own'*.[71] The purpose of the poem's closure is to enter the poet not just into a community of the dead but also into a community of sympathetic feeling about the dead, and to suggest the consolatory force of fellow-feeling in general, even in circumstances of implied suicide. Yet the earlier version of the poem, seen by Gray's friend, William Mason, and containing four stanzas rejected for usage in the final version, ends on an entirely different note, with an exhortation by the poet to the reader:

> No more with Reason & thyself at strife;
> Give anxious Cares & endless Wishes room
> But thro' the cool sequester'd Vale of Life
> Pursue the silent Tenour of thy Doom.[72]

The consolatory reasoning here is entirely different, with Gray advocating a middle-way, similar to Greville's 'Half-pleased' contentment, between rational control on the one hand and the unsettling volatility of 'Cares' and 'Wishes' on the other. The way that we should cope with the hardships and vicissitudes of life is merely through stoical fortitude, through plodding on with as much indifference as we can muster.

Gray's *Elegy* is one of many major eighteenth-century literary works to be touched by the issue of melancholy, even perhaps suicidal melancholy. Gray and other eighteenth-century poets, moralists and philosophers, viewed unhappiness as an invariable human malaise, though one that could still be treated or moderated. Though, of course, melancholy was identified and treated at the time as a distinct medical condition, the medical response vied with a number of other discourses intended to help people make sense of their depressive feelings and to cope with them. I hope to have shown something of the range of these alternative discourses: ones spanning from the religious to the moralistic to the philosophical. Most importantly, the chapter has tried to show something of philosophy's complex dealings with melancholy, perhaps best symbolized by the ambiguity in eighteenth-century nomenclature about what it meant to be 'pensive'. Melancholy could be seen as a precondition for philosophical inspiration, or as an occupational hazard uniquely incident to philosophers. Philosophers such as Hartley and Beattie tried to fit melancholy within complex formulations about how the mind worked or sometimes failed to work, and the idea of emotional indifference, deriving from classical Stoicism, provided an influential, though much disputed, form of consolation to those enduring the symptoms of what we would now call depression.

3
'Strange Contrarys': Figures of Melancholy in Eighteenth-Century Poetry

John Baker

'Unhappy happiness'

In the poetry it has inspired over time, melancholy has left memorable and precious tracks and traces. This chapter will address the question of how poetry finds terms for, and how it comes to terms with, melancholy in the eighteenth century, focusing in particular on the first half and the middle decades, with the cult of darkness and gloom manifest in the graveyard poetry tradition, and concluding with William Cowper. The voices are various and distinct, and only a few will be heard here, but it will soon be apparent that melancholy provokes (and inspires) an ambivalent response, is as much praised and prized as it is feared and endured.

Mental affliction no doubt changes over time both in the way it is experienced from within and perceived from without, and yet it does have a recognizable continuity, a face and a figure. This can be said of the poetry of melancholy as well as of its representations in the world of art. Enigmatic, brooding, silent, at once sluggish and intense, melancholy lends itself to iconographical representations with a remarkable permanence in the reproduction of the same basic image, a usually seated figure staring off into an internal, private space and distance that expresses, to use Henri Michaux's words, a 'remote within' ('lointain intérieur').[1] This image, with the head propped up by an arm bent at the elbow, has an almost obsessive continuity, as in a hall of mirrors, down the centuries. The acknowledged Mona Lisa of these images is Albrecht Dürer's *Melencolia I* (1514). The crowded engraving (the title itself is enigmatic: was there to be a sequel?) brings many things to mind. Among them two qualities can be privileged, immobility and introspection. The seated (but not fallen) angel is motionless and its open eyes and fixed, intense stare give the impression of profound thought, of someone looking deep within, involved and lost in some inextricable meditation, despite the apparently outward gaze.

This image of melancholy was joined by many others, past and present, in the exhibition conceived and organized by Jean Clair in Paris and Berlin in 2005–6. On leaving the Paris exhibition the final image that the visitor encountered was that of the work *Untitled (Big Man)* (2000) by Ron Mueck: a large, pink man with a shaven head, disturbingly lifelike and more than life-size, sitting hunched up, exposed and naked in a corner, surrounded not by a clutter of instruments to measure time and space but by a perfectly empty space, with a similarly intense and yet directionless stare to that of Dürer's angel. Melancholy's disordered intellectual paraphernalia have gone; the void, the immobility and a stark vulnerability have become more palpable.

The poet and translator Yves Bonnefoy opens the catalogue to that exhibition with a preface entitled 'La mélancolie, la folie, le génie – la poésie'.[2] Bonnefoy provides a metaphysical genealogy and backdrop for melancholy. Melancholy would have its source in the perception that with the advent of language there took place a fundamental divorce between immediate experience and conceptual thought, leading to an abiding sense of ontological loss. Language and conceptual thinking have, as it were, created a henceforth insuperable distance between 'true life' and its representation. Poetry is the refusal to accept this situation and thus partakes of the impossible, but vital, quest to at least draw closer to this lost unity, the desire to accede once more to an at-one-ment, a real presence in the world. Bonnefoy proposes a careful definition of melancholy, alluding to Keats's nightingale:

What is melancholy? Deep down, it seems to me, it is a hope at once always being reborn and endlessly disappointed: but less a true desire for a 'true life' than the lack in this desire of a real need to attain satisfaction. The song of the bird is heard, in its 'elsewhere'. You set off towards it, with a map you think you have, and think you like to have. In your mind there is an idea of the place in which you could live and the way you would live there, but this idea is already spelt out, put into words, a conceptual thought, already a simple image and not the actual presence, and it follows that these paths turn, and turn back on themselves, and the person who has taken them has to acknowledge his illusion, an illusion he may well prefer to the 'over there' that he cannot get back to.[3]

Following this reading, poetry would be both the promise (but *only* the promise) of a way back to some lost land or time and the sign or symptom of what has been lost. Art, Bonnefoy continues, is 'an incentive to this lucid dream, this unhappy happiness ('ce bonheur malheureux'): melancholy. Throughout the history of the West, it has come to be the magnified mirror image and expression of this oxymoron at the heart of existence'.[4] Melancholy is thus far from being simply a curse and an affliction. Here again it is associated with creativity, albeit a creativity spurred on by a sense of lack and loss. A rather different, more dramatic and strident formulation of this ontology of loss is evident in Edward Young's *Night Thoughts* and will be evoked further on.

Such a reading goes some way to explaining why melancholy should so often be invoked rather than shunned by poets. The poets of the eighteenth century, often enthusiastically, call on the muse of melancholy to inspire their own musings and poetic compositions. Melancholy is frequently a tutelary figure, a companion, a help and a consolation. Anne Amend reminds us that melancholy can be read in a polar way, along two signifying chains, a 'positive' one oriented towards philosophy, a second 'negative' one towards medicine, psychiatry and pathology. Poetic invocations of melancholy are so abundant, Amend suggests, that it would be justifiable to consider melancholy as a tenth muse. The dual and problematic nature of melancholy resurfaces in another guise: 'It is thus possible to glorify melancholy, to praise it to the skies, making it into a tenth muse, the source of artistic creativity, or to discredit it, labelling it as a sickness.'[5]

'Probably more of the leading poets were melancholic in the eighteenth century than in any other comparable span of English history', writes John F. Sena in an article published in 1971.[6] He goes on to list sixteen of the (un)fortunate elect, all of them male: 'Pope, Tickell, Young, Parnell, Thomson, Blair, Thomas Warton, Shenstone, Broome, Hammond, Collins, Gray, Moore, Watts and Whitehead, all came before melancholy's altar with varying degrees of devoutness'. Sena redresses the gender balance in part as his study, devoted to ambivalence, melancholy and poetry, features two women poets of the period, Anne Finch and Elizabeth Carter.

Several key poets in the eighteenth century suffered from deep mental distress. One, Thomas Chatterton, is commonly believed to have committed suicide, though this version of events is disputed.[7] William Cowper was to attempt suicide on several occasions and endured recurrent episodes of severe depression in the course of his life. William

Collins, Christopher Smart and Cowper spent periods in madhouses. Yet this bleak picture is only a part of the story of melancholy and poetry in the period, and only a part of the story of the poetry of those writers. The eighteenth century would indeed appear to be a high (or low) point for melancholy, a period in which poets, writers, physicians and sometimes physician-poets[8] described and expressed not only the symptoms, the enigmas, the suffering but also (to modern ears and eyes) the more unexpected and unlikely pleasures and joys associated with the melancholic experience and condition.

At the heart of this situation, there are several paradoxes. One is that poetry is a ritualized, carefully structured, highly self-conscious use of language. Yet melancholy as it is sometimes represented (as in *Melencolia I* and as Sigmund Freud was to present it in 'Mourning and Melancholia')[9] can be the very antithesis of movement, of energy and expression. One can picture it, in this respect, as language lacking affect, unable to make or sustain connections and relations. It can be imagined as broken language, language routed or obscure, its syntax dislocated, fragmented and incoherent. This modern view corresponds not only to changes and experiments in poetic form in the last century but also to the influence of psychoanalysis and in particular *The Interpretation of Dreams* (1900) and the close attention Freud paid to the unconscious in language and the language of dreams, its uses and ruses. William B. Ober addresses these questions in his study 'Madness and Poetry: A Note on Collins, Cowper, and Smart', acknowledging, however, that it is a parlous enterprise to seek out the symptoms of a future 'depressive psychosis' in the syntax, diction or, indeed, content of a poem. Ober refers in particular to William Collins and his 'Ode on the Poetical Character' but his comments here concern Collins's odes in general and the impression of difficulty created by the involved syntax and imaging process:

If we add to a passive, withdrawn diction the disjunctive, incoherent syntax and both of these to a poetic content expressing fear and anxiety as well as an inadequacy of affect, it is possible to outline a constellation of effects which, taken together, suggest depressive psychosis as that form of mental disturbance most likely to develop. To this extent Collins's mania was expressed and can be detected post hoc in his poems. But such interpretations are subject to the caution that many poets wrote on melancholy, on thwarted love, on their fears and anxieties, and only a few developed clinical psychosis.[10]

This blending of a clinical prognosis and a literary and linguistic analysis, language as symptom, does require caution, but the observations that Ober makes no doubt needed (and need) to be made. Dustin Griffin invites vigilance too when he writes of Collins: 'It now seems clear that his madness did not appear until about 1751, that it recurred, that it left him lucid intervals, and that none of his poems was written under its influence.'[11]

The relations between poetry and melancholy are, then, complex and ambivalent, and melancholy cannot be understood 'only' as a peculiar form of madness. It is often referred to as a sickness of the soul, a spiritual or existential malaise. Anxiety and a sense of foreboding about the future and the afterlife were far from being absent during the first half of the eighteenth century if one judges from the number of poems on the Four Last Things, and in particular on the Day of Judgement. The eighteenth-century graveyard poetry tradition, a useful label however loose and questionable it may be, can be said to commence with Thomas Parnell's 'A Night-Piece on Death' (1721),[12] written after the death of his wife, and was to reach its apogee in Thomas Gray's *Elegy Written in a Country Churchyard* (1751), the latter poem serving as a watershed for the two comprehensive early twentieth-century critical studies devoted to poetry and melancholy, Amy Louise Reed's *The Background of Gray's Elegy* (1924) and *The Gloomy Egoist* (1932) by Eleanor M. Sickels.[13] Other unquiet concerns and meditations, no less pervasive, were expressed in poems centred on the *vanitas* topos, and in paraphrases of the book of Job, which explored the question of theodicy, the desire to find a rational explanation for the unaccountable and 'unjustified' pain and suffering inherent in the human condition.

One theme that often recurs in the poetry on melancholy in the eighteenth century is that of the cure, with poetry itself, implicitly or explicitly, viewed by some as a remedy, a form of redemption or, in a more didactic guise, as a purveyor and vehicle of sound advice. These aspects will be apparent in several poems and poets discussed here.

The chronological eighteenth century conveniently opens for our purposes with two contrasting poems, both of which were to become famous in their own right, *The Choice* (1700) by John Pomfret[14] and 'The Spleen' (1701) by Anne Kingsmill Finch, Countess of Winchilsea.[15]

On John Pomfret: 'The dark Recesses of the Mind'

The Choice, an immensely popular poem,[16] a recipe for the good life, a programme for the well-to-do, would-be *beatus vir*, appears on the

face of it to be quintessentially Augustan in its form, ethos and pre-
cepts, and light years from the melancholic mode. Not too little, not too
much. In this good-natured but unreal universe of (male) retirement and
contentment, there is no place for the spleen, even as a weekend hobby
or pastime.

Contentment here goes hand in hand with containment, and the
title of the poem underlines the role of reason and judgement in
the creation of this carefully managed 'ideal' life. And yet the poem
remains strangely unbalanced. The moderation itself is excessive. The
profusion of modals (*would*s and *should*s in particular) undermines the
reassuring message at each and every step, almost at each and every
rhyming couplet. The whole performance is a vast hypothesis, a castle
(or country house) in the air, what Fairer and Gerrard call 'an escapist
fantasy of an English landed gentleman's life of rural leisure'.[17] Samuel
Johnson, himself the author of *The Vanity of Human Wishes* (1749),
apparently approved Pomfret's exercise in wishful thinking without a
second thought: 'His *Choice* exhibits a system of life adapted to common notions and equal to common expectations; such a state as affords
plenty and tranquillity, without exclusion of intellectual pleasures'.[18]

There is something unrealized and unrealizable in this manifesto of
normalcy for the happy few (God willing). The poem starts with an 'if',
and it is a very big 'if', as Pomfret is well aware:

> If Heav'n the grateful Liberty wou'd give,
> That I might chuse my Method how to live:
> And all those Hours propitious Fate shou'd lend,
> In blissful Ease, and Satisfaction spend.
>   Near some fair Town I'd have a private Seat,
> Built Uniform, not little, nor too great. (1–6)[19]

Having passed in review the various activities and *divertissements* that
would fill the speaker's days, and having cursorily evoked (and bracketed
off) the inconveniences, anxieties and excesses to be avoided, the poem
concludes with another big 'if': 'If Heav'n a Date of many Years wou'd
give, / Thus I'd in Pleasure, Ease, and Plenty live' (154–5).

Pomfret is in search of 'A permanent, sincere, substantial Bliss' (97), a
modest but comfortable heaven on earth. Edward Young was later in the
century to seek permanence in his turn but located it not in this world
but after death: 'Bliss! sublunary Bliss! proud words! and vain: / Implicit
Treason to divine Decree!' (*Night Thoughts*, 1.198–9).[20] The unfortunate
irony of the matter is that Pomfret was to die only two years after

the publication of the poem, after contracting smallpox, aged 35. But Pomfret was, like Young, the author of poems on the Last Day, 'On the General Conflagration and Ensuing Judgment. A Pindaric Essay' and 'Dies Novissima, or the Last Epiphany', and he shared the latter writer's anxiety not only about death and the afterlife but also about the precarious possibility of happiness in this life.

Several of Pomfret's poems are thus far removed from the benign social and moral ideal of retirement and contentment cheerfully delineated in *The Choice* and reveal a close concern with human suffering. In the consolatory poem entitled 'To his Friend under Affliction' (1702), the comfort Pomfret brings to his friend comes in the form of a reassurance that he is not alone in his distress, and that all mankind is united in a community of anxiety and unrest:

> To be from all things that disquiet, free,
> Is not consistent with Humanity.
> Youth, Wit and Beauty are such charming Things,
> O'er which, if Affluence spreads her Gaudy Wings,
> We think the Person, who enjoys so much,
> No Care can move, and no Affliction touch.
> Yet cou'd we but some secret Method find
> To view the dark Recesses of the Mind;
> We there might see the hidden Seeds of Strife,
> And Woes in Embrio rip'ning into Life. (21–30)[21]

The reference to 'some secret Method' can almost be read as a premonition of the 'invention' of psychoanalysis and the 'dark Recesses of the Mind' as an intuition of the unconscious.

'A Prospect of Death' (1701), another poem by Pomfret that was to appear along with Anne Finch's 'The Spleen' in 1709, is itself a graveyard cum deathbed poem that looks beyond the grave to eventual hoped for rewards or to the less desirable prospect of eternal retribution. Again the depiction of the human condition is bleak. The best we can do is to bear our ills patiently (things could be worse), lead a virtuous and blameless existence, and put our hope in religion and a happy outcome on the Last Day.

> The Tongue's unable to declare
> The Pains, the Griefs, the Miseries we bear:
> How Insupportable our Torments are.
> Musick no more delights our deaf'ning Ears,

Restores our Joys, or Dissipates our Fears.
But all is Melancholly, all is sad,
    In Robes of Deepest Mourning Clad
For Ev'ry Faculty, and Ev'ry Sence
Partakes the Woe of this dire Exigence. (50–8)[22]

Several characteristics of the melancholy humour surface here, the powerlessness of language to express distress, and the inability of previous
pleasures like music to distract and provide solace. All the senses are
dulled; everything is covered with the pall of melancholy. This all-
enveloping, all-invasive quality was to be most memorably expressed
by Pope in the consummate portrait of Melancholy as an animate force
he gives us in *Eloisa to Abelard* (1717):[23]

But o'er the twilight groves, and dusky caves,
Long-sounding isles, and intermingled graves,
Black Melancholy sits, and round her throws
A death-like silence, and a dread repose:
Her gloomy presence saddens all the scene,
Shades ev'ry flow'r, and darkens ev'ry green,
Deepens the murmur of the falling floods,
And breathes a browner horror on the woods. (163–70)

Eloisa's address to the absent Abelard is an attempt to fill the 'craving
Void' (94), but she succeeds at least in expressing her grief and passion
at their hopeless situation, in finding a way to voice her distress. The
poetry provides a form of redemption. And in this symmetry where a
poet takes up the theme, relays and eternalizes the memory, there is
something that prefigures the concluding tableau in Gray's *Elegy*, where
the poet literally involves the reader in the graveyard scene, inviting him
or her to enter the poem to read the epitaph in their turn: ' "Approach
and read (for thou can'st read) the lay, / Graved on the stone beneath
yon aged thorn" ' (115–16).[24]

   In the closing lines of *Eloisa to Abelard* the poet again makes absence
present and palpable, and thus brings a consolation of sorts, an identification, the sharing of a 'sad similitude of griefs':

And sure if fate some future Bard shall join
In sad similitude of griefs to mine,
Condemn'd whole years in absence to deplore,
And image charms he must behold no more,
Such if there be, who loves so long, so well;

Let him our sad, our tender story tell;
The well-sung woes will sooth my pensive ghost;
He best can paint 'em, who shall feel 'em most. (359–66)

Such 'well-sung woes' (and the specular image of these lines where Eloisa appears to be anticipating Pope's poem: 'some future Bard') are the heart of some of the best melancholy poetry in the eighteenth century, poetry that at once describes, expresses and transcends melancholy.

On Anne Finch: 'Thro' thy black Jaundice I all Objects see'

Such can be said of the poetry of Anne Finch who wrote several remarkable poems on melancholy and related themes, among which the best-known is 'The Spleen. A Pindarique Ode' (1701). It can be considered as the most impressive poem written both on, and out of, melancholy in the eighteenth century. Finch presents in miniature an anatomy of the spleen in the course of the poem. It is the discriminating analysis of someone who has both lived with melancholy[25] and been able to stand back, observe and cast a cold and critical eye on it as a social phenomenon.

The form of the poem itself, a Pindaric ode, with the studied irregularity of its 150 lines and the variable length of its stanzas, reflects the nature of the elusive, baffling object that Finch is pursuing. From the outset it is clear that the spleen is not prized or invoked in the positive sense, but is something to be endured and fought with. The image often employed here, as in the poem 'Ardelia to Melancholy',[26] is that of a contest, a struggle which ends, in both cases, with the resigned avowal of an inevitable defeat.

The poem begins with an apostrophe, a reprimand in the form of a question in which Finch rebukes the spleen as if addressing someone she knows well, and then goes on to describe the complexity of the affliction in metaphorical terms:

What art thou, *SPLEEN*, which ev'ry thing dost ape?
    Thou *Proteus* to abus'd Mankind,
    Who never yet thy real Cause cou'd find,
Or fix thee to remain in one continued Shape.
    Still varying thy perplexing Form,
    Now a Dead Sea thou'lt represent,
    A Calm of stupid Discontent,
Then, dashing on the Rocks wilt rage into a Storm. (1–8)[27]

As Jonathan Culler usefully reminds us, 'poetry uses apostrophe repeatedly and intensely'.[28] This form of address is sustained throughout the poem and is widely manifest in the poetry of melancholy. The use of apostrophe is, however, no simple convention. It is a curiously forceful poetic event and drama, an exchange (albeit one-sided), that Finch conjures up, where the 'object' spleen plays the role of a fully-fledged actor and animate force, as the present participles in the opening stanza show: 'varying', 'dashing', trembling', 'intruding'. Culler's commentary on the function of apostrophe seems especially relevant to Finch's poem:

> to apostrophize is to will a state of affairs, to attempt to call it into being by asking inanimate objects to bend themselves to your desire. In these terms the function of apostrophe would be to make the objects of the universe potentially responsive forces: forces which can be asked to act or refrain from acting, or even to continue behaving as they usually behave. The apostrophizing poet identifies his universe as a world of sentient forces.[29]

The question Finch bluntly asks concerns the identity of the spleen. She addresses an absent entity (not a person, then, but *as* a person), takes its existence for granted. And yet she is unable to say what it is, an essential element of the identity of the spleen being precisely that it eludes definition. Absence and presence (like loss) form part of the mystery that surrounds the object/subject melancholy.[30] There is clearly a need to humanize it, to give it a form and a face, an identity. The address, 'What art thou …?', is as much a reproach as it is a question.

Finch presents the spleen in its habitual guise as shapeless, indefinable, causeless, as something that can vary in temper from a state of total insensibility to one of uncontrollable violence. The sea metaphor is employed as will be the case also in other poems that treat of melancholy and despair, in Young's *Night Thoughts* and Cowper's 'The Cast-away'. The liquid element allows the poet to illustrate and play out the drama of changing and contrasting moods. The spleen's fickleness and its serial identity literally know no bounds: 'In ev'ry One thou dost possess, / New are thy Motions, and thy Dress' (44–5). It is presented as a maleficent, devious agent that appropriates people, takes them over. Part of the irony of melancholy, part of its malleable and fickle nature and identity, is that it comes to be seen by some as desirable. The infirmity can even be imitated as a sign of sensibility, intelligence and refinement, something modish, itself something to be put on and displayed, a phenomenon analysed by Clark Lawlor in Chapter 1 above.

Various remedies are evoked in the form of beverages, infusions and 'noble Liquors' (132), along with the soothing delights of soft music, but nothing brings relief. The portrait that Finch draws is of a living, debilitating, active force; a mystery, for as the poem draws to a close, the enigmatic identity and source of the spleen remain unclear, the opening question, unanswered.

But this 'objective' anatomy is only half the story. An earlier climax comes in the middle of the poem when Anne Finch recounts her own subjective confrontation with the spleen which (or who) is addressed as both intimate acquaintance and arch-enemy. Again melancholy colours everything, and its colour is black:

> O'er me, alas! thou dost too much prevail:
> I feel thy Force, whilst I against thee rail;
> I feel my Verse decay, and my crampt Numbers fail.
> Thro' thy black Jaundice I all Objects see,
> As Dark, and Terrible as Thee,
> My Lines decry'd, and my Employment thought
> An useless Folly, or presumptuous Fault. (74–80)

What is at stake here is Finch's poetic self, her identity as a writer and (in the lines that follow) as a woman writer. The spleen is portrayed as a destructive force which prevents her from writing, or leaves her a prey to self-doubt and self-deprecation. The obvious paradox, as in all poetic accounts of depression or melancholy that have seen the light of day, is that the lines the reader is reading are proof of Finch's own victory and that of her poetry, despite the fact that she openly acknowledges her defeat.

William Stukeley, physician and antiquarian, was to include Finch's poem in his handsome treatise on the spleen published in 1723, the transcription of the Gulstonian Lecture he had delivered before the Royal College of Physicians the previous year.[31] This co-existence of 'readings' and analyses of the spleen from two very different angles was a noteworthy and unexpected initiative. In his address 'To the Reader', Stukeley refers to 'the admirable poem on the spleen (which I obtain'd leave to insert) I judg'd necessary, to help out my own description of the disease'.[32]

At least two characteristics of the spleen are highlighted in the accounts, poetic and medical. Stukeley, like Finch, recalls from the out-set the elusive nature of the spleen, not of the infirmity but of the physical organ and its function, seeming to echo Finch's final stanza: 'it seems no easy task to answer the great problem of its use, after all the most famous Anatomists have fail'd in the attempt'.[33] Where Finch and Stukeley clearly part company is on the subject of remedies. For Finch the spleen can be neither understood nor vanquished. Stukeley, like George Cheyne and other physicians, will see the development of the spleen as related to changes in 'modern' lifestyle. Already in the early eighteenth century an accusing finger was being pointed at sedentary occupations, excess and inactivity:

> Our leaving the country for cities and great towns, coffeehouses and domestick track of business, our sedate life and excesses together, have prepar'd a plentiful harvest for these disorders. The remedy therefore is obvious; and without the concurrence of chearfulness, exercise, open air and conversation, all medicine is impotent.[34]

Stukeley evokes 'the golden mean necessary in every thing'.[35] Laughter is one remedy, as it stimulates and sets the spleen in motion:

> Wisely therefore did our ancestors keep their jesters to entertain them at dinner, to make 'em laugh and digest well, the first topick of health, whence they begat an athletic and hardy race, that did such wonders in arms. Quite contrary to the practice in religious houses, colleges, where the scripture is preposterously read at meal-times, and a superfluous demureness of countenance prepares them for all the diseases of an unactive spleen.[36]

Such conventional 'remedies' for Anne Finch quite simply do not work, as she writes in both 'The Spleen' – 'In vain to chase thee ev'ry Art we try, / In vain all Remedies apply' (128–9) – and in 'Ardelia to Melancholy':

> I have apply'd
> Sweet mirth, and musick, and have try'd
> A thousand other arts beside,
> To drive thee from my darken'd breast,
> Thou, who hast banish'd all my rest. (6–10)[37]

On Matthew Green: 'Laugh and be well'

Remedies such as laughter and exercise (as well as conversation) were, however, to figure prominently on the agenda of Matthew Green's *The Spleen* (1737),[38] a second notable poem to feature one of the characteristic early eighteenth-century terms for melancholy in its title.

At once an implicit anatomy of the illness and its diverse but (here) relatively benign manifestations, it is above all a list of remedies, and indeed a therapy in itself. It is an agreeable, amusing but nonetheless, to use Green's expression, 'joco-serious' (176) ramble, an attempt to stave off the spleen, a poetic exercise in preventive medicine. Its satire can be read as a self-administered remedy. And yet, suggests Amy Reed, satire (even light-hearted) can be read as being closely related to, rather than the opposite of, despair:

> much of seventeenth and eighteenth century satire may well be regarded as the poetry of despair. Nevertheless, since a sense of superiority is an essential element in the satiric spirit, the satirist never feels himself actually engulfed by the weltering waters of melancholy. He may be a castaway, but he is still riding the waves on the plank of intellect. Nor does he give direct expression to his feeling of depression, but conceals it by an attack on the folly or wickedness of other men, or of the world in general.[39]

The *topos* of the sea voyage, the journey through life's troubled waters, and sartorial imagery, are often in evidence in this poem that takes the outward-looking, convivial and relaxed form of the epistolary poem.[40] In the journey through life, if one wishes to arrive in port safely, the wisest path is to steer a middle course in religion and politics, and not to rock the boat. Moderation in all things is Green's motto if one wants to avoid both the Scylla of Enthusiasm and the Charybdis of Melancholy. In his echoing the attention drawn in medical discourses by Stukeley, Blackmore and Cheyne (and later in poetic form by Armstrong) to the importance of diet, the lower echelons of society were no doubt relieved to know they had not been forgotten in Green's insistence on the benefits of simple fare:

> I always choose the plainest food
> To mend viscidity of blood.
> Hail! water-gruel, healing power,
> Of easy access to the poor. (53–6)

Hunting is to be preferred to lying in bed. Get out and about, be sociable, avoid all forms of excess, exercise your mind and body – such are Green's exhortations:

> To cure the mind's wrong bias, Spleen;
> Some recommend the bowling-green;

Some, hilly walks; all, exercise;
Fling but a stone, the giant dies.
Laugh and be well. (89–93)

And he is not alone in extolling the benefits of fresh air and an active life. In the section of *Of The Spleen* devoted to laughter, Stukeley suggests, referring to the organ itself, that 'the ancients had a more than metaphorical reason to assign this part the honor of mirth and jollity, health and love, &c.' He goes on to elaborate on the physiological reasons for this, and we see that 'mirth and jollity' are intimately associated with the spleen, and the illness itself, 'the spleen', is thus provoked by an organ that is defective, inactive. A link between the contraries that are mirth and melancholy is thus established on purely medical grounds: 'A fit of laughter has often cur'd a fit of the spleen. Laughter is a passion proper to the human race, and certainly is assisted by the spleen; as in that convulsion, the diaphragmatic and phrenic branches give and receive blood readily to it.'[41] Green will say no more (but in fewer, less technical words) in suggesting that the spleen can literally be laughed off. His own form of chit-chat (in this he anticipates Cowper's entertaining digressions in *The Task*) dispels the clouds of spleen almost before they gather. The sartorial imagery indicates that moods would appear to be something one can put on or take off more or less at will, a sort of disguise, a choice rather than something one is subjected to:

Sometimes I dress, with women sit,
And chat away the gloomy fit;
Quit the stiff garb of serious sense,
And wear a gay impertinence. (182–5)

Green would gossip his way (and have us gossip our way) out of the doldrums. Poetry, however, he suggests in a moment of self-directed irony, is a waste of breath: 'You friend, like me, the trade of rhyme / Avoid, elab'rate waste of time' (502–3). The outside world, the environment and weather have their influence on one's morale. But Green is always on hand with advice. The climate of the physical world quickly affects the weather of the mind. 'In rainy days keep double guard' (154), he warns.

And when the time comes, Green (like Pomfret) hopes for a painless departure from this world. Everything is measured and controlled. Anything that could give rise to the spleen is held in check and defused in the poem. Death itself thus becomes a natural, banal and above all unalarming phenomenon, nothing more dramatic than a ripe piece of fruit falling to the ground; the daunting prospect and promise of eternity is whittled down to an unassuming 'perhaps', the afterworld reduced to a cautious afterword:

> Unhurt by sickness' blasting rage,
> And slowly mellowing in age,
> When Fate extends its gathering gripe,
> Fall off like fruit grown fully ripe,
> Quit a worn being without pain,
> Perhaps to blossom soon again. (710–15)

This vade-mecum of remedies and reassuring counsel no doubt provides distraction and entertaining advice for those feeling a bit down and suffering from a momentary attack of the blues, but may well prove to be less effective for those who are constitutionally prone to depression or melancholy. It does, however, suggest the pervasiveness of the infirmity at the time, as well as its eminently social identity.

The hence and hail mode

A dialogue between the poetry on and of melancholy and medical discourse is thus manifest in the course of the eighteenth century. It appears in both Finch, where the medical world signally fails to find a cure for the spleen, and in Green's poem, where common sense, moderation and good humour are advanced as means of prevention or remedies, a Popean avoidance of overreaching oneself, the ability to know and accept one's limits. The dialogue is especially audible in the poet-physician John Armstrong's didactic *The Art of Preserving Health* (1744) with its four books, 'Air', 'Diet', 'Exercise' and 'The Passions'.[42]

In Book 4, Armstrong, addressing the psychological manifestations of melancholy, distinguishes between 'Thought' (4.35), the positive employment of the mind in the exercising of reason, and 'painful thinking' (4.36) or 'sickly musing' (4.91). Armstrong exhorts his readers to be wary of the 'restless mind' (4.85), a mind that has no occupation, no fixed object to pursue, that turns in on itself, 'creating Fear / Forms out of nothing; and with monsters teems / Unknown in hell' (4.99–101):

> Quite unemploy'd, against its own repose
> It turns its fatal edge, and sharper pangs
> Than what the body knows embitter life.

Chiefly where Solitude, sad nurse of care,
To sickly musing gives the pensive mind.
There madness enters; and the dim-ey'd Fiend,
Sour Melancholy, night and day provokes
Her own eternal wound. (4.87–94)

The mind thus becomes its own place, here a hell of its own making, and the source of a negative, destructive creativity, feeding on its own unhappiness. But in the many poems influenced and inspired by the young Milton's twin poems 'L'Allegro' and 'Il Penseroso' (1645),[43] it is not a medical or psychological perspective that is privileged but a poetic vision. Two discourses, the two very different directions recalled above by Anne Amend,[44] are at once identified and dissociated. This illustrates the argument of Lawrence Babb that one should, and Milton clearly does, distinguish between two melancholies, that of the Galenic tradition ('utterly loathsome') and the divine goddess associated with Aristotle and Ficino.[45]

In Milton's diptych, the almost symmetrical companion poems oppose mirth and melancholy, though one is left throughout with the distinct feeling that these strange contraries are two sides of the same coin. In the life-approving address to Euphrosyne, or Mirth, one of the three graces, Milton having repudiated Melancholy, 'Of Cerberus, and blackest Midnight born' ('L'Allegro', 2),[46] goes on to embrace Mirth and Liberty, and petitions 'To live with her, and live with thee / In unre-proved pleasures free' (39–40). The poet of *Paradise Lost* goes on to portray a pastoral, idyllic world where ploughman, milkmaid, mower and shepherd live in perfect peace and harmony with nature.

In 'Il Penseroso' the poet abruptly dismisses such 'vain deluding Joys' (1). He has no time for 'The brood of Folly without father bred' (2) and aspires to live 'Far from all resort of mirth' (81). The 'delights' of mirth with which the poet means to live at the end of 'L'Allegro' are thus exchanged for the 'pleasures' of melancholy at the end of 'Il Penseroso'. Mirth opens the dance but melancholy has the last word in this quasi (but not totally) reversible universe.

Milton, then, not only associates and contrasts mirth and melan-choly, giving each a fair hearing, petitioning both, but also identifies and opposes two melancholies. The carefully crafted balance of Milton's dip-tych was, significantly, to become much more one-sided in the poems on melancholy in the eighteenth century. It is the melancholy of con-templation and meditation, but with a marked taste also for the gothic, the sensational, or the macabre elements of graveyardism, that will be apparent in poems by Dart, Young and Thomas Warton, for instance. In all three poems but especially the first two, mirth and joy are sent packing in the true 'hence and hail' tradition.

Thus John Dart commences his *Westminster-Abbey: A Poem* (1721, 1742)[47] by dismissing Venus and Love:

> Hence sportive *Venus*, and thy fading Joys,
> Thy wanton Sparrows, and thy blooming Boys;
> Hence *Love*, far hence, thy flaming Torches throw,
> Thy shining Arrows, and intending Bow:
> Trifling Amusements I no more pursue,
> By riper Thought inclin'd to sober View. (1–6)

Dart proceeds by negation, describing in an ambivalently positive manner what he rejects:

> I pensive now to solemn Scenes retire;
> Where, not the laughing Goddess makes Retreat,
> But sober Piety selects her Seat;
> [...]
>   Where, not the distant grove invites the Eyes,
> But Snow-white Towers in awful Reverence rise;
> Where murmuring Floods no pleasing Musick share,
> But Bells, far tolling, fix the Traveller's Ear.
> Where no aspiring Trees their Arms display,
> Thick wov'n, endeavouring to exclude the Day;
> Beneath whose chequer'd Shade and fragrant Air
> The Shepherd sleeps serene, recluse from Care:
> But Roofs wide bending rear their Arches high
> In antique Pride, and tire th'erected Eye;
> Where thro' the painted Glass the Beams invade,
> With rich stain'd Light, and cast a painted Shade. (22–4, 29–40)

The pleasures mentioned and dismissed are appealingly and generously described. If one removes the linguistic negation, one has a pleasant pastoral scene, with the agreeable music of the streams, the aspiring trees, the shepherd's repose. Émile Benveniste resumes as follows the paradoxical nature of this form of negation:

> What characterizes linguistic negation is that it can only annul what has been affirmed, that it must explicitly advance something in order

to suppress it, that a judgement of non-existence has also necessarily the formal status of a judgement of existence. Negation is thus initially admission.[48]

Edward Young begins his poem 'Cynthio' (1727)[49] in similar vein but with greater gusto and the immortal opening, 'I Hate the *Spring*':

> I Hate the *Spring*, I turn away
> From gaudy Scenes of flow'ry *May*,
> The vocal Grove, the painted Mead,
> The lucid Brook, the quiv'ring Shade,
> Where *Mirth*, and *Love*, (Phantastick Pair!)
> Laugh at the clouded Brow of Care.
>   The Death of Nature, the severe
> And wintry Waste, to me more dear.
> Yes, welcome Darkness! welcome Night!
> Thrice welcome every dread Delight! (1–10)

If darkness and gloom carry the day, Young still finds space and time to evoke the rejected charms of spring.

Thomas Warton, who was to provide a handsome, annotated edition of Milton's shorter poems in 1785,[50] was already clearly influenced by Milton when he wrote *The Pleasures of Melancholy* in 1745, aged 17.[51] The poem commences with Warton's own adaptation (and inversion) of the hence and hail address in which he invokes the 'Mother of musings, Contemplation sage' (1) and asks her to conduct him to a cheerless, nocturnal scene. Mirth and the spring day-world have lost their attraction, but the two worlds are again set side by side:

> O lead me, queen sublime, to solemn glooms
> Congenial with my soul; to chearless shades,
> To ruin'd seats, to twilight cells and bow'rs,
> Where thoughtful Melancholy loves to muse,
> Her fav'rite midnight haunts. The laughing scenes
> Of purple Spring, where all the wanton train
> Of Smiles and Graces seem to lead the dance
> In sportive round, while from their hands they show'r
> Ambrosial blooms and flow'rs, no longer charm;
> Tempe, no more I court thy balmy breeze,
> Adieu green vales! ye broider'd meads, adieu! (17–27)

In the relatively short space of this poem (315 lines) Warton manages to include just about all the gothic, nocturnal, graveyard elements one can imagine. They feature as at once enchanting and dismal details. All are the source of the poet's pleasure and the delight he paradoxically takes in his meditation on the ephemeral elements of human existence, markers and emblems of mutability and human finitude:

> Then let my thought contemplative explore
> This fleeting state of things, the vain delights,
> The fruitless toils, that still our search elude,
> As thro' the wilderness of life we rove. (80–3)

Warton invokes and aligns these elements not only to express his preference for gloom and 'mystic visions' (63) sent by the 'sacred Genius of the night' (62) but to associate them with a poetic programme, with the poetry of Spenser and Milton, as well as Pope's *Eloisa to Abelard*.

That such a sombre, gloomy, sorrow-laden world should so entrance the poet (and other poets of the time) may seem puzzling but, for Warton, the suffering soul, the man of sensibility, is held up as a paragon, embodying new ways of seeing and feeling, and writing poetry. The contraries here again are evoked and sustained. Mirth does not disappear because of its negation; suspended, rejected, it remains present, but the creative muse is clearly melancholy.

On Edward Young: 'The great Magician's dead!'

David B. Morris has written that the middle of the eighteenth century ushered in 'a new death-centered literature for which the prevailing mood is melancholy'.[52] The *genre sombre*, as the literary expression of the English taste for darkness and gloom came to be known in France, was diffused abroad in particular from the 1740s on. It included various often intertwined strands, the elegiac mode, poetry of loss and mourning, the themes of the passing of time and of mutability, a heightened awareness of mortality and finitude, the 'Death the Leveller' *topos*, all amplified by the expression of sentiment and sensibility.[53] The 'graveyard school' was in no sense an organized movement. It was a disparate grouping of separate poems by very different poets (notably Parnell, Blair, Young and Gray) who associated graveyard imagery and references with a shared chronotope (the time was evening or night, the place a graveyard).

The acknowledged central figure in the graveyard school and the *genre sombre* is the poet and dramatist Edward Young, best remembered for his *Night Thoughts* published in nine 'Nights' between May 1742 and January 1746. It is a complex, philosophical poem, a protracted meditation, whose full title is *The Complaint: Or, Night-Thoughts on Life, Death, & Immortality*. Despite the melancholy and invasive obscurity of the opening pages, the poem taken as a whole can be read not only as a passage from doubt, despair and darkness to light, as Mary S. Hall has convincingly argued,[54] a poem working essentially within the Christian framework of belief (hardly surprising for an Anglican churchman), but also as a redemption of a rather different kind, one where man becomes aware of his untapped creativity and potential, of an embryonic identity, an unknown other self, 'the stranger within',[55] a voyage, then, of self-discovery, even a conversion narrative in its peculiar way.

'Night the First' presents in the opening lines a tableau of insomnia and distress where the poet, as Anne Finch does in 'The Spleen', uses the sea metaphor to express the agitation and the turbulent nature of his mental state:[56]

> I wake, emerging from a sea of Dreams
> Tumultuous; where my wreck'd, desponding Thought
> From wave to wave of *fancy'd* Misery,
> At random drove, her helm of Reason lost;
> Tho' now restor'd, 'tis only Change of pain,
> A bitter change; severer for severe:
> The *Day* too short for my Distress! and *Night*
> Even in the *Zenith* of her dark Domain,
> Is Sun-shine, to the colour of my Fate. (1.9–17)

The cause of this distress is not immediately identified but will become apparent, without detail, some 200 lines on in an energetic apostrophe to Death:

> Death! Great Proprietor of all! 'Tis thine
> To tread out Empire, and to quench the Stars;
> The Sun himself by thy permission shines,
> And, one day, thou shalt pluck him from his sphere.
> Amid such mighty Plunder, why exhaust
> Thy *partial* Quiver on a Mark so mean?
> Why, thy *peculiar* rancor wreck'd on me?
> Insatiate Archer! could not One suffice?

Thy shaft slew thrice, and thrice my Peace was slain;
And thrice, e'er thrice yon Moon had fill'd her Horn. (1.204–13)

This is what Young calls in his 'Preface' '*the Occasion*' of the poem. The poet mourns the passing of not one but three close relations, his stepdaughter, Elizabeth ('Narcissa'), his stepdaughter's husband and a close friend, Henry Temple ('Philander'), and his wife, Lady Elizabeth ('Lucia'). Around these three deaths and the lessons to be drawn from them, Young weaves a dramatic, albeit patently lopsided, dialogue in which time and space while being centre stage are also strangely elusive. The two protagonists that are 'present' throughout the poem (rather than being present by their absence, as is the case with the deceased) are the first-person *persona*, 'I', the poet himself, and Lorenzo, whom James E. May calls an 'apostate *adversarius*',[57] the poet-preacher's sparring partner, a free-thinker and libertine, at once antagonist and friend, for whom no precise identity outside the poem has been established.

Young, like Webster (and Donne), was much possessed by death. At the heart of his poetry, there is a constant sense of disquiet, a deep-rooted anxiety about the transience of all things, about death itself, and the possibility of an afterlife. Young travels constantly between two poles, two extremes, between a dread of death and above all of annihilation, of non-being, and an apology for the afterlife and the immortality of the soul, expressed in an enthusiastic and, at times, ecstatic rhetoric of the beyond. Both poles create a rarefied atmosphere, a curiously empty but resonant poetic and mental landscape.

The deaths of Philander, Narcissa and Lucia give rise at first, as one might expect, not to a message of comfort and solace, but to grief and despair, the feeling that the world has been emptied of its substance, that something irretrievable has been lost, that a vital, enchanted bond, a charm, has been broken. Young relates first the emotion he feels on the death of Philander. The tableau is preceded by an admonition that is addressed to Lorenzo and, beyond him, no doubt, to the congregation of readers at large:

>   beware
> All joys, but joys that never can expire:
> Who builds on less than an *immortal* Base,
> Fond as he seems, condemns his joys to Death.
>   Mine dy'd with thee, *Philander!* thy last Sigh
> Dissolv'd the charm; the disenchanted Earth
> Lost all her Lustre; where, her glittering Towers?

> Her golden Mountains, where? all darken'd down
> To naked Waste; a dreary Vale of Tears;
> The great Magician's dead! Thou poor, pale Piece
> Of out-cast earth, in Darkness! what a Change
> From yesterday! (1.340–51)

This sudden change, the experience of an inner void, recalls the phenomenon of mourning as described by Freud in 'Mourning and Melancholia'. The world becomes the shadow of itself. Freud was to distinguish between mourning, the inevitable at once intimate and customary (socially acknowledged) reaction to the loss of someone close, or to some prized object, with the often conflicting emotions involved, and the illness of melancholia, characterized by an 'unknown loss'.[58] In the latter, the withdrawal, the loss of taste and appetite for the world (physical, emotional and moral), becomes not a passing and 'productive' phase (the 'work of mourning')[59] but a pathological, and seemingly unending and inexplicable phenomenon.

This broken spell, as in a fairy tale (or in Keats's 'Ode to a Nightingale' and 'La Belle Dame sans Merci'), where the protagonist wakes to find him or herself forlorn, abandoned and exiled from an enchanted world, is reworked and reformulated to similar effect with the death of Narcissa. The same use of pathos is made to express a fall, the charm that has gone from the world, and a natural world left 'Unharmonious' (3.89).

Young will extend this sense of individual loss to the notion of an exile that informs and defines the human condition. This endemic dissatisfaction in the poet's eyes is paradoxically read as proof of man's divine calling. Here he compares the condition of man and beast:

> Is it, that Things Terrestrial can't content?
> Deep in rich Pasture, will thy Flocks complain?
> Not so; but to their Master is deny'd
> To share their sweet *Serene*. Man, ill at Ease,
> In this, not *his own* Place, this Foreign Field. (7.37–41)

Young's melancholy has at least three faces and voices in these *Night Thoughts*. The first is that of the bereaved poet, the individual, overborne by the loss of his loved ones. This grief soon, simultaneously as it were, gives rise to a general reflection on the human condition. This second, 'moral' melancholy is presented in such a way that it becomes a source of hope, and Young the mourner becomes the prophet of worlds to come. The third, more unexpected, manifestation of melancholy is the expression of metaphysical and religious despair, voiced with some precaution and much vigour in 'Night the Seventh'.

The world as graveyard

In 'Night the First', moving from personal bereavement to a universal vision, Young conjures up the image of the world's 'melancholy map':

> A Part how small of the terraqueous Globe
> Is tenanted by man? the rest a *Waste*,
> Rocks, Deserts, frozen Seas, and burning Sands;
> Wild haunts of Monsters, Poisons, Stings, and Death:
> Such is Earth's melancholy Map! But far
> More sad! this Earth is a true Map of *man*. (1.284–9)

This 'true Map of *man*' includes fate, woes, sorrows, troubles, calamities and passions, what are called elsewhere 'the Moral maladies of Man' (5.284). This world picture, where the moral and physical coincide and correspond, differs from other physico-theologies presented by the Boyle lecturers[60] in that while it still observes analogies between the microcosm and the macrocosm, between human nature and the natural world, man and the universe, nevertheless states that this moral and very imperfect map is one that faithfully reflects an essentially hostile and stark physical environment. Young's vision comes closer to Thomas Burnet's sublimely fallen world or 'damaged paradise', as Basil Willey was to dub it, the world as 'a mighty ruin, a damaged paradise – majestic, no doubt (the work of the divine architect could scarcely be otherwise, even in decay), but a ruin none the less'.[61]

Having set the scene and deplored the loss of his loved ones, Young very quickly intersperses reflexive passages by which he effects a fundamental inversion. The graveyard thus becomes not only 'a Place of Graves' as the Irish poet and essayist Thomas Parnell calls it in 'A Night-Piece on Death' (1721) but also a source of life and hope; it becomes our 'subterranean Road to Bliss' (7.10), and death thus becomes eminently desirable (and 'vital') as the necessary passage to '*real* life' (1.128). The idea that this world is the true graveyard is vividly portrayed in the last 'Night' in this address to Lorenzo:

> What is the World itself? *Thy* World? - a Grave!
> Where is the Dust that has not been alive?
> The Spade, the Plough, disturb our Ancestors;

> From human Mould we reap our daily Bread:
> The Globe around Earth's hollow Surface shakes,
> And is the Ceiling of her sleeping Sons:
> O'er Devastation we blind Revels keep;
> Whole bury'd Towns support the Dancer's Heel. (9.91–8)

Having completed this uncompromising portrait of the world, in which he recalls above all man's mortal nature, Young is capable of conjuring up a quite different vision in a passage where he puts the onus on man's untapped creative capacities, 'creator' of the world through the senses, a prime actor in his own destiny.

Young develops a moral and poetic vision that Cowper[62] and Wordsworth were later to express.[63] Young's melancholy is here transformed and the world becomes re-enchanted. This aesthetic and poetic recreation and enthusiasm is the counterweight to Young's melancholy, a poetic cure through the combination of the senses and the imagination, a hymn to the beyond within. The 'it' in question here is man's '*true* Treasure' (6.413), his senses and divine calling, which make him 'the soul of all he sees' (6.440):

> Seek it in Thyself;
> Seek in thy naked Self, and find it There.
> In *Being* so Descended, Form'd, Endow'd;
> Sky-born, sky-guided, sky-returning Race!
> Erect, Immortal, Rational, Divine!
> In *Senses*, which inherit Earth, and Heavens;
> Enjoy the various riches *Nature* yields;
> Far nobler! *give* the riches they enjoy;
> Give tast to Fruits; and harmony to Groves;
> Their radiant beams to Gold, and Gold's bright Sire;
> Take in, at once, the Landscape of the world,
> At a small Inlet, which a Grain might close,
> And half create the wonderous World, they see.
> Our *Senses*, as our *Reason*, are Divine.
> But for the magic Organ's powerful charm,
> Earth were a rude, uncolour'd Chaos still. (6.415–30)

Young has moved far from the melancholy that informs the opening lines and books of the poem. He expresses a belief in man's capacities, in his senses and imagination, the restoration of the lost 'charm' that melancholy had obliterated. But Young will go on to envisage a further form of radical loss in 'Night the Seventh', where he imagines the belief in the afterlife as an empty promise, a delusion. Here, the loss is anticipated and imagined rather than recalled and experienced but is no less devastating for that.

'No Futurity'

In the preface to 'Night the Sixth', the first part of 'The Infidel Reclaim'd', Young writes that the dispute about religion '*may be reduced to this single Question*, Is Man Immortal, or is he not?'[64] In the 'Contents' to 'Night the Seventh', after affirming that 'Immortality *alone renders our Present State Intelligible*', he says that space will be given to the voice, as he puts it, of '*The natural, most melancholy, and pathetic Complaint of a Worthy Man under the Persuasion of no* Futurity'.[65] This extended passage (7.645–843) is a remarkable expression of religious despair of a peculiar kind, both a diatribe against an absent and indifferent God, one who has lost interest in his Creation, and the expression of anguish at the prospect of annihilation, of the non-existence of the soul after death. Lorenzo here is, once again, the addressee but the object of the invective is God himself, and, as in the book of Job, the vehemence, anger and the *ressentiment* are as violent as they are unexpected.[66] Nevertheless, this indirect address to the Deity (quite other to that – 'A *Night*-Address to the Deity' – which will conclude the night cycle in 'Night the Ninth and Last') is held at a remove, and put between quotation marks. Young can safely let off steam and give full expression to his own 'Dark Doubts' (4.701) and 'dark Distrust' (7.642).

In this extended passage on the prospect of absolute loss, Lorenzo's libertine or supposedly Epicurean vision of a life whose term is death for both body and soul, provokes in Young's mind a vision of horror and the prospect of annihilation. Man's fate is felt to be worse than Satan's and Young adopts a sublime Miltonic voice to express the extent of his hopelessness, as man is ' "hurl'd headlong, hurl'd at once / To Night! To Nothing! Darker still than Night" ' (7.659–60). If there is no afterlife, Young's system is reduced to ruins, self-knowledge becomes anathema. Here the despairing and desperate poet is in full stride in this scathing reversal and rebuttal of the 'nosce teipsum' and Christian traditions:

"To *know myself*, true Wisdom? - No, to shun
"That shocking Science, Parent of Despair!
"Avert thy Mirror; If I see, I die.
  "*Know my Creator?* Climb His blest Abode

"By painful Speculation, pierce the Veil,
"Dive in His Nature, read His Attributes,
"And gaze in Admiration - on a Foe,
"Obtruding Life, with-holding Happiness?
"From the full Rivers that surround His Throne,
"Not letting fall one Drop of Joy on Man;
"Man gasping for one Drop, that he might cease
"To curse his Birth, nor envy Reptiles more!
"Ye sable Clouds! ye darkest Shades of Night!
"Hide *Him*, for ever hide Him, from my Thought... (7.677–90)

Arguably the first eight books of the *Night Thoughts* are a hymn to loss in its various forms and aspects. There is real loss in the poem, the triple bereavement is the purported stimulus for the work, and yet Young's 'melancholy Map' is more general, indeed universal in scope. The moral map of human kind, of human actions, aspirations, imper-fections and fears is the map not only of a necessarily lost world but also of an embryonic world, a world to come, a world to be created. In this sense, the contraries, the experience and the expression of loss and the promise they engender can recall and strangely echo Bonnefoy's reference to the poetic map of melancholy, 'a map you think you have'. No single, simple map of melancholy comes to light. Each poet comes to terms with melancholy in his or her own way. William Cowper in 'Retirement' opens and peruses 'the map of God's extensive plan' (147)[67] but will live to the end of his days with the bitter, damning conviction that he himself will 'Come Home to Port no more'.[68]

On William Cowper: 'such a destin'd wretch as I'

' "An Outcast from Existence!" ' (7.822) is how Young's '*Worthy Man under the Persuasion of no* Futurity' describes himself (and he stands for all mankind) in the diatribe directed against God in 'Night the Seventh'. William Cowper was to leave a powerful, spare and moving self-portrait in the poem he wrote towards the end of his life, 'The Cast-away'. Cowper, who trained to be a barrister at the Middle Temple and then the Inner Temple, at first unmindful of religion, was converted to evan-gelicalism in 1764 following a period of depression. His life was to be governed by the rhythm of recurring episodes of depression, the first dating from 1753 when he was 22. After the time spent in Dr. Nathaniel Cotton's 'Collegium Insanorum' in St Albans (1763–5) following a severe crisis in 1763, he lived in the country, Huntingdon in Cambridgeshire, Olney and Weston Underwood in Buckinghamshire, and, for his last years, East Dereham in Norfolk, cared for, retired and protected from the world by friends and family. He enjoyed intervals of respite, but was to remain vulnerable to further episodes of depression, and attempted to commit suicide on several occasions. He died, ill and depressed, in 1800. The last poem he was to write in English, 'The Cast-away', written in March 1799, conjures up themes of abandonment, despair and isolation that were to pervade his poetry, intermittently, from his first serious emotional setback as a young man in 1753 when his hopes of marrying his cousin Theadora Cowper came to naught.

In Cowper's poetry an image that returns time and again is that of a being adrift, utterly alone, his fate sealed. Cowper was to consider himself as a lost, damned soul for much of his life and such was definitively the case from 1773 on. Baird and Ryskamp recall the circumstances when Cowper seemed to reach the point of no return: 'Then on 24 January he had the dream which changed everything. A voice spoke the words "Actum est de te, periisti"—"it is all up with you, you have perished." ' The judgement for Cowper was a divine judgement and according to his understanding of his Calvinistic religion was irrevocable. Baird and Ryskamp go on to comment: 'From that day forth Cowper never entered a church, never attended a prayer meeting, never said a prayer, never so much as said grace at his table, for in God's eyes, so he thought, he had already ceased to exist.'[69] How such a deep despair translates in his poetry is complex, and as with other poets who suffered from mental affliction, such as Christopher Smart, his poetry remains very varied in form and theme. Despair does not dominate Cowper's poetry, as is evident from the fine variety of voices and themes that go to make up his major poem *The Task* (1785). To conclude, however, I will evoke briefly some poems that seem to resonate with Cowper's last English poem.

Already in 'Doom'd, as I am, in solitude to waste', a poem composed towards the end of 1757 (or later), he had written, following the end of his hopes of marriage with his cousin Theadora and the death of a close friend, Sir William Russell:

See me – ere yet my destin'd course half done,
Cast forth a wand'rer on a wild unknown!
See me neglected on the world's rude coast,
Each dear companion of my voyage lost! (15–18)[70]

In October 1780 Cowper received a letter that contained a poem from the Reverend John Newton, the former slavetrader, also a convert to evangelicalism, and with whom Cowper was to compose the *Olney*

Hymns. Viewing the sea from the cliffs above Ramsgate, looking back on his life, Newton feels a sense of relief that he is now, at last, on safe ground. The sea, here employed yet again as a metaphor for the world, was no longer felt to be a threat to the man who had made several voyages as master of ships engaged in the slave trade. He seems appeased. Cowper replies a few days later with the poem 'To Mr. Newton On His Return From Ramsgate', in which he expresses the very different feelings he experiences when contemplating the sea from the same vantage point. For Cowper the prospect is disquieting and alarming. The same view conjures up quite contrary sentiments and reminiscences, hopes for the future or deep forebodings, in the two men:

> That Ocean you of late survey'd,
>   Those Rocks I too have seen,
> But I, Afflicted and dismay'd,
>   You tranquil and Serene. (1–4)[71]

This poem reiterates the verdict that Cowper was to live with from 1773 on when he felt he had received confirmation of being 'chosen' in the sense of marked out as eternally damned, 'in a fleshly tomb... / Buried above ground', as he was to write in 'Hatred and Vengeance, My Eternal Portion'.[72] He expresses his situation and feelings thus in the final stanzas of the poem addressed to Newton:

> To me, the Waves that ceaseless broke
>   Upon the dang'rous Coast,
> Hoarsely and ominously spoke
>   Of all my Treasure lost.
>
> Your Sea of Troubles you have pass'd,
>   And found the peacefull Shore;
> I, Tempest-toss'd, and wreck'd at last,
>   Come Home to Port no more. (9–16)

Such poems seem to rehearse and lead inexorably to 'The Cast-away'.[73] If the meaning accorded to the term 'castaway' from the end of the eighteenth century on is that of someone who has been shipwrecked, the earlier meaning given in the *Oxford English Dictionary*, 'reprobate', is obviously relevant to Cowper's predicament and his own estimation of himself.

Similar concerns to those that appear in Pope's *Eloisa to Abelard* and Gray's *Elegy* surface at the end of the poem concerning the relationship between the poet, poetry, the reader, melancholy and despair. Cowper puts into verse (in a ballad form) the story of a seaman lost overboard during a storm narrated in Richard Walter's account (1748) of Commodore George Anson's voyage around the world on the *Centurion*. The poem immortalizes the tragic scene of the seaman swimming hopelessly to save himself, farther and farther from the ship, 'His floating home' (6), with no salvation possible. At first within sight of his shipmates, then within earshot, his voice still heard above the waves, and finally totally alone and lost, he 'waged with Death a lasting strife / Supported by despair of life' (17–18). Cowper, recalling the drama, identifies with the seaman and his destiny. In evoking the 'delight' to be found in misery, Cowper seems to echo Eloisa's words quoted above when she talks of a 'sad similitude of griefs to mine':

> No poet wept him, but the page
>   Of narrative sincere
> That tells his name, his worth, his age,
>   Is wet with Anson's tear,
> And tears by bards or heroes shed
> Alike immortalize the Dead.
>
> I, therefore, purpose not or dream,
>   Descanting on his fate,
> To give the melancholy theme
>   A more enduring date,
> But Mis'ry still delights to trace
> Its semblance in another's case. (49–60)

The final twist plunges the reader into even deeper perplexity, when Cowper returns to his own destiny as a damned soul, and the sea again takes on a violent, indifferent and unforgiving face. Here there is no headstone to read, no burial, no names, message and dates to pore over, no visible and material trace, but a cry, a voice above the waves that is soon no longer heard. But the poem, like Richard Walter's account, serves to commemorate the lost seaman and his plight. A curious *mise en abyme* is wrought here: Anson's log, the narrative of Anson's voyage and the seaman lost overboard, the poet who recounts the story, the immediate identification of the 'I' with the seaman in the opening stanza – 'such a destin'd wretch as I' (3) – and the merging of the pronouns at the end. The 'he' and the 'I' become 'we' but separate in the same (last) breath, with Cowper's mental and moral drowning appearing an even more terrible fate than the seaman's. As with Young in 'Night the Seventh', the divine and the hope of salvation are evoked by their absence; Cowper's fate is beyond even the extreme anguish of the 'outcast mate' (23). The linguistic negation again serves to signal what has been lost, or rather the absence of divine intercession:

> No voice divine the storm allay'd,
>   No light propitious shone,
> When, snatch'd from all effectual aid,
>   We perish'd, each, alone;
> But I, beneath a rougher sea,
> And whelm'd in deeper gulphs than he. (61–6)

The poetry of the eighteenth century that addresses melancholy, mirrors its subject both in its volatility and its stability, is paradoxical itself in its diversity and in its predictability, in the ambivalence at work in those 'strange contrarys', the mixed sentiments of attraction and repulsion, the convergent and divergent poles of pain and pleasure John Norris was to evoke in his own 'Ode to Melancholy' (1687):

> Strange contrarys in thee combine,
> Both *Hell* and *Heaven* in thee meet
> Thou greatest bitter, greatest sweet.
> No *Pain* is like thy Pain, no *Pleasure* too like *thine*.[74]

Melancholy recalls, reinstates and reaffirms the central place of loss and death in life. Its 'strange contrarys' are our own ambivalence, at once acknowledging, drawn to and fleeing from the realities of finitude, loss and mortality, seeing in another's demise our own destiny, fascinated by disaster, always tempted to approach the brink. If melancholy has a figure of speech, it could very well be, as Bonnefoy suggests, the oxymoron – Young's 'Delightful gloom!' (5.205), a yoking together of opposites while maintaining the conflict and tension between them. In his 'Ode on Melancholy', Keats was to acknowledge in his turn the fascination that melancholy exercises, its aesthetic and poetic potential, in his own version of Norris's opposition between pleasure and pain:

> Ay, in the very temple of Delight
>   Veil'd Melancholy has her sovran shrine. (25–6)[75]

The eighteenth century opens and closes with Finch and Cowper, with very different, but intense, poetic and personal expressions of melancholy and loss; both are moving, both are lucid. In both, also, melancholy is pictured as a force that takes over the individual, and the idea and the poetic images of a state of absolute helplessness are a poignant expression of abandonment that tallies with accounts of depression closer to us in time, still associated with the ideas of vulnerability, of introspection, of isolation, of suffering, but also of creativity. A helplessness belied, at least in part, by the poetry it creates, and which gives it and leaves us precious voices and traces.

4
Despair, Melancholy and the Novel

Stuart Sim

Religious melancholy, generated by a belief in one's utter worthlessness in the eyes of God, was a widely acknowledged phenomenon in the seventeenth century, drawing criticism from such as Robert Burton and Richard Baxter (for whom it was a cause of 'overmuch sorrow');[1] although, as Jeremy Schmidt has pointed out, for many others at the time it could also be interpreted as a spiritually promising sign of concern for the state of one's soul.[2] One of the major channels for expressing such experiences, and that concern, proved to be the genre of spiritual autobiography. The influence of spiritual autobiography on the development of the early novel has been well documented, and we find the narrative structure and concerns of the former being taken over by such practitioners as Daniel Defoe and Samuel Richardson in works like *Robinson Crusoe* and *Pamela*.[3] The structure dictates recurring cycles of sin to repentance in the protagonist's life until an epiphany delivers what they believe to be evidence of divine grace being extended – the 'conversion experience' (the genre is also sometimes referred to as 'conversion narrative'). Along with the structural pattern also comes a psychological landscape in which despair plays a critical role, with authors making extensive use of the term. The passage to a state of grace is never easy, and involves much mental torture that tests individuals to the limit of their endurance.

John Bunyan's frequent references to despair in his own spiritual autobiography, *Grace Abounding to the Chief of Sinners*, show how central the state was to the process of conversion, with each episode forcing the individual to confront his or her own worst fears – of rejection by God and likely damnation, for example, a matter of overwhelming concern in such a deeply devout historical period. Bunyan's record of his personal experience of despair is harrowing, and it is fairly clear that we

are dealing with someone who, in modern terms of reference, is suffering from depression (there is a distinctly manic-depressive character to
be noted in the trajectory of Bunyan's life, with emotional highs and
lows alternating in disruptive fashion).[4] The religious system Bunyan
lived by, Calvinism, encouraged this condition, especially if one became
as obsessed with its predestinarian components as the author plainly
did, and it gave him a narrative line to help deal with the experience.
Life turned into an arduous journey through despair and anxiety to
the final security of salvation: a severe, but ultimately rewarding trial
of character. Through recourse to theological doctrine Bunyan could
make sense of his feelings – even if the message the doctrine yielded was
not always a very comforting one to receive. Selected passages from the
Bible were as likely to speak of divine vengeance as divine grace, to scare
the reader as to quell his or her anxieties. The question of whether religion caused the despair or merely provided a convenient explanation for
its development in the individual remains, however, a tantalizing one.
Speculation inevitably arises as to whether Calvinism creates manic-
depressives or attracts them; whether it is to be viewed as cause or cure
of personal despair and the breakdown that can so often accompany
this. (It is always worth remembering in this context, as Jeremy Schmidt
has observed, that despair was not confined to Calvinists;[5] but it seems
fair to say that Calvinism generally intensified the experience.)

Despair is carried over into Bunyan's fictionalized spiritual autobiography *The Pilgrim's Progress* (as in the figure of Giant Despair),[6]
and is appropriated from there into Defoe's Robinson Crusoe (the
hero marooned on what he christens his '*Island of Despair*').[7] Whether
Crusoe's despair, again apparently religiously derived as concerning his
spiritual prospects, ever reaches the depth or intensity of its source
is more questionable – like most of Defoe's protagonists, Crusoe can
be a very slippery character who evades precise classification as to his
motives or beliefs.[8] Nevertheless, Defoe's handling of the topic, and
his considerable influence on subsequent generations of novelists, puts
religious despair firmly on the agenda of the new literary form, which
becomes a prime site for exploring its complex and highly varied nature
and the social and political ramifications that follow on from this.
The interplay between the spiritual and the secular, the individual and
the society within which he or she lives, becomes a fascinating phenomenon to observe in eighteenth-century fiction, and this will now be
investigated in a range of key works from *The Pilgrim's Progress* in the
late seventeenth century through to James Hogg's *The Private Memoirs
and Confessions of a Justified Sinner* in 1824. Although Hogg's work falls

slightly outside the dates for this volume, it is included because it provides such a natural frame for the debate on the relationship between religion and despair from Bunyan onwards. Effectively, we can say that Hogg deconstructs the genre of spiritual autobiography by revealing its gaps and contradictions, thus undermining the tradition of religious enthusiasm stretching back into seventeenth-century British life in the process. After Hogg, it is very difficult indeed to make much of an argument for the virtues of that tradition: its dangers are far more evident.

This chapter asks us to consider whether we are dealing with specifically religious despair in each case, curable by some form or other of the conversion experience, or whether religion is merely the conventional means of expressing depressive states (that is, a narrative framework to which any believer, but particularly one from a nonconformist background, has ready access). It will be argued that religion proves to have less ability to provide solace for the psychologically beleaguered individual as we move through the period, allowing something more like the modern form of depression to take shape. Melancholy, for example, becomes an increasingly fashionable way of responding to depressing circumstances from the mid-eighteenth century onwards (the popularity of Laurence Sterne's work in particular encouraging this), although by this stage it is a different phenomenon from the religious variety of the previous century and is more secular in its orientation – less fixated on personal salvation, for instance, and also less clear as to where to lay the blame for the experience of 'overmuch sorrow'. Establishing the nature of the relationship between the individual and the narrative framework can tell us a great deal about changing attitudes towards despair over the long eighteenth century, as well as helping us to discriminate more precisely between despair and depression. The former can be overcome if circumstances change for the better; the latter, especially in a culture with by modern standards fairly rudimentary medical and health care, is a far more debilitating state, where the physical and the metaphysical feed off each other in a destructive manner. The source of despair, in other words, can be either circumstantial or ontological; religion can be either the cure or the disease, although its curative powers do seem to wane as we move through our period.

John Bunyan and the fictionalization of despair

The Pilgrim's Progress stands as one of the most powerful fictionalizations of the state of despair in world literature, a handbook to generations of readers on how to cope with, and eventually overcome, the experience of chronic despair in one's personal life. Its protagonist, Christian, is beset with demons and enemies over the course of a perilous journey from his home in the City of Destruction to the Celestial City, and he undergoes psychological torments in his epic struggle to reach the destination where his salvation will be confirmed. Despair is an omnipresent threat to the character throughout that journey, a condition he consistently falls into; but for the roots of the author's obsession with despair we need to turn first to his own life history, as detailed in *Grace Abounding*.

Grace Abounding is now regarded as a classic example of spiritual autobiography, the only one from the period to hold any kind of substantial readership through into our own time. It records the progress of the author from swaggering and sinful young man to eventual belief in his coming salvation, and then on to his subsequent career as a lay preacher in the Baptist Church. So far, so conventional, that is the kind of journey we expect to hear about in spiritual autobiography. What marks Bunyan's version out from the crowd, however, is the sheer intensity of his experiences: an intensity which bespeaks a depth of despair in the author's character that can make for painful reading much of the time. The author's pronounced mood swings certainly suggest someone caught up in a manic-depressive pattern: 'Now was the battel won, and down I fell, as a Bird that is shot from the top of a Tree, into great guilt and fearful despair', as he graphically describes his state of mind at one critical juncture.[9] Bunyan is to remain prey to such destabilizing emotional shifts until he is given what to him will count as proof of his own forthcoming salvation:

> But one day, as I was passing in the field, and that too with some dashes on my Conscience, fearing lest yet all was not right, suddenly this sentence fell upon my Soul, *Thy righteousness is in Heaven*...Now did my chains fall off my Legs indeed, I was loosed from my afflictions and irons, my temptations also fled away: so that from that time those dreadful Scriptures of God left off to trouble me; now went I also home rejoycing, for the grace and love of God.[10]

The sense of exaltation about having the means henceforth to keep despair and disablingly depressive thoughts at bay is palpable. Even if residual doubts and anxieties do still creep into the author's mind on occasion afterwards, they are never on the scale of pre-conversion existence and can be borne: his narrative is now in place.

Despair is seen in purely religious terms by Bunyan, as indicative of a lack of faith on his part, thus a negative sign, strongly suggestive of impending damnation. Bunyan is a believer in predestination, meaning that he considers the decision about his spiritual fate to have been made by God before he was born, and to be irrevocable.[11] Individuals can do no more than examine their daily thoughts and actions for signs of grace from God hinting at salvation: they are powerless before the decision itself and can only await confirmation of the verdict one way or the other. Calvinism turns the screw on this by claiming that although individuals can take no credit for their salvation, they are nevertheless responsible for their own damnation – on the grounds that all humankind is guilty of original sin and none of us therefore deserves to be saved: 'man falls according as God's providence ordains, but he falls by his own fault', in Calvin's typically stern words.[12] To become a member of the elect is a privilege that none of us should expect, and not surprisingly this can induce anxiety and despair in believers – in Bunyan's case, acute anxiety and despair:

> For about the space of a month after, a very great storm came down upon me, which handled me twenty times worse then all I had met with before: it came stealing upon me, now by one piece, then by another; first all my comfort was taken from me, then darkness seized upon me; after which whole flouds of Blasphemies, both against God, Christ, and the Scriptures, was poured upon my spirit, to my great confusion and astonishment.[13]

Nowadays, such an experience, highly suggestive of clinical depression in the violence of the mood swing it records, would be very likely to prompt some kind of medical treatment. The sheer volume of such episodes over the course of Bunyan's life, as well the length of time they lasted (years in some cases), would hardly go unnoticed in a world that now has such diagnostic aids as the American Psychiatric Association's *Diagnostic and Statistical Manual–IV* to call upon[14] (Allan Ingram will be considering the pros and cons of such material in Chapter 6). For Bunyan, however, the context is metaphysical rather than physical. He processes his physical symptoms through his theological system, which tells him they are to be read as signs of his soteriological status. Despair is to be contained within a religious framework, even if we would have to say that it is the framework itself which is triggering a great deal of the despair – or at any rate exaggerating it. Again the question of cause or cure presents itself, and Bunyan is an intriguing figure in this regard: someone in whom circumstantial and ontological factors are so entangled that it is difficult to see how they can be overcome, one side always being capable of setting off the other.

The Pilgrim's Progress takes the author's personal experience into the fictional domain, allegorizing his physical symptoms – the Slough of Despond, Doubting-Castle, Giant Despair, etc. Christian has to struggle against an array of formidable obstacles to his journey, and these often bring him to the brink of desperation. Whenever doubts about his salvation come into Christian's mind, and they do so on a regular basis despite his early receipt from a group of angels of a scroll to be handed in at the Celestial City to gain admission there, then he sinks into a condition of despair recalling that of his author in its intensity. In the Slough of Despond, for example, Christian, accompanied by a neighbour of his from the City of Destruction, Pliable, is rendered almost completely helpless in what is a particularly striking image of religious melancholy:

> Here therefore they wallowed for a time, being grievously bedaubed with the dirt; And *Christian*, because of the burden that was on his back, began to sink in the Mire. Pli. *Then said* Pliable, *Ah, Neighbour* Christian, *where are you now? Chr.* Truly, said *Christian*, I do not know.[15]

The burden that Christian carries around on his back is a visible symbol of his problematical soteriological state, yet even after he has managed to shed it (energized by a vision of Christ on the cross) despair continues to dog him, as in the encounter he and his fellow pilgrim Hopeful have with Giant Despair:

> So when morning was come, he goes to them in a surly manner, as before, and perceiving them to be very sore with the stripes that he had given them the day before; he told them, that since they were never like to come out of that place, their only way would be, forthwith to make an end of themselves, either with Knife, Halter or Poison: For why, said he, should you chuse life, seeing it is attended with so much bitterness.[16]

The pilgrims eventually escape from the Giant's clutches, but despair is to come back to haunt Christian as he crosses over the River of Death, where we are told, a great darkness and horror fell upon *Christian*, so that he could not see before him ... [A]ll the words that he spake, still tended to discover that he had horror of mind, and hearty fears that he should die in that River, and never obtain entrance in at the Gate[.][17]

Clearly, despair is deeply rooted in Christian's character, and he needs constant reinforcement from his religious belief if he is to function effectively enough to maintain his progress. His life can come to appear as one large round of desperately striving to keep despair at bay, and he is never completely free from its hold over him. Religion nevertheless provides more solace than anxiety overall, and just scores as cure in this case – as it does with Bunyan himself.

Daniel Defoe: despair and the isolated self

Defoe trades heavily on the pattern of spiritual autobiography in his fiction, with the intriguing exception of *Roxana*, which will be considered later. Crusoe and Moll Flanders certainly use the pattern to make retrospective sense of their lives, although the suspicion always lingers that there may be an opportunistic quality to the exercise, that adopting the form enables them to present themselves to best advantage to the reader and to gloss over their catalogue of sins. Crusoe is harshly punished for the sin of going against the will of his father in order to seek out a life of adventure (a 'fatal ... Propension' on his part as he is to admit in retrospect),[18] but he remains a headstrong character to the last, tempting providence yet again by embarking on another long-range seafaring adventure at the age of almost sixty (to be outlined in detail in *The Farther Adventures*). Moll, whose catalogue of sins is far more extensive than Crusoe's, only finds repentance while under sentence of death in Newgate Prison for a life of crime, and her 'editor' openly queries her sincerity in this respect, remarking that, in her later life, she 'was not so extraordinary a Penitent, as she was at first'.[19] Moll's despair is brought on by circumstances rather than by personal psychology; she seems otherwise a fairly outgoing type, not overly given to self-reflection. One suspects that the prospect of hanging would affect most that way, so we cannot necessarily assume great spiritual depths to the character because of her highly emotional reaction to her plight: 'I cry'd out all Night, Lord! What will become of me? Lord! what shall I do? Lord! I shall be hang'd, Lord have mercy upon me, and the like.'[20]

Crusoe, in contrast, is more successful at communicating a sense of religious conviction when on his 'Island of Despair', even if this is never quite so evident in his post-island life when he reverts to the adventuring, entrepreneurial ways that landed him in trouble initially. In the early days after his shipwreck, however, it is his faith which enables him to endure his situation; Bible-reading eventually providing him with a series of comforting messages (much in the manner that it does for Bunyan in *Grace Abounding*) to convince him that he is not really alone:

> This was the first Time that I could say, in the true Sense of the Words, that I pray'd in all my Life; for now I pray'd with a Sense of my Condition, and with a true Scripture View of Hope founded on the Encouragement of the Word of God; and from this Time, I may say, I began to have Hope that God would hear me.[21]

Once assured of providentialism being extended in his favour, Crusoe's despair gradually dissipates, and he applies himself to establishing his own little kingdom on the island. Any anxiety he may feel after the 'Extasy of Joy' marking out his conversion experience, is provoked by external circumstances, such as the footprint he discovers on the shore, or the arrival of cannibals from the mainland, rather than by his spiritual prospects.[22] Although these events can scare him, his conviction that he is now under divine protection means that any fear he experiences is temporary. Despair need no longer be part of his individual narrative.

Roxana is an altogether more interesting case, and despair pursues her right through to the end of the narrative. Her life gives ample reason for the development of such feelings: abandoned by her husband and forced into a life of prostitution in order to keep her five young children fed, she becomes outstandingly successful in her new career amassing a fortune over the years by becoming the mistress of various wealthy men, if at a considerable psychological cost. She has to live a life of subterfuge and secrecy (even 'Roxana' is an assumed name) and, although corrupted by her financial success, still manages to suggest an overall sense of moral unease at her situation: 'the Devil himself cou'd not form one Argument, or put one Reason into my Head *now*, that cou'd serve for an Answer, no, not so much as a pretended Answer to this Question, *Why I shou'd be a Whore now?*'[23] There is no indication in the narrative of a conversion experience on the heroine's part, and one could regard *Roxana* as a failed spiritual autobiography, the record of someone inexorably heading for damnation and unable to arrest the process. The critical point comes when her daughter Susan, farmed out to foster-parents in line with Roxana's policy of continuing her career as unencumbered as possible, returns as a young woman to haunt her, claiming a recognition Roxana cannot countenance: 'this impertinent Girl, *who was now my plague*', as she complains bitterly of Susan's increasingly desperate attempts to confront her.[24] It is implied that Susan is done away with by Amy, Roxana's loyal servant, although this is never confirmed nor exact details given; all we have are some tantalizing allusions on Roxana's part. From that episode onwards, however, Roxana gives the impression of being consumed by guilt, and the narrative ends on a chillingly despairing note:

> Here, after some few Years of flourishing, and outwardly happy Circumstances, I fell into a dreadful Course of Calamities, and *Amy* also; the very reverse of our former Good Days; the Blast of Heaven seem'd to follow the Injury done the poor Girl, by us both; I was brought so low again, that my Repentance seem'd to be only the Consequence of my Misery, as my Misery was of my Crime.[25]

Roxana's despair may well have a religious foundation, her recognition of the immorality of her lifestyle and how this breaks the code of Christian ethics on which her society is, at least officially, structured (plus, of course, the prohibition against murder); yet it seems to transcend that framework and become more of a general reaction to the pressures exerted on her by a patriarchal system. She becomes the victim of a society constructed on double standards, where sexual transgression is considered acceptable for males but not for females, and where women are permanently preyed on by men. Susan becomes the all-too-visible symbol of the penalties exacted on women for sexual transgression – even for someone as discreet and professionally organized as Roxana proves herself to be over the course of her career. Roxana's is an existential despair about the condition of being a woman in a patriarchal society, where both social convention and biology conspire against you: in a society without effective methods of birth control, pregnancy is a constant threat and women are made to bear the shame for this. Religion is providing no comfort for that state of affairs. Guilty though Roxana may be of vanity and avarice, as she openly admits ('These were my Baits, these the Chains by which the Devil held me bound'),[26] these sins pale beside the abuses that women are subjected to by men in general. There is no way out of that situation for Roxana, and her final cry of despair is only too warranted. We could say that religion has failed her, leaving her far more isolated and bereft of comfort than Crusoe ever was, for all his solitary existence.

Despairing of patriarchy: Samuel Richardson, Frances Burney and Mary Hays

Samuel Richardson's *Pamela* and *Clarissa* both feature women reduced to a state of despair by men taking full advantage of the power granted them by patriarchal society, and they have many similarities to Roxana's situation. As we shall go on to see below, that is also the case in the fiction of Frances Burney and Mary Hays, authors heavily influenced by Richardson. Both Pamela and Clarissa are pursued relentlessly by male rakes, and find themselves being trapped in morally compromising positions that cause them considerable anguish. The overweening power of patriarchy, which acts much in the manner of fate as far as women are concerned, closing off their options at almost every turn, registers strongly in both instances. And whereas Roxana is by the moral standards of her society a sinner, and thus can only expect a certain amount of sympathy from her contemporary readers (harsh though that may seem to us now, given the mitigating circumstances), neither Pamela nor Clarissa can be held guilty of this, so their treatment is even less justifiable.

Pamela is the lighter of the two works and it is often very comic in tone, but the seriousness of the heroine's plight is still apparent. Pamela's virginity must be protected at all costs, otherwise she runs the risk of becoming a social outcast, as her parents keep warning will be her fate should her vigilance ever slip. Her personal integrity will be destroyed if Mr. B succeeds in his efforts to seduce her, and she becomes a highly symbolic figure of morality under stress, a female version of Christian. Her adventures are often played for fun by Richardson, yet this is no less of a spiritual autobiographical journey that is being enacted all the same. Pamela is hounded by Mr. B and forced out of necessity to develop a character that can withstand the trials he insistently visits upon her, well aware of the essential weakness of her position as a servant in his household, thus his social as well as gender inferior. Salvation in this instance will be achieved only by marriage, and the road to it is at least as tortuous as that faced by Christian in his struggle to reach the Celestial City, as conducive of despair as Pamela's resolve is constantly put under pressure by the determined Mr. B.

Pamela's despair comes to a head when, having been kidnapped by Mr. B and imprisoned on another of his estates, she is brought low enough emotionally to contemplate suicide by drowning. Only by an effort of will, and by reflecting on the religious prohibitions against the act itself, can she steel herself to go on and resist Mr. B as best she can.

There is a sense of the conversion experience about the episode, with Pamela deciding that a higher power is putting her virtue to the test and that it is therefore her duty to abide by its dictates:

> [W]ilt thou, to shorten thy *transitory* griefs, *heavy* as they are, plunge both body and soul into *everlasting* misery! Hitherto, Pamela, thought I, thou art the innocent, the suffering Pamela; and wilt thou, to avoid thy sufferings, be the guilty aggressor? How do I know but that the Almighty may have permitted these sufferings as trials of my fortitude, and to make me, who perhaps have too much prided myself in a vain dependence on my own foolish contrivances, rely wholly on his grace and assistance?[27]

Eventually, she does win out and Mr. B accepts her terms and marries her, but she is regularly subjected to assaults on her person in the interim, as Mr. B comes very close to raping her on occasion – often with help from his only too willing staff, eager to prove their allegiance to their master. Marriage to Mr. B secures Pamela's social position and, as Part II records, her life settles down into a happy round of child-rearing and charitable activities in her local neighbourhood; nevertheless, the precariousness of her situation has been made very clear. Pamela may have escaped social disgrace, but that will not be true of all the other women whom Mr. B, and numerous rakes like him, have pursued – and will continue to pursue. Religion has been an aid in bolstering Pamela's resistance to Mr. B's advances, but it does not always work out that way and others sink into longer-lasting despair instead, as in the case of one of Mr. B's earlier conquests, Sally Godfrey. Having started an affair with Miss Godfrey, Mr. B is put under heavy pressure by her family to marry her when they discover the liaison. In characteristically cavalier rake fashion he resists, leaving the unfortunate woman pregnant. After the birth, which nearly kills her, she resettles in Jamaica, asking Mr. B to provide for the child, which he does. Mr. B professes to 'abhor my past liberties, and pity poor Sally Godfrey', but one can only speculate at the state of mind of the mother, separated from her child and family on the other side of the world, and forced to pass for a young widow in order to contract a marriage and attain an appearance of respectability.[28] One could hardly interpret her story as a successful spiritual autobiography: Mr. B definitely has the better of the bargain, with Pamela even agreeing to bring up the child as her own after their marriage.

Clarissa is an altogether more disturbing narrative, with the protagonist in effect being driven to death because of her inability to overcome the despair she feels at her maltreatment by both her family and her seducer Lovelace. Clarissa proceeds to give up after her rape, refusing to be part of a world in which such evil can exist – and even escape much in the way of censure, rakes like Lovelace simply being considered part of the normal order of things. Again, it is the existential condition of womanhood that is found wanting, and though Clarissa can turn to religion for some comfort in her distress, it is only to make it easier for her to die:

> When these lines reach your hands, your late unhappy niece will have known the end of all her troubles; and as she humbly hopes, will be rejoicing in the mercies of a gracious God who has declared that He will forgive the truly penitent of heart … [H]owever sharp my afflictions have been, they have been but of short duration; and I am betimes (happily as I hope) arrived at the end of a painful journey.[29]

If anything, religion intensifies the despair that Clarissa feels as a rape victim, since she can no longer meet its ideals of female moral purity.

Clarissa's sense of despair is initiated by her parents, who attempt to force her into marriage with someone she detests, their unpleasant neighbour Solmes, with the explicit desire to enlarge the family estate through the union. The heroine is treated like property, to be dealt in to further the family fortunes, with no regard at all for her personal feelings in the matter. She is expected to submit meekly to the family's wishes, and when she refuses to do so the intense pressure that is subsequently placed on her soon takes its toll as she realizes the vulnerability of her situation. The social conventions of the time dictate that there is no acceptable way for her to live outside the family unit unless she is married, but her family controls access to her, leaving her with little or no say in her future (even the right of veto, supposed to be respected by families at the time, being denied her). When Lovelace starts making overtures to her, having switched his attentions from her sister, then her plight worsens. She declares herself disgusted by Lovelace's immoral lifestyle and firmly rejects his advances; but her family, who have now taken against him, suspect, totally unfairly, that she is encouraging him secretly, and she finds herself caught between the two parties, with no-one to call on for help. When she escapes her family using Lovelace's assistance, her reputation is severely endangered. As in Crusoe's case, the will of the father has been ignored; an even more serious breach in the case of a young woman than a young man.

Clarissa's descent into despair is only too understandable, and she becomes one of the most celebrated victims of patriarchy in eighteenth-century fiction: a martyr to female powerlessness in a society where religion cannot be relied upon to act as a check on male conduct. Lovelace's reflections in the immediate aftermath of his rape of Clarissa show how easily the desire for power can overcome considerations of morality in the male sex:

> *Abhorred be force!–be the thoughts of force! There's no triumph over the will in force!* This I know I have said. But would I not have avoided it if I could?–Have I not tried every other method? And have I any other recourse left me? ... I'll teach the dear charming creature to emulate me in contrivance!–I'll teach her to weave webs and plots against her conqueror![30]

Post-rape, Clarissa retreats into her own private world, where she will listen to none of the entreaties being made by her friends that she should either accept Lovelace's offer of marriage in penitence or stop allowing herself to waste away. Instead, she sets about systematically, and depressingly single-mindedly, preparing herself for death: 'believe me, gentlemen, the shorter you tell me my time is likely to be, the more comfort you will give me', as she informs the doctors attending her as her health steadily declines.[31] Shortly afterwards she visits an undertaker's shop to arrange for the making of her coffin, which is then duly delivered to her room: Clarissa telling the startled onlooker, Lovelace's friend Belford, that 'it is all to save *you* trouble'.[32] Behaviour of this nature would most likely lead to a far more interventionist style of medical care now, being interpreted as symptomatic of depression – at the very least, psychiatric counselling would be recommended. Any counselling in the period would have a religious dimension of course, but Clarissa is to become a symbol of religion's limitations: it cannot protect her from male power, and neither can it provide her with the strength of will to go on upholding a morality which is being broken with impunity by much of the male sex on a regular basis. Her decline is rapid and apparently unpreventable. Although she dies a devout believer, that belief has not been enough to sustain her through the trials visited upon her by the self-interested, self-centred, representatives of patriarchy; it does not enable her to be a survivor in the approved spiritual autobiographical manner, resigning herself to God's will as Pamela so dutifully does.

Religion does not come out of the narrative particularly well, hard though Richardson tries to transform Clarissa into a saint-like figure in her final days (otherwise, there is more than a hint of suicide about her death). Spiritual autobiography is a far harder task for a woman to construct than a man, and Clarissa simply opts out of the game. We can begin to wonder just how religious a society we are dealing with; as seen from Clarissa's perspective, it is a deeply hypocritical one instead, and her choice of death rather than life as what her society will conceive of as a ruined woman is a condemnation of everything that society stands for.

Frances Burney offers another take on the Clarissa narrative in her novel *Cecilia*, where we observe the heroine being reduced to a state of physical and mental breakdown by the machinations of a patriarchal society concerned to keep women in a state of subjection. In this instance the heroine survives, but it is a close-run thing, with her friends fearing for her sanity and even her life:

> About noon, Cecilia, from the wildest rambling and most perpetual agitation, sunk suddenly into a state of such utter insensibility, that she appeared unconscious even of her existence; and but that she breathed, she might already have passed for being dead.[33]

What brings her to this extremity is that her parents' will contains a clause which challenges the patriarchal order: the requirement that to inherit her estate she must obtain her future husband's agreement to include her family name in his. Failure to do so will mean the loss of the inheritance, and thus of the significant financial power that £3,000 per year represents at the time. Not surprisingly this creates problems, with her eventual suitor, Mortimer Delvile, finding his father resolutely opposed to complying with the condition, as he is obliged to report in a letter to Cecilia: 'My father, descended of a race which though decaying in wealth, is unsubdued in pride, considers himself as the guardian of the honour of his house, to which he holds the name of his ancestors inseparably annexed.'[34] All attempts by Cecilia and Mortimer to discover a way round the provision fail, and the heroine eventually collapses under the strain and comes close to death. The price of marriage to the man she loves proves to be the loss of her fortune, and Cecilia has to resign herself to following the will of patriarchy. The irony of her dilemma having been created in the first place because of demands being made by the heroine's own patriarchal line, using women as pawns yet again, is not lost on us.

Until marriage Cecilia, like Pamela and Clarissa before her, has to fend off the attentions of a succession of rakes, with her three guardians signally failing to offer her any substantial help or guidance (something of an unholy trinity in this regard). Indeed, in the case of one of them, Cecilia is to find herself being financially exploited to stave off creditors pursuing the profligate Harrel for settlement of his substantial debts. Fashionable society in general proves to be a source of constant emotional stress for Cecilia, reaching a climax in the sudden suicide of Harrel in Vauxhall Gardens, in front of a party of friends including Cecilia, in desperation at his impossible financial situation. Even in the immediate aftermath of this horrifying event she is to find herself being pestered by a would-be admirer, and erstwhile acquaintance of Harrel, Sir Robert Floyer. On being asked to perform a friend's duty and attend the body until an undertaker arrives, Floyer shows himself to be far more concerned at pressing his suit with a shocked and disgusted Cecilia: ' "Will you promise, then," he answered, "not to go away till I come back? for I have no great ambition to sacrifice the living for the dead." '[35]

Despite the fact that Cecilia's eventual situation is far preferable to Clarissa's, one does gain a sense of lingering depression at the end of the narrative, as Cecilia reflects on what she has been compelled to do in order to marry: give up her fortune and become completely dependent financially on her husband. The conclusion she draws is that this is the best she could have hoped for under the circumstances, but no attempt is made by the author to pretend that it is anything other than a defeat for women at the hands of the patriarchal system. It has to be borne with resignation, and although Cecilia manages to muster this, the unfairness built into the social order, and its depressive effect on women, unmistakably registers:

> [S]he knew that, at times, the whole family must murmur at her loss of fortune, and at times she murmured herself to be thus portionless, tho' an HEIRESS. Rationally, however, she surveyed the world at large, and finding that of the few who had any happiness, there were none without some misery, she checked the rising sigh of repining mortality, and, grateful with general felicity, bore partial evil with chearfullest resignation.[36]

Burney is no romantic; marriage tends to come across in her work, after her first novel *Evelina* anyway, as little better than the least of several evils facing women – a means of circumscribing male predatoriness as much as anything. Neither is there any suggestion that a turn to religion might help to alleviate such evils.

Yet another novel that trades on the *Clarissa* theme can be found in Mary Hays's *The Victim of Prejudice*, published a half-century later when a feminist movement was beginning to develop in England. Again, we have a heroine who is raped by a villainous rake and reduced to a condition of despair in a society where, as the author puts it in the most uncompromising terms in the 'Advertisement to the Reader',

> *Man* has hitherto been solicitous at once to indulge his own voluptuousness and to counteract its baneful tendencies: not less tragical than absurd have been the consequences!...Let *man* revert to the source of these evils; let him be chaste himself, nor seek to reconcile contradictions. – Can the streams run pure while the fountain is polluted?[37]

It is the patriarchal system that ruins the life of the protagonist, Mary Raymond, whose memoirs rail bitterly against 'the injustice and barbarity of society' and how it has forced her as one of its victims to derive 'courage from despair'.[38] Unlike Clarissa, this is a wronged woman who is determined to leave evidence behind of her mistreatment at the hands of the male sex, and her memoirs constitute a savage indictment of male behaviour and how it can break women's spirit. Hays is definitely an angrier author than Richardson, and is notably free in her use of the word 'despair'. As with Burney, she is also disinclined to see any specifically religious dimension to women's travails.

Mary's case is all the more poignant in that she has been raised an orphan after her mother, who has drifted into a life of prostitution since being seduced as a young girl, becomes an accomplice to murder and is hanged. In her final letter from prison to Mr. Raymond, a former friend whom she asks to become Mary's guardian, she recounts her sorry tale, making it plain how devastating an effect patriarchal power has on women:

> Man, however vicious, however cruel, reaches not the depravity of a shameless woman. *Despair* shuts not against him every avenue to repentance; *despair* drives him not from human sympathies; *despair* hurls him not from hope, from pity, from life's common charities, to plunge him into desperate, damned, guilt.[39]

Mary is to find herself similarly reduced to despair by male deceit, when she is abducted by the boorish Sir Peter Osborne, who has been pursuing her over a period of years, and then raped by him after having been kept prisoner for several days in his London home.

There is a horrible inevitability as to how events then unfold: her reputation tarnished by gossip that spreads around London, Mary struggles to find regular employment and eventually is arrested for debt, refusing her rapist's offer of help if she will agree to become his mistress. She is freed by the intercession of an ex-servant of her guardian, with whom she goes to live in the country, but they run into debt and he dies, leaving her friendless and unprotected. Meanwhile Sir Peter Osborne continues to pester her, and she is so repelled by him that, following Clarissa's lead over Lovelace, she refuses his offer of marriage. Soon enough she is arrested again for debt and brought to the brink of suicide: 'Despair nerves my hand; despair justifies the need.'[40] Rescued once more after several years in jail, she sinks into a state of depression, complaining that 'the tone of my mind was destroyed':[41] a situation not helped by the subsequent death of her benefactors. Like Christian and Bunyan, her life seems a constant round of trying to keep despair at bay.

Henry and Sarah Fielding: despair at human nature

Henry Fielding offers a very different worldview to the nonconformist tradition, and is more interested in the fate of society than of the individual. Hence the narrator's dismissive reference in *Tom Jones* to,

> the painful and voluminous historian, who to preserve the regularity of his series, thinks himself obliged to fill up as much paper with the detail of months and years in which nothing remarkable happened, as he employs upon those notable eras when the greatest scenes have been transacted on the human stage.[42]

Narratives like *Robinson Crusoe*, where the protagonist's inner life (such as his struggle with religious despair) takes precedence, immediately come to mind. Despair does put in an appearance in Fielding's work, most notably in the person of the Man of the Hill in *Tom Jones*, but is portrayed as an overreaction to the faults in human nature. Sarah Fielding's view of human nature is darker, particularly in *Volume the Last* of *David Simple*, ultimately lacking the guarded optimism that her brother can summon, so it is instructive to compare the two authors in this respect. Both are critical of the way that self-interest has come to dominate in human affairs, but whereas Henry sees this as a trait which can be policed and kept in check for the greater public good (assuming a wise ruling class, which has learned the virtue of prudence) Sarah is more exercised by its destructive potential.

The Man of the Hill is an embittered and misanthropic individual whose despair about the failings of human nature – 'everywhere the same, everywhere the object of detestation and scorn', as he insists[43] – has caused him to withdraw from society altogether. He recounts a litany of mean and spiteful, even criminal, acts committed by himself in his youth, and then eventually against him by his friends and acquaintances, who prove no better than he does in moral terms. Tom Jones chides him for 'taking the character of mankind from the worst and basest among them', and advocates a more generous view of humanity and its motives, arguing of wickedness and evil that 'much of this arrives by mere accident'.[44] Nevertheless, we are made aware of just how base human nature can be, and how easily this can induce despair in those who care to dwell on it – as the Man of the Hill plainly has, secluding himself away for just this purpose. Having been highly motivated by self-interest himself in his wild days, and then betrayed by friends and lovers eager to further their own cause at his expense, the Man of the Hill is well versed in the damage that self-interested individuals can inflict on each other. His eventual assessment of humanity is couched in terms of existential despair:

> Man alone, the king of this globe, the last and greatest work of the Supreme Being, below the sun; man alone hath basely dishonoured his own nature; and by dishonesty, cruelty, ingratitude, and treachery, hath called his Maker's goodness in question, by puzzling us to account how a benevolent being should form so foolish and so vile an animal. Yet this is the being from whose conversation you think, I suppose, that I have been unfortunately restrained, and without whose blessed society, life, in your opinion, must be tedious and insipid.[45]

The sentiments are worthy of Jonathan Swift, and recall Gulliver in his final stages, almost unable to bear the company, or even the sight, of other human beings, referring caustically to humanity as 'a Lump of Deformity, and Diseases both in Body and Mind'.[46]

Sarah Fielding's *David Simple* follows the adventures of its eponymous protagonist, a rather naive and gullible individual, through a world where self-interest rules and almost no-one can be considered reliable or trustworthy. Shocked by the grasping behaviour of his brother over their father's will, David sets himself the task of moving through London society to find a true friend, but wherever he goes he meets with deceit and moral corruption. When he pays suit to Nanny Johnson, a young woman he meets in his travels around the city, for example, she soon switches her affection to a richer suitor, archly proclaiming, 'I will have the Riches, that is positive', leaving David aghast, especially as his rival is old and ugly.[47] Other acquaintances he makes, such as the men-about-town Spatter and Varnish, abuse their friends behind their backs and come to sum up the hypocrisy that is rife in fashionable London life. The more behaviour of this kind he encounters then the more that David comes to despair of human nature in general.

Eventually he does manage to put together a circle of true friends: the brother and sister Valentine and Camilla (later to become David's wife), and Cynthia (who marries Valentine). All of them have suffered at the hands of their family, with close relatives prosecuting their own self-interest to the trio's individual disadvantage. They proceed to form a small community, supportive of each other but wary of the rest of humanity. As long as they remain this way then despair can be kept at bay, and the narrative ends on a relatively optimistic note:

> Every little Incident in Life was turned into some delicate Pleasure to the whole Company, by each of them endeavouring to make every thing contribute to the Happiness of the others...It was this Care, Tenderness, and Benevolence to each other, which made *David*, and his amiable company happy.[48]

Volume the Last, a continuation to *David Simple* added after nine years, takes the narrative into more sombre territory. Financial difficulties have come to trouble the group, David losing most of his estate in fighting a lawsuit unfairly brought against him, with the consequence that Valentine and Cynthia find it expedient to emigrate to Jamaica in a bid to restore their fortunes. Events begin to turn against David with depressing regularity, and he is repeatedly let down by his apparent friends and associates. Then Valentine dies in Jamaica, Cynthia loses her estate in a swindle, and Camilla dies also. David himself subsequently dies a broken man, bewailing the state of the world in a tone of genuine despair:

> When I revolve in my Thoughts all my past Life, the Errors of my Mind strike me strongly. The same natural Desire for Happiness actuated me with the rest of Mankind: But there was something peculiar

in my Frame; for the Seeds of Ambition or Avarice, if they were in me at all, were so small they were imperceptible. Friendship and Love were the only Images that struck my Imagination with Pleasure; there therefore I fixed my Pursuit, and in these I felt the Sharpness of every Disappointment[.][49]

As with Clarissa, it is clear that religion is failing to provide the support needed to keep the character going (even if in each case they are shining examples of the kind of moral virtue that religion seeks to promote); all it can do is make it easier for him to accept death. David's faith cannot sustain him in the face of the corruption he has found all around him in society, a point underlined by the author:

I chuse to think he is escaped from the Possibility of falling into any future Afflictions, and that neither the Malice of his pretended Friend, nor the Sufferings of his real ones, can ever again rend and torment his honest Heart.[50]

It is a depressing conclusion to reach on behalf of her character; a damning judgement of human nature in general that it can harry sensitive individuals into such a condition of 'victimhood', as Linda Bree has noted, that they lose the will to live.[51]

Laurence Sterne: melancholy as default

It is Sterne more than anyone who turns melancholy into a fashionable condition that can encompass a range of feelings running from sadness, often of a pleasurable kind, through to misery and despair – the 'strange contrarys' John Norris speaks of in his ode on the subject (as discussed by John Baker).[52] Melancholy is a powerful presence in Sterne's fiction, almost a default emotional position for the main characters in *Tristram Shandy*, who find themselves unable to exert much in the way of meaningful control over the progress of their lives. For all the author's clerical background, religion has a very low profile in the text, and it is striking how little individuals turn to it for either comfort or an explanation of why they in particular seem to have been picked out as targets for the arbitrariness of fate: on the occasions when they do, we have a sense of their beliefs being gently mocked by the author. Resignation, often rather wry in form, is the more general reaction to their plight and, although this is a Christian virtue, that side of it is rarely drawn attention to throughout the text.

Underlying the narrative, however, are some complex theological issues, such as the role of pain and suffering in God's plan for humanity, and why some are given an unequal share of this. Theologians are grappling with such topics at the time, and as an Anglican clergyman Sterne is aware of those debates and how unsettling they can be.[53] The recourse to melancholy as a method of dealing with such intractable problems is very suggestive of some doubts creeping into religious belief, a fear that perhaps there really is no external force to appeal to for help in such situations (belief in particular providentialism being on the decline in English life by this point). Sterne's characters are forced instead to go inside themselves to find any comfort for their unfortunate fate as the 'sport of what the world calls Fortune'.[54] When Crusoe does that, God answers; not so with Tristram. The despair and depression consequent on the experience of the harsh side of human existence seem less amenable to the narrative frameworks of conventional religious belief than they were for Bunyan earlier: melancholic resignation becomes the mode instead, and one senses that despair is often there just under the surface.

It is a metaphysical problem with which Tristram and his associates are wrestling: that there appears to be no discernible pattern to their life or its development.[55] This is spiritually disconcerting, and the exact antithesis of Christian's experience, structured as this was by a particular providentialism which was steadfastly watching out for his welfare. It is a world out of joint, and theology no longer seems to explain it – nor tell us how we should make our way through it such that eventually we can reach a state of security. Uncle Toby is an instructive example of our essential vulnerability, his life having been profoundly affected by the accident of being at a particular spot during a battle and sustaining an unfortunate injury there: 'a blow from a stone, broke off by a ball from the parapet of a horn-work at the siege of *Namur*, which struck full upon my uncle *Toby's* groin'.[56] There appears to be no way to guard against such events, life being, as Walter Shandy ruefully observes at another point in the narrative, one 'long chapter of chances' that the individual has to muddle through[57] – and the Shandy family seem to experience more than their fair share of misfortune.

Given 'chances' such as Toby's injury, the mangling of Tristram's nose at birth and then his near castration by a falling window frame as a young boy, it is not surprising that the characters so often retreat into melancholy, their only consolation being a sentimental recognition that we are all in the same boat – defenceless against the workings of fate.

We just have to accept that 'we live amongst riddles and mysteries', and that 'even the clearest and most exalted understandings amongst us find ourselves puzzled and at a loss in almost every cranny of nature's works'.[58] And the biggest riddle and mystery of all is death, which looms over the narrative. Yorick's memory evokes a black page, symbolising the sheer impenetrability of this phenomenon, in striking contrast to Bunyan's dramatic account of Christian's engagement with the River of Death in *The Pilgrim's Progress*. The tale of Le Fever's death then prompts some of the most melancholic reflections in the whole work. Add in the sudden death of Tristram's brother, Bobby, and the precariousness of human existence becomes very clear. 'Philosophy has a fine saying for every thing.–For *Death* it has an entire set', as Tristram is moved to observe, but it is a set which seems to offer little consolation to the grieving Shandy family.[59] Religion, meanwhile, barely intrudes on the scene.

Melancholy is arguably an even more pervasive presence in Sterne's *A Sentimental Journey*, with the author constantly mocking his own pretensions, as in informing the reader at an early point in his travels that '[i]t had ever . . . been one of the singular blessings of my life, to be almost every hour of it miserably in love with some one'.[60] He flatters himself that his various encounters with women will develop into something romantic, but almost invariably they leave him looking foolish instead, compelling him to admit that '[i]t is a miserable picture which I am going to give of the weakness of my heart'.[61] In characteristic fashion, one such episode, where he has felt himself to be rebuffed by a fellow traveller, soon gravitates towards pathos (albeit it with a dubious sexual overtone):

> upon turning her face towards me, the spirit which had animated the reply was fled – the muscles relaxed, and I beheld the same unprotected look of distress which first won me to her interest – melancholy! to see such sprightliness the prey of sorrow. – I pitied her from my soul; and though it may seem ridiculous enough to a torpid heart, – I could have taken her into my arms, and cherished her, though it was in the open street, without blushing.[62]

A sense of melancholy seems to lie just under the surface of most human encounters, waiting to catch us unawares, and all we can do is to empathise with each other's experience of it.

For all the book's humour, there is a definite air of sadness to its picture of human relations, where we are so often guilty of misinterpreting each others' feelings. It is only too characteristic as well that a monk with whom the author has a misunderstanding, then a reconciliation, during his time in Calais, turns out to be dead the next time he passes through the town, leaving the author in tears at his graveside. Any of us might be so afflicted, and we remain susceptible to the 'damp upon my spirits' the author suffers on receiving this unwelcome news.[63] Whether religion can always reconcile us to the causes of our melancholy is becoming more problematical; there seems to be far more evidence of arbitrariness in the progress of our lives than of providential patterning. Adopting a phrase from William Empson's poem *The Last Pain*, A. Alvarez postulates that Sterne has fashioned 'a style from a despair' in *A Sentimental Journey*, and that can make us wonder about the efficacy of religion in confronting the many reasons we have for 'overmuch sorrow', especially when it is a clergyman addressing us.[64]

William Godwin: despair without religious solace

William Godwin's *Caleb Williams* can certainly be approached as a spiritual autobiography, as Pamela Clemit has noted, but the context this time is overtly political.[65] Caleb's life is blighted by being made party to his master Falkland's secret that he is a murderer, who has allowed others to be executed for the crime he has committed in earlier life to avenge his highly developed sense of honour. Flight from Falkland to escape his depressive influence turns Caleb into a fugitive who is pursued by both Falkland's agents and those of the state (Falkland being a pillar of the establishment and able to call on such assistance at will), leaving the unfortunate Caleb in an almost permanent state of despair, never able to settle anywhere for any length of time or to achieve even the semblance of a normal life.

Godwin himself had a Calvinist background, and although he subsequently drifted away from the faith there is a distinctly Calvinist air to the narrative of *Caleb*, which resonates with a sense of fear and foreboding about one's fate (Calvinists always assuming the worst unless provided with incontrovertible proof to the contrary). The protagonist is damned to a life of desperation because of an action undertaken by someone else before his birth, and no action of his own can seem to remove the stain this leaves on his character. Eventually, he does manage to confront his accuser and force a public confession out of him, but it proves to be a conversion experience yielding no relief for the victorious hero. Caleb is left devastated by Falkland's death a few days after his admission of guilt, and has nothing to fall back on to alleviate his feelings of despair:

> I thought that, if Falkland were dead, I should return once again to all that makes life worth possessing. I thought that, if the guilt of Falkland were established, fortune and the world would smile upon my efforts. Both these events are accomplished; and it is only now that I am truly miserable.[66]

The book's original ending is considerably more bleak, with Caleb imprisoned and Falkland still successfully protesting his innocence of the charges Caleb has brought against him. This leaves Caleb on the verge of madness, a despairing, defeated creature without hope for his future:

> At present, I by no means find myself satisfied with the state of my intellects. I am subject to wanderings in which the imagination seems to refuse to obey the curb of judgment. I dare not attempt to think long and strenuously on any one subject.[67]

There is no sense of a world governed by a just divinity, and the individual seems to have no-one, or system of belief, to turn to for solace. Despair appears to be the individual's destiny – and it is not only Caleb who discovers this to be so. Falkland too, we are made aware, is racked with guilt at his action in murdering his adversary Tyrrel (an unpleasant enough individual, it should be said), and his life has been turned into one long episode of despair in consequence, culminating in his anguished public confession.

James Hogg: deconstructing a genre

If Defoe raises doubts as to the sincerity behind spiritual autobiography in the case of Moll, *The Private Memoirs and Confessions of a Justified Sinner* comes close to sounding its death knell as a genre capable of offering comfort to the afflicted. *The Pilgrim's Progress* gave us an example of spiritual autobiography being used to overcome despair, but in Hogg's hands we find the form being abused by the protagonist Robert Wringhim to justify inhuman acts. In this demolition of the Calvinist mindset, religion presents very much in the guise of a disease. Robert follows the antinomian line on predestination that argues the saved can do no wrong, that all their actions are justified in the eyes of God, no matter how they may appear to the rest of humanity, and this belief leads him to commit a series of savage murders against supposed enemies. He is prompted to do so by his doppelganger, Gil-Martin, his exact look-alike as Robert first perceives him, who turns out, however, to be invisible to most others, or of a different appearance each time around if ever he is reported in Robert's company. After being told by his father, the Rev. Wringhim, that he has been designated as one of the elect and need no longer worry about his spiritual fate – 'your redemption is sealed and sure'[68] – Robert, egged on by Gil-Martin, proceeds to see signs of his superiority wherever he looks, becoming progressively more daring in his actions.

The narrative turns into a bleakly cautionary tale of the dangers inherent in the theology behind Calvinist spiritual autobiography. The fact that the conversion experience is a self-validating exercise means it is entirely contingent on the psychology of the individual, and this can put the rest of humankind at risk if we are dealing with, say, a psychotic personality. The depth of your belief becomes a guarantee of the truth of the belief. Given his strict religious upbringing according to Calvinist principles, Robert can only interpret his experience through the scheme of predestination (the Rev. Wringhim being an uncompromising advocate), and with the assistance of Gil-Martin he finds constant justification for his actions. The possibility that the signs could be interpreted in other ways never enters Robert's mind, and he discounts any opposition he meets on this score – as from his half-brother, George, who becomes one of his many victims. Antinomianism closes off other interpretations, signifier and signified joining together totally unproblematically for the believer, who cannot conceive of slippage of meaning occurring; everything constitutes proof of election. What this signals for Robert is that it is his destiny to become an avenging angel for the Lord, ridding the world of sinners, a crusade he undertakes with no little zeal, even to the extent of murdering a minister – on the pretext that he does not accept the Calvinist line on salvation.

Before embarking on his self-appointed mission, however, Robert goes through the ritual experience of religious despair:

> About this time, and for a long period afterwards, amounting to several years, I lived in a hopeless and deplorable state of mind; for I said to myself, 'If my name is not written in the book of life from all eternity, it is in vain for me to presume that either vows or prayers of mine, or those of all mankind combined, can ever procure its insertion now.' I had come under many vows, most solemnly taken, every

one of which I had broken; and I saw with the intensity of juvenile grief, that there was no hope for me.[69]

This is a character who knows his spiritual autobiography, expertly fitting his experience into the genre's framework and adopting its approved narrative line. The despair is eventually banished by his father's declaration of his election, and then the attentions of his double, whose sophistry from their first encounter onwards encourages Robert to consider himself an exalted being beyond all standard conceptions of morality: 'And now that you have taken up the Lord's cause of being avenged on *his* enemies, wherefore spare those that are your own as well as his?'.[70] As long as Gil-Martin is in attendance then Robert is fearless in his conduct, although when he deserts him on occasion the despair and doubts about the reality of his conversion can re-emerge.

Despair returns with a vengeance in Robert's final days, when he contemplates his coming fate, having entered into a compact with his double to commit suicide. His belief system has ultimately failed him, and he is reduced to a state of terror in his last moments:

But, ah! who is yon I see approaching furiously–his stern face blackened with despair! My hour is at hand.–Almighty God, what is this that I am about to do! The hour of repentance is past, and now my fate is inevitable.–*Amen, for ever!*[71]

In a similar situation in *The Pilgrim's Progress*, Christian finds a key 'called *Promise*' in his pocket, that effects his escape from Doubting-Castle;[72] but no such aid is to be extended to Robert in his distress.

Conclusion: the secularization of despair

While it is natural to turn to religion as a way of dealing with despair in the early part of our period, as Bunyan so successfully does, it becomes progressively less effective a move for later generations, who are more disposed to see the hand of man rather than God behind their troubles. Despair becomes secularized and individuals are forced to find other ways than religion of coping with the heavy strain it puts on their system. This leaves them more exposed psychologically, and there is no doubt that religion had been something of a lifesaver to figures like Bunyan, as well as fictional creations like Crusoe and Pamela, who could contextualise themselves within a socially sanctioned narrative. Even a theology as harsh as predestinarian Calvinism could be therapeutic in effect – if the individual could work his or her way through its severe trials. At least with religious melancholy you knew what you were up against.

Ontological despair minus the religious framework could be a much more debilitating condition, however, since there was no apparent explanation for it; it could only be taken as arbitrary, an unfortunate twist of fate. Not everyone was temperamentally capable of being stoic about this either, which could only exacerbate the effects of the 'black dog', in Samuel Johnson's arresting phrase.[73] Alternatively, the condition could have been brought about by the actions of an unjust society which no longer feared divine retribution, with all the depressing implications this had for vulnerable individuals – women most particularly. Mary Raymond's memoirs raise just that issue when she proclaims, 'If, as I have been taught to believe, a Being existeth, who searcheth the heart, and judgeth not as man judgeth, to Him I make my last appeal'.[74] The emphasis seems very much on the 'if', and the plight she finds herself in suggests that her appeal might well be pointless, that despair has lost its spiritual significance.

Belief itself does not disappear over the period, but belief in particular providentialism clearly goes into decline, and with it the provision of a readily available scheme by which to make sense of despair. The medical world does eventually step into the breach, but it will take a great deal of trial and error before it can replace the support system offered by religion, and most notably by the Bible. A Bunyan or Defoe character can always assume the possibility of a dialogue with God through the Bible; and where this fails to materialize, as with Roxana, know how to interpret its absence – painful though this can be to the character in terms of what it says about her likely fate. Spiritual matters still loom large on the psychological horizon, and whatever happens in individuals' lives is covered by their theology – with the Bible as the approved method for decoding its meaning. Whether cause or cure, religion endows despair with an important role in human affairs that helps to map out the nature of the relationship between the individual and God.

As we edge closer to modern times, however, that link between theology and psychology begins to weaken, as does the belief in there being a pattern to individual existence. This partly explains the turn to a Shandean style of melancholy, with its sense of resignation, wry or otherwise, in the face of life's many ills. Spiritual autobiography gave the individual a sense of being at the centre of a cosmic drama between good and evil, holding out the prospect of ultimately winning through to the security of salvation. Melancholy, as we note in Sterne, tends towards the bathetic instead, with individuals beginning to suspect, however reluctantly, their insignificance in the overall scheme of things and the unlikelihood of anything like a conversion experience coming to their rescue. Concern over soteriological status gradually gives way to concern over social, political and gender status, and these are far more diffuse, as well as less easy to narrativize. Religion may have offered a false resolution to the experience of despair (although modern-day evangelicalism, where the personal relationship with God is still felt to obtain, would beg to differ), especially since its effect was to conflate the ontological and circumstantial sources of the condition; but it gave a meaning to it for which we are still largely searching to find a substitute in our own world. The eighteenth-century novel constitutes an invaluable resource for tracing the shift that was taking place in English society from a theology-led to a medicine-led conception of depression (as Allan Ingram will be discussing in detail in Chapter 6), and the advantages and disadvantages this involved at the level of the individual stand vividly revealed in the journey from Bunyan through to Hogg.

5
Melancholy, Medicine, Mad Moon and Marriage: Autobiographical Expressions of Depression

Leigh Wetherall-Dickson

The issue of identity or 'who am I?' has been endlessly posed, as Roy Porter has already observed, by philosophers, poets, psychiatrists and people at large, and 'if the question has stayed the same, the answers have changed over time'.[1] And if the answer to that question has changed over time so has the answer to 'what is wrong with me?' when asked in relation to a dejected state of mind. The rise of auto-biography is one of the ways in which attempts have been made to answer these questions. It has been suggested that there is a close corre-lation between the development of self-portraiture and autobiography, which has been attributed, in part, to the development of good mir-rors in Europe.[2] Paul Delaney observes that Albrecht Dürer is the best example of an early Renaissance artist using the mirror as tool for self-analysis and introspection; his first recorded work, at the age of 13 in 1484, is a drawing of himself with the inscription 'made out of a mirror'.[3] Dürer's self-portraits change radically through a variety of costumes, settings and expressions, from a handsome young man that holds a good-luck charm in 1493 to the nude and broken *Man of Sor-rows* in 1522, which suggests either a trying-on of various guises or a search for a sense of self that proves to be elusive. As well as painting multiple versions of himself by way of exploring the notion of iden-tity, Dürer also engraved, as John Baker has already noted, the iconic pictorial representation of the nature of melancholia. The enigmatic figure is surrounded by redundant tools and symbols of systems of knowledge, all of which hint at some integral meaning and yet the meaning remains as elusive as the inner self that he tried to capture in his self-portraits. Although not under discussion here the figure of Dürer brings together the two themes of this chapter: the exploration of the meaning of 'self' and the interpretation of the meaning of melancholia in relation to that search for the self as represented in written self-portraits.

In literature, Montaigne describes the elusiveness of that inner-self which he wished to present to the world:

> Others form man, I only declare what he is; and I represent a particular one...Now, tho' the features of my picture alter and vary, there is still a likeness...I do not paint its being, I paint its passage, not a passage...from seven years to another seven; but from day to day, minute to minute.[4]

The pursuit of the elusive inner-self as a preoccupation is still in evidence today; Bethan Benwell and Elizabeth Stokoe begin their discussion on how identity is formed by discursive structures with a transcript from the television programme, *What Not to Wear*:

> JANE [member of the public]: I think I have given up somewhere along the line.
> TRINNY [expert]: The *real* you is so different from the image you are portraying and if it's inside you we've got to get it and haul it out, Jane, and, you know, put it on the outside.[5]

As Benwell and Stokoe highlight, this programme raises a number of issues about the question of identity, such as its nature and how it can be manipulated, but there is one thing that Trinny, her fellow expert, Susannah, and Jane all appear to be in agreement about and that there is some real 'inner self' that Jane has not been able to locate and has, for years, been presenting instead a drab, inauthentic version of herself. The idea that even though people may present themselves differently in different contexts there lurks underneath an essential, prediscursive and stable identity is a popular one throughout history. Autobiography, observes Felicity Nussbaum, is a means by which this inner-self can be located and represented, though arguing that the sense of 'self' that is predominant in eighteenth-century autobiography is one that is an ideological construct 'that is recruited into place within specific historical formations rather than always present as an eternal truth'.[6] Nussbaum also suggests that the autobiographies of eighteenth-century England are of particular interest because it is a period when established forms of narrative models, such as spiritual autobiographies, were 'stretch[ed] to "represent" new kinds of consciousness and experience', and were also a place to 'resist dominant cultural constructions of [the self] and substitute alternatives'.[7]

As a genre evolving in the eighteenth century, autobiography, which also includes diaries and journals, is a space where prevailing notions of identity are experimented with, revised and resisted, and a sense of self coalesces via a revisiting and reinterpreting experience through the act of writing. However, if the notion of identity as a unified, internal phenomenon can be revisited and reinterpreted, then there is the possibility, as Katharine Hodgkin has observed in her work on autobiography and madness in the seventeenth century, of the need to negotiate a threatened collapse or disintegration of what was thought to be the coherent self.[8] Elspeth Graham notes the continuing dominance of the theme of the fragile self into the present day:

> Our current preoccupation with autobiography, the prime genre of selfhood, very often seems to be, in fact, a pre-occupation with threats to selfhood, with issues of collapse and absence of self, with the very fragility or the impossibility of a concept and sense of the self.[9]

If one aspect of autobiography is about definitions of the self, another is about elucidating the dangers to, and disturbance of, that self. If, as Nussbaum proposes, we need to take into account the historical, social and cultural factors, such as religion, rank and gender that operate to construct a viewpoint of the self, then we also need to consider that it is these factors that affect how any form of disturbance is perceived.

Building on Richard Terry's discussion on the semantics of melancholy, this chapter will present four autobiographical accounts of depression that demonstrate four interpretations of a shared lexicon and set of symptoms. However, whereas Terry gives an overview of how meanings evolved over the long eighteenth century, I have chosen a much shorter timescale to review which may, at first, seem perversely restricting given the wealth of material available. The four accounts presented here were written within thirty years of each other in the first half of the period, and are chosen to demonstrate that a flexibility of meaning existed even within this narrow timeframe. Two of the accounts are written within the apparently rigid framework of the spiritual autobiography and two are diaries, in which a religious framework exists but is not the *raison d'être* for their production. There are two male voices and two female voices represented here and, following Nussbaum's example, they are paired in order to try to strike a balance rather than inadvertently to privilege one gendered experience as somehow more legitimate than the other. For the same reason all of the four voices are relatively unknown and are therefore not in danger of being overshadowed by a larger presence, which may have the effect of diminishing what they are trying to tell us.

Depressed states, though now diagnosed with standardized criteria that appear to be universal, can be looked at as a relationship between an individual and society, as it uncovers how an individual relates to society, but also how society affects individuals and how they perceive themselves. In so far as the historical antecedents to depression are disorders of the self, different ideas about the self will generate different ways of understanding what being depressed actually meant to those who experienced it in this period when the very essence of the self was also under such close examination. Stanley Jackson has already commented on how a dejected state 'of one form or another seems to have been part of the world of Western man as far back as his literature allows one to look', and has observed how the terms to describe these states, like today's use of depression, are not only familiar but have also been used 'sometimes carefully and sometimes carelessly'.[10] Mental disorder was explained, interpreted and treated in a number of different ways in this period, and medicine, as will be discussed in the next chapter, provided one language for describing and explaining the experience, but it was not the only one. As Hodgkin has already demonstrated, alongside the formal medical ideas about what constituted the causes and appropriate cures for this threat to the self, there was a 'vernacular and popular understanding, sometimes borrowing from science, sometimes ignoring it'.[11] What the autobiographical representations of these altered states of mind reveal is the lay person's view of what they understood their experience of depression to mean outside the medical discourse, and also how the act of writing about it gives shape and meaning to an otherwise destabilising experience.

Middle-class mind, body and soul: memoirs of 'A Private Gentleman'

As Stuart Sim has already mentioned in Chapter 4, the genre of the spiritual autobiography was, in his words, one of the major channels for exploring and expressing concern about the state of one's soul. The narrative of conversion is, essentially, one of a journey from a psychological state of anxiety and despair to a state of peace and joy. The writers strive for reconciliation between the spiritual, inner self, or the soul that belongs to God, and the physical, outer self which exists in the material world. However, as Hodgkin notes, there are problems with reading spiritual autobiographies for their descriptions of mental disturbance:

> as every good Protestant knows what will be found in the self: sin. To look into the self is to look into a pit of ugliness, and if what is found is not pride, selfishness, vanity, greed, hypocrisy, then it means that the sinner is not looking hard enough.[12]

Religious despair and being a good Christian go hand in hand, so a boundary between religious affliction and the illness of melancholy is very difficult to establish, and yet if what we are looking for are signs of what would now be labelled as depression, as identified by specific diagnostic criteria, then the experiences described by the spiritual autobiographers would definitely fit the bill. They describe feelings of worthlessness, guilt, thoughts of suicide, diminished pleasure in previously enjoyable activities; symptoms which lie at the core of the diagnostic criteria of a Major Depressive Episode as outlined by the *Diagnostic and Statistical Manual of Mental Disorders; Fourth Edition*, more commonly referred to as the *DSM–IV*. However, for the spiritual autobiographers, the experience of what looks to us like a major depressive episode has a deeper significance than just as a cluster of symptoms that demarcate a period of mental ill-health, and the period of profound despair is often described as a necessary, and even positive, stage of transition from being a miserable sinner to a reclaimed soul admitted to God's grace.

As a genre it is the most prescriptive form of autobiography as its purpose was to chart the journey from earthly sin to heavenly rebirth as a child of God. D. Bruce Hindmarsh describes the well-established pattern of the conversion narrative as a series of linear steps towards salvation via worldliness, an awakening of conscience, self-exertion towards moral rectitude, doubt and despair which leads to sincere repentance and divine forgiveness, and 'as a climax...a psychological release from guilt'.[13] A difficulty with the genre, however, is that the accounts of religious despair are often written retrospectively and to read them, as in any autobiography, is to read an exercise in creativity, selection, suppression and arrangement.[14] This process of selection and arrangement is particularly pertinent for the genre of spiritual autobiography as it is one that is operating from within two conflicting religious discourses, as identified by both Hodgkin and Nussbaum, in that the genre requires introspection yet must avoid appearing to be self-absorbed, which is suspiciously close in proximity to pride and arrogance.[15] As a prescribed form of autobiography, the production of a textual identity is one that, according to Nussbaum, is 'consensually agreed upon'.[16] Nussbaum argues that the search for salvation is the search for an identity, but one that has been agreed upon as acceptable by the standards of the community to which the individual belongs. The 'I' conveys a sense of an individual, one who claims to be unlike all others, but this individuation is demarcated with stock-in-trade shorthand, such as 'chief of sinners', that gives an illusion that the individual is known to the congregation.[17] However, this apparently prescriptive genre does not completely annihilate the individual expression of experience, even though the writing itself is an exercise in attempting to fit a lived experience within the parameters of an existing framework in order to make the experience intelligible.

The anonymity of the author of *An Abstract of the Remarkable Passages in the Life of a Private Gentleman* (1715) draws attention away from the individuality of the author altogether, the emphasis being upon the events that led him, and that can lead others, to spiritual disaster. As Hodgkin notes, 'childhood – like marriage, like parenthood, happens to everyone in more or less the same way'.[18] The aim of the narrative is to dismantle the sinful self rather than to express it, and show how individuality and the true self are defined by one's own spiritual experiences. It is the focus upon the events of the inner life that is important. Similarly, the exact nature of the 'black scenes' of the author's life are not elaborated upon because 'to tell of some crimes is to teach them'.[19] The hints he gives, he believes, are enough for his readers to recognize the form of his sins, referring to a vice that is so common at school that 'the Conceit that it is harmless, as it's reputed by heedless youth, and the Secresie of Acting it, contribute to its Prevalency'.[20] It would be a fair assumption that the unnamed vice was masturbation, which may have been viewed as harmless by those practising it but was considered extremely damaging to their moral, physical and spiritual welfare by the anonymous author of *Onania; of the Heinous Sin of Self-Pollution, and All its Frightful Consequences, in both SEXES*, a remarkably popular book that was first published in 1710 and which had run to twenty editions by 1760. Masturbation had dire consequences for mind, body and soul; believed to be both a symptom and cause for melancholy because the act was undertaken in isolation, it depleted vital energy and fluids and went against the 'natural' carnal practices as ordained by God in the name of procreation, being carried out 'without the Assistance of

Others'.[21] It is the notion of 'self-pollution' that is important here: it is an act by and upon the physical body, but the lasting damage is upon the conscience, or the inner self. The author of *Onania* places on the title page a quotation from the book of Revelation which declares that heaven would never admit 'any Thing that defileth, or Worketh Abomination' (Rev. 22:27). Richard Baxter (1615–91), nonconformist cleric and author, identified masturbation as one of the primary causes of melancholy and similarly warned against this most solitary of all vices, as 'venerous Crimes leave deep wounds in the Conscience; [and] are often cast into long and lamentable Troubles, by letting Satan once into their Phantasies'.[22] This would prove to be the case with the 'private gentleman'.

The frequent repetition of it abated his aversion to it, but the real problem lay in the fact that his sins 'burst not forth, as in others, thro' Fear and Shame; yet they smother'd too much within'.[23] Rather than a natural course of sin, shame and confession, this young man 'attended not to the Purity of Heart, but *Pharisee* like, contented [his] Self in keeping the outside of the Cup clean',[24] thereby adding hypocrisy to the performance of the shameful secret act. 'The Plague', he bemoans, 'is not more contagious than Ill company', and he finds it impossible to maintain piety within such 'polluting' discourses, and every breach of integrity made it easier to commit the next sin, and thereby allowing his 'whimsies [to] multiply'.[25] It is not only the indulgence of these other unnamed vices by his outward self that threatens his inner purity but the self-complacency concerning the salvation of his soul that is engendered because of the lack of immediate divine retribution.

There is no great moment of awakening from his sense of spiritual security, rather a gradual awareness of his going through the motions of everyday life due to an enervating absence of God's spirit, which had withdrawn itself because of what he later perceives to be his ingratitude for previous signs of God's grace. Prayers become formal and meaningless, reading ceases to be a source of comfort, enjoyment and inspiration, and 'Study and Recreations had lost all their power'.[26] The more he felt God calling to him in his distress the more he 'striv[ed] to find new Bypaths to run from him'.[27] He seeks counsel from ministers but does not feel that the wounds of his sins were probed deeply enough. He tries to distract himself by attending the theatre, which leaves him feeling even more degenerate. Every place was, for him, 'full of Dread and Horror; [and he] longed for Rest, but dreaded Bed'.[28] He hated company but hated even more to be left alone with his own thoughts, and this cycle of despair eventually drives him to contemplate suicide. At last it 'pleased God to bless the use of Opiates'[29] in order to give himself respite from his shaking terrors and dreadful foreboding. This relief proves to be short-lived, however, and the final breakdown occurs when, once more, he resolves to draw up some new rules for living, but feels his 'Mind gradually withdrawing; till at length I found I could no longer under-prop my Soul with the Hopes and Resolutions I lately rely'd on'.[30] The terrifying climax of his condition is described in terms of a demonic possession:

> Towards the Decline of the Day, I was more Restless, till at length I fell into surprizing Transports, wild Postures, extravagant Expression; all concurring to express the Convulsions of my very Soul...I plainly discerned, I was acted by another Spirit more than my own: Such strange Emotions in Soul and Body ensued, as perfectly convinced me they were preternatural[.][31]

He speaks of a physical and psychological battle with the devil, who appears in his most common manifestation as a tempter in order to exploit the innate inner depravity of human beings; as he says in his introduction, the private gentleman was born bad, a 'Traytor...a Viper in [God's] Bosom'.[32] It is a struggle for control of the private gentleman's body and, more importantly, his mind; the devil wages psychological war by compelling him to commit the worst sin of all, that of despair in his belief that God had abandoned him. However, it eventually 'pleased God...to scatter this dreadful Tempest [and] The glorious Son...arising with healing in his Wings [began] to dawn my relief'.[33] The storm passes as he begins to recover his faith, primarily as a result of what he calls gentle conversation with a poor and illiterate man who was apparently blessed by God in his sincerity.

The author makes a careful distinction between what he has suffered, which was nothing less than a battle to reclaim his soul from damnation through wilful neglect and 'meer [sic] Melancholy', a condition that originates in either the mind or the body but which 'immediately affect one the other mutually'.[34] A doctor is called in to attend to him as his 'Bed of Terrors' was initially attributed to 'the power of the Spleen', the biological source of symptoms of melancholia as the producer of black bile, and he was 'treated accordingly', though he does not elaborate on what this consisted of, but to no avail.[35] It is rare, states the 'private gentleman', that melancholy continues as 'a meer natural Disease', and only does in 'some very peculiar Cases, where God may, for some wise Reasons, restrain Satan'.[36] If the sufferer of melancholy has sinned against his soul or his inner self, which belongs to God, then God spots an opportunity to test and improve the sinner by allowing Satan to assault him with temptations. Therefore, in the author's opinion, melancholy is either physical in origin and is a natural temper or it begins in the mind and is caused by a series of afflictions, but whatever the origin the condition will lead to being 'tormented with black, desponding Thoughts, till they turn their own Executioner'.[37] If the source of melancholy is physical or mental it can be treated; if a sufferer of mere melancholy seeks help from a minster he will be directed towards a doctor. However, the doctor can only help if the melancholy is not compounded by a guilty conscience, in which case he is obliged to call back upon the minister. It is a necessary form of suffering, sanctioned by God, in order to set the sinner back on the path of moral rectitude. The author also observes that it is common to adopt 'the *Hyppo* [as] a fashionable Term of Art, and Preten[d] to it',[38] and he declares that this posturing is a smokescreen of guilt that is hiding the horrors of a corrupt conscience. If not suffering from the terrors of true melancholy then, warns the author, be thankful. He also warns against mistaking the 'Terrors for Conversion': it may seem like the 'Pangs of a New Birth' but more often than not it 'goes off without Delivery'.[39] He states it is only when Jesus appears directly to the soul can it be considered a conversion, otherwise the 'legal Terrors' are a legitimate and divinely ordained reminder about the need to maintain a strict watch over one's own spiritual welfare.

Having knowingly committed sins against his soul, or his inner self, the author's uneasiness compelled him to keep everything to himself; by giving no vent to his distress he exacerbated the problems against which he was struggling, whereas disclosing them would have weakened them. Subscribing to an early version of the talking cure, he urges his readers not to allow the 'Nature of these Sores to fester and Throb' but to 'confess your faults one to another' by way of diminishing their magnitude.[40] The work itself is offered up as a public admission by way of seeking absolution for his sins, as he pleads with God to 'please accept my Confession for Christ's sake'.[41] The act of confession implies that there are secrets that need to be brought out into the open, secrets which, in this case, appear to be the foundation for the gentleman's emotional distress. The act of writing and the public presentation of an unflattering portrait of himself, even though the work was published anonymously and the sins he committed are not actually named, lays the foundation for his own cure by bringing out into the open his sins so that he can wipe the slate clean; as Oscar Wilde was later to quip, it is the confession, not the priest, which gives us absolution. Bernard Mandeville, in his *Fable of the Bees: or Private Vices Publick Benefits* wrote that 'Man need not conquer his Passions, it is sufficient that he conceals them',[42] but for the 'private gentleman' the concealing of his natural inclinations added to the problem of indulging in them in the first place, and the laying bare of his vices was not only a way of 'knowing himself' and regulating his own behaviour but also a way of disciplining and regulating the behaviour of others by reminding them of their duty to themselves, their class and to God:

> [This work] now lies within the Reach of the middle Sort of People, who are for cheap Purchases but who are above Alms...As the Author could have no Design in Displaying these black scenes of his Life (so much to the Prejudice of his Character) but that glorious one of doing Good...May bad Men be startled, and reclaim'd: the Almost-Christian perfected: Doubting Souls establish'd: the Despondent comforted[.][43]

The 'private gentleman' experiences and displays his own weakness not only as a Christian subject but also as a class-bound one, of the 'middle sort'; his description of himself as a 'private gentleman' does not completely obliterate the individuation of his account, but flags up his status and means, as does riding his own horse and taking holidays by way of a cure for his despair.

His written reconstruction of his despair is for the purpose of maintaining a pattern of appropriate behaviour that aligned his inner and outer selves to that broad band of the population that was above the lower class and beneath the aristocracy, a class-conscious self-awareness that Nussbaum notes was rapidly developing during the eighteenth century.[44] Michel Foucault describes the confessional model as a 'technology of the self', and views it as a way of regulating the interiority of the self into a prescribed pattern of behaviour.[45] Therefore the spiritual crisis of the 'private gentleman' can be read as how the author's sense of his authentic self had been shored up by what Ulrich Beck terms a 'constructed certitude'[46] or ideological model of behaviour as prescribed and proscribed by the twin institutions of religion and class. The crisis the 'gentleman' underwent was as a result of his deviation from an outward model of behaviour which was at odds with the proclivities of his inner self, the model to which he aspired having appeared to have cast out the ambiguities and ignored the complexities of what it meant to be human, nasty habits and all.

Religious despair and medical desire: Anne Dutton

To be 'out of oneself' or 'beside oneself' not only threatens one's individual salvation but also has consequences for the demarcation of appropriate social behaviour, and if class is an important consideration when reading accounts of religious despair, then the same can be said of gender. Within the spiritual autobiographies written by women there is a resistance to the hegemonic characterization of the female as passive non-participants; while adopting the patterns and language authorized by male dissenters, women carve out occasions for oppositions to gender restrictions and the gendered hierarchy within the dissenting sects. Anne Dutton presents her experiences of religious despair in such a way as to elevate her status within the Church. Dutton's *A Brief Account of the Gracious Dealings of God, with a Poor, Sinful, Unworthy Creature* (1750) was published under the initials 'A.D'. *A Brief Account of the Gracious Dealings of God* was originally published in 1743 but was expanded in 1750 into a three-part work. The first two parts cover her early years and conversion, and her opportunities for worship and spiritual training. The third part consists of her experiences of the Lord's help with publishing her work, an appendix that describes her efforts to get her work published in America and a letter that defends the 'Lawfulness of a Woman's Appearing in Print'. So even though the initials of 'A.D.' are gender neutral, Dutton makes no bones about flagging up that the writer is a woman. As Hindmarsh points out Dutton was ambitious to have a clearly defined role within the Church, 'not withstanding her efforts to chasten this ambition and spiritualise it'.[47] She was caught between wanting to yield to God and the teachings of the Holy Scripture, which taught the subjugation of women to supporting roles within the Church, and the desire to fulfil a useful role by taking the mission of the Church to the masses. However, the same dynamic of evangelical conversion that impelled men to preach impelled Dutton to write and publish, and within *A Brief Account of the Gracious Dealings of God* she provides comprehensive lists of her previously published religious tracts.

Nussbaum's observation that dissenting women 'rarely reflect on their decision to write [and that] few wrote with the expectations of publication during their lifetime'[48] clearly does not apply in this case. Dutton negotiates the boundaries between public and private by insisting in her letter, addressed to 'Such of the Servants of Christ who May Have any Scruple about the Lawfulness of Printing any Thing written by a Woman', that 'Book-Teaching is *private*...and permitted to *private*

Christians', and asking her readers to imagine that when her books arrive in their houses 'that I am come to give you a *Visit*; (for indeed by *them* I do)'.[49] Dutton's account of God's brief dealings with her follows the prescribed pattern of spiritual autobiography, which charts her transition into high Calvinism within the Baptist Church order and the highs and lows of her search for signs of her status as one of the elect. However, her account of her periods of doubt and despair are described in a specifically gendered manner that sanctifies her ambition to take an active role within the Church.

Throughout Dutton's narrative Jesus is her 'sweet Lord', 'beloved', 'royal bridegroom', by whom she was 'wonderfully favoured with intimate Communion [and] the sweetness of private fellowship'.[50] In comparison, on the rare occasion her two husbands, both of whom predeceased her, are mentioned they are simply referred to as her 'Yoke-fellow[s]'.[51] Their deaths cause Dutton some distress but nothing like 'the hungering and thirsting for the Enjoyment of him' that the absence of Jesus causes. If, as Hindmarsh notes, this language of intimacy is not unusual within female-authored spiritual autobiography,[52] then what is striking is how the depths of her despair because of the perceived absence of Jesus in her life are registered in language that is medical as well as religious in application. The periods of Dutton's deepest sorrow are when she describes herself as being '*sick of Love*':

> As saith the *Spouse*, when she sought her absent Lord, charging *the Daughters of Jerusalem*, that is they saw him, they should tell him, *she was sick of Love* Song [of Solomon 5:] v.8.[53]

Although Dutton's illustration of the phrase love-sick by way of explaining her malady as a spiritual one that has a biblical origin, 'lovesickness' was also recognized as a distinct category of mental illness.

Robert Burton's *The Anatomy of Melancholy*, first published in 1621, traces the history, symptoms and cures of 'Love Melancholy' from classical literature up to his own time. Although there is no modern equivalent to lovesickness as a distinct category of depression, Frank Tallis observes that 'many of the symptoms of lovesickness can be found distributed through the ICD (*International Classification of Diseases and Related Health Problems*) and the DSM ... classification systems [indicate that] being in love produces a symptom profile that would ordinarily suggest significant psychiatric disturbance'.[54] Tallis is in agreement with Burton's observation that 'the state of mind induced by love is one which is in itself insane'.[55] Lesel Dawson similarly observes a correlation between the symptoms of classical lovesickness and those of depression, such as insomnia, loss of appetite, exhaustion, mental fixations and speechlessness, rendering the sufferer 'pale and emaciated; [with] hollow, sunken eyes, and...subject to intense, fluctuating emotions'.[56] Interestingly, these are also the same physical symptoms described in *Onania*, and suffering from unrequited love, as initially in Dutton's case because the object of her desire was spiritual rather than physical, and masturbation are solitary pursuits which were deemed to affect both physical and psychological well-being. Lovesickness had various forms according to Burton – lust, jealousy, obsession – but by far the most common was that of unfulfilled desire, all of which, if left to fester, could result in melancholy, mania or even death. Dawson also notes that lovesickness is often characterized as having two alternating states; the lover is filled with and overwhelmed by a hot and fiery passion for the object of their desires, followed by a stage of melancholy in which the unfulfilled lover feels fear and sorrow.[57] Dutton's spiritual development is an emotional rollercoaster of ecstasy when she discerns Christ's favour, and an 'oppression of the soul'[58] when he is absent and hides his intentions from her. Even though the object of Dutton's desire is an inner, spiritual one, she describes the need for her desires to be met in distinctly physical terms.

On first seeing a vision of Christ, she recounts that she saw 'such ravishing Beauty, and transcendent Excellency [that] nothing but himself could satisfy me'.[59] Dutton's recounting of her first encounter with Jesus' love that extended even to her, the worst of all sinners, is written in the language of that desire gratified, having experienced a 'Soul-ravishing, Heart-attracting Revelation of Christ' that lifted her from the 'Depths of Misery to the Heights of Glory'.[60] Her desperation for him in his absence results in Dutton's soul being 'pained with Love – Desires, for want of a wished enjoyment [her] Soul was ready to faint [and] she groaned out [her] desires thus: "Oh that the Lord would give...but Himself" '.[61] The least degree of Jesus' absence from her causes her to cry out, 'Love me, my Lord, or else I die', and she describes her 'Soul [as] solitary and [she] mourn'd in secret; like the Dove that has lost her mate, because [her] beloved had withdrawn himself'.[62] Dawson equates the sufferer of lovesickness with Tantalus, as the lover is 'teased by an ever-present yet elusive image of the beloved',[63] which results in an excessive contemplation of the desired object. Yet when the desired object is a union with a spiritual rather than physical object, as with Dutton, then within the context of a spiritual autobiography it is a case of there never being enough contemplation rather than too much.

Located within this context, Dutton's descriptions of her emotional highs and lows and accounts of her worthlessness are entirely appropriate and are underpinned by what Hodgkin describes as a 'widespread assumption that true spiritual faith should be emotionally and powerfully expressed'.[64] In Dutton's case the power of her language also underlines her femininity.

In the eighteenth century lovesickness had shifted from being a masculine state of elevated emotion and intellectually inspired genius towards a lower form of illness that was specifically located in the female body and the female nature, and exemplifies a shift from the male metaphysical to the female 'bodily need for sex'.[65] Indeed, as Dawson notes, one of the recommended cures for lovesickness was sexual intercourse, preferably with the object of desire but not necessarily, as much to dispel the lover's fixation as to supply a physical release.[66] This physical gratification of desire as a cure was obviously not available to Dutton, but in the way she presents her case she does appear to be intimating a connection between her sexual maturity and her spiritual desires, and how she channels those physical longings into something altogether more elevating.

Dutton's lovesickness appears to have begun with the onset of puberty and began as a bodily desire that needed satisfying. Dutton claims an early conversion at the age of thirteen, prior to which the adult Dutton describes her very young self as a vain and arrogant little girl who felt her salvation was secure because she professed to prefer praying to playing. Before her spiritual awakening, Dutton remembers this prepubescent stage as one of peace, albeit also recognizing it, in retrospect, as a 'false Peace from my supposed *Goodness*'.[67] It is with the onset of menstruation and therefore puberty and awakening sexual maturity that both her troubles and signs of salvation begin:

> I was *cast out in the open Field, to the Lothing* [sic] *of my Person.* But the God of all Grace *pass'd by me, and saw me polluted in mine own Blood*; cover'd all over with Nature's Defilement: And lo! He said unto me, when I was in my Blood, *live*…For *my Time was the Time of Love*…&c. of Love's Manifestation[.][68]

Dutton flags up her debased female nature as both polluted and ripe for cleansing and it is the relationship between Christ, love and the feminine subject that defines Dutton's bouts of doubt and despair.

Like the 'private gentleman', she uses shorthand to depict her sinful and sorrowful self; echoing Bunyan she casts herself as the 'very *Chief* of sinners' and as full of 'Filth and Abomination'.[69] On recovering from an illness that nearly killed her Dutton asks of God, 'Oh *Why me! Why me*, when *Thousands* perish!'[70] The emphasis upon the singular 'me' and the vast number who perish everyday highlights Dutton as special. The answer to her question soon becomes clear as it coincides with her recovery from lovesickness; as much as Christ stimulates a desire that needs to be gratified in Dutton, the feeling is apparently mutual. According to Dutton Jesus refers to her as 'thou fairest among women', and he tells her that:

> *Thou hast ravished my* Heart, my *Sister, my Spouse; thou hast ravished my* Heart *with one of thine Eyes, with one Chain of thy Neck*, Song [of Solomon, 4:] v.9.[71]

From here on in Dutton makes no reference to being 'sick with love' and refers to the Bible not by way of explaining the malady under which she has been labouring but to sanction her ambition within the Church. She is Jesus' chosen consort, her desire for him has been gratified and she describes feasts that he prepares for her himself, the splendid robes she wears as only befitting the chosen bride of Christ, and his attendance upon her:

> I thought he might have said, I'll *send* for thee, but he said I'll *come*. I saw that this was the Language of my *kind Bridegroom*: And like as if a tender husband having his dear Bride at a distance should not be content with sending his *Servants* for her, but will come *himself* to fetch her Home.[72]

Such is her position within God's grace, she even states that she planned to use her 'Interest at the Throne, and pray'd to Christ to use *his*' to prevent a move she was unwilling to undertake,[73] apparently to no avail; yet in retrospect the larger plan for her becomes clear. When her second 'Yoke-fellow', Benjamin Dutton, is called to minister at the Baptist church of Great Gransden Dutton is similarly compelled. She lays out the argument she has with God which states that she could not possibly take up such a responsibility, protesting not only personal weakness but also that of all her sex, yet God insists and 'encourag'd [her] from *his* infinite *All-sufficiency* ... Tho' [she] hast no Ability [my] God would not suffer me to be ashamed, [she] attempted the Work'.[74] Her suffering has proved her worth and Dutton brings forth a host of biblical sources in answer to those criticisms she has already pre-empted of her ability to undertake even the '*meanest* Service that could be done for [the] Lord'.[75]

From the vilest of all God's creatures to Jesus' chosen bride, Dutton's period of depression negotiates a conversion not away from her family and religious community but into it more deeply and more actively. Through the written emphasis of her unworthiness and her depiction of despair which was born of a physical desire and a spiritual one, Dutton found a way to negotiate the conflicting demands in a creative way. Dutton's narrative is not a purge like that of the private gentleman, but a call for recognition that her suffering has elevated her into a position of divinely sanctioned authority. If, as Hodgkin writes, the spiritual autobiography 'has its origins in the often anguished and complex reinvention of the self that goes with spirituality',[76] then Dutton also rewrites a medical condition that perceives a natural inferiority in women that feeds into their limited role within the Church. Dutton rewrites a physical need into a spiritual calling, transforming the negative connotations of the illness, through its association with the feminine, into a positive sign of her elevated status within not only the Church but also in Christ's affections.

Matrimonial misery: Elizabeth Freke

Spiritual autobiographies are narratives of transformation that depict a shift from a self that has become fractured by suffering to one that emerges whole, cleansed and redeemed. Paul John Eakin remarks that the 'taking up of one's life in language...testifies to the author's particular involvement in the world, a landing rather than a hovering',[77] and this certainly applies to both the private gentleman and Anne Dutton. They both look back upon their earlier selves from their new position as a transformed subject and thank the Lord that their period of misery is now over. Their spiritual autobiographies construct a coherent story from what Carolyn A. Barros describes as the 'tattered remains of [their] experience[s]'.[78] As retrospective accounts of their depressed episodes there are clearly issues with memory and the representation of what Hodgkin calls 'the truth of a life',[79] especially one that has been written with a specific aim and audience in mind. As Allan Ingram has already commented, for the writers of spiritual autobiographies their suffering is 'firmly enclosed by the perspective of their redemption through God. Suffering is dealt with...but its presence is unproblematic in so far as its telling is able to make it mean in a context of temptation, transgression and salvation'.[80] Diaries and journals promise a more immediate relationship between the writer and the reality of their bouts of depression as the form resists the imposition of plot, the end of the story being not already known. However, even though there is not a beginning, middle or end, and they are not generally written for consumption by a wider audience, Nussbaum argues that diaries and journals can be considered as legitimate autobiography as the form represents an attempt to examine and shape character by the writer within existing social relations.[81]

Linda Anderson observes the rise in popularity of the diary form in the seventeenth and eighteenth centuries, which she attributes to the expansion of literacy and the receding authority of the State and the Church.[82] The two diaries under examination here were written within the first half of the eighteenth century; Elizabeth Freke began to write her diary in 1702 and continued it until shortly before her death in 1714, and Edmund Harrold's covers the years from 1712 to 1715. The secular nature of these documents co-exists alongside, rather than succeeds, the spiritual autobiography of the 'private gentleman' and both predate that of Dutton. Ostensibly a private document, within the pages of the diary the individual could broach the issues and problems of their everyday life, instead of being urged to transcend it. The central preoccupation of both diaries is the author and they present us with minute details about the respective domestic worlds of an early eighteenth-century gentry-woman and a tradesman that are missing from the spiritual accounts. The class and gender of both diarists are indicated and formed in relation to these details, as are their experiences of low spirits. Ramona Wray recognizes that it is the accumulation, repetition and reoccurrence of the minutiae of everyday life within these documents that gives the reader a 'potent impression of repeated disappointments, deep dissatisfactions and continuous blows to a fragile self-esteem'.[83] The diaries are repositories for what Wray describes as 'long-term and low-level emotional flux' rather than being 'self-confessed and often public embodiments'[84] of psychic disturbance.

Freke's depressed state is more visible than that of Harrold as she begins her diary retrospectively, and the motivation for her writing is made immediately apparent:

> Some few remembrances of my misfortuns have attended me in my unhappy life since I were marryed, which was November the i4, i67i.[85]

Freke begins the first version of her diary at least twenty-six years after the date of the first entries: there is a postscript of 1702 in an entry dated 1676 that states that her son who was crippled at birth 'now goes straight and well, [and is] the father of two lovely boys in Ireland, November i4, 1702'.[86] Roger Anselment notes that changes in handwriting indicate that the entries in the first, white-vellum bound manuscript of her diary were written fairly soon after the entry dates, however, and that she was writing up a second fair copy of the diary consecutively with the first.[87] It is the first version of the diary that we are concerned with here as it is the most immediate expression of her fluctuating emotional states, filled with emotional outbursts and deletions that belie the more composed and sanitized version of events in the second diary.[88] So even though Freke begins her diary with an apparent imposition of plot, as indicated in her opening statement, she did catch up with herself, although it is impossible to determine exactly at what point, and the diary-writing becomes contemporaneous with her unhappiness.

If the cause and the cure of Anne Dutton's episodes of lovesick melancholy were spiritual in nature, then Elizabeth Freke's unhappiness is the opposite: a distinctly terrestrial and unhappy marriage to her cousin, Percy Freke. After being engaged for seven years, it is not clear why the marriage was undertaken without her father's knowledge but a clue to the long engagement, the secret marriage and the subsequent years of debilitating unhappiness lies in an entry dated 15 September 1673, in which she writes that she was 'being governed by [her] affecttions in this [her] marrying and without the consentt of any of [her] frinds'.[89] As neither her family nor friends wanted Freke to rush into a marriage with Percy there were clearly misgivings about his abilities as a potential husband that Freke's affections overrode. That his daughter's happiness was of paramount importance to Ralph Freke is indicated by a second marriage ceremony that took place in his presence on 26 July 1672, eight months after the first ceremony. Ralph had a close bond with his four daughters, of whom Freke was the youngest, as he had raised them along with a maternal aunt after their mother's early death. The closeness between father and daughter contrasts markedly with that of wife and husband, and the kindnesses of Freke's father appear to be an attempt to offset what Anselment describes as the 'neglect and treachery of husband [and] son'.[90]

Percy Freke's irregular financial dealing with his wife's money is compounded by his neglect of her person. As he chips away at the basis of her financial security he also chops away at her emotional wellbeing:

September i5 Aboutt the midle of September Mr Frek endeavouring to place my fortune on an estate in Hampshire ... Thus was three of my unhappy years spentt in London in a marryed life, and I never had, as I remember, the command of five pounds of my fortune. Wher I miscaried twice and had very little of my husband's company, which was no small grife to me[.][91]

Having married for affection she keenly feels the lack of it from her husband, who apparently has no compunction at leaving his wife to fend for herself for months, and even years in one instance, at a time. Freke's father is a constant source of emotional and financial support until his death 13 years after her marriage. An entry dated 'Agust i5' records that during a visit to her father she was 'looking a little malloncoly on some past reflections'.[92] Assuming the reason for her sadness was a lack of money, Ralph Freke disappeared to 'his closet and brought [her] downe presently in two bags two hundred pounds [and] he charged [her] to keep privatt from [her] husbands knowledge'.[93] She does tell her husband and she wryly observes that he 'presently found a use for itt'.[94] Her father wished Freke to remain with him so that they might take care of each other until he died, a proposal to which she readily agreed. However, her husband had different ideas about whose side she should be at, even though he had effectively abandoned her on several occasions, and arrived at her father's house to take her back to Ireland. The 'greatt allterration' she found there that made her so unhappy was the contrast between the supportive love of her father and the mercenary interest of her husband, for which she was clearly ill prepared.

In the early years Percy Freke's irregular appearances in the life of Freke is usually associated with a hunt for money or assets to sell, and when he leaves it is usually in a flurry of angry words, the shock of which clearly never left Freke:

> i682/3, Febeary i8 ... Besides his last parting wish att Kingsaile (which was) <deleted: thatt he might never se my face more>; and this stuck deep in my stomack, tho to this day (i712 <originally: i702>) I never lett my father know the least difference between us or any unkind usage ... for fear of grieving him[.][95]

The diary becomes the confidante of misery that she cannot share, and also the site of her explosive anger and emotional outbursts that she could not, observes Effie Botonaki, discharge elsewhere.[96] Alongside the numerous examples of her husband's neglect and irresponsibility, Freke records a succession of unhappy moves to empty houses (seven in total between Ireland, Norfolk and London), clashes with her husband's family, her dependency upon the generosity and support of others, clashes with her tenants and neighbours at Norwich, and an increasingly strained relationship with her son, who apparently treats Freke with the same callous disregard as her husband. After a very difficult birth, during which it was proposed that the baby should be cut into pieces in order to save her life, after nursing him through numerous dangerous illnesses and supplying continued financial support in later life, which included purchasing him a baronetcy, Freke clearly felt that she was owed at least a sense of gratitude even if she was not given any respect. She frequently writes to her son about his need to 'open [his] eyes to see [his] errors, and Mollyfye [his] heart, [and consider his] unduttyfulness' towards 'A diseased Malloncoly Aged Mother (66 years of Age)'.[97]

The accumulative effect of all the conflicts, slights and disappointments that Freke records 'much Aded to [her] Greatt Misery & sickness'.[98] Freke draws a correlation between her recurring bouts of physical illness and her emotional low-points. Her first recorded bout of serious illness occurred during the four and half years she spent in Ireland. In an entry dated 12 November 1692 Freke records her arrival at Rathbary and her discovery that the house had burnt down and there was 'neither a bed, table, or chair, or stool fit for a Christion to sett on'.[99] So miserable was she that she states she 'was sick all the whole time that [she] hardly wentt downe stairs butt as [she] were carryed to the garden', the origin of her sickness was 'being frightted att my first coming to see whatt a place I were to come to'.[100] Frights, fear and emotional upset seem to precipitate periods of ill health; after an unpleasant clash with her son and daughter-in-law, whom she describes on more than one occasion as 'cruel', over her denied request to keep her favourite grandson with her, Freke falls into a 'violent sickness for above six weeks I thought would have binn my last'.[101] Anselment notes that Freke's periods of incapacity as a result of her 'tissick' often occurs immediately after family disputes such as this and suggests that there is an element of hypochondria in the modern sense of illusory symptoms and convenient illness.[102] However, Freke would have perceived a direct connection between her physical illness, her emotional distress and the ill-usage of her by her husband and son.

In 1708 Freke consulted a Doctor Jeffreys[103] whom she considered to be 'the most excellent doctter of this country'.[104] She went to the doctor because, from 1700 onwards, Freke records increasingly serious attacks of what she calls 'tissick', a vernacular form of 'phthisic' which, in turn, refers to tuberculosis, better known in the long eighteenth century as consumption. Doctor Jeffreys's prognosis was not good:

> As soon as he saw mee, he told me twas too late: grife had brought me into the condition I were in; and thatt I were wasted all in my inward parts, both my kidnys and back ulcerated from some fall I had lately had, which on the least stoppages of flew up to my unhapy head and caused my greatt shortness of breath, which would sudenly take me off. Therfore [he] advised me nott to be alone or expectt ever to be cured of my missery, which he said must bee very greatt by my watter.

Clark Lawlor observes that up until the end of the nineteenth century it was taken as a matter of fact that consumption could be 'brought on through disorder of the mind and emotions...that somatic problems were often likely to have a psychological origin and vice versa'.[105] Freke's condition would have been described as a 'growing consumption' rather than what Lawlor terms the ' "proper" and "true" ' form of the disease; growing consumptions were curable but only if treated in time, and were apparently infinite in variety:

> Growing consumptions fall under numerous headings: 'hypo-chondriack; scorbutic; amorous; of grief; studious; apostlematick; cancerous; ulcerous; dolorous; aguish; febril; cachetick; verminous; of rickets; pockie; poysonous; bewitch'd; of the back; of the kidneys; of the lungs' and so on.[106]

Freke complains bitterly about the 'many slights and Disrespects' that have 'broke [her] Hartt and brought [her] to the Condition [she is] in'.[107] The variety of causes of growing consumptions listed above is both mental and physical and they converge in 'one basic effect: the wasting of the body'.[108] The doctor's diagnosis is that Freke is going to die of misery because of the attendant physical symptoms that deep-rooted melancholy has caused as a result of the years of sorrow inflicted upon her, first by her husband and then by her son.

Anselment notes that Freke's representation of herself offers no apology or justification, she pays lip service to neither 'the cultural ideal of maternal strength...nor emphasises the traditional, secondary role of the loving wife'.[109] Freke does demonstrate obedience towards her husband; she apparently cannot refuse his summons to Ireland and to Bath when he lies there ill, despite being seriously ill herself. She has little choice but to allow him to live with her at West Bilney, in Norfolk, when he arrives on her doorstep, though she did resist his earlier attempts to force her to sell the place. Even when she prays for his safe passage to and from Ireland, it smacks of protocol rather than true sentiment. The diary becomes her place of refuge, resistance and relief; in it she was allowed to speak with criticism in a way that, as Botonaki observes, her 'heavily censored female mouth' could not.[110] Freke, like Dutton, is an example of what Nussbaum describes as eighteenth-century women who 'found leverage for resistance to their co-optation by becoming the autobiographical subject rather than the object of the textual representations of their lives'.[111]

In her examination of female-authored diaries Harriet Blodgett describes depression as 'the companion to female devaluation and powerlessness' and utilizes Martin E. P. Seligman's 'learned helplessness' theory to explain:

> [Seligman suggests] 'that what produces self-esteem and a sense of competence, and protects against depression, is not only the absolute quality of experience, but the perception that one's own actions controlled the experience.' In short, if one concludes that she is controlled by life, rather than controlling it, she is likely to become depressed.[112]

This certainly applies to Freke in that she is helpless in economic and financial terms, and her dependence upon others affects her self-esteem. Despite Freke's acknowledgment of a providential framework to which she, perhaps grudgingly, attributes the preservation of her husband and son after perilous crossings to Ireland, there is no suggestion that she must submit to it with reference to the treatment she receives from them. This is the diary of a strong-willed woman intent upon asserting herself against familial neglect and legal abuse, and struggling against culturally acceptable modes of feminine behaviour. Within it she emphasizes years of personal struggle and resistance, and it is no coincidence that towards the end of the diary and after she takes full and legal possession of West Bilney, and after her husband's death, we see Freke grow in stature, despite increasingly frail health. She maintains an iron-like grasp of her finances, making detailed lists of her expenditures and material wealth, and is not afraid to enter in legal wrangles to defend her property rights, and even her choice of minister. She writes to show that it is she that is now in control of the purse strings, and to make sure that her ungrateful son and his cruel wife are aware of the fact. Money becomes for her a measure of self-definition amidst sickness, isolation and insecurity.

'Mad moon' and masculine melancholy: Edmund Harrold

Edmund Harrold, a wig-maker from Manchester, also writes his diary because of his lack of control, but in this instance it is his lack of control over himself. Whereas it would be a reasonable assumption that Freke wrote her diary for posterity, hence the two versions and the swearing of the truth to each entry, Harrold's was more likely to have been written for his own personal consumption as it itemizes his actions and failings as a pious man and offers critical self-assessments and ways in which he could improve himself in the future. Craig Horner observes that this is a diary of a 'flawed and vulnerable human being, a man with a drink problem, struggling with the demons in his personal, spiritual and professional life'.[113] Harrold's diary is a meticulous record of his daily life: like that of Freke, it is thick with domestic detail. He records details about business transactions, customers and costs, church attendance and non-attendance, reading matter, marital status, sexual activity, and his drinking habits, which had an adverse effect on all of the above. Harrold simply could not help himself when it came to drink:

> 7 {July, 1712} This morn I had my old malancholy {*sic*} pain seized me wth a longing desire for drink. So I went and p[ai]d my rent, yn I s[ol]d J[ames] G[rantham] a lock of hair, pro loss 5^s 6^d. Yn I spent 2^d wth Hall etc. Yn 4^d with Mr Allen, [at]tourney, yn fought wth S:[amuel] B[oardman] at Janewins about a hat. Yn had a hurrey wth wife on bed etc. Yn went into ye [Hanging] Ditch [for] a rambl[e] [at the] Keys, [the] Dragon and Cas[t]le, and [the White] Lyon till near 12 cl[oc]k, till I was ill drunken. Cost me 4$^{1/2d}$ from 6 till 12. I made my self a great foole etc.[114]

The cost of Harrold's drinking is represented here in terms of economics and his pride. His failure to resist the urge to drink is the basis of his own form of depression as it signifies his failure to conduct himself in an appropriate manner as a businessman and a provider for his family.

The inevitable hangovers are accompanied with remorse about how his behaviour affects his family, his reputation and his peace of mind:

9 {July, 1712} This day I lay in bed till almost 11 cl[oc]k {…} Ive drank no ale to day, yet on 6 at night I'm vext about my ramble last night. I've mist pub:[lic] [and] private prayers 2 times. It's a very great trouble to me, yt I thus expose my self, hurt my body, offend against God, set bad example, torment my mind and break my rules, make my self a laughing stock to men, greive {*sic*} ye holy spirit, disorder my family, fret my wife now quick, wch is al[l] against my own mind when sober. Besides loss of my credit and reputation in ye world, what must I do? {…} I'm very much indisposed, yet very dull and melancholy, but work close al[l] day.[115]

So much of a reputation for drunkenness did Harrold have that a minister refused to perform a marriage ceremony for him and his third wife, Anne, saying that it was because Harrold was 'a madman in drink, and yt ye woman run her ruin in marriing [sic]' him.[116] Harrold also describes his drinking as a kind of madness; he noted on 22 June 1713 that 'Charles went mad' with drink, a permanent state he had thus far escaped but constantly bordered upon, observing that he 'wickedly ended June and begune July 1st madly…tis mad moon'.[117] It is the loss of himself during these episodes of madness that is central to his unhappiness for, as Hannah Barker notes, it is the 'struggle for self-control [that was] central to [Harrold's] sense of identity, not just in terms of maintaining honour and reputation…but also as concerned with [his] inner consciousness'.[118] He strives for sobriety as a way of restoring a sense of inner peace as 'it makes every thing pleasant and easy [and] causes one to sleep well, when one has done their duty to God and man as far as ye can, always endeavouring to keep a good conscience'.[119] He prays to God that he will never let Harrold 'dye in drink' because of the lack of preparation needed to prepare his soul for entry into heaven. Harrold views his drinking as a sin; he despairs that this 'sin brings great sorrow and shame, pain and loss always' and as having 'too long served ye fflesh and ye lusts thereof'[120] rather than attending to his spiritual welfare.

Harrold's sense of identity is shaped by his sense of duty not only as a good Christian but also as the head of a household. His desire for a stable domestic background is evident in the swiftness of his remarriage after the deaths of his first and second wives; Horner's research shows that Harrold married Sarah within nine months of the death of Alice Bancroft, and was engaged in courtship only three months after Sarah's death.[121] He approached and was turned down by two women, before being accepted by Ann Horrocks – who was warned by the minister that marriage to Harrold would be her ruin. His role within the family would have been informed by his favoured reading material of seventeenth-century theological texts, as Barker points out:

> There is little explicit discussion of gender in such theological works, although Harrold appears to have accorded with the view expressed by Isaac Ambrose, that his role in his family was that of 'chief governor' who should be affectionate to his wife and 'wisely maintain and manage his authority over her' while remembering that 'He that provideth not for his own, and especially for those of his own house, he has denied the faith and is worse than an infidel'.[122]

Harrold's desire to set up and maintain a household has attached to it the prime importance of not only providing for his family but also of behaving towards them in a decent Christian manner. In contrast to the shameful and solitary sexual activity of the 'private gentleman', the numerous and intimate details about how often he has sex with his wife, in what position and where were part of his record of his manly duty to his wives in the name of Christian procreation, yet this is the only area in which he succeeds in his masculine and Christian duties. Barker cites the work of Jeremy Gregory, in which he demonstrates how 'the neglect of religious priorities was frequently depicted as "unmanly" in much eighteenth-century literature where right conduct in society was portrayed as "the hallmark of masculine religiosity", allowing men to avoid the "feminine" failing of vice'.[123] Harrold's depression is fuelled by his sense of disgust because he is unable to control himself and despair because he perceives himself a failure as both a man and a Christian.

Harrold does demonstrate a sincere desire to reform, and his periods of obeying his rules of sobriety are written up with a joy that contrasts markedly with the despair that follows his relapses. As Barker notes, Harrold follows a long tradition of diary-keeping as a means of religious self-scrutiny, and conduct literature of the eighteenth century also encouraged the keeping of a journal as 'a means to monitor one's performance within a more temporal context'.[124] Harrold's diary-keeping is scrupulous in that every day is accounted for, even the ones he can't remember:

> 16 {January, 1715} This day till noon. Made a sad week, ram[bling] and ill. 17 18 19 20 21 22 23 24 25 Worse of all{.}
> 26 Ill.
> 27 Worse
> 28 Mended

29 As so.
30 Under pennance {*sic*}.[125]

The gaps within the diary and the lack of words to describe his state of mind are eloquent of Harrold's sense of disappointment in himself and his deepening struggle with depression.

Harrold's meticulousness has much in common with practices of diary and journal keeping as espoused by John Wesley, whom Nussbaum notes used diary-keeping as a means of organizing the working week and its labour and insisted upon 'attention to detail ... a rigorous work ethic and a commitment to redeeming the moment'.[126] Harrold's diary is certainly rich with detail, and was as rigorous at recording how much time and money was lost through drinking as he was at recording how much money he had made and how he intended to proceed. It is also this attention to detail that reveals his desperation and deepening depression as he continues to fail to live up to his own expectation of himself. By creating an almost daily journal of his failings as well as his infrequent successes, Harrold makes an attempt to rein in his life which appears to be spiralling out of his control. His attention to the more insalubrious details is a way of preserving it against forgetfulness and of keeping the habits of the mind, body and soul constantly under review. Anderson describes the function of the diary as an '*aide-memoire* ... it was a place to return to in order to contemplate one's self, or one's own character'.[127] Harrold notes his own practice of keeping a record of his character:

April ye 1st 1715 Fell off and never writ in this b[oo]k till ye 18th day of May, when on reflecting of all ye time past how madly it was spent, I writ the great folly of intemperance in drinking out ye Meditations of a Divine soul, whc God knows I have too much experienced true.[128]

This entry, written approximately eight months before the last entry, reads as though Harrold has finally made his peace with himself, yet sadly this does not appear to be the case. The penultimate entry records how, after what appears to be a three-day drinking session, he came home and 'brok[e] knuckles [and] head and other p[ar]ts'.[129] The diary's function as a mirror, within which Harrold could subject himself to intense self-scrutiny in the same manner that Dürer sought the elusive inner self, failed to produce the desired result of character reformation. In the end, it was merely a poor reflection of Harrold's failings and unrealized good intentions.

Balancing the books

What the diaries of both Harrold and Freke have in common, that is lacking in the spiritual narratives of Dutton and the 'private gentleman', is an ongoing discussion of money; they both tot up accounts of what is owed and what has been paid. Harrold measures what he has earned against what he spends on drink and his despair is rooted in the difference. For Freke money becomes a measure of certainty and self-definition in her increasingly isolated state, and her diary includes lengthy and minutely detailed lists of not only what she has spent on other people but also what she possesses in material terms. Money or the lack of it, in the diaries of Harrold and Freke, becomes an indicator of self-worth. Stuart Sherman has noted how early diarists absorbed the form and purpose of the accountant's ledger in order to 'track self, health, soul and salvation as though these too were questions of debit and credit'.[130] The financial record-keeping of Harrold and Freke translates into a form of moral accounting, and this can also be identified as the motivation that impelled Dutton and the 'private gentleman'. Their narratives can be read as an audit of character, and their books are presented as proof that all is now in order after a period of moral deficit upset the balance, and where there was a deficit there was the onset of despair and depression.

The fundamental difference between the accounts of Dutton and the 'private gentleman', and Harrold and Freke, however, is that the former present their accounts believing that all debts have been settled, whereas for Harrold and Freke the audit is ongoing. For all of them, though, the writing is driven not only by the need to prepare for the spiritual day of reckoning, which produced its own kind of anxiety, but also by the search for self-knowledge. The eighteenth century is synonymous with pushing the boundaries of knowledge and, as Roy Porter has succinctly observed, 'plenty of eighteenth-century minds launched themselves in voyages of self-understanding, flying the flag of philosophical doubt'.[131] But a little self-knowledge can be a dangerous thing; the minute exploration of one's own feelings and failings is always at the risk of the development of further sorrow, rather than finding reassurance. As John Baker's chapter has shown, the pleasure of introspection is often outweighed by the pain of discovery. Self-loathing is the product of Harrold's ongoing attempt at self-understanding, but the retrospective accounts by Dutton and the 'private gentleman' both demonstrate the precarious nature of mental equilibrium. Although they have a temporal vantage point over Harrold's perspective of himself, their accounts flag up the futility in trying to guarantee the future by committing a past version of the self to paper. Even Freke's sense of security and order in later life is undermined by the apparently compulsive need to list and re-list every item that she owns, the very richness of her possessions becoming a sad reflection of the very emptiness of her life. No life bears much looking into, and those who try, certainly in these examples, risk opening up the very emptiness that their writing was intended to fill.

6
Deciphering Difference: A Study in Medical Literacy

Allan Ingram

Being normal

As Leigh Wetherall-Dickson has shown in the previous chapter, coming to terms with oneself, especially through the medium of language, even within a private context, is a hazardous and painstaking enterprise, and one that is by no means guaranteed to end successfully. For those whose sense of self is clouded by doubts, self-recriminations and recurrent feelings of unworthiness, the process can involve an agonizingly long series of negotiations for which life itself, perhaps, provides insufficient time. This chapter seeks to place the quest for that elusive core of the depressive identity in terms of medical change, both the changes in medical practice between the eighteenth century and our own period, and also the changes in response that different medical approaches seem to have met with from patients then and now. This leads to the key question, both in this book and in terms of society's attitudes towards its depressed individuals: how far were, and are, medical responses actually helping the 'troubled in mind', and how far were, and are, they actually contributing to the problem.

In a recent book on treating mental illness, the clinical psychologist Richard Bentall relates the experience of 'Andrew', a former patient diagnosed by his psychiatrist as schizophrenic, who became unduly upset at his grandmother's funeral, in consequence of which one of his brothers alerted his doctor. He in turn 'called out the psychiatric team'. As a result, Andrew was visited at home by 'the social worker and community psychiatric nurse ... accompanied by six policemen', who duly escorted him to a local psychiatric ward where he was detained. When Dr Bentall visited him a few days later, 'just before the Christmas holiday', he found him 'sitting quietly, wearing a suit, and reading a novel'. The duty doctor 'could not give me a credible explanation why he had been sectioned, but explained that he would remain under observation in the hospital over the Christmas period'. Questioning one of the psychiatric nurses about her impression of Andrew, he is told that 'He's excessively polite.' Pressed a little further, the nurse adds: 'Well, we're trying to work out whether his politeness is part of his normal personality or his illness.'[1]

At least one of the many reviews of the book gives prominence to the story. Writing in *The Guardian*, Daniel Freeman begins with the case, calling it a 'darkly comic anecdote' and adding that it is 'unlikely to assuage general worries about the desirability of psychiatric treatment'.[2] Freeman goes on to draw attention, too, to the somewhat random quality that psychiatric diagnoses share with what might, or might not, be perceived as symptoms. ('Andrew's' being smartly dressed, Bentall has pointed out, was marked in his clinical notes 'as evidence that he was "grandiose"'.)[3]

> Diagnostic classifications were invented, Bentall reminds us, not discovered – and their validity is often questionable. Back in the early 1990s, Bentall published a paper lampooning the psychiatric diagnoses of schizophrenia by proposing that there were stronger grounds to classify happiness as a psychiatric disorder ('major affective disorder, pleasant type').[4]

Sally Vickers picks up on the same point about classifications in her review for *The Observer*: 'diagnostic concepts', she writes,

> arise out of a collective decision, rather than scientific discovery (you can't test for schizophrenia in the way you can for diabetes). Schizophrenia and bipolar disorder (once called 'manic depression') are merely the names given to a loose collection of 'symptoms' and the decision to plump for one diagnosis over another will be influenced by the doctor's interpretation of the current psychiatric scoreboard.[5]

Or, as Bryan Appleyard in *The Sunday Times* puts it:

> Psychiatrists use reference books that sub-divide mental categories – most familiarly manic depression (bipolarity) and schizophrenia – that are, in fact, simply ways of making mental illnesses as definable as physical disorders.[6]

And symptoms themselves, in fact, can be as randomly defined as the diagnoses that are based on them, and what might lead one doctor to one conclusion could take another, with a slight difference in perspective, in a different, or differently emphasized, direction, with consequent difference in prescribing and even, it follows, a different interpretation of what constitutes 'cure'.

When the dramatist Nathaniel Lee, who was himself confined in Bedlam in the 1680s, joked, 'They said I was mad; and I said they were mad; damn them, they outvoted me',[7] he was putting his finger on something that has ever since haunted discussions and diagnosis of insanity in most of its forms, and which underlies the story of 'Andrew': how does one know what is normal? Is normality, as Lee implies, simply a matter of what the majority thinks it is? And is to depart from that normality therefore inevitably to attract a definition of madness? Moreover, and here the question is even more pertinent in the face of a serious professional orthodoxy, is the enforcement of what is normal ultimately reliant upon the coercion that can be exercised by force of numbers – by six policemen and a community psychiatric nurse, say?

Perhaps the most disturbing feature of Lee's remark, though, is the implied fluidity of madness. If one of 'them' had been sick that day, or if Lee had had a friend with him, he might not have been defined as mad at all, or at least as less mad. Indeed, had Lee had two friends he might have won, and then he would have been sane and the medical enforcers would have been mad. It all depends upon where you stand, and, while seriously disruptive of our sense of stability, both social and psychological, there is also a fascination in the prospect. That fascination was a particular preoccupation for writers and artists of the eighteenth century, from Swift and Pope, through Fielding and Sterne, to Hogarth, Rowlandson and Gillray, and many more, and on to Blake, Wordsworth, Crabbe, Godwin, Hogg and after them Dickens and Browning. Of two parallel worlds, apparently similarly constituted and held to with conviction, albeit by perhaps a single person, only one can be validated as normal – but which one? Gulliver's or Colley Cibber's, or Christopher Smart's or William Cowper's, or, to choose less extreme cases, Thomas Gray's or Samuel Johnson's? Few eighteenth-century writers, of course, felt that raving madmen should be allowed to wander the streets creating mayhem, following whatever promptings their version of reality seemed to demand, but other forms of mental disturbance, not least depression, posed more subtle questions and required more sensitive distinctions to be made between what was normal for one and normal for many, or rather what was normal for some of the time for one and normal for most of the time for many. As James Boswell puts it, on one of his bad days: the 'Hypochondriack' 'knows that his mind is sick' but 'his gloomy imagination is so powerful that he cannot disentangle himself from its influence, and he is in effect persuaded that its hideous representations of life are true'.[8]

'Doctoring the mind'

For Bentall, what is unquestionably true is the increasingly pervasive influence on doctors and on their prescribing of the pharmaceutical industry. Sales figures alone demonstrate this:

> The global market for antipsychotic medication is currently about $15 billion per year. Between 1997 and 2004 the number of US citizens receiving these drugs rose from 2.2 million to 3.4 million and expenditure on them tripled. In Britain, in the period between 1991 and 2001, antipsychotic drug prescriptions for patients living in the community increased by a (less dramatic) 23 per cent.[9]

The story in relation to antidepressants is even more striking, especially once selective serotonin re-uptake inhibitors (SSRIs) were in production, with vigorous marketing by manufacturers and wide publicity through the media:

> Beginning with Prozac, the SSRIs were marketed with enormous hype, even by the already extravagant standards of the industry, with dramatic claims about their superior efficacy compared to the older tricyclic antidepressants. That these efforts were successful is evident from the number of antidepressant prescriptions written by family doctors. Between 1991 and 2001, these rose by 173 per cent in Britain. In the United States, the total number of antidepressant prescriptions tripled between 1995 and 2004.[10]

The very breadth of prescribing is matched by the latitude of diagnoses for which such prescriptions can be written. In the case of schizophrenia, Bentall reproduces a checklist from the third version of the *Diagnostic and Statistical Manual* (*DSM–III*), produced by the American Psychiatric Association, in its successive versions virtually the Bible of American psychiatric diagnosing. *DSM–III*'s test for schizophrenia is the presence of 'at least one of the following during a phase of the illness'. There are six possible broad categories of symptoms, including 'bizarre delusions', 'somatic, grandiose, religious, nihilistic or other delusions', 'delusions with persecutory or jealous content', 'auditory hallucinations' and 'incoherence' with 'marked loosening of associations, markedly illogical thinking, or marked poverty of content of speech' when associated with delusions or hallucinations.[11] The extraordinary range of tolerance within a single diagnosis has meant that many people with different symptom patterns can find themselves in the same category when their conditions in fact have little in common, something that would scarcely be credible with a physical illness like diabetes, measles or even cancer. Because there are other diagnostic manuals both in the United States and across the globe, including the World Health Organization's *International Classification of Diseases* (*ICD–10*), the criteria for deciding on a diagnosis of schizophrenia can vary enormously. In a recent study by the Dutch psychiatrist Jim van Os, in which patients were diagnosed using several different systems, 'the number of schizophrenic patients varied between 268 and 387, and the number of patients with bipolar disorder ranged between 6 and 66'.[12]

At the same time, the influence that the *DSM* (of which a fifth version is in preparation) exerts over American psychiatric diagnosing, and therefore on prescribing, is considerable, not least because psychiatrists and psychologists 'are obliged to give *DSM* diagnoses in order to obtain payment from their patients' medical insurance schemes'.[13] This effectively means conducting a consultation along the lines laid down in the *DSM* structured-interview schedules, which include 'lists of questions that should be asked during diagnostic interviews'.[14] The Structured Clinical Interview (SCID) was first published in 1992, though other schedules published by other bodies both preceded and followed it. When we look at the schedule for depression from the Structured Clinical Interview for *DSM–IV* (SCID I), published in 1997, we see the nature of the straitjacket that is placed upon the relation between doctor and patient, between diagnosis and symptoms. Questions relating to a 'Major Depressive Episode' move through a list of symptoms:

A1. In the past month has there been a period of time when you were feeling depressed or down most of the day, nearly every day? (What was that like?)
    IF YES: How long did it last? (As long as 2 weeks?)
A2. What about losing pleasure or interest in things you usually enjoyed?
    IF YES: Was it nearly every day? How long did it last? (As long as 2 weeks?)

A direction at the foot of this page instructs:

> If **neither** A1 **nor** A2 is "+" during the current month, check for
> past Major Depressive Episode by asking questions A1 and A2 again
> looking for lifetime episodes, beginning with 'Has there EVER...'
> IF AT LEAST ONE PAST DEPRESSED PERIOD: Have you had more than
> one time like that? Which one was the worst?
> If **neither** A1 **nor** A2 has ever been '+', go to **A16**, page 8 (*Manic
> Episode*).

Subsequent questions ask about weight loss (A3), sleep patterns (A4),
restlessness (A5), energy levels (A6), feelings of worthlessness and guilt
(A7), trouble concentrating (A8), and thoughts of death and self-
harming (A9). Question A10 is a direction to the clinician: '**AT LEAST
FIVE OF A(1)-A(9) ARE "+" AND AT LEAST ONE OF THESE IS ITEM
A(1) OR A(2).**' This is followed by another instruction at the foot of the
page:

> If **A10** above is '-' (i.e., fewer than five are '+'), ask the following if
> unknown:
> Have there been <u>other</u> times when you've been depressed and had
> even more of the symptoms that we've just talked about?
> If 'yes,' go back to **A1**, page 3, and ask about that episode.
> If 'no,' go to **A16**, page 8 (*Manic Episode*).[15]

While clearly giving a sense of order and scientific control over the
proceedings, and over the pattern of knowledge to be acquired, the
questions are curiously detached, personal in that they want to know
about feelings and living patterns, but disengaged, as if asking about the
persistence of a rash or the appearance of a lump, something with few
implications, as far as its origins are concerned, for the patient's own
personality. As Bentall puts it (with reference to schizophrenia):

> The meaning of the patient's symptoms, and the context in which
> they have occurred, are therefore seen as irrelevant, and efforts made
> by the patient to discuss them, and to have his story heard, are often
> discouraged.[16]

What lies behind these proceedings is the conviction that mental
disturbances, and from our point of view depression in particular, are
biological in origin and can therefore be best treated with medication.

Symptoms are important because they first of all confirm for the clinician the nature of the illness and therefore a diagnosis, and then can be used to indicate the particular drug that is likely to be effective. DSM is predicated on the assumption that there will be a prescription, and prescriptions mean the pharmaceutical industry, that has spent 'enormous sums on persuading mental health professionals, lay people and politicians that patients suffering from chemical imbalances in the brain can only be cured by medication'.[17] And the list of available drugs for depression alone is a long one, as Lewis Wolpert finds out for his memoir/history, *Malignant Sadness: The Anatomy of Depression*. The older tricyclic drugs include Imipramine, Nortriptyline, Protriptyline, Doxepin and Dothiepin. Their side effects might be

> difficulty urinating, constipation, rapid heartbeats, feeling faint when standing, a feeling of drowsiness due to a sedative action, and confusion. There can be effects on heart rhythm. Taking an overdose poses serious risks and can cause death.[18]

There are also withdrawal symptoms, possible after both a short and a long period of taking tricyclics, which can include anxiety, headache and tremor, and, after a longer period, confusion, nausea and convulsions. The newer SSRIs include Fluvoxamine, Fluoxetine (Prozac), Paroxetine and Sertraline. Side effects are less severe, but can include nausea, insomnia, agitation and anxiety, while possible withdrawal symptoms are 'delirium, nausea, fatigue and dizziness, so the ending of a treatment should take place over a period of several weeks'. Then there are the Monoamine Oxidase Inhibitors (MAOIs), which are contemporaries of the tricyclics and work by inhibiting the enzyme MAO. These include Phenelzine and Tranylcypromine. Their side effects include 'lowering of the blood pressure leading to dizziness and fainting, headaches and sleep disturbances', while withdrawal can produce headaches and nightmares. In addition, the drugs can react adversely with certain foods, such as 'mature cheese and pickled fish'. Drugs listed for manic depression are Lithium Carbonate, Carbamazepine and Sodium Valproate. Here the list of side effects is considerable:

> Lithium has a variety of side effects – a reduction in thyroid function, excessive thirst, a fine tremor of the hands can be observed in a significant number of patients. In early pregnancy lithium can about

double the risk of congenital malformation. As some patients develop lithium toxicity in which there is a coarse tremor, nausea, diarrhoea and, in more severe cases, vomiting, its concentration in the blood needs monitoring. Carbamazepine can cause nausea, dizziness, an itchy rash and a lowering of the white blood cell number. With valproate there may be nausea, stomach cramps, and, on occasion, liver failure.[19]

In his 1991 memoir of depression, William Styron gives a patient's experience both of the psychiatric consultation and of the drug prescription. He is hardly the first to point out the irony of medication intensifying some of the symptoms it was intended to alleviate, and even of its bringing about new effects that make the existence of the depressed person more miserable. Styron's depression is already severe when he first visits a psychiatrist, whom he calls (surely with intended irony) 'Dr. Gold':

> I had never before consulted a mental therapist for anything, and I felt awkward, also a bit defensive; my pain had become so intense that I considered it quite improbable that conversation with another mortal, even one with professional expertise, could alleviate the distress.[20]

His specific purpose in seeing a psychiatrist, he states, 'was to obtain help through pharmacology – though this, too, was alas! a chimera for a bottomed-out victim such as I had become'. Nevertheless, the interview proceeds, with 'Dr. Gold' going through the routine questions and getting textbook responses, though, as Styron's narrative makes clear, those responses are far from the full story, indeed represent only the very tip of the iceberg:

> He asked me if I was suicidal, and I reluctantly told him yes. I did not particularize – since there seemed no need to – did not tell him that in truth many of the artifacts of my house had become potential devices for my own destruction: the attic rafters (and an outside maple or two) a means to hang myself, the garage a place to inhale carbon monoxide, the bathtub a vessel to receive the flow from my opened arteries. The kitchen knives in their drawers had but one purpose for me. Dr. Gold and I began to chat twice weekly, but there was little I could tell him except to try, vainly, to describe my desolation.[21]

The outcome is sadly predictable:

> His platitudes were not Christian but, almost as ineffective, dicta
> drawn straight from the pages of *The Diagnostic and Statistical Manual
> of the American Psychiatric Association* ... and the solace he offered me
> was an antidepressant medication called Ludiomil.[22]

Ludiomil is a market name in the US for Maprotiline, a tetracyclic drug
related to the tricyclics, and one to be used with particular caution in the
case of suicidal patients. (Its use was discontinued in Britain in 2006.)
The consequence of this medication for Styron, equally predictably, is
dreadful.

> The pill made me edgy, disagreeably hyperactive, and when the
> dosage was increased after ten days, it blocked my bladder for hours
> one night. Upon informing Dr. Gold of this problem, I was told that
> ten more days must pass for the drug to clear my system before start-
> ing anew with a different pill. Ten days to someone stretched on such
> a torture rack is like ten centuries – and this does not begin to take
> into account the fact that when a new pill is inaugurated several
> weeks must pass before it becomes effective, a development which
> is far from guaranteed in any case.[23]

As Styron goes downhill, the visits continue, but with little expectation
of benefit:

> So I found little of worth to anticipate in my consultations with Dr.
> Gold. On my visits he and I continued to exchange platitudes, mine
> haltingly spoken now – since my speech, emulating my way of walk-
> ing, had slowed to the vocal equivalent of a shuffle – and I'm sure as
> tiresome as his.[24]

Psychiatry, however, has one more trick up its sleeve: another pill.

> I had been driven (I could no longer drive) to Dr. Gold's office, where
> he announced that he had decided to place me on the antidepressant
> Nardil, an older medication which had the advantage of not causing
> the urinary retention of the other two pills he had prescribed. How-
> ever, there were drawbacks. Nardil would probably not take effect in
> less than four to six weeks – I could scarcely believe this – and I would
> have to carefully obey certain dietary restrictions, fortunately rather

epicurean (no sausage, no cheese, no pâté de foie gras), in order to avoid a clash of incompatible enzymes that might cause a stroke.[25]

So far so not very good. But then comes the bombshell, not a bombshell on the medical level as such, but more on the level of patient–psychiatrist wave lengths.

> Further, Dr. Gold said with a straight face, the pill at optimum dosage could have the side effect of impotence. Until that moment, although I'd had some trouble with his personality, I had not thought him totally lacking in perspicacity; now I was not at all sure. Putting myself in Dr. Gold's shoes, I wondered if he seriously thought that this juiceless and ravaged semi-invalid with the shuffle and the ancient wheeze woke up each morning from his Halcion sleep eager for carnal fun.[26]

At a professional level, of course, Dr. Gold is merely fulfilling his obligation to inform the patient of all possible side effects. But at the level of personal interaction and trust, he has blown it. Had he actually been listening all those months? Has be been so conditioned and DSM-ed that he can no longer see his patient other than as a collection of SCID I diagnostic signs? Is there no glimmer of sensitivity to what it must be like to be inside Styron at that moment?

Styron begins the preparations for suicide that evening, and the fact that he fails to go through with it is down not to pharmacy or psychiatry but to the accidental watching of a film with Brahms on the soundtrack. The *Alto Rhapsody* 'pierced my heart like a dagger' and reminded him 'of all the joys the house had known':

> All this I realized was more than I could ever abandon, even as what I had set out so deliberately to do was more than I could inflict on those memories, and upon those, so close to me, with whom the memories were bound. And just as powerfully I realized I could not commit this desecration on myself.[27]

He has himself admitted to hospital, an almost victim of the cure being worse than the condition.

The final chilling piece in the jigsaw, for Bentall, is coercion. Styron is not a resisting patient, but he is a despairing one for whom a lucky chance intervenes in the apparently inevitable spiral through depression, insensitive medical orthodoxy, drugs and their side effects to

suicide. But too often less lucky patients, caught up in the pincer movements of state systems, find themselves faced with a stark choice should
they, like Styron, try to decide that enough is enough – enough urine
retention, enough insomnia or even enough being not listened to.

> Research shows that coercion is commonplace in traditional services.
> It is not only that psychiatrists have become more willing to use their
> powers of involuntary detention...but that informal methods of
> leverage are often used to persuade patients to do as directed. In these
> circumstances the psychiatric interview is often reduced to a polite
> meeting in which the patient's adherence to the prescribed regimen
> is the one item on the agenda, and which finishes when the patient
> agrees to conform. Patients may be told that their access to benefits
> or housing, or even their right to raise their own children, will be
> rescinded unless they follow instructions. This increasing resort to
> intimidation...has culminated in many countries with the introduc-
> tion of community treatment orders (CTOs), which require patients
> to continue their treatment (invariably medication) after discharge
> from hospital on the threat of some kind of sanction (usually a return
> to the locked ward).[28]

Six policemen again. No state, after all, can allow the chaos of a minority
of its citizens running around, or shuffling around, bringing madness
and despair, or seriously neglecting their children, and no drug company can afford to see its research and development, or its publicity
campaigns, wrecked on the shoals of patient choice. But public order is
not the real issue in terms of what this chapter is exploring, any more
than pharmaceutical profits. The issue is one of appropriateness.

A promiscuity of symptoms, a plethora of cures

We have seen in Chapter 1 how productive eighteenth-century medical men were in identifying and distinguishing between symptoms
of melancholy and its associated conditions. John F. Sena's 'plurality
of melancholies',[29] as Clark Lawlor argues, is thoroughly exemplified
in the physical and psychological manifestations of the condition
noted by physicians. Many were inherited from classical sources and
accepted, therefore, as unimpeachable marks of the melancholy temperament – causeless fear and sorrow, for example, and an association
with genius and creativity. Many, too, were passed on from Burton:

digestive problems, especially to do with wind and heaviness; wakefulness and insomnia; irritability, restlessness, resentment and the desire
to be alone; suspicion and watchfulness, imagined slights and snubs;
fear and anxiety; sadness and inertia; conviction of sin and the certainty of damnation and, its counterpart, belief in some kind of destiny
or appointed role, especially when alternating with a sense of personal
worthlessness; visions both pleasing and terrifying; and, ultimately, a
weariness of all things human and divine. Equally, the different terms
adopted during the period reflect partly, as Lawlor points out, changing
trends and fashions both diagnostic and linguistic, but also the attempt
to distinguish between shades of causes and effects: spleen and vapours,
hypochondria and its manifold subdivisions.

At the same time, and partly because this was an age of medical
laissez-faire, both physicians and quacks offered and championed a stag-
gering range of treatments for melancholy conditions, some of them
plausible, but many of them, one would think, dangerous and even life-
threatening. Quite apart from the ubiquitous bleeding for virtually any
complaint, physical, mental or indeed imaginary, and baths, sometimes
hot but usually cold, where anything involving the mind was concerned, different schools and different one-off eccentrics developed their
own distinctive methods. Some of these were within the realm of what
was medically orthodox at the time, depletion being a trusted favourite,
based on the assumption that what was within the body causing the
problems had very much better be out of it. This was the principle of
bleeding, as standard in Bethlem Hospital for the Insane and elsewhere
at the end of the century as it was at the beginning, and as enthusiastically practised by Bryan Crowther as surgeon there between 1790 and
1815 as it was when James Carkesse experienced it as a patient in the
late 1670s. Other methods of achieving depletion included vomits and
purges, which were almost exclusively the treatment employed by John
Woodward in the first two decades of the eighteenth century, and which
were still being defended by John Monro, the physician to Bethlem, in
the 1750s and administered under the direction of his son, Thomas,
who succeeded him as physician, from 1791. Also widely practised were
cupping and scarification (drawing blood from scratches, rather than
opening a vein, by placing a cupping glass over them), blistering (artifi-
cial blisters caused by some such irritant as mustard), issues (a cut or sore
kept open to enable secretion), leeches, trepanning, the administration
of a salivation in order to encourage depletion through abundance of
saliva (often involving mercury taken orally), or an errhine to accom-
plish the same through sneezing, or a diaphoretic (also known as a

sudorific) to achieve it through perspiration, or a diuretic, operating to stimulate the discharge of urine. If these failed in their purpose it was always possible to employ mechanical means, and to swing your patients in a revolving chair, as Joseph Mason Cox did in the last years of the eighteenth century and into the nineteenth, until they either vomited or defecated, or both, prior to passing out.

Such therapies were employed most frequently with patients who had already been diagnosed as insane, rather than on the merely melancholy or hypochondriac, though vomits, purges and bleeding were difficult to avoid even as a sane patient. But refinements of the full range, certainly, could be tried even on the fee-paying individuals who voluntarily consulted their physicians, rather than those who were confined and so had less say in the matter. John Woodward, for example, whose cases were conducted entirely as a private practitioner, gives detailed accounts of the treatments he prescribes. A William Rockcliff, who exhibits the symptoms of a classic hypochondria, including dreadful gastric problems together with fearful dreams, melancholy thoughts and jealousies,[30] is given 'two Ounces of the Oil of Sweet Almonds' and a 'few volatile and vinous Spirits' by way of preparation:

> But the main Stress of the Cure was put upon Clysters and Purges, of which some were given very strong, with Oils interposed, in considerable Quantity, to temper the Acrimony of the Biliose Salts, put an End to their Colluctations, smear over, defend, and lubricate the Stomach and Guts.[31]

Woodward, in apparent surprise, describes the effects – 'It is hardly credible what a Quantity of bilious Matter, scalding hot, excessively sharp and excoriating, with Froth and Wind, was brought down by this Means' – and the happy consequences for Mr. Rockcliff's state of health:

> The greater Discharge was made, the Bile being first tamed by the Oils, and rendered harmless, the greater Relief he ever found, the easier his Stomach presently became, the better his Appetite and his Rest, the brisker his Spirits, the greater his Strength, the less his Fears, Melancholy, and other Affections of his Mind.[32]

In the course of relating the case, Woodward also mentions the prescription of the previous physician consulted by Rockcliff, a Dr. Colbatch, who, observes Woodward sniffily, 'neither directed Vomits nor Clysters' but

Steel, with Purges at Intervals, also Acids, Juice of Lemon, and Spirit of Vitriol, Cremor Tartari, and Tartarus Vitriolatus. He directed him to abstain wholly from Malt Liquors and Wine, and to drink only Punch and Cyder. He ordered Volatil Spirits, Tincture of Castor, and Asafœtida, Infusions of Pæony Root, and Bryony Root, in Spring Water; Misleto and Camphire in Electuaries; Plaisters with Galbanum and Spices to his Feet; likewise *Hampstead* and *Bath* Waters; but all to very little Advantage, and sometimes to his Detriment. The Acids ever made him worse, and heightened all the Symptoms.[33]

While the deterioration in his condition is hardly surprising, the quantities of medication that Rockcliff was prepared to take was truly heroic.

Other physicians followed other drums. Nicholas Robinson, in his *A New System of the Spleen, Vapours, and Hypochondriack Melancholy*, advocates for hypochondriack melancholy 'Vomits of mineral Preparations' which 'greatly avail in removing that Load of viscid, glewy Humour, that lies impacted in the Fibres of the Brain, and chains down the noble Faculties of the Soul to this Gloomy Way of Thinking'.[34] Bleeding in certain circumstances is also recommended, and, once the vomits have begun to do their work, he advocates

the Effects of the Cold Bath, which, in all Splenetick and Hypochondriack Cases . . . I look upon to be a Remedy second to none; for it purses up the over-lax *Machinulæ* of the Fibres, restores their impair'd Contractions, and by that Means revives the Action of the several Organs.[35]

George Cheyne, famously, champions diet in order to counteract the onset of the English Malady, preceded by bleeding and purging, which were achieved by the administration of such substances as mercury and valerian,[36] while Sir Richard Blackmore, advising against bleeding, prefers 'Vomitive Remedies'[37] followed by 'Steel and Chalybeate Waters',[38] a remedy sanctioned by the influential seventeenth-century clinician Thomas Sydenham. For his part, the mid-century Edinburgh physician George Young wrote strongly in favour of opium, for a wide range of medical conditions, not least for 'lowness of spirits' and 'melancholia *and* mania'.[39] This has proved such a 'very successful remedy' that he 'doubted not but that it acted as a specific, and only failed in other peoples hands, because they gave it in too small doses'.[40]

One particular set of treatments newly available to the eighteenth-century medical world involved those procedures made possible by science. Some of them employed variations on kinds of mechanical apparatus, but of particular promise was electricity. John Birch, in the 1790s (he later treated Catherine Blake for rheumatism, apparently very successfully), was a huge enthusiast, using

> a moderate-sized cylinder, conductor, and Leyden jar, with an insulating chair and electrometer; a glass mounted director with a wooden handle, to the extremity of which a glass ball and wooden point are fitted, and a brass director mounted in wood.
>
> When I wish to apply the fluid, I connect by a smooth wire the glass-mounted director to the conductor with a point at it's extremity, and the radii are projected from it to the part affected. When desirous of propelling the sparks, I change the point for the ball. When the shock is intended, the circuit of the Leyden jar must be made ... [41]

Birch has found this treatment 'in many cases exclusively eminent and efficacious', not least in that 'it often affords relief where every other hope is lost'.[42] In the case of melancholy, he has met with some significant success, treating, he relates, 'a porter of the India warehouses', who cannot recover his spirits after 'the death of one of his children',[43] a singer who 'from a variety of distressing causes, became extremely melancholy', so much so 'that he was incapable of taking employment',[44] and a 'gentleman who had been long a patient of Dr. Monro's, with a moping melancholy, and who had reached the age of 26 without any relief'.[45] The results of electrification are, in fact, not wholly convincing, with the porter at first regaining his spirits, but apparently relapsing after four years, upon which Birch, curiously, tells him 'to apply for medical aid, and to the hospital'.[46] The gentleman allows Birch to pass a series of increasingly strong currents through his head on several occasions, but gains no improvement from it. Only the singer, who had been suicidal prior to consulting Birch, apparently gains permanent benefit. He rejoices at finding his mind so cleared by it that he 'becomes sensible of' a 'divine interposition' in preventing his intended suicide, so

> that he found himself able to return thanks; and this relief of mind was followed by a refreshing sleep, from which he awoke a new being: that he felt sensible of the powers of electricity every day after it's application, being capable of mental exertions immediately. He could

not be satisfied, he said, without making this declaration to me, as no one but himself could have an adequate idea of the sudden change the first electric shocks wrought in his mind.[47]

This patient's enthusiasm for the wonders made possible by science is matched by Birch, too, who even seems to look upon himself as something of a showman: 'The ingenuity', he observes, 'with which these simple modes of application may be varied, to puzzle and deceive the observation of a by-stander, is unbounded...'[48]

Clearly the energies put into science during the seventeenth and eighteenth centuries were always going to have spin-off effects for medicine, and those who specialized in the mind were foremost in recognizing the potential in new processes, chemical and pharmaceutical as much as mechanical and electrical. While this left the way open for the makers of spurious elixirs and nostrums, and for celebrated performance artists like Anton Mesmer, clearly others in the more legitimate areas of the medical profession were genuinely stimulated by new ideas, alert to both the potential mental benefits as well as the profits to be made from the harnessing of scientific advance.

Profits and losses

There were many factors that distinguished medical attitudes towards the disturbed mind during the long eighteenth century, and particularly towards the many varieties of melancholy experience to be met with. One, certainly, was the almost completely free hand physicians, surgeons, alienists, apothecaries, mad-doctors and interested amateurs had in prescribing. Whatever the patient was willing to undergo, or could be coerced into undergoing, was likely to be acceptable, short of actually killing – and sometimes even that too.[49] Another was the vitality of the medical market place, with society physicians like George Cheyne becoming rich on the fashionable sick. Equally, with new theories concerning the body and the mushrooming, therefore, of ways to be ill, the way was open for therapies and applications promising relief, especially for a clientele with cash to spare.

Some two or three centuries later, many of these circumstances still prevail in both Britain and the United states. Certainly it is an age, and has been increasingly so for the past hundred years, in which science, it is believed, is capable, given time, resources and its head, of solving virtually anything, be it a race to the moon, a cure for cancer or for the common cold. With each new breakthrough on the depression front, another set of branded (and copyrighted) drugs enters the market, at first displacing those of longer standing but later, perhaps, falling back, as unforeseen, or understated, side effects persist as problems – urine retention, insomnia, anxiety or liver failure. But our faith in science remains: if not this one, then perhaps the next – if not steel and chalybeate water, then perhaps opium, or even electricity. The contemporary medical market place, of course, is more sophisticated than its eighteenth-century counterpart, with technology and multinationalism both major factors, and marketing techniques, therefore, with such resources behind them, being aimed ruthlessly at specific targets in ways simply not available for those relying on broadsheets, posters and the occasional newspaper insertion. Indeed, if money was a key driving force behind eighteenth-century medical approaches to depressive illnesses, this is indisputably so, in a wider variety of ways, within the present-day market place.

State medicine, in Britain, as we well know, is both enormously costly and subject to constant monitoring: a huge proportion of its running costs, though, is accounted for by its drugs bill, while other sectors, including the psychiatric service, are often seen as the Cinderellas of the health system. In the United States, much of the cost of health is borne by insurance schemes, either occupational or personal, and occasionally state. As such, as we have seen, psychiatric care has a strong tendency to gravitate towards the systematized, with DSM classification and SCID interview formats necessarily observed in order to trigger the practitioner's fee, and also the recommended prescription. Both kinds of monitoring, financial scrutiny by the state and DSM straitjacketing through insurance mechanisms, mean that today's specialists in mental conditions are subject to far more restriction than their eighteenth-century predecessors, and while this can work, of course, to patients' enormous advantage (they are much less likely, for example, to be killed by their consultants, except perhaps by accident), there are also losses.

A model physician

First published in 1711, and in an expanded edition in 1730, Bernard Mandeville's *A Treatise of the Hypochondriack and Hysteric Diseases* (as it was finally known) was distinctive among eighteenth-century medical works in being constructed in the form of a series of dialogues. Drawing upon models that included the dialogues of Galileo and the French writer Fontenelle, rather than the conventional English medical treatise, which until the late seventeenth century was normally written in Latin and still had a relatively set formula, Mandeville, as Stephen H. Good has observed in his edition of the 1730 text, chose this form because it 'allows him to demonstrate the proper procedure for a physician in treating hypochondria and hysteria, diseases which demand that psychological factors be considered'. Indeed, 'the manner of Philopirio, the physician, is as important in the dialogues as are the actual discussions of symptoms, causes and remedies'.[50] Mandeville actually has Misomedon, the male hypochondriac patient in the dialogues, and a loose self-portrait, declare towards the end of 'The First Dialogue':

> You and I must be better acquainted, *Philopirio*; if your Medicines do me no good, I am sure your Company will: One thing above the rest I admire in you, and that's your Patience, which must be unaffected, because you can be gay in the Exercise of it. You can't imagine, how a pertinent lively Discourse, or any thing that is sprightly, revives my Spirits.[51]

Misomedon adds, in a remark that provides a link with our modern understanding of hypochondria, in which patients are never happier than when discussing their variety of illnesses with their physician, 'I don't know what it is that makes me so, whether it be our talking together, the Serenity of the Air, or both; but I enjoy abundance of Pleasure, and this Moment, methinks, I am as well as ever I was in my Life.'[52]

Philopirio's method of consulting is at the heart of the treatise, even though Mandeville also frequently gives his physician's medical prescriptions, recommended for both Misomedon and for his wife, Polytheca, who appears in the 'The Third Dialogue'. Some of the conversation is in fact largely monologue, particularly when his patients give to Philopirio the histories of their conditions intertwined with their life stories, and some consists of what appear to be digressions, on previous medical treatises, for example, or on different aspects of science, including mathematics. But the core, always returned to, is the relationship between doctor and patient, even before the relation between patient and illness. As Misomedon puts it during 'The Third Dialogue': 'What I do now is only to pay you for the Trouble I have given you, and the Time you have spent with me. — But is this, pray, the general Method you take with all Hypochondriacks, *mutatis mutandis*, which now you have prescrib'd to me?'[53] Philopirio's reply triggers a conversation about medical practice, which places Mandeville and his alter ego (for Philopirio is also a version of the author himself) at a distinct remove from many physicians of his time.

Phil. Mutatis mutandis it is; but that is all in all, for as the Symptoms differ, so I alter my Method; and I never saw yet two hypochondriacal Cases exactly alike.

Misom. Then what is your Secret in the Cure of this difficult Distemper?

Phil. I have several: I allow my self time to hear and weigh the Complaints of my Patients.

Misom. The first I have experienced to be true, and I have no Reason to doubt of the latter.[54]

What Philopirio says next in effect defines a model for the ideal physician:

Phil. I take pains to be well acquainted with the manner of living of my Patients, and am more curious in examining them than there is occasion for a Man to be in any other Distemper; not only to penetrate into the Procatartick Causes, but likewise the better to consult the Circumstances as well as *Idiosincrasy* of every particular Person: Some have strange Aversions as to Diet; others peculiar Antipathies against some excellent Remedies; and every wholesome Exercise suits not with all People. A third Secret is, that I am very careful in endeavouring to distinguish between the Efforts of Nature, whom I would assist, and those of the Distemper, which I am to destroy.[55]

For Philopirio, individual temperament, habits, preferences come first, those features that tend to make a person distinctive. Yet, it seems, that was not quite what Misomedon had in mind: 'But I meant Medicines,' he explains, 'when I spoke of Secrets.' Philopirio sets less store by medicine, yet acknowledges there is a place for it, as long as what is prescribed is appropriate both for the temperament and the condition:

Phil. Then I must answer you, that I have not one but what I am willing to impart to any Patient, as generous as your self, that for his private Use, after having receiv'd some extraordinary Benefit from it, asks me for the Prescription. For tho' I make use of Chymical as well as Galenical Preparations, yet I have no *Nostrums* that I intend either to magnify or conceal . . . The Medicines I make use of are such as others have likewise recommended in the same Cases; and all the Mystery I know in Physick, as to Remedies, consists in the Choice and Application of them.[56]

The physician's skill, in other words, consists of attentive listening in order to be able to decipher difference, to identify what is distinctive and to treat the patient in whatever way his total condition seems to require – including, as he eventually prescribes for Polytheca, 'no Medicines at all'.[57]

A secular priesthood

We argued in the introduction to this work that medical attitudes towards the troubled in mind in the long eighteenth century owed a lot to, but lagged far behind, the practical and pastoral curacy of the Nonconformist ministry. The compilation made in 1716 by Samuel Clifford, himself a minister in London, from the works of Richard Baxter, entitled *The Signs and Causes of Melancholy, with Directions Suited to the Case of those who are Afflicted with it*, is a testimony to the attentiveness enjoined upon those wider members of the congregation whose Christian duty it is to recognize, engage with and help to cure those fellow believers unfortunate enough to fall into this condition. Its divisions, into 'The Nature of Melancholy', 'The Signs of Melancholy', 'The Causes of Melancholy', 'Directions to the Melancholy' and, as quoted earlier, 'Directions to those who are concerned in the Care of Melancholy Persons',[58] provide a practical guide to recognition of the illness and to understanding it, and then, like the good physician, to managing it, to overcoming it and to bringing about a return to assurance of the love of God. The signs are there for all to see, if we are willing to do so:

1. Melancholy Persons are commonly *exceeding fearful*, cause[les]sly or beyond what there is Cause for: Every thing which they hear or see, is ready to increase their fears ...
2. Their Fantasie most erreth in aggravating their *Sin*, or *Dangers* or *Unhappiness*: Every ordinary Infirmity they are ready to speak of with Amazement, as an heinous Sin ...
3. They are still addicted to Excess of *Sadness*, some weeping they know not why, and some thinking it *ought* to be so; and if they should Smile or speak merrily, their Hearts smite them for it, as if they had done amiss.[59]

Specialized knowledge, it is implied, is not necessary, but intelligent sympathy and alertness to changes in mood are:

1. A great part of their Cure lieth in *pleasing* them, and avoiding all displeasing Things, as far as lawfully can be done ...

> If you know any lawful thing that will please them in Speech,
> in Company, in Apparel, in Rooms, in Attendance, give it them.
> If you know at what they are displeased, *remove* it.... Could you
> put them in a *pleased* Condition you might *Cure* them.
>
> 2. As much as you can, *divert* them from the Thoughts which are
>   their Trouble; keep them on some other Talk or Business; break in
>   upon them, and interrupt their Musings; raise them out of it, but
>   with loving Importunity.
>
> 3. Often set before them the great Truths of the Gospel, which are
>   fittest to comfort them: And reading to them informing comfort-
>   ing Books, and live in a loving cheerful manner with them.[60]

The process, in fact, is a kind of seduction, whereby the melancholy
person is gradually to be weaned away from habitually gloomy thoughts
to enjoyment of others, and of God.

This is a process we can see in practice in various first-person accounts
of the experience of melancholy, and even of despair. The future
Nonconformist minister George Trosse, for example, confined in a madhouse at Glastonbury in 1656 after one of his early mental breakdowns,
and believing himself forsaken of God, describes how the '*Gentlewoman*
of the House', one Mrs. Gollop and 'a very *religious* Woman', not only
'*pray'd* in the *Evenings* at least with her Servants in the Family' but also
made every effort, covert as well as open, to bring him to a true belief:

> She was very well acquainted with the Scriptures, insomuch, that I
> sometimes received a Letter from her with a Hundred and odd Proofs
> in the Margin, fitted in good Measure to comfort poor *tempted* and
> *dejected Souls*. She had great Compassion upon me; would many times
> sit and discourse with me; would give me good Directions, and offer
> me considerable Encouragements: But all was, for some Time, lost
> upon me, who understood *little* or *nothing* of what was said to me,
> and would apply nothing to my *Soul* for my Comfort and Ease in
> such a *dreadfully* sinful and woful Condition.[61]

In spite of his obstinacy, Trosse, looking back at the time of writing, adds: 'However, this I may say, if any one was more *eminently
Instrumental* in my *Conversion* than another, *She* was the Person.'[62]

We can see the same attempts, with initially the same effect, over a
century later, when William Cowper describes his experience as a patient
in Nathaniel Cotton's madhouse at St Alban's. Cotton, as Michelle
Faubert reminds us, was an evangelical Christian as well as a medical

man, who believed 'that the most Christian way to live is also the most psychologically healthful'.[63] Cowper commends both Cotton's 'skill, as a physician' and also, like Philopirio, 'his well-known humanity, and sweetness of temper'.[64] The doctor makes it his business, as if following the Baxter prescription, to engage his patient in conversation: Cowper 'laughed at his stories, and told him some of my own to match them'.[65] But Cotton, apparently, also works in mysterious ways, or at least more stealthy ways than Mrs. Gollop, and Cowper tells of coming upon 'a Bible on the bench in the garden':

> I opened it upon the 11th of St. John, where Lazarus is raised from the dead; and saw so much benevolence, mercy, goodnes, and sympathy with miserable man, in our Saviour's conduct, that I almost shed tears even after the relation; little thinking that it was an exact type of the mercy which Jesus was on the point of extending towards myself. I sighed, and said, "Oh, that I had not rejected so good a Redeemer, that I had not forfeited all his favours!" Thus was my heart softened, though not yet enlightened. I closed the book, without intending to open it again.[66]

The book, however, whether placed by the doctor's ministry or merely there by chance, has had its effect, and it is followed up the next day when, with 'the cloud of horror, which had so long hung over me ... every moment passing away',[67] Cowper happens upon yet another casually placed Bible:

> I flung myself in a chair near the window, and seeing a Bible there, ventured once more to apply to it for comfort and instruction. The first verse I saw was the 25th of the 3d of Romans: 'Whom God hath set forth to be a propitiation through faith in his blood, to declare his righteousness for the remission of sins that are past, through the forbearance of God.' Immediately I received strength to believe, and the full beams of the Sun of Righteousness shone upon me ... In a moment I believed, and received the gospel.[68]

The first steps in the seduction have worked, and Cotton is now more explicit in pushing home in his conversations with Cowper the efficacy of his prescription:

> In a short time, Dr. C. became satisfied, and acquiesced in the soundness of my cure; and much sweet communion I had with

him concerning the things of our salvation. He visited me every morning while I stayed with him, which was near twelve months after my recovery, and the gospel was the delightful theme of our conversation.[69]

'In a process that seems to be a kind of spiritual talk-therapy,' says Faubert, 'Cotton made himself a kind of priest for his patient'.[70] Cowper later described his experience under Cotton in terms that echo, in religious terms, Misomedon's more secular delight in his consultations with Philopirio:

> I reckon it one instance of the Providence that has attended me throughout this whole event, that...I was carried to Dr Cotton...[for] I had so much need of a religious friend to converse with...The doctor was as ready to administer relief to me in this article likewise [i.e. religious anxiety], and as well qualified to do it as in that which was more immediately his province.[71]

Cowper, continues Faubert, 'even implies that Cotton's religious approach to psychological cure surpassed both that of the priests who lacked psychological knowledge and the doctors who lacked religious knowledge'.[72]

How to read

Subtlety in patient seduction, be it towards spiritual or mental health, was one crucial feature of what some early psychologist physicians shared with Nonconformist cure. The second was the case history. Just as a large part of Mandeville's semi-fictitious work is taken up with patient monologue, published accounts by doctors of actual cases sometimes include substantial amounts of material, supplied by the patient, relating to the history of their condition and often their personal histories from birth. Dorothy and Roy Porter have shown how rarely eighteenth-century physicians were interested in anything but immediate symptoms, and were frequently prepared to prescribe without actually having met, let alone examined, the so-called patient.[73] In these circumstances the kinds of detailed histories that Misomedon provides and those that the actual physician, John Woodward, inserts in his *Selected Cases, and Consultations, in Physick* are exceptional. 'He was born *August* 26, 1684,' writes Woodward of William Rockcliff, the hypochondriac mentioned above, and in *December* following his Father died of a Phthisis, at the Age of thirty-three. His Mother was healthy and strong, and lived to sixty-three Years of Age, but fell finally into a Cholic and Pleurisy, of which she died. As to this Gentleman, their Son, in his Infancy his Lips were apt to be chapped and cracked, but chiefly in the Winter. This Disposition continued upon him until about the Year 1706. He was also subject to Kernels, or an Hardness of some Parts of the Parotid Glands, as likewise to spitting of a frothy Matter. From his Infancy his Eyes were annoyed with a sharp hot Humour; by the Acrimony whereof, at the Age of three Years, he lost his Right Eye.[74]

It is some seven or eight pages before the history moves closer to the moment of consultation with Woodward, and therefore to the immediate need for a physician.

The patient has clearly been ready to supply what we have to assume is a lengthy spoken account of his past, even to the minutiae of relatively minor childhood conditions (the chapped lips in winter), some of which might well amount to hearsay within the immediate family, and the physician, equally clearly, has had both the time and interest not only to listen but also to take detailed notes. Transferred to a religious setting, this suggests on one hand the situation of the confessional, with a resident professional listening to a self-selected personal narrative and expected, at the end, to diagnose a spiritual distemper, with appropriately prescribed penance. It has, though, perhaps more in common in its forms not with Roman Catholic procedures but, again, with Nonconformist practice, and specifically with the growing habits of keeping a spiritual journal and the publishing of spiritual autobiographies, whose very purpose, as Stuart Sim and Leigh Wetherall-Dickson have discussed in Chapters 4 and 5, was to probe at the weak spots of one's soul, to expose their frailties and to render them healthy and whole in terms of a renewed relationship with God. William Law, for one, sets the tone by demanding in his *Serious Call to a Devout and Holy Life*, first published in 1729, daily spiritual scrutiny of the most searching and intense kind, a scrutiny that also involved providing an account of the reasons why certain actions had been taken: 'every good man', according to Law, should make it 'a constant part of his night recollection, to examine how, and in what degree, he has observ'd' his own rules for 'holy living', and to 'reproach himself before God, for every neglect of them'.[75] Stuart Sim has shown the influences of spiritual autobiography and its conventions on the novel, and particularly on the engagement with despair and melancholy within the novel framework.

The 'interplay between the spiritual and the secular' he observes at work there is also a factor, we now suggest, in the form and function of the narrated case history.

To return to George Trosse, for example, his *Life*, so titled, is certainly that to an extent, but it is a 'life' in which knowledge of later events, in his case spiritual despair, serve as the filter for what is highlighted, beyond the bare facts, of his earlier, pre-despairing, years:

> I was born in Exon, *Octob.* 25th, in the Year 1631. of *Wealthy Parents, honourable Citizens*...They gave me the usual Education of those Days amongst such as were no Friends to *Puritans*...I was taught the *Principles* of *Religion*, call'd upon to read the *Scriptures*, forbidden to sport or play upon the *Lord's-Day*, made to frequent the *Publick Assemblies* for Worship on *that Day*, and to sit demurely there; and should be reprov'd and corrected, if in these Respects I transgress'd. Yet, *too often* I thus offended: I sported and play'd with others upon the *Lord's-Day*...I never car'd to understand, or to retain, what I heard in Publick; never, as I can remember, being call'd to an account by my *Parents*, after the Sermon and Service was over.[76]

This lack of parental attentiveness means that Trosse is being 'call'd to an account' so many years later by a far greater authority than his slack parents: hence his state of religious despair.

Medical patients are not 'call'd to an account' in quite the same way, but it is nevertheless the case that perhaps unnoticed signs from the past, trivial events or characteristics, take on new significance when seen in the light of a developed physical or, for us, psychological condition. The newly attentive sufferer, like the religiously alert sinner, can hardly fail to revisit their own past in a spirit of inquiry, while the physician, like a secular priest, picks up on the early signs and symptoms of malaise being revealed in the context of a remembered life. And just as, in spiritual cure, each soul is regarded as unique and individual, the single part of an identity that cannot be replicated, and is therefore beyond all value, so the case history, with its distinct sequences of events, impressions, reactions, accidents of birth and nature, and with the inevitable temperamental gloss given, consciously or unconsciously, by the teller, is the one thing that marks each patient as him or her self. What priest or spiritual adviser would dare to ignore such glaring evidence of the state of his charge's soul? What physician would be so foolish as to regard the uniqueness of each patient as being of no account? And what definition, what treatment, could possibly be a perfect fit for them all?

John Woodward is remarkable for the detail and length of his patient histories, sometimes even filling them out with his own speculations on the wider implications of certain symptoms, not only for the individual but also for his own understanding of medicine. As we have seen, however, Woodward's inevitable remedies are purges, vomits and clysters of varying types and strengths (successfully, apparently): the physician may be sensitive to patient difference and to the individuality of their stories, but that is no reason not to purge them. A physician, however, who seems genuinely not only to have listened to his patients' accounts but also to have been unusually sensitive to differences in personality in his choice and approach to treatment is Peter Shaw. Shaw had a distinguished career, practising in London through a large proportion of the eighteenth century until his death in 1763. He was physician to George II and, for a short while, to George III. His two-volume *A New Practice of Physic* was first published in 1726 and extended to seven editions, the last being published in 1753. In many respects he was relatively conventional, and certainly recommended, for example, in cases of madness, that 'universally' the head should be shaved, 'to encourage a free perspiration in that part' together with the 'cold bath, once a day, if necessary, from *May* to *August*, inclusive, not only to mitigate the influence of the summer solstice, but to forward the cure itself'.[77] The 'cure itself' is nothing other than purges, clysters, issues, blisters and the standard range of treatments for the mad. It is when he turns to melancholy madness, though, that Shaw begins to strike a distinctive note:

> To cure a melancholy madness, requires a different process. This is defined a delirium without a fever, joined with fear and sadness.
>
> The diet here should be moist and lubricating. Wine may be allow'd in moderation; and chearful conversation, a clear air, exercise, and especially riding, contribute to the cure, wherein also emetics, epispastics, cephalic drops, and sternutatories should be freely used; but phlebotomy and purgatives more sparingly...
>
> The cold bath is good in this species also.[78]

Epispastics are applied to the skin to produce blisters, cephalic drops are preparations applied to the head for relief of pain, and sternutatories are anything designed to cause sneezing, which together with emetics represent as unpalatable an array of treatments, especially with the cold bath to come, as any modern mental pharmacopoeia, though probably with less capacity to inflict lasting damage to the liver or any other vital organ. But what makes the link to Baxter, and with him the whole Nonconformist tradition, as opposed to the increasing secularity of orthodox medicine, is the insistence too on social methods of cure. Shaw's 'chearful conversation', like Baxter's '*divert* them from the Thoughts which are their Trouble' and his 'keep them on some other Talk or Business', places a main emphasis on relationships in the cure of the melancholy mad, and recognition, therefore, of the part the patient is capable of occupying, has occupied and will occupy again, within the common intercourse of his circle, once drawn away from the gloomy preoccupations that possess him.

One striking instance of Shaw's consultative practice (and one that I discussed in my book *The Madhouse of Language*)[79] is related in his 1724 publication, *The Juice of the Grape: or, Wine Preferable to Water*, a book that deals with the wine aspect of his treatment as well as the conversational. This cheerful volume contains a number of cases where Shaw has successfully, he reports, induced persons with melancholy or hypochondriac fancies to collude with him, usually without their awareness that they are doing so, in effecting a cure. The most interactive concerns a 'Maiden Gentlewoman of a considerable Fortune' who has been 'for many Years subject to the hysterical Disease (which is the same in Females as the Hippo in Men)'. She has been spending 'Eighty Pounds *per Annum*' on medicines and is 'worn almost to a Skeleton, and appearing with a very meagre Look, and wanting all manner of Appetite' by the time she consults Shaw. 'She was also', says Shaw, 'full of Whimsies and strange Fancies; daily foretelling at what Minute of Time she shou'd expire the next Day; now crying, now laughing, now singing, and then dancing; with many other ridiculous Gestures and Vagaries.'[80] Shaw's approach is to employ his patient's attention in her own treatment, and thereby to make the method of cure the cure itself.

> I said to her with an Air of Chearfulness, Madam, your several Physicians were very ingenious Gentlemen, and have perform'd all within the Compass of Art, so that I find nothing left for me to do in the ordinary Road, suffer me therefore to put you into a new Method, and to shew you how you may become your own Physician. Be pleas'd, Madam, said I, in the Presence of her Sister, to slice the Rind of two *Sevil* Oranges, and set it to steep, for a Day or two, in a Quart Bottle of Sherry; and of this Liquor, when strain'd, take half a Wine-Glass every Morning, fasting; as much an Hour before Dinner, and again the like when you go to Bed. Walk about your Chamber as much as your Strength will permit, let your Diet be light, and easy of Digestion,

eat little at once, but often; and drink a Glass or two of *Mountain* or *Canary* at your Meals; for, continued I, your Stomach is weak, but this Method, if you fail not in the Performance of your Part, will restore your Appetite and give you Strength; the things you now stand most in need of.[81]

To her objection that 'I must have Physick, some Bolusses, and a Cordial, or I shall never live till Morning', Shaw replies that his design is 'to make you your own Physician' and to 'have you take to your self the Care and the Honour of the Cure'.[82] Her agreement, aided by the fact that 'when in her Health' she had had 'a great Inclination to Physick', leads to the desired effect. Shaw, apparently honouring her supposed condition, as well as her distinctive interests, and genuinely engaging her within the envelope of his own 'Chearfulness', successfully seduces his lady away from her current mode of being. She had previously never been 'better pleas'd', he says,

> than in preparing some cordial Water or Conserve; so that she soon came to take Pleasure in making her own Wine, as her Intervals gave her leave. And when I made my next Visit, she propos'd to improve my Medicine, by an Addition of some Spices. This Opportunity I took to recommend Gentian-Root, and a little Galangal, which she complied with, and kept to for several Days; 'till, in fine, her Appetite and Strength began to return, and as these increas'd, her Fits of crying and other Symptoms left her so far, that coming to take the Air on Horseback, and continuing the Use of her bitter Wine, she, without any other Remedy, recover'd a good State of Health, and a fine Complexion, and is at this Day a comely hearty Woman.[83]

The treatment may be nothing but a placebo. Richard Bentall, after all, draws attention to the 'Dodo bird conjecture' with regard to different forms of psychotherapies. The allusion is to Lewis Carroll: 'At last the Dodo said, "Everybody has won and all must have prizes." '[84] That is, all psychotherapies have effect and the differences in their effectiveness could be down to the nature of the 'therapeutic alliance', the likelihood that 'the differences in effectiveness between therapists carrying out the same type of psychotherapy often exceed the differences observed between different psychotherapies'.[85] Shaw, evidently, is supreme at gaining his patients' confidence and at manipulating them in the pursuit of their own good. As such, his skills as a doctor are way ahead of the rudimentary applications available to him.

Shaw was a society physician. He visited his patients, they paid him handsomely, which clearly encouraged him to find methods of dealing with them that worked by stealth rather than authority. At the very end of our period, and into the nineteenth century, the example of the Quaker madhouse, The Retreat, near York, presents a very different part of the social spectrum and a very different set of relations between the patient and the nature of medical authority. As we outlined in the introduction to this book, treatment at The Retreat was based on moral principles, on leading the patient towards a state of self-management through recognition, in spite of his madness, of his obligations towards 'the Family', and on regarding each member as a distinct individual. And just as Shaw draws his gentlewoman away from dwelling on her problems by attracting her into the mechanics of her own cure, so at The Retreat the method, with melancholics at least, is to 'seduce the mind from its favourite but unhappy musings, by bodily exercise, walks, conversation, reading, and other innocent recreations'.[86]

Particularly striking, in Samuel Tuke's *Description of The Retreat*, is the history of a melancholic gardener, 'a patient much afflicted with melancholic and hypochondriacal symptoms', who had walked two hundred miles from his home with a friend in order to be admitted 'by his own request'. The very walk, apparently, had improved his mental condition, and he 'found much less inclination to converse on the absurd and melancholy views of his own state, than he had previously felt'.[87] The superintendent, George Jepson, realizing therefore that employment was beneficial to this man, put him to work in the gardens, where his knowledge showed itself as 'very superior'.[88] Before long, however, he began to show 'a reluctance to regular exertion, and a considerable disposition to wandering, which had been one of the previous features of his complaint':

> The poor man rambled several times from the grounds of the Institution; which, in his state of mind, excited considerable anxiety in the family. Of course it became necessary to confine him more within doors.[89]

The jealousy of the head gardener, apparently, means that he cannot be trusted to keep the man to his tasks, and Jepson therefore takes on this role:

> the superintendent took many opportunities to attend him into the fields or garden, and to engage him for a time in steady manual

labour. As his disorder had increased, it became difficult to induce him to exert himself; but even in this state, when he had been some time employed, he seemed to forget his distressful sensations and ideas, and would converse on general topics with great good sense.[90]

The sensitivity shown to this patient's state of mind (and the writing, though Tuke's, is clearly dependent on the spoken recollections of Jepson, with whom Tuke had several interviews in preparing the *Description*) is remarkable, and indicates possible far-reaching implications of the kind of therapy that, as an ideal, was seen as a goal at The Retreat:

> In this truly pitiable case, the superintendent several times tried the efficacy of long walks, where the greatest variety and attraction of circumstances were presented; but neither these, nor the conversation which he introduced, were able to draw the patient out so effectually from the 'moods of his own mind,' as regular persevering labour. It is not improbable, however, that the superior manner in which the patient was able to execute his work, produced a degree of self-complacency which had a salutary effect; and that, had his education enlarged his curiosity, and encouraged a taste and observation respecting the objects of nature and art, he might have derived much greater advantage, as many patients obviously do, from variety of conversation and society.[91]

Just as Shaw's gentlewoman is to have 'the Honour of the Cure', and so enters into the spirit of her treatment as to suggest her own improvements, so Jepson recognizes the importance not just of occupation but also of self-regard in combating melancholy.

The ideal of self-management, however, is never achieved by this patient who, unlike the gentlewoman, is not in a position to afford 'Eighty Pounds *per Annum*', or anything like it, on buying attention for his condition, much to Jepson's regret:

> The circumstances of this patient did not allow him a separate attendant, and the engagements of the superintendent were too numerous and important, to permit him to devote to this case the time and attention which it seemed to require. He has frequently expressed to me, the strong feelings of regret, which were excited in his mind, by the unsuccessful treatment of this patient . . .[92]

Like many melancholics, apparently, this man was capable of being seduced away from his preoccupations, but only by constant attention from a skilled and sensitive companion, and that could not be afforded. The patient, concludes Tuke, 'after remaining several years in the house, died of an acute inflammation of the bowels. His situation for a considerable time previously to his death, was most deplorable.'[93]

The study of life

In an influential article, 'The Disappearance of the Sick-Man from Medical Cosmology, 1770–1870', published in 1976, the sociologist N. D. Jewson has argued that there took place a distinct shift in medical outlook in the western world between the eighteenth century and the nineteenth, one that remains the basis for medical thought and practice in the modern era. In the period of what he calls 'Bedside Medicine', corresponding largely to the later eighteenth century, the 'morbid forces' responsible for illness

> were located within the context of the total body system rather than within any particular organ or tissue. Furthermore, in addition to physical disposition, all aspects of emotional and spiritual life were deemed relevant to the understanding of the functions of the constitution. It was also believed that each individual had his own unique pattern of bodily events which the practitioner had to discern in each case.[94]

During the first decades of the nineteenth century, however, particularly with the growth of the large Paris hospital schools, 'Bedside Medicine' begins to give way to 'Hospital Medicine', in which

> Medical investigators concentrated upon the accurate diagnosis and classification of cases rather than upon the prognosis and therapy of symptom complexes. The sick-man became a collection of synchronized organs, each with a specialized function.[95]

Our present phase, which Jewson calls 'Laboratory Medicine', develops out of 'Hospital Medicine', which means that now

> The study of medicine is focused upon the recurring, objective, quantitative characteristics of categories of the sick rather than upon the unique, subjective, qualitative differences between individuals. The

universe of medical discourse is seen to be composed of inanimate objects. Living organisms and their ailments are conceptualized as law-like combinations of non-living elements and substances, life and death as physico-chemical processes. The study of life is replaced by the study of organic matter.[96]

In consequence, 'personal rapport in the consultative relationship' and the location of the 'sick-man' 'in all his aspects' as 'the focal point of medical knowledge', his 'perception of himself as a unique individual with specific personal problems of physical and mental health',[97] are all replaced. Instead of rapport there is a 'public guarantee of the safety and efficacy of theories and therapies', and the 'sick-man' himself, 'in all his aspects', is cast in the role of object, or 'patient': 'As such he was designated a passive and uncritical role in the consultative relationship, his main function being to endure and to wait.'[98]

It would be hard to name a single aspect of 'physical health' that has not been unrecognizably improved by the advent of 'Hospital', and subsequently 'Laboratory', medicine, over the days when bloodletting was standard practice for virtually everything, when they took off limbs without anaesthetic, and when Peter Shaw could define a doctor as 'a Man who writes Prescriptions, till the Patient either dies, or is cured by Nature'.[99] How confidently, though, could we assert the same for 'mental health', which cannot be confidently tested for in a laboratory, and especially for depressive illnesses? Did we, instead of gaining, actually lose something irreplaceable, a moment of opportunity, when psychiatry followed other branches of medicine down the road to a more purely scientific future, to 'objective quantitative, characteristics of categories', albeit ones that could lead to seriously discrepant diagnoses depending upon which interview structure one was using, and away from 'the unique, subjective qualitative differences between individuals'? Did treatment of the mind actually sell the pass of patient difference by throwing in so much of its lot with the technology of cure, the pharmacopoeia of the drugs industry?

Kay Redfield Jamison, for one, testifies convincingly and movingly to the crucial role played by medication, as well as the importance of psychotherapy, in bringing about her recovery from severe depression, and in maintaining her sanity:

At this point in my existence I cannot imagine leading a normal life without both taking lithium and having had the benefits of psychotherapy. Lithium presents my seductive but disastrous highs, diminishes my depressions, clears out the wool and webbing from my disordered thinking, slows me down, gentles me out, keeps me from ruining my career and relationships, keeps me out of hospital, alive, and makes psychotherapy possible. But, ineffably, psychotherapy *heals*. It makes some sense of the confusion, reins in the terrifying thoughts and feeling, returns some control and hope and possibility of learning from it all.[100]

It is a powerful statement, and worth bearing in mind in any balanced account of psychiatric practice, both in the United States and in Britain. There is no clear solution, and any attempt to cast drugs as inevitably the villains of the piece will risk disaster.

At points during the eighteenth century, though, before 'Bedside' became 'Hospital', a Shaw, a Woodward, a Jepson and even a Philopirio could, each with distinctive and differing modes of engagement, come close to something 'unique' in their sick men and women and, having deciphered what made them different, make progress towards their healing, unhampered by the advantages of a modern drugs market or a systematized diagnostic structure. Perhaps for the only time in our history, in between the long centuries of religious orthodoxy and the newer reign of established medical procedures, this period, for all its medical impoverishment in so many other ways, seems to have allowed access to a vocabulary in which doctors, or certain doctors, and their patients could, if not speak the same language, where depression was concerned, at least read successfully between each others' lines. In an age like our own, when it takes six policemen to bring a man in for suspected politeness, and when a trained psychiatrist can warn a near suicidal depressive about a possible falling off in his sex drive, it is hard not to believe that medicine took a wrong turn, somewhere, in its attitudes towards the melancholy mind. Perhaps it was when we allowed technology to take over from attention to language and what it might tell us and put our faith in drugs and their production rather than in people.

Notes

Introduction: Depression before Depression

1. Kay Redfield Jamison, *An Unquiet Mind: A Memoir of Moods and Madness* (New York: Alfred Knopf, 1995), pp. 217–18.
2. See, for example, Jennifer Radden (ed.), *The Nature of Melancholy from Aristotle to Kristeva* (Oxford: Oxford University Press, 2000), pp. ix–xi.
3. Samuel Johnson, Letter to Hester Thrale, 28 June 1783, *Letters of Samuel Johnson*, ed. Bruce Redford, The Hyde Edition, 5 vols (Oxford: Oxford University Press, 1994), IV, p. 160.
4. See Cecil Price, *Theatre in the Age of Garrick* (Oxford: Basil Blackwell, 1973), p. 143.
5. Ben Jonson, *Every Man In His Humour* [1601], III i 87–124, *The Complete Plays*, ed. F. E. Schelling, 2 vols (London: Dent, 1964), vol. I, pp. 584–5.
6. James Boswell, *The Hypochondriack* [October 1780], *Boswell's Column, 1777–1783*, ed. Margery Bailey (London: William Kimber, 1951), p. 200.
7. Alexander Pope, *The Rape of the Lock* [1714], *The Poems of Alexander Pope: A One-volume Edition of the Twickenham Text, with Selected Annotations*, ed. John Butt (London: Methuen, 1963), IV 23–4, 35–6 (pp. 232–3).
8. James Boswell, *The Private Papers of James Boswell from Malahide Castle*, ed. Geoffrey Scott and Frederick A. Pottle, 18 vols (New York: privately printed, 1928–34), vol. XVI, p. 57.
9. William Shakespeare, *Hamlet* [1601?], ed. Harold Jenkins (London: Methuen, 1982), I ii 76–86 (pp. 183–4).
10. Ibid., II ii 303–8 (pp. 253–4).
11. Ibid., III i 66, 81–2 (pp. 278, 279–80).
12. Alexander Pope, *Moral Essays: Epistle IV. To Richard Boyle, Earl of Burlington* [1731], *Poems*, ed. Butt, l. 114 (p. 592).
13. Bernard Mandeville, *A Treatise of the Hypochondriack and Hysterick Diseases* [1730], 2nd edn, intro. Stephen H. Good (New York: Scholars' Facsimiles and Reprints, 1976), pp. 46–7.
14. Ibid., pp. 48–9.
15. Michel Foucault, *Madness and Civilization* (Histoire de la folie, 1961), trans. Richard Howard (London: Routledge, 1967), p. 104.
16. Miguel de Cervantes Saavedra, *The Adventures of Don Quixote* [1605, 1615], trans. Tobias Smollett, as *The History and Adventures of the Renowned Don Quixote*, 2 vols (London: A. Millar et al., 1755), vol. I, p. 105.
17. Ibid., vol. I, pp. 380–1.
18. Boswell, *The Hypochondriack*, December 1780, p. 209.
19. Cervantes Saavedra, *Don Quixote*, vol. I, p. 112.
20. Ibid., vol. II, pp. 461–2.
21. John Hill, *Hypochondriasis: A Practical Treatise* [1766], ed. G. S. Rousseau (Los Angeles: Augustan Reprint Society, no. 135, 1966), p. 14.

22. Laurence Sterne, *A Sentimental Journey through France and Italy* [1768], ed. Graham Petrie (Harmondsworth: Penguin Books, 1967), p. 137.
23. Ibid., p. 138.
24. Hannah Allen, *A Narrative of God's Gracious Dealings With that Choice Christian Mrs. Hannah Allen* [1683], in Allan Ingram (ed.), *Voices of Madness: Four Pamphlets, 1683–1796* (Stroud: Sutton Publishing, 1997), p. 16.
25. Ibid., p. 19.
26. Timothy Rogers, *A Discourse Concerning Trouble of Mind and the Disease of Melancholly* (London: Thomas Parkhurst and Thomas Cockerill, 1691), p. v.
27. Richard Baxter, *The Signs and Causes of Melancholy*, collected by Samuel Clifford (London: Cruttenden and Cox, 1716), pp. 81–3.
28. *First Report. Minutes Of Evidence Taken before The Select Committee appointed to consider of Provision being made for the better Regulation of Madhouses, in England* (London: The House of Commons, 1815), p. 95.
29. Samuel Tuke, *Description of The Retreat, An Institution Near York* [1813], ed. Richard Hunter and Ida MacAlpine (London: Dawsons, 1964), pp. 134–5.
30. Boswell, *The Hypochondriack*, December 1780, p. 209.
31. Ibid., p. 210.
32. Tuke, *Description of The Retreat*, pp. 151–2.
33. John Haslam, *Observations on Insanity* (London: Rivington, 1798), pp. 77–80.
34. Anne Finch, 'The Spleen' [1713], *The Poems of Anne Countess of Winchilsea*, ed. Myra Reynolds (Chicago: University of Chicago Press, 1903), p. 252.
35. Ibid., l. 6; Thomas Gray, *Letters*, ed. Paget Toynbee and Leonard Whibley (Oxford: Oxford University Press, 1935), Gray to West, 27 May 1742.
36. See John Bunyan, *The Pilgrim's Progress* [1678, 1684], ed. J. B. Wharey and Roger Sharrock, 2nd edn (Oxford: Clarendon Press, 1962), p. 113.
37. Daniel Defoe, *The Life and Strange and Surprizing Adventures of Robinson Crusoe* [1719], ed. Thomas Keymer (Oxford: Oxford University Press, 1983, 2007), p. 60.

1   Fashionable Melancholy

1. James Makittrick Adair, *Medical Cautions, for the Consideration of Invalids; those especially who resort to Bath: Containing Essays on fashionable disease; the dangerous effects of hot and crouded rooms; an enquiry into the use of medicine during a course of mineral waters; on quacks, and quack medicine, and lady doctors; and an appendix, containing a table of the relative digestibility of foods, with explanatory observations* (Bath: R. Cruttwell; London: J. Dodsley and C. Dilly, 1786).
2. The problem of equating melancholy with depression is perceptively discussed by Jennifer Radden (ed.) in *The Nature of Melancholy from Aristotle to Kristeva* (Oxford: Oxford University Press, 2000), and 'Is This Dame Melancholy?: Equating Today's Depression and Past Melancholia', *Philosophy, Psychiatry, & Psychology* (2003), 10:1, pp. 37–52. Richard Terry discusses the issues arising from labelling 'normal' sadness as melancholy in Chapter 2 of the present volume, following on from the excellent work in the contemporary field of depression studies by Allan V. Horwitz and Jerome C. Wakefield, *The Loss of Sadness: How Psychiatry Transformed Normal Sorrow into Depressive Disorder* (Oxford: Oxford University Press, 2007).

3. For the concept of cultural capital, see Pierre Bourdieu, 'The Forms of Cultural Capital', in J. G. Richardson (ed.), *Handbook for Theory and Research for the Sociology of Education*, trans. R. Nice (New York: Greenwood Press, 1986), pp. 241–58, p. 242.

4. John F. Sena, 'The English Malady: The Idea of Melancholy from 1700–1760', PhD thesis (Princeton University, 1967), p. 64.

5. Ibid., p. 66.

6. Ibid., p. 67.

7. Ibid., p. 68.

8. Ibid., p. 69.

9. See Andrew Scull, *Hysteria: The Biography* (Oxford: Oxford University Press, 2009); and Elaine Showalter, *The Female Malady* (New York: Pantheon, 1987).

10. Sena 'English Malady', p. 70. Henry Fielding's Captain Booth gives a sense of the difficulties of definition in this period when describing the eponymous Amelia's condition: 'A Disorder very common among the Ladies, and our Physicians have not agreed upon its Name. Some call it the Fever on the Spirits, some a nervous Fever, some the Vapours, and some the Hysterics': Fielding, *Amelia* (London: A. Millar, 1752), Vol. 1 Bk III. Ch. VII, p. 218. Roy Porter has argued that the use of the term melancholy in medical works declined in this period in response to the changing conception of the body and a nervous entity and the decline of humouralism: see Porter, *Mind Forg'd Manacles: A History of Madness in England from the Restoration to the Regency* (London: Penguin, 1990), pp. 47–61.

11. Sena, 'English Malady', p. 85.

12. Angus Gowland, 'The Problem of Early Modern Melancholy', *Past & Present*, 191:1 (2006), pp. 77–120, p. 86.

13. Ibid., p. 87.

14. Thomas Willis, *Two Discourses Concerning the Soul of Brutes*, ed. Samuel Pordage (London: Dring, Harper, and Leight, 1683), XI, pp. 188–201, esp. 188–9, 192–3, 199–201; see also Gowland, 'Problem of Early Modern Melancholy', p. 87.

15. Nicholas Robinson, 'Of the Hypp', *Gentleman's Magazine*, 2 (November 1732), pp. 1062–4, p. 1062; Sena, 'English Malady', p. 74.

16. Robinson, 'Of the Hypp', p. 1063.

17. Robinson, 'Of the Hypp', p. 1062.

18. Robinson, 'Of the Hypp', p. 1063. But Robinson notes that if a male 'begins to think he is with Child, or is turn'd into an Egg, a Tea-pot, a Glass Bottle, &c.' (see Alexander Pope's 'Cave of Spleen' in *The Rape of the Lock* for a literary connection) the doctor has to resort to trickery, and Robinson goes on to recount the example of the scholar from Oxford (see Robinson's main text and our previous discussion in this chapter).

19. I am grateful to Charlotte Holden, whose work on this subject is forthcoming, for sharing some of her early research with me and the other participants at our conference on depression in eighteenth-century Britain and Europe.

20. Bernard Mandeville, *Treatise of Hypochondriack and Hysterick Passions* (London: printed for the Author, 1711), p. 270.

21. See Anita Guerrini, *Obesity and Depression: The Life and Times of George Cheyne* (Norman, Oklahoma: University of Oklahoma Press, 2000), p. 105.

22. Stanley W. Jackson, *Melancholia and Depression: From Hippocratic Times to Modern Times* (London: Yale University Press, 1986), p. 4.
23. Aristotle, *Problems* xxx, in Radden (ed.), *Nature of Melancholy*, p. 57.
24. Raymond Klibansky, Erwin Panofsky and Fritz Saxl, *Saturn and Melancholy: Studies in the History of Natural Philosophy, Religion, and Art* (New York: Basic Books, 1964).
25. Radden (ed.), *Nature of Melancholy*, p. 58.
26. See also Lawrence Babb, *The Elizabethan Malady: A Study of Melancholia in English Literature from 1580 to 1642* (East Lansing, Michigan: Michigan State College Press, 1951), p. 59.
27. Arthur Kleinman, *Social Origins of Distress and Disease: Depression, Neurasthenia, and Pain in Modern China* (New Haven, Connecticut: Yale University Press, 1986), p. 44.
28. Ibid., p. 47.
29. Radden, 'Is This Dame Melancholy?', p. 44.
30. Lawlor, *Consumption and Literature*, p. 4; David B. Morris, *Illness and Culture in the Postmodern Age* (Berkeley, California: University of California Press, 1998).
31. Lawlor, *Consumption and Literature*, pp. 4–5.
32. Kay Redfield Jamison, *Touched with Fire: Manic-depressive Illness and the Artistic Termperament* (New York: Free Press, 1993).
33. Radden (ed.), *Nature of Melancholy*, p. 57.
34. Babb, *Elizabethan Maladay*, p. 35; Robert Burton, *The Anatomy of Melancholy* [1621], ed. Thomas C. Faulkner, Nicolas K. Kiessling and Rhonda L. Blair; commentary J. B. Bamborough and Martin Dodsworth, 6 vols (Oxford: Clarendon Press, 1989–2000), vol. 1, p. 243 ('Idleness a Cause').
35. Burton, *Anatomy*, vol. 1, p. 243.
36. Ibid., p. lxix, lines 1–8.
37. Ibid., pp. lxx–lxxi, lines 35–40.
38. Thomas Gray, *Letters*, ed. Paget Toynbee and Leonard Whibley (Oxford: Oxford University Press, 1935), Gray to West, 27 May 1742.
39. See Lawlor, *Consumption and Literature*, p. 30.
40. Burton, *Anatomy*, vol. 1, p. 120.
41. Ibid., p. 121.
42. Ibid., p. 21.
43. Ibid., p. 21.
44. Ibid., p. 21.
45. Ibid., p. 21.
46. Ibid., p. 120.
47. The divergence between evolutionary biology's explanations of depression's causes and sociological and psychoanalytic ones is a case in point. See Horwitz and Wakefield, *Loss of Sadness*, for a lucid discussion of these perspectives.
48. James Boswell, *The Life of Samuel Johnson, LL.D.*, 4 vols, 3rd edn (London: Charles Dilly, 1799), vol. 3, p. 443, Johnson, Letter to Boswell, 27 October 1779.
49. Diane Buie, 'Melancholy and the Idle Lifestyle in the Eighteenth Century', PhD thesis (University of Northumbria, 2010), p. 213. My thanks to Diane Buie for her permission to cite this material.

50. Anonymous, *An Abstract of the Remarkable Passages In the Life of a Private Gentleman* (London: Joseph Downing, 1715), p. 108.
51. Alexander Pope, 'The Rape of the Lock' [1714], *Alexander Pope: The Major Works*, ed. Pat Rogers (Oxford: Oxford University Press, 2006), pp. 77–100, IV, ll. 57–8, 37–8.
52. Boswell, *Life of Samuel Johnson*, vol. 3, p. 208.
53. Samuel Johnson, *The works of Samuel Johnson, LL.D. A new edition, In twelve volumes. With an essay on his life and genius, by Arthur Murphy*, 12 vols (London: printed for T. Longman, B. White and Son, B. Law, J. Dodsley, H. Baldwin, 1792), vol. 1, p. 85.
54. Boswell, *Life of Samuel Johnson*, vol. 1, p. 42.
55. Ibid., p. 171.
56. Ibid., p. 171.
57. Boswell, *Life of Samuel Johnson*, vol. 3, p. 450.
58. Ibid., p. 450.
59. James Boswell, 'The Hypochondriack No. V', *London Magazine* (January 1778), pp. 58–60, p. 58.
60. Ibid., p. 58.
61. Sena, 'English Malady', p. 176; Boswell, 'Hypochondriack No. V', p. 58.
62. Boswell, *Life of Samuel Johnson*, vol. 1, p. 39.
63. Katharine Hodgkin, *Madness in Seventeenth-Century Autobiography* (London: Palgrave, now Basingstoke: Palgrave Macmillan, 2007), pp. 82–3. Heather Meek, 'Creative Hysteria and the Intellectual Woman of Feeling', *Before Depression: The Representation and Culture of Depression in Britain and Europe, 1660–1800 (Figures et culture de la dépression en Grande-Bretagne et en Europe, 1660–1800), European Spectator*, vol. 11, forthcoming.
64. In an intriguing combination of science and literature not uncommon in the eighteenth century, Finch's poem was published within William Stukeley's [1723] *Of the Spleen, Its Description and History, Uses and Diseases, Particularly the Vapors, With Their Remedy* (London: Printed for the Author, 1723), 'Diseases', Sect. XVII, pp. 64–9, including Ann[e] Finch, 'A Pindaric Ode on the Spleen', pp. 6–9; reprinted in facsimile in Clark Lawlor and Akihito Suzuki (eds), *Literature and Science, 1660–1834*, Part I, Vol. 2: *Sciences of Body and Mind* (London: Pickering & Chatto, 2003), pp. 69–72.
65. Lawlor and Suzuki, *Literature and Science*, pp. 70–1.
66. Lawlor and Suzuki, *Literature and Science*, p. 71.
67. Samuel A. Tissot, *Three Essays: First, On the Disorders of People of Fashion, Second, On Diseases Incidental to Literary and Sedentary Persons, Third, On Onanism: Or, a Treatise upon the Disorders produced by Masturbation: or, the Effects of Secret and Excessive Venery*, trans. Francis Bacon Lee, M. Danes, A. Hume, M.D. (Dublin: James Williams, 1772).
68. Ibid., p. 18.
69. Ibid., p. 17.
70. Ibid., pp. 15–17.
71. Ibid., p. 18.
72. Ibid., p. 18.
73. Ibid., p. 18.
74. Ibid., pp. 18–19.
75. Ibid., p. 19.

76. Ibid., p. 21.
77. Ibid., p. 21.
78. Ibid., p. 20.
79. Ibid., pp. 14, 15.
80. Ibid., p. 27.
81. Ibid., p. 27.
82. Ibid., p. 28.
83. Ibid., p. 28.
84. Ibid., p. 28.
85. Ibid., p. 28.
86. Ibid., p. 29.
87. Thomas Trotter, *A View of the Nervous Temperament; being a practical enquiry into the increasing prevalence, prevention, and treatment of those diseases commonly called nervous, bilious, stomach and liver complaints; indigestion; low spirits; gout, etc,* 2nd edn (London: Printed by Edw. Walker, Newcastle, for Longman, Hurst, Rees, and Orme, 1807).
88. Tissot, *Three Essays,* p. 31.
89. Ibid., p. 31.
90. Ibid., p. 31.
91. Ibid., p. 32.
92. See G. S. Rousseau, 'Nerves, Spirits, and Fibres: Towards Defining the Origins of Sensibility', in R. F. Brissenden and J. C. Eade (eds), *Studies in the Eighteenth Century* (Toronto: University of Toronto Press, 1976), pp. 137–57; G. J. Barker-Benfield, *The Culture of Sensibility: Sex and Society in Eighteenth-Century Britain* (London: Routledge, 1992).
93. Tissot, *Three Essays,* p. 33.
94. Ibid., pp. 32–3.
95. Ibid., p. 34.
96. Ibid., p. 34.
97. Ibid., p. 35.
98. Ibid., p. 35.
99. G. S. Rousseau, 'Towards a Semiotics of the Nerve', *Nervous Acts: Essays on Literature, Culture and Sensibility* (Basingstoke: Palgrave Macmillan, 2004), p. 261.
100. See Guenter B. Risse, 'Medicine in the Age of the Enlightenment', in Andrew Wear (ed.), *Medicine in Society: Historical Essays* (Cambridge: Cambridge University Press, 1992), pp. 149–98, pp. 160–3.
101. The literature on sensibility is vast, but a useful start would include: Barker-Benfield, *Culture of Sensibility*; John Mullan, *Sentiment and Sociability: The Language of Feeling in the Eighteenth Century* (Oxford: Clarendon Press, 1988); Ann Jessie van Sant, *Eighteenth-Century Sensibility and the Novel: The Senses in Social Context* (Cambridge: Cambridge University Press, 1993); Janet Todd, *Sensibility: An Introduction* (London: Methuen, 1986); Anne C. Vila, *Enlightenment and Pathology: Sensibility in the Literature and Medicine of Eighteenth-Century France* (Baltimore: Johns Hopkins University Press, 1998).
102. See Lawlor, *Consumption and Literature,* pp. 105–7.
103. See Roy Porter, 'Introduction', in *Thomas Trotter, An Essay, Medical, Philosophical, and Chemical, on Drunkenness, and its Effects on the Human Body* (London: Routledge, 1988), pp. ix–xl, p. xxxiv.

104. Risse, 'Medicine in the Age of the Enlightenment', pp. 163–5.
105. Ibid., pp. 165–7.
106. Eleanor M. Sickels, *The Gloomy Egoist: Moods and Themes of Melancholy from Gray to Keats* (New York: Columbia University Press, 1932).
107. Charlotte Turner Smith, *The Collected Letters of Charlotte Smith*, ed. Judith P. Stanton (Bloomington, Indiana: Indiana University Press, 2003), p. 627. My thanks to Pauline Morris for her insights into Charlotte Smith's depression.

2   Philosophical Melancholy

1. See entry of 15 April 1802, in Dorothy Wordsworth, *The Grasmere and Alfoxden Journals*, ed. Pamela Woof (Oxford: Oxford University Press, 2002), p. 85.
2. William Wordsworth, 'Daffodils', *The Poetical Works of William Wordsworth*, ed. E. de Selincourt, 2nd edn, 5 vols (Oxford: Clarendon Press, 1952), 2: 216–17, lines 13–16, 20.
3. For discussion of issues of creative ownership in the relationship between William and Dorothy, see John Barrell, 'The Uses of Dorothy: "The Language of the Sense" in "Tintern Abbey" ', *Poetry, Language and Politics* (Manchester: Manchester University Press, 1988); Jane Spencer, *Literary Relations: Kinship and the Canon 1660–1830* (Oxford: Oxford University Press, 2005), pp. 164–87; and Tilar Mazzeo, *Plagiarism and Literary Property in the Romantic Period* (Philadelphia: University of Pennsylvania Press, 2007), pp. 62–70.
4. Cited from Laurence Sterne, *The Life and Opinions of Tristram Shandy, Gentleman* [1759–67], ed. Melvyn New and Joan New, with an introductory essay by Christopher Ricks (London: Penguin Books, 2003), p. 451.
5. See Geoffrey Chaucer, 'The Miller's Tale', *The Riverside Chaucer*, gen. ed. Larry D. Benson, 3rd edn (Oxford: Oxford University Press, 1987), Fragment 1, line 3339 (p. 70).
6. See Samuel Johnson, *A Dictionary of the English Language* (London: W. Strahan et al., 1755) – Sorrow: 'Grief; pain from something past; sadness; mourning. Sorrow is not commonly understood as the effect of present evil, but of lost good.'
7. The changing denotation of these two terms is discussed in Richard Terry, *Mock-Heroic from Butler to Cowper: An English Genre and Discourse* (Aldershot and Burlington, Vermont: Ashgate, 2005), pp. 171–72.
8. Eric G. Wilson, *Against Happiness: In Praise of Melancholy* (New York: Sarah Crichton Books, 2008), p. 34. For other works dealing with the role of happiness and sadness in human life, see: Harvie Ferguson, *Religious Transformation in Western Society: The End of Happiness* (Routledge: London, 1992); and Lewis Wolpert, *Malignant Sadness: The Anatomy of Depression*, 3rd edn (London: Faber and Faber, 2006).
9. The statistic is taken from Allan V. Horwitz and Jerome C. Wakefield, *The Loss of Sadness: How Psychiatry Transformed Natural Sorrow into Depressive Disorder* (Oxford: Oxford University Press, 2007), p. 4.
10. Andrew Solomon, *The Noonday Demon: An Anatomy of Depression* (London: Vintage, 2002), p. 443.

11. Horwitz and Wakefield, *Loss of Sadness*, pp. 8–9, 14.
12. See ibid., pp. 27–52, 52.
13. Timothie Bright, *A Treatise of Melancholie* (London: Thomas Vautrollier, 1586), p. 90.
14. Felix Platter, *Praxeos Medicae* (1602), cited from Horwitz and Wakefield, *Loss of Sadness*, p. 63.
15. Robert Burton, *The Anatomy of Malancholy* (1621), cited from Horwitz and Wakefield, *Loss of Sadness*, pp. 63–4. For general discussion of depression as 'sadness without cause', see Stanley W. Jackson, *Melancholia and Depression: From Hippocratic Times to Modern Times* (New Haven: Yale University Press, 1986), pp. 315–17; Jennifer Radden (ed.), 'Introduction', *The Nature of Melancholy: From Aristotle to Kristeva* (Oxford: Oxford University Press, 2000), pp. 37–9; and Horwitz and Wakefield, *Loss of Sadness*, pp. 53–71.
16. Johnson's first definition is 'A disease, supposed to proceed from a redundance of black bile'; his second, 'A kindness [sic] of madness, in which the mind is always fixed on one object'; and his third, 'A gloomy, pensive, discontented temper'.
17. Cited from Elizabeth Singer Rowe, *The Works of Mrs. Elizabeth Rowe: including original poems and translations by Mr. T. Rowe. To which is added the life of the author*, 4 vols (London: John and Arthur Arch, 1796), 3: 123.
18. 'On the anniversary return of the day on which Mr *Rowe* died', in Rowe, *Works*, 3: 125.
19. The poem is cited from David Nichol Smith (ed.), *The Oxford Book of Eighteenth Century Verse* (Oxford: Clarendon Press, 1926), pp. 309–12.
20. Cited from Samuel Johnson, *The Rambler*, in *The Yale Edition of the Works of Samuel Johnson*, ed. W. J. Bate and Albrecht B. Strauss (New Haven: Yale University Press, 1958–), 3: 252–8, 254.
21. Ibid., 3: 255, 258.
22. Isaac Barrow, *Of Contentment, Patience and Resignation to the Will of God* (London: J. Round, J. Tonson and W. Taylor, 1714), p. 14.
23. Ibid., pp. 20, 22.
24. Joseph Addison and Richard Steele, *Spectator* 574 [30 July 1714], *The Spectator*, ed. Donald F. Bond, 5 vols (Oxford: Clarendon Press, 1965), vol. 5, pp. 561–5, pp. 561–2.
25. Addison and Steele, *Spectator* 387 [24 May 1712], *Spectator*, vol. 3, pp. 451–4, pp. 451, 452.
26. Ibid., pp. 453–4. For a poetic invocation of the merits of cheerfulness, see Mark Akenside, 'Hymn to Chearfulness', *Odes on Several Subjects* (London: R. Dodsley, 1745), pp. 23–31. He calls upon the abstraction to help him counteract his 'mind's oppressive gloom' (p. 23).
27. Richard Allestree, *The Art of Patience and Balm of Gilead under all Afflictions* (London: John Marshall, 1702), pp. 80–5.
28. Cited from Henry Fielding [1743], *Miscellanies*, ed. Henry Knight Miller, Wesleyan Edition of the Works of Henry Fielding, vol. 1 (Oxford: Clarendon Press, 1967–), see pp. 212–25, 224.
29. Ibid., p. 215.
30. Ibid., p. 225. Fielding's 'Remedy' and the consolatory tradition to which it belongs are discussed in Henry Knight Miller, *Essays on Fielding's Miscellanies: A Commentary on Volume One* (Princeton, New Jersey: Princeton University

Press, 1961), pp. 228–71. For a general discussion of the relation between melancholy and bereavement, see the chapter on 'Grief, Mourning, and Melancholia', in Jackson, *Melancholia and Depression*, pp. 311–24.

31. Fielding, *Miscellanies*, p. 212.
32. John Locke, *Essays on the Law of Nature . . . together with Transcripts from Locke's Shorthand in his Journal for 1676*, ed. W. von Leydon (Oxford: Clarendon Press, 1970), pp. 265, 267–8.
33. David Hartley, *Observations on Man, His Frame, His Duty, and his Expectations*, 2 vols (London: James Leake and William Frederick, 1749), 1: 399.
34. James Beattie, *Dissertations Moral and Critical . . . On Memory and Imagination* (Dublin: Exshaw et al., 1783), pp. 241–2, 243–7.
35. Hartley, *Observations*, 1: 399.
36. Beattie, *Dissertations Moral and Critical*, p. 245.
37. The letter, entitled 'A Kind of History of My Life', is printed as an appendix to David Fate Norton (ed.), *The Cambridge Companion to Hume* (Cambridge: Cambridge University Press, 1993), pp. 345–50. Here, pp. 347, 345, 350.
38. Ibid., pp. 346–8.
39. David Hume, *A Treatise of Human Nature* [1739–40], ed. David Fate Norton and Mary J. Norton (Oxford: Oxford University Press, 2001), 1. 4. 7. para. 1 (pp. 171–2). Hume's melancholy scepticism is discussed in John Sitter, *Literary Loneliness in Mid-Eighteenth-Century England* (Ithaca, New York: Cornell University Press, 1982), pp. 27–32.
40. Hume, *Treatise of Human Nature*, pp. 174, 176.
41. Ibid., pp. 172, 175.
42. Eleanor M. Sickels, *The Gloomy Egoist: Modes and Themes of Melancholy from Gray to Keats* (New York: Columbia University Press, 1932). The phrase 'deliberate melancholizing' is used on p. 40. For other significant treatments of melancholy poetry in the mid-eighteenth century, see: Amy Louise Reed, *The Background of Gray's Elegy: A Study in the Taste for Melancholy Poetry, 1700–1751* (New York: Columbia University Press, 1924; New York: Russell and Russell, 1962); and Sitter, *Literary Loneliness*.
43. Cited from James Thomson, *The Seasons* [1730], ed. James Sambrook (Oxford: Oxford University Press, 1981), p. 186.
44. Letter to Dr. William Cranstoun, probably sent September or October 1725, cited from James Thomson, *James Thomson (1700–1748): Letters and Documents*, ed. Alan Dugald McKillop (Lawrence, Kansas: University of Kansas Press, 1958), p. 16.
45. For Thomson's 'Hymn on Solitude', see James Thomson, *Liberty, The Castle of Indolence and Other Poems*, ed. James Sambrook (Oxford: Clarendon Press, 1986), pp. 280–3. For Warton's 'Ode to Solitude', see Joseph Warton, *Odes on Various Subjects* (London: R. Dodsley, 1746), pp. 46–7.
46. Joseph Warton, *The Enthusiast or the Lover of Nature* (London: R. Dodsley, 1744), pp. 14–15.
47. Thomas Warton, *The Pleasures of Melancholy. A Poem* (London: R. Dodsley, 1747), sig. A2.
48. Thomson, *Seasons*, pp. 84–6.
49. For a larger consideration of the received knowledge about druids during the eighteenth century and their role within literary culture, see Richard Terry, 'Thomson and the Druids', in Richard Terry (ed.), *James Thomson:*

Essays for the Tercentenary (Liverpool: Liverpool University Press, 2000), pp. 141–63.

50. Warton, *Pleasures of Melancholy*, p. 23.
51. Cited from William Shakespeare, *Hamlet* [1601?], ed. Harold Jenkins (London: Methuen, 1982), III. i. 84–5 (p. 280).
52. Dryden's remark comes from his *Discourse Concerning the Original and Progress of Satire* [1693], *Of Dramatic Poesy and Other Critical Essays*, ed. George Watson, 2 vols (London: J. M. Dent & Sons, 1962), 2: 122; Cooke's comment is made in *Comedian*, no. 9 [December 1732], p. 5, cited here from Martin C. Battestin with Ruthe R. Battestin, *Henry Fielding: A Life* (London: Routledge, 1989), p. 156.
53. The general relevance of stoic ideas to the study of melancholia is discussed by Jackson, *Melancholia and Depression*, see pp. 17–19, 313–14.
54. On the tenets of Stoic thought, see Tad Brennan, *The Stoic Life: Emotions, Duties and Fate* (Oxford: Clarendon Press, 2005). A range of Stoic ideas are documented and explicated in A. A. Long and D. N. Sedley, *The Hellenistic Philosophers*, 2 vols (Cambridge: Cambridge University Press, 1987), see Vol. 1, *Translation of the Principal Sources with Philosophical Commentary*.
55. See 'Thoughts on Various Subjects', in Jonathan Swift, *Prose Writings*, ed. Herbert Davis et al., 14 vols (Oxford: Blackwell, 1939–74), 1: 244; Samuel Johnson (1971), 'The Vanity of Human Wishes' [1749], *The Complete English Poems*, ed. J. D. Fleeman (London: Penguin, 1971), line 344, p. 91.
56. The exemplum is discussed, and various sources for it noted, in Miller, *Essays on Fielding's Miscellanies*, p. 231.
57. Richard Fenton, 'Ode to the Scavoir Vivre Club', *Poems*, 2 vols (London: E. and T. Williams, 1790), 1: 23; Alexander Pope, *Essay on Man* [1733–34], *The Twickenham Edition of the Poems of Alexander Pope*, ed. John Butt et al., 11 vols (London: Methuen, 1939–69), vol. 3 (1950), ed. Maynard Mack, II. 101, p. 67.
58. Cited from Miller, *Essays on Fielding's Miscellanies*, p. 241. For discussion of the attempt to reconcile Stoic and Christian consolatory wisdom during the early modern period, see Andrea Brady, *English Funerary Elegy in the Seventeenth Century: Laws in Mourning* (Basingstoke: Palgrave, now Palgrave Macmillan, 2006), pp. 37–43.
59. Henry Fielding, *The History of Tom Jones: A Foundling* [1749], ed. Martin C. Battestin, Wesleyan, Edition of the Works of Henry Fielding, 2 vols (Oxford: Clarendon Press, 1974), vol. 1, pp. 116–17.
60. Oliver Goldsmith, *The Vicar of Wakefield* [1766], ed. Arthur Friedman, with an introduction and notes by Robert L. Mack, World's Classics (Oxford: Oxford University Press, 2006), see Chapter XXIX ('The equal dealings of providence demonstrated with regard to the happy and the miserable here below'), pp. 144–7, 144.
61. Henry Fielding, *Joseph Andrews* [1742], ed. Martin C. Battestin, Wesleyan Edition of the Works of Henry Fielding (Oxford: Clarendon Press, 1967), see pp. 264–7 ('Containing the Exhortations of Parson *Adams* to his Friend in Affliction') and 308–10.
62. Samuel Johnson, *The History of Rasselas, Prince of Abissinia* [1759], ed. Paul Goring (London: Penguin, 2007), pp. 45–7.
63. Fielding, *History of Tom Jones*, vol. 1, p. 230.

64. For a survey of anti-stoical opinion, see Henry W. Sams, 'Anti-Stoicism in Seventeenth- and Eighteenth-Century England', *Studies in Philology*, 41 1 (1944), pp. 65–78.
65. Lady Mary Chudleigh, *Essays upon Several Subjects in Prose and Verse* (London: R. Bonwicke et al., 1710), p. 65.
66. Ibid., pp. 67, 75.
67. Ibid., pp. 76, 77, 78–9.
68. See Roger Lonsdale (ed.), *Eighteenth-Century Women Poets* (Oxford: Oxford University Press, 1990), p. 190. The poem itself occupies pp. 192–4.
69. Greville's poem is discussed in Janet Todd, *Sensibility: An Introduction* (London: Methuen, 1986), pp. 61–3. The tenor of the poem was rejected in Helen Maria Williams, 'To Sensibility', *Poems*, 2 vols (London: Thomas Cadell, 1786), vol. 1, pp. 21–8.
70. For discussion of the competition between stoic and Christian impulses, see Ian Jack, 'Gray's *Elegy* Reconsidered', in Frederick W. Hilles and Harold Bloom (eds), *From Sensibility to Romanticism: Essays Presented to Frederick A. Pottle* (New York: Oxford University Press, 1965), pp. 139–69; Roger Lonsdale's headnote to the poem in his edition of *The Poems of Thomas Gray, William Collins and Oliver Goldsmith*, Longmans' Annotated English Poets (London: Longman, 1969), pp. 103–16; and more recently in Eric Parisot's unpublished PhD thesis 'The Paths of Glory: Authority, Agency and Aesthetics in Mid-Eighteenth-Century Graveyard Poetry' (University of Melbourne, 2008), see pp. 114–17, on 'Stoic Resolve in Gray's "Stanzas" '.
71. The poem is cited from Lonsdale (ed.), *Poems of Thomas Gray, William Collins and Oliver Goldsmith*, pp. 117–40, pp. 313–17.
72. Lonsdale (ed.), *Poems of Thomas Gray, William Collins and Oliver Goldsmith*, p. 131.

3 'Strange Contrarys': Figures of Melancholy in Eighteenth-Century Poetry

1. Henri Michaux, *Plume précédé de Lointain intérieur* (Paris: Gallimard, [1938] 1963).
2. Yves Bonnefoy, 'La mélancolie, la folie, le génie – la poésie', in Jean Clair (ed.), *Mélancolie, génie et folie en Occident* (Paris: Réunion des musées nationaux/Gallimard, 2005), pp. 14–22. The exhibition took place at the Galéries nationales du Grand Palais, Paris (10 October 2005–16 January 2006) and the Neue Nationalgalerie, Berlin (17 February–7 May 2006).
3. Ibid., p. 15. All translations from French into English in the chapter are my own.
4. Ibid., p. 16.
5. Anne Amend, 'Mélancolie', in Michel Delon (ed.), *Dictionnaire européen des Lumières* (Paris: Presses Universitaires de France, 1997), pp. 698–701, p. 698.
6. John F. Sena, 'Melancholy in Anne Finch and Elizabeth Carter: The Ambivalence of an Idea', in *The Yearbook of English Studies* (1971), vol. 1, pp. 108–19, p. 116.
7. Nick Groom argues that 'the seventeen-year-old Thomas Chatterton died from an accidental overdose of arsenic and opium (laudanum)' (Nick Groom,

'Chatterton, Thomas (1752–1770)', in *Oxford Dictionary of National Biography* (Oxford: Oxford University Press, 2004), vol. 11, p. 240).

8. Among whom may be mentioned Richard Blackmore, the author of *A Treatise of the Spleen and Vapours* (1725) and *A Critical Dissertation upon the Spleen* (1725), and John Armstrong whose didactic poem *The Art of Preserving Health* appeared in 1744. See Michelle Faubert, *Rhyming Reason: The Poetry of Romantic-Era Psychologists* (London: Pickering and Chatto, 2009).

9. Sigmund Freud, 'Mourning and Melancholia' [1917], *On Metapsychology: The Theory of Psychoanalysis*, trans. James Strachey, Penguin Freud Library, vol. 11, gen. ed. Angela Richards (London: Penguin, 1984), pp. 245–68.

10. William B. Ober, 'Madness and Poetry: A Note on Collins, Cowper, and Smart' [1970], *Boswell's Clap and Other Essays: Medical Analyses of Literary Men's Afflictions* (Carbondale and Edwardsville, Illinois: Southern Illinois University Press, 1979), pp. 137–92, p. 153.

11. Dustin Griffin, 'Collins, William (1721–1759)', in *Oxford Dictionary of National Biography* (Oxford: Oxford University Press, 2004), vol. 12, p. 740.

12. Alexander Pope edited his friend and fellow Scriblerian Thomas Parnell's *Poems on Several Occasions* (London: Printed for B. Lintot, 1722).

13. Amy Louise Reed, *The Background of Gray's Elegy: A Study in the Taste for Melancholy Poetry, 1700–51* (New York: Columbia University Press, 1924); Eleanor M. Sickels, *The Gloomy Egoist: Moods and Themes of Melancholy from Gray to Keats* (New York: Columbia University Press, 1932).

14. Published in December 1699 but has an imprint dated 1700.

15. Anne Kingsmill Finch's *The Spleen. A Pindarick Ode* was printed anonymously in Charles Gildon (ed.), *A New Miscellany of Original Poems, On Several Occasions* (1701). A slightly modified version appeared in 1709 with Pomfret's *A Prospect of Death*, and the poem was finally to appear under Anne Finch's name (the Right Honourable Anne, Countess of Winchilsea) in *Miscellany Poems, On Several Occasions* of 1713. The 1713 poem, the text quoted here, is the same as that published in 1701.

16. Samuel Johnson wrote: 'Perhaps no composition in our language has been oftener perused than Pomfret's *Choice*' (Samuel Johnson, 'Pomfret', *Lives of the English Poets* [1779–81], ed. George Birkbeck Hill (Oxford: Clarendon Press, 1905), vol. 1, p. 301.

17. David Fairer and Christine Gerrard (eds), *Eighteenth-Century Poetry: An Annotated Anthology* (Oxford and Malden, Massachusetts: Blackwell, 1999), p. 1.

18. Johnson, *Lives*, vol. 1, p. 302.

19. The text of *The Choice* (1700) is that of the first edition, reproduced in Fairer and Gerrard (eds), *Eighteenth-Century Poetry*, pp. 1–5.

20. All quotations from Young's *Night Thoughts* are referenced in the text and follow Stephen Cornford's 1989 edition, *Edward Young: 'Night Thoughts'* (Cambridge: Cambridge University Press).

21. John Pomfret, *Miscellany Poems, On Several Occasions* (London: Printed for John Place, 1702).

22. Ibid.

23. Alexander Pope, *The Rape of the Lock and Other Poems* [1714], ed. Geoffrey Tillotson, Twickenham Edition, vol. 2 (London and New York: Routledge, 1993).

24. Thomas Gray, *Elegy Written in a Country Churchyard* [1751], in Roger Lonsdale (ed.), *The Poems of Thomas Gray, William Collins, Oliver Goldsmith* (London: Longman, 1969).

25. As Myra Reynolds notes: 'Her poem on the *The Spleen* is of the first-hand, naturalistic order' (Anne Kingsmill Finch (Countess of Winchilsea), *The Poems of Anne Countess of Winchilsea*, ed. Myra Reynolds (Chicago: University of Chicago Press, 1903), p. xliii).

26. Finch, *Poems*, pp. 15–16.

27. Anne Kingsmill Finch (Countess of Winchilsea) *Miscellany Poems, On Several Occasions* (London: Printed for John Barber, 1713).

28. Jonathan Culler, *The Pursuit of Signs: Semiotics, Literature, Deconstruction* (London: Routledge & Kegan Paul, 1981), p. 136.

29. Ibid., p. 139.

30. Charles H. Hinnant observes in his study *The Poetry of Anne Finch: An Essay in Interpretation* (Newark, Delaware: University of Delaware Press; London and Toronto: Associated University Presses, 1994), p. 218: 'throughout the poem—and not just in the opening lines—the spleen is a presence that can be conceived only as an absence—as an entity that is accessible to us only through its effects, never as a cause'.

31. William Stukeley, *Of the Spleen, Its Description and History, Uses and Diseases, Particularly the Vapors, with their Remedy* (London: Printed for the Author, 1723).

32. Ibid., p. 3.

33. Ibid., p. 2.

34. Ibid., p. 73.

35. Ibid., p. 75.

36. Ibid., p. 73.

37. Finch, *Poems of Anne Countess of Winchilsea*, p. 15.

38. Matthew Green, *The Spleen, and Other Poems* with a Prefatory Essay by J. Aikin, M.D. (London: Printed for T. Cadell, junr. and W. Davies, [1737] 1796).

39. Reed, *Background of Gray's Elegy*, p. 26.

40. The poem was addressed to Green's friend Mr. Cuthbert Jackson and published posthumously by Richard Glover in the year of Green's death, 1737.

41. Stukeley, *Of the Spleen*, p. 72.

42. John Armstrong, *The Art of Preserving Health: A Poem* (London: Printed for A. Millar, 1744).

43. John Milton, *Complete Shorter Poems*, ed. John Carey, Longman Annotated English Poets (London: Longman, 1978), pp. 130–46. First published in 1645, 'L'Allegro' and 'Il Penseroso' are thought to have been composed around 1631.

44. See note 5.

45. Lawrence Babb, *The Elizabethan Malady: A Study of Melancholia in English Literature from 1580 to 1642* (East Lansing, Michigan: Michigan State College Press, 1951), p. 178.

46. It would appear that in Milton's time too, even on poetic themes, one of the most effective ways to insult someone was to attack their parents and origins.

47. John Dart, 'Westminster Abbey: A Poem' (1721). The version quoted here is that published in John Dart, *Westmonasterium or The History and Antiquities of The Abbey Church of St. Peter's Westminster* (London: Printed for T. Bowles and J. Bowles, 1742).

48. Émile Benveniste, ''Remarques sur la fonction du langage dans la découverte freudienne', *Problèmes de linguistique générale I* (Paris: Gallimard, 1966), p. 84.

49. Edward Young, *Cynthio: On the Death of John Brydges, Marquis of Carnarvon* (London: Printed for J. Roberts in Warwick-Lane, 1727). John Brydges, son of the 1st Duke of Chandos, died from smallpox in 1727, aged 24.

50. John Milton, *Poems Upon Several Occasions, English, Italian, and Latin, With Translations, by John Milton*, with notes critical and explanatory, and other illustrations, by Thomas Warton (London: Printed for J. Dodsley, 1785).

51. The text cited is not that of 1747 but a revised version that appeared in Dodsley's *Collection of Poems by Several Hands*, vol. 4 (London, 1755), and reproduced with notes and commentary in Fairer and Gerrard's *Eighteenth-Century Poetry*, pp. 367–74.

52. David B. Morris, 'A Poetry of Absence', in John Sitter (ed.), *The Cambridge Companion to Eighteenth-Century Poetry* (Cambridge: Cambridge University Press, 2001), pp. 225–48, p. 234.

53. See Robert N. Essick and Morton D. Paley, 'Introduction: The Poet in the Graveyard', *Robert Blair's 'The Grave' Illustrated by William Blake: A Study with Facsimile* (London: Scolar Press, 1982), pp. 3–17.

54. Mary S. Hall, 'On Light in Young's *Night Thoughts*', *Philological Quarterly*, 48 (1969), pp. 452–63.

55. '[D]ive deep into thy bosom; learn the depth, extent, biass, and full fort of thy mind; contract full intimacy with the stranger within thee…' (*Edward Young's 'Conjectures on Original Composition'* [1759], ed. Edith J. Morley (Manchester: Manchester University Press, 1918), p. 24).

56. In 'Night the Eighth' Young addresses the ocean thus: 'Too faithful Mirror! How dost thou reflect, The melancholy Face of human Life!' (8. 174–5).

57. James E. May, 'Young, Edward (*bap.* 1683, *d.* 1765)', in *Oxford Dictionary of National Biography* (Oxford: Oxford University Press, 2004), vol. 60, pp. 882–7, p. 885.

58. Freud, 'Mourning and Melancholia', p. 254. This brings to mind the famous definition of melancholy, cited by Robert Burton: 'The common sort define it to bee *a kinde of dotage without a feaver, having for his ordinary companions, feare, and sadnesse, without any apparant occasion*' (Robert Burton, *The Anatomy of Melancholy* [1621], ed. Thomas C. Faulkner, Nicolas K. Kiessling and Rhonda L. Blair; commentary J. B. Bamborough and Martin Dodsworth, 6 vols (Oxford: Clarendon Press, 1989–2000), vol. 1, p. 162).

59. Freud, 'Mourning and Melancholia', p. 253.

60. The Boyle Lectures were a series of annual lectures or sermons in defence of natural and revealed theology, delivered from 1692 to 1732, and named after the natural philosopher and writer Robert Boyle (1627–91) who made provision for them in his will. Their purpose was to defend Christianity against attacks from its enemies and detractors: '*proving the Christian Religion against notorious Infidels, viz., Atheists, Theists, Pagans, Jews, and Mahometans*'. Boyle's codicil, annexed to his will and dated 28 July 1691, is quoted (in a footnote) in the 'Dedication' (n. pag.) to Thomas Tenison, Lord

Archbishop of Canterbury, in William Derham, *Physico-Theology* (London: Printed for W. Innys, 1713; facs. edn, Hildesheim; New York: Georg Olms, 1976).

61. Basil Willey, *The Eighteenth Century Background: Studies on the Idea of Nature in the Thought of the Period* (London: Chatto and Windus, [1940] 1963), p. 28. The reference is to Thomas Burnet's *Sacred Theory of the Earth* or *Telluris Theoria Sacra* (London: 1681?–89?).

62. 'I gazed, myself creating what I saw' (William Cowper, 'The Winter Evening' (4.290), *The Task, A Poem, In Six Books* [1785], *The Poems of William Cowper*, vol. 2, *1782–5*, ed. John D. Baird and Charles Ryskamp (Oxford: Clarendon Press, 1995)).

63. See 'Lines Written a Few Miles above Tintern Abbey', where Wordsworth at once remembers and forgets a reference to Young in a note to line 107 (William Wordsworth and S. T. Coleridge, *Lyrical Ballads* [1798], 2nd edn, ed. R. L. Brett and A. R. Jones (London and New York: Routledge, 1991)).

64. Young, *Night Thoughts*, p. 147.

65. Ibid., p. 177.

66. Job 7:11: 'Therefore I will not refrain my mouth; I will speak in the anguish of my spirit; I will complain in the bitterness of my soul' (King James Version).

67. William Cowper, 'Retirement', *The Poems of William Cowper*, vol. 1, *1748–82*, ed. John D. Baird and Charles Ryskamp (Oxford: Clarendon Press, 1980), p. 381.

68. Cowper, 'To Mr. Newton On His Return From Ramsgate', composed 12–13 October 1780, *Poems of William Cowper*, vol. 1, p. 224.

69. John D. Baird and Charles Ryskamp, 'Cowper and His Poetry, 1731–82', in William Cowper, *The Poems of William Cowper*, ed. Baird and Ryskamp, vol. 1, pp. ix–xxv, p. xx.

70. Cowper, 'Doom'd, as I am, in solitude to waste', ibid., pp. 62–3.

71. Cowper, 'To Mr. Newton On His Return From Ramsgate', ibid., p. 224.

72. Cowper, 'Hatred and Vengeance, My Eternal Portion', ibid., pp. 209–10.

73. Cowper, 'The Cast-away', *The Poems of William Cowper*, vol. 3, *1785–1800*, ed. Baird and Ryskamp (1995), pp. 214–16.

74. John Norris, *A Collection of Miscellanies: Consisting of Poems, Essays, Discourses, and Letters, Occasionally Written* (Oxford, 1687); facs. edn (New York and London: Garland Publishing, 1978), pp. 130–1.

75. John Keats, 'Ode on Melancholy', *John Keats: The Complete Poems*, ed. John Barnard, 2nd edn (Harmondsworth: Penguin, 1977).

4 Despair, Melancholy and the Novel

1. See Robert Burton, *The Anatomy of Melancholy* [1621], ed. Thomas C. Faulkner, Nicolas K. Kiesling and Rhonda L. Blair; commentary J. B. Bamborough and Martin Dodsworth, 6 vols (Oxford: Clarendon Press, 1989–2000); and Richard Baxter, *Preservatives Against Melancholy and Overmuch Sorrow* (London: Printed for W.R., 1713).

2. See Jeremy Schmidt, *Melancholy and the Care of the Soul: Religion, Moral Philosophy and Madness in Early Modern England* (Aldershot and Burlington, Vermont: Ashgate, 2007).

3. See particularly: G. A. Starr, *Defoe and Spiritual Autobiography* (Princeton, New Jersey: Princeton University Press, 1965); and also J. Paul Hunter, *The Reluctant Pilgrim: Defoe's Emblematic Method and Quest for Form in Robinson Crusoe* (Baltimore: Johns Hopkins University Press, 1966).

4. Vera J. Camden, a psychoanalyst as well as literary critic, makes a similar point when she notes that in *Grace Abounding's* narrative, 'Bunyan places his account of his encounter with the Ranters following his meeting with the poor women of Bedford. The Bedford Baptists and the Ranters project the extremes of his own bipolarity' (Vera J. Camden, 'Blasphemy and the Problem of Self in *Grace Abounding*', *Bunyan Studies*, 1:2 (1989), pp. 5–21, p. 8).

5. See Schmidt, *Melancholy and the Care of the Soul*, pp. 54–7, for example.

6. John Bunyan, *The Pilgrim's Progress* [1678, 1684], ed. J. B. Wharey and Roger Sharrock, 2nd edn (Oxford: Clarendon Press, 1960), p. 113.

7. Daniel Defoe, *The Life and Strange and Surprizing Adventures of Robinson Crusoe* [1719], ed. Thomas Keymer (Oxford: Oxford University Press, 1983, 2007), p. 60.

8. For a discussion of this side of Defoe's practice, see Laura A. Curtis, *The Elusive Daniel Defoe* (London and Totowa, New Jersey: Vision Press and Barnes and Noble, 1984).

9. John Bunyan, *Grace Abounding to the Chief of Sinners* [1666], ed. Roger Sharrock (Oxford: Clarendon Press, 1962), p. 43.

10. Ibid., p. 72.

11. The impact of predestination on Bunyan's fiction is discussed in: John Stachniewski, *The Persecutory Imagination: English Puritanism and the Literature of Religious Despair* (Oxford: Clarendon Press, 1991); and Stuart Sim, *Negotiations with Paradox: Narrative Practice and Narrative Form in Bunyan and Defoe* (Hemel Hempstead: Harvester Wheatsheaf, 1990).

12. John Calvin, *The Institutes of the Christian Religion*, I–II [1536], trans. Ford Lewis Battles (London: SCM Press, 1961), I, p. 957.

13. Bunyan, *Grace Abounding*, p. 31.

14. See Michael B. First, Robert L. Spitzer, Miriam Gibbon and Janet B. W. Williams, *Structured Clinical Interview for DSM–IV Axis I Disorders – Clinician Version (SCID–CV)* (Washington DC: American Psychiatric Press, 1997).

15. Bunyan, *Pilgrim's Progress*, p. 14.

16. Ibid., pp. 114–15.

17. Ibid., p. 157.

18. Defoe, *Robinson Crusoe*, p. 6.

19. Daniel Defoe, *The Fortunes and Misfortunes of the Famous Moll Flanders* [1722], ed. G. A. Starr (Oxford: Oxford University Press, 1981), p. 5.

20. Ibid., p. 283.

21. Defoe, *Robinson Crusoe*, p. 83.

22. Ibid.

23. Daniel Defoe, *Roxana: Or, The Fortunate Mistress* [1724], ed. John Mullan (Oxford: Oxford University Press, 1996), p. 201.

24. Ibid., p. 302.

25. Ibid., pp. 329–30.

26. Ibid., p. 202.

27. Samuel Richardson, *Pamela; Or, Virtue Rewarded* [1740], ed. Peter Sabor (Harmondsworth: Penguin, 1980), p. 213.
28. Ibid., p. 505.
29. Samuel Richardson, *Clarissa: Or, The History of a Young Lady* [1747–48], ed. Angus Ross (London: Penguin, 1985), p. 1375.
30. Ibid., p. 879.
31. Ibid., p. 1249.
32. Ibid., p. 1304.
33. Fanny Burney, *Cecilia, or Memoirs of an Heiress* [1782], ed. Peter Sabor and Margaret Anne Doody (Oxford: Oxford University Press, 1988), p. 911.
34. Ibid., p. 561.
35. Ibid., p. 418.
36. Ibid., p. 941.
37. Mary Hays, *The Victim of Prejudice* [1799], ed. Eleanor Ty (Peterborough, Ontario: Broadview Press, 1994), p. 1.
38. Ibid., p. 3.
39. Ibid., p. 67.
40. Ibid., p. 168.
41. Ibid., p. 170.
42. Henry Fielding, *The History of Tom Jones, a Foundling* [1749], ed. John Bender and Simon Stern (Oxford: Oxford University Press, 1996), p. 67.
43. Ibid., p. 417.
44. Ibid., p. 421.
45. Ibid., pp. 419–20.
46. Jonathan Swift, *Gulliver's Travels* [1726], ed. Claude Rawson (Oxford: Oxford University Press, 2005), p. 276.
47. Sarah Fielding, *The Adventures of David Simple* [1744, 1753], ed. Malcolm Kelsall (Oxford: Oxford University Press, 1969), p. 37.
48. Ibid., pp. 304, 305.
49. Ibid., p. 430.
50. Ibid., p. 432.
51. Linda Bree, *Sarah Fielding* (New York: Twayne, 1998), p. 39.
52. John Norris, *A Collection of Miscellanies: Consisting of Poems, Essays, Discourses, and Letters, Occasionally Written* (Oxford, 1687); facs. edn (New York and London: Garland, 1978), p. 130.
53. See Peter Green, ' "Job's Whole Stock of Asses": The Fiction of Laurence Sterne and the Theodicy Debate', PhD thesis (Open University, 2010).
54. Laurence Sterne, *The Life and Opinions of Tristram Shandy, Gentleman* [1759–67], ed. Ian Campbell Ross (Oxford: Oxford University Press, 1983), p. 10.
55. For a discussion of the philosophical side of Sterne's work, see: John Traugott, *Tristram Shandy's World: Sterne's Philosophical Rhetoric* (Berkeley and Los Angeles: University of California Press, 1954); and James E. Swearingen, *Reflexivity in Tristram Shandy: An Essay in Phenomenological Criticism* (New Haven, Connecticut, and London: Yale University Press, 1977).
56. Sterne, *Tristram Shandy*, ed. Jack, pp. 54–5.
57. Ibid., p. 224.
58. Ibid., p. 233.

59. Ibid., p. 285.
60. Laurence Sterne, *A Sentimental Journey Through France and Italy* [1768], ed. Ian Jack (London: Oxford University Press, 1968), p. 43.
61. Ibid., p. 18.
62. Ibid., pp. 18–19.
63. Ibid., p. 21.
64. A. Alvarez, 'Introduction', in Laurence Sterne, *A Sentimental Journey through France and Italy* [1768], ed. Graham Petrie (Harmondsworth: Penguin, 1967), pp. 7–19, p. 17; William Empson, *The Last Pain, The Complete Poems of William Empson*, ed. John Haffenden (London: Allen Lane, 2000), l.36.
65. Pamela Clemit, *The Godwinian Novel: The Rational Fictions of Godwin, Brockden Brown, Mary Shelley* (Oxford: Clarendon Press, 1993), p. 55.
66. William Godwin, *Caleb Williams* [1794], ed. David McCracken (Oxford: Oxford University Press, 1977), p. 325.
67. Ibid., Appendix I, p. 331.
68. James Hogg, *The Private Memoirs and Confessions of a Justified Sinner* [1824], ed. John Carey (Oxford: Oxford University Press, 1990), p. 115.
69. Ibid., p. 100.
70. Ibid., p. 146.
71. Ibid., p. 240.
72. Bunyan, *Pilgrim's Progress*, p. 118.
73. Samuel Johnson, Letter to Hester Thrale, 28 June 1783, *Letters of Samuel Johnson*, ed. Bruce Redford, The Hyde Edition, 5 vols (Oxford: Oxford University Press, 1994), IV, p. 160.
74. Hays, *Victim*, p. 3.

5   Melancholy, Medicine, Mad Moon and Marriage: Autobiographical Expressions of Depression

1. Roy Porter (ed.), *Rewriting the Self: Stories from the Renaissance to the Present* (London and New York: Routledge, 1997), p. 1.
2. Paul Delaney, *British Autobiography in the Seventeenth Century* (London: Routledge & Kegan Paul, 1969), p. 12.
3. Ibid., p. 13.
4. Michel de Montaigne, *The Essays of Michael Seigneur de Montaigne, Translated into English, 4 Volumes, 8ᵗʰ Edition* (Dublin: James Potts, 1760), III, 226.
5. Bethan Benwell and Elizabeth Stokoe, *Discourse and Identity* (Edinburgh: Edinburgh University Press, 2006), p. 2.
6. Felicity A. Nussbaum, *The Autobiographical Subject: Gender and Ideology in Eighteenth-Century England* (Baltimore, Maryland, and London: Johns Hopkins University Press, 1989), p. xii.
7. Ibid., p. xiii.
8. Katharine Hodgkin, *Madness in Seventeenth-Century Autobiography* (London: Palgrave, now Basingstoke: Palgrave Macmillan, 2007), p. 26.
9. Elspeth Graham, ' "Oppression Makes a Wise Man Mad": The Suffering of the Self in Autobiographical Tradition', in Henk Dragstra, Sheila Ottway and Helen Wilcox (eds), *Betraying Our Selves: Forms of Self-Representation in*

Early Modern English Texts (London and New York: Macmillan/St. Martins Press, 2000), pp. 197–214, p. 198.

10. Stanley W. Jackson, 'Acedia the Sin and Its Relationship to Sorrow and Melancholia', in Arthur Kleinman and Byron Good (eds), *Culture and Depression: Studies in the Anthropology and Cross-cultural Psychiatry of Affect and Disorder* (Los Angeles and London: University of California Press, 1985), pp. 43–62, p. 43.

11. Hodgkin, *Madness*, p. 40.

12. Ibid., p. 23.

13. D. Bruce Hindmarsh, *The Evangelical Conversion Narrative: Spiritual Autobiography in Early Modern England* (Oxford: Oxford University Press, 2007), pp. 51–2.

14. Ibid., p. 246.

15. Hodgkin, *Madness*, p. 23; Nussbaum, *Autobiographical Subject*, p. 64.

16. Nussbaum, *Autobiographical Subject*, p. 64.

17. Ibid., p. 64.

18. Hodgkin, *Madness*, p. 25.

19. Anonymous, *An Abstract of the Remarkable Passages In the Life of a Private Gentleman* (London: Joseph Downing, 1715), p. 7.

20. Ibid., p. 8.

21. Anonymous, *Onania; of the Heinous Sin of Self-Pollution, and All its Frightful Consequences, in both SEXES, Fourth Edition* (London: Printed for the Author, 1718), p. 1.

22. Quoted in Richard Hunter and Ida Macalpine (eds), *Three Hundred Years of Psychiatry 1535–1860* (Oxford: Oxford University Press, 1961), p. 240.

23. Anonymous, *An Abstract*, p. 8.

24. Ibid., p. 8.

25. Ibid., pp. 24, 21.

26. Ibid., p. 20.

27. Ibid., p. 21.

28. Ibid., p. 71.

29. Ibid., p. 63.

30. Ibid., p. 70.

31. Ibid., p. 76.

32. Ibid., p. 6.

33. Ibid., p. 82.

34. Ibid., p. 86.

35. Ibid., p. 41.

36. Ibid., p. 87.

37. Ibid., p. 85.

38. Ibid., p. 108.

39. Ibid., p. 112.

40. Ibid., p. 42.

41. Ibid., p. 107.

42. Bernard Mandeville, *Fable of the Bees; or Private Vices Publick Benefits* (London: J. Roberts, 1714), p. 63.

43. Anonymous, *An Abstract*, p. iv.

44. Nussbaum, *Autobiographical Subject*, p. xiv.

45. Michel Foucault, *The History of Sexuality, Vol. 1: An Introduction*, trans. Robert Hurley (New York: Vintage Books, 1980), p. 58.
46. Ulrich Beck, *Risk Society: Towards a New Modernity* (London: Sage, 1992), cited in Benwell and Stokoe, *Discourse and Identity*, p. 22.
47. Hindmarsh, *Evangelical Conversion Narrative*, p. 299.
48. Nussbaum, *Autobiographical Subject*, p. 176.
49. Anne Dutton, *A Brief Account of the Gracious Dealings of God, in Three Parts* (London: J. Hart, 1750), III, 178 (emphasis in the original as will be in all subsequent quotations unless otherwise stated).
50. Ibid., II, 16.
51. Ibid., II, 29; II, 142.
52. Hindmarsh, *Evangelical Conversion Narrative*, p. 299.
53. Dutton, *Brief Account*, II, 35.
54. Frank Tallis, *Love Sick: Love as a Mental Illness* (London: Century, 2004), p. 54.
55. Robert Burton, *The Anatomy of Melancholy* [1621], ed. Thomas C. Faulkner, Nicolas K. Kiessling and Rhonda L. Blair; commentary J. B. Bamborough and Martin Dodsworth, 6 vols (Oxford: Clarendon Press, 1989–2000 (1994)), III, 163.
56. Lesel Dawson, *Lovesickness and Gender in Early Modern English Literature* (Oxford: Oxford University Press, 2008), pp. 17–18.
57. Ibid., p. 20.
58. Dutton, *Brief Account*, III, 25.
59. Ibid., I, 19.
60. Ibid., I, 13.
61. Ibid., II, 38.
62. Ibid., I, 40; II, 35.
63. Dawson, *Lovesickness*, p. 23.
64. Hodgkin, *Madness*, p. 7.
65. Dawson, *Lovesickness*, p. 92.
66. Ibid., p. 23.
67. Dutton, *Brief Accounts*, I, 8.
68. Ibid., I, 9.
69. Ibid., I, 12.
70. Ibid., I, 31.
71. Ibid., II, 43; III, 23.
72. Ibid., III, 119.
73. Ibid., II, 95.
74. Ibid., III, 8–9.
75. Ibid., II, 150.
76. Hodgkin, *Madness*, p. 27.
77. Quoted in Carolyn A. Barros, *Autobiography: Narrative of Transformation* (Ann Arbor, Michigan: The University of Michigan Press, 1998), p. 208.
78. Ibid.
79. Hodgkin, *Madness*, p. 20.
80. Allan Ingram, *The Madhouse of Language: Writing and Reading Madness in the Eighteenth Century* (London: Routledge, 1991), p. 120.
81. Nussbaum, *Autobiographical Subject*, pp. xiii, xxi.
82. Linda Anderson, *Autobiography* (London: Routledge, 2001), p. 35.

83. Ramona Wray, 'Depressive Patterns and Textual Solutions in Seventeenth-Century Women's Autobiography', conference paper presented at *Before Depression: The Representation and Culture of Depression in Britain and Europe, 1660–1800*, 19–21 June 2008, Northumbria University. This paper is due to be published as an article in a forthcoming edition of the *European Spectator*.

84. Ibid.

85. Elizabeth Freke, *The Remembrances of Elizabeth Freke, 1671–1714*, ed. Raymond A. Anselment (Cambridge: Cambridge University Press, 2001), p. 37. The original spelling is preserved in this entry and all subsequent ones.

86. Ibid., p. 42.

87. Ibid., p. 2.

88. Anselment's edited edition of Freke's diary contains both versions.

89. Freke, *Remembrances*, p. 39.

90. Raymond A. Anselment, 'Elizabeth Freke's Remembrances: Reconstructing a Self', *Tulsa Studies in Women's Literature*, 16:1 (1997), pp. 57–75, p. 59.

91. Freke, *Remembrances*, p. 39.

92. Ibid., p. 49.

93. Ibid.

94. Ibid.

95. Ibid. The text in between < brackets> is inserts by Anselment in his edition of Freke's *Remembrances* to show deletions, insertions and the like, see n. 88.

96. Effie Botonaki, 'Early Modern Women's Diaries and Closets', in Dan Doll and Jessica Munns (eds), *Recording and Reordering: Essays on the Seventeenth- and Eighteenth-Century Diary and Journal* (Lewisberg, Pennsylvania: Bucknell University Press, 2006), pp. 43–64, p. 55.

97. Freke, *Remembrances*, pp. 89–90.

98. Ibid., p. 76.

99. Ibid., p. 61.

100. Ibid.

101. Ibid., p. 81.

102. Ibid., p. 14.

103. Anselment notes that Freke is possibly referring to a John Jefferie of Neatishead, ten miles north-east of Norwich, who is described by a contemporary source as 'a local quack of great repute', and who may also be the same Dr. Jefferies that advertised in the *Norwich Gazette*. She also called in a Dr. Jefferies for her husband's final sickness. For the sake of consistency I will retain Freke's own spelling when referring again to this doctor.

104. Freke, *Remembrances*, p. 98.

105. Clark Lawlor, *Consumption and Literature: The Making of the Romantic Disease* (London and New York, now Basingstoke: Palgrave Macmillan, 2006), p. 21.

106. Ibid., pp. 19–20.

107. Freke, *Remembrances*, p. 98.

108. Lawlor, *Consumption*, p. 20.

109. Anselment, 'Reconstructing a Self', p. 58.

110. Botonaki, 'Diaries and Closets', p. 43.

111. Nussbaum, *Autobiographical Subject*, p. 126.

112. Harriet Blodgett, *Centuries of Female Days: Englishwomen's Private Diaries* (New Brunswick, New Jersey: Rutgers University Press, 1967), p. 211.

113. Edmund Harrold, *The Diary of Edmund Harrold, Wigmaker of Manchester 1712–1715*, ed. Craig Horner (Aldershot and Burlington, Vermont: Ashgate, 2008), p. x.
114. Ibid., pp. 16–17. All inserts in [brackets] are editorial inserts made by Craig Horner (see above note). My own inserts within quotations from the primary text will therefore appear as {brackets}. Harrold uses the term 'ramble' throughout his diary to denote a prolonged drinking session.
115. Ibid., p. 17.
116. Ibid., p. 85.
117. Ibid., pp. 78–9.
118. Hannah Barker, 'Soul, Purse and Family: Middling and Lower-Class Masculinity in Eighteenth-Century Manchester', *Social History*, 33:1 (2008), pp. 12–35, p. 26). I would like to take this opportunity to thank Hannah Barker for sharing this paper with me before it was published.
119. Harrold, *Diary*, p. 14.
120. Ibid., p. 18.
121. Ibid., p. xiii.
122. Barker, 'Soul, Purse and Family', p. 27.
123. Ibid.
124. Ibid.
125. Harrold, *Diary*, p. 115.
126. Nussbaum, *Autobiographical Subject*, p. 87.
127. Anderson, *Autobiography*, p. 35.
128. Harrold, *Diary*, p. 119.
129. Ibid., p. 123.
130. Stuart Sherman, 'Diary and Autobiography', in John Richetti (ed.), *The Cambridge History of Literature 1660–1780* (Cambridge: Cambridge University Press, 2005), pp. 649–72, p. 651.
131. Roy Porter, *Madmen: A Social History of Madhouses, Mad-Doctors & Lunatics* (Stroud: Tempus, 2004), p. 102.

6 Deciphering Difference: A Study in Medical Literacy

1. Richard Bentall, *Doctoring the Mind: Why Psychiatric Treatments Fail* (London: Allen Lane, 2009), pp. 111–12.
2. Daniel Freeman, 'Health in Mind', *The Guardian* (25 July 2009), p. 6.
3. Bentall, *Doctoring the Mind*, p. 111.
4. Freeman, 'Health in Mind'.
5. Sally Vickers, 'See a psychiatrist? Are you mad?', *The Observer* (21 June 2009), p. 19.
6. Bryan Appleyard, 'Have we lost all reason?', *Sunday Times* (5 July 2009), 'Culture', p. 45.
7. Cited in Roy Porter, *Mind-Forg'd Manacles: A History of Madness in England from the Restoration to the Regency* (London: The Athlone Press, 1987), p. 2, citing Max Byrd, *Visits to Bedlam* (Columbia, South Carolina: University of South Carolina Press, 1974), p. 75.
8. James Boswell, *Boswell's Column, 1777–1783*, ed. Margery Bailey (London: William Kimber, 1951), p. 209.

9. Bentall, *Doctoring the Mind*, p. 13.

10. Ibid., p. 208.

11. Ibid., p. 99.

12. Ibid., p. 100, citing J. van Os et al., 'A Comparison of the Utility of Dimensional and Categorical Representations of Psychosis', *Psychological Medicine*, 29 (1999), pp. 595–606.

13. Bentall, *Doctoring the Mind*, p. 83.

14. Ibid., p. 97.

15. Michael B. First, Robert L. Spitzer, Miriam Gibbon and Janet B. W. Williams, *Structures Clinical Interview for DSM–IV Axis I Disorders – Clinician Version (SCID–CV)* (Washington DC: American Psychiatric Press, 1997), pp. 2–4.

16. Bentall, *Doctoring the Mind*, p. 14.

17. Ibid., p. 275.

18. Lewis Wolpert, *Malignant Sadness: The Anatomy of Depression*, 3rd edn (London: Faber and Faber, 2006), p. 139.

19. Ibid., pp. 139–40.

20. William Styron, *Darkness Visible: A Memoir of Madness* (London: Jonathan Cape, 1991; repr. London: Vintage, 2001), p. 51.

21. Ibid., pp. 52–3.

22. Ibid., p. 53.

23. Ibid., pp. 53–4.

24. Ibid., p. 55.

25. Ibid., pp. 59–60.

26. Ibid., p. 60.

27. Ibid., pp. 66–7.

28. Bentall, *Doctoring the Mind*, p. 271.

29. John F. Sena, 'The English Malady: The Idea of Melancholy from 1700–1760', PhD thesis (Princeton University, 1967), p. 64.

30. John Woodward, *Select Cases, and Consultations, in Physick* (London: The Royal Society, 1757), p. 31.

31. Ibid., p. 43.

32. Ibid.

33. Ibid., p. 41.

34. Nicholas Robinson, *A New System of the Spleen, Vapours, and Hypochondriack Melancholy* (London: A. Bettesworth, W. Innys and C. Rivington, 1729), pp. 386–7.

35. Ibid., p. 391.

36. George Cheyne, *The English Malady: or, A Treatise of Nervous Diseases of all Kinds* (London: G. Strahan and J. Leake, 1733), pp. 134, 136.

37. Sir Richard Blackmore, *A Treatise of the Spleen and Vapours: or, Hypochondriacal and Hysterical Affections* (London: J. Pemberton, 1726), p. 167.

38. Ibid., p. 169.

39. George Young, *A Treatise on Opium, Founded upon Practical Observations* (London: A. Millar, 1753), pp. 101–8.

40. Ibid., p. 106.

41. John Birch, *A Letter to Mr. George Adams, on the Subject of Medical Electricity* (London, for the author, 1792), pp. 5–6.

42. Ibid., p. 4.

43. Ibid., p. 45.
44. Ibid., p. 47.
45. Ibid., p. 49.
46. Ibid., p. 47.
47. Ibid., pp. 48–9.
48. Ibid., p. 6.
49. See, for example, the death by drowning of a patient in Bethlem, one Fowler, about which the Parliamentary Enquiry questioned the then apothecary to Bethlem, John Haslam, in 1815. *First Report. Minutes of Evidence Taken before The Select Committee appointed to consider of Provision being made for the better Regulation of Madhouses, in England* (London: The House of Commons, 1815), p. 104.
50. Bernard Mandeville, *A Treatise of the Hypochondriack and Hysterick Diseases* [1730], 2nd edn, intro. Stephen H. Good (New York: Scholars' Facsimiles and Reprints, 1976), p. ix.
51. Ibid., p. 45.
52. Ibid., pp. 45–6.
53. Ibid., p. 343.
54. Ibid.
55. Ibid., p. 344.
56. Ibid., pp. 344–5.
57. Ibid., p. 282.
58. Samuel Clifford, *The Signs and Causes of Melancholy . . . Collected out of the Works of Mr. Richard Baxter* (London: S. Cruttenden and T. Cox, 1716), p. xlvii.
59. Ibid., pp. 5–6.
60. Ibid., pp. 120–2.
61. George Trosse, *The Life of the Reverend Mr. George Trosse* [1714], ed. A. W. Brink (Montreal: McGill-Queen's University Press, 1974), p. 96.
62. Ibid.
63. Michelle Faubert, *Rhyming Reason: The Poetry of Romantic-Era Psychologists* (London: Pickering and Chatto, 2009), p. 47.
64. William Cowper, *Memoir of the Early Life of William Cowper, Esq.* [1816], in Dale Peterson (ed.), *A Mad People's History of Madness* (Pittsburgh: University of Pittsburgh Press, 1982), pp. 65–73, p. 69.
65. Ibid., pp. 69–70.
66. Ibid., p. 71.
67. Ibid.
68. Ibid., p. 72.
69. Ibid., p. 73.
70. Faubert, *Rhyming Reason*, p. 42.
71. Faubert, *Rhyming Reason*, p. 43, citing R. Walsh, 'The Life of Dr Cotton', in *The Works of the British Poets, with Lives of the Authors* (Boston, Massachusetts: Charles Ewer and Timothy Bedlington, 1822), vol. 35, pp. 313–17, pp. 315–16.
72. Faubert, *Rhyming Reason*, p. 47.
73. See, for example, Dorothy Porter and Roy Porter, *Patient's Progress: Doctors and Doctoring in Eighteenth-Century England* (London: Polity Press, 1989), pp. 72–8, including a section on 'Prescribing by Post'.

74. Woodward, *Select Cases*, p. 21.
75. William Law, *A Serious Call to a Devout and Holy Life* (London: William Innys, 1729), p. 483. I am grateful to Diane Buie for alerting me to this passage.
76. Trosse, *Life*, p. 47.
77. Peter Shaw, *A New Practice of Physic* [1726] (London: Thomas Longman and Thomas Shewell, 6th edn, 1745), 2 vols, vol. 1, p. 28.
78. Ibid., 1, 29.
79. Allan Ingram, *The Madhouse of Language: Writing and Reading Madness in the Eighteenth Century* (London: Routledge, 1991), pp. 50–3. Parts of the present discussion are also touched upon in different sections of this book.
80. Peter Shaw, *The Juice of the Grape: or, Wine Preferable to Water* (London: W. Lewis, 1724), p. 43.
81. Ibid., pp. 43–4.
82. Ibid., p. 44.
83. Ibid., p. 45.
84. Lewis Carroll, *Alice's Adventures in Wonderland . . .* [1865] (London: Nonesuch Press, 1963), p. 27.
85. Bental, *Doctoring the Mind*, pp. 248–9 and n.
86. Samuel Tuke, *Description of The Retreat, An Institution Near York* [1813], ed. Richard Hunter and Ida MacAlpine (London: Dawsons, 1964), pp. 151–2.
87. Ibid., p. 152.
88. Ibid., p. 153.
89. Ibid., pp. 153–4.
90. Ibid., p. 154.
91. Ibid., p. 155.
92. Ibid.
93. Ibid., p. 156.
94. N. D. Jewson, 'The Disappearance of the Sick-Man from Medical Cosmology, 1770–1870', *Sociology*, 10 (1976), pp. 225–44, p. 229.
95. Ibid.
96. Ibid., p. 232.
97. Ibid., p. 234.
98. Ibid., p. 235.
99. Peter Shaw, *The Reflector: Representing Human Affairs, As they are; and may be improved* (London: T. Longman, 1750), p. 227.
100. Kay Redfield Jamison, *An Unquiet Mind: A Memoir of Moods and Madness* (New York: Alfred A. Knopf, 1995), pp. 88–9.

Bibliography

Primary sources

Adair, James Makittrick, *Medical Cautions, for the Consideration of Invalids; those especially who resort to Bath: Containing Essays on fashionable disease; the dangerous effects of hot and crouded rooms; an enquiry into the use of medicine during a course of mineral waters; on quacks, and quack medicine, and lady doctors; and an appendix, containing a table of the relative digestibility of foods, with explanatory observations* (Bath: R. Cruttwell; London: J. Dodsley and C. Dilly, 1786).

Addison, Joseph, and Richard Steele, *The Spectator*, ed. Donald F. Bond, 5 vols (Oxford: Clarendon Press, 1965).

Akenside, Mark, *Odes on Several Subjects* (London: R. Dodsley, 1745).

Allen, Hannah, *A Narrative of God's Gracious Dealings With that Choice Christian Mrs. Hannah Allen* [1683], in Allan Ingram (ed.), *Voices of Madness: Four Pamphlets, 1683–1796* (Stroud: Sutton Publishing, 1997).

Allestree, Richard, *The Art of Patience and Balm of Gilead under all Afflictions* (London: John Marshall, 1702).

Anonymous, *An Abstract of the Remarkable Passages In the Life of a Private Gentleman* (London: Joseph Downing, 1715).

Anonymous, *Onania; of the Heinous Sin of Self-Pollution, and All its Frightful Consequences, in both SEXES, Fourth Edition* (London: Printed for the Author, 1718).

Armstrong, John, *The Art of Preserving Health: A Poem* (London: Printed for A. Millar, 1744).

Barrow, Isaac, *Of Contentment, Patience and Resignation to the Will of God* (London: J. Round, J. Tonson and W. Taylor, 1714).

Baxter, Richard, *Preservatives Against Melancholy and Overmuch Sorrow* (London: Printed for W. R., 1713).

—— *The Signs and Causes of Melancholy*, collected by Samuel Clifford (London: Cruttenden and Cox, 1716).

Beattie, James, *Dissertations Moral and Critical...On Memory and Imagination* (Dublin: Exshaw et al., 1783).

Birch, John, *A Letter to Mr. George Adams, on the Subject of Medical Electricity* (London: for the author, 1792).

Blackmore, Sir Richard, *A Treatise of the Spleen and Vapours: or, Hypochondriacal and Hysterical Affections* (London: J. Pemberton, 1726).

Boswell, James, *Boswell's Column, 1777–1783*, ed. Margery Bailey (London: William Kimber, 1951).

—— 'The Hypochondriack No. V', *London Magazine* (January 1778), pp. 58–60.

—— *The Life of Samuel Johnson, LL.D*, 4 vols (London: 1799).

—— *The Private Papers of James Boswell from Malahide Castle*, ed. Geoffrey Scott and Frederick A. Pottle, 18 vols (New York: privately printed, 1928–34).

Bright, Timothie, *A Treatise of Melancholie* (London: Thomas Vautrollier, 1586).

Bunyan, John, *Grace Abounding to the Chief of Sinners* [1666], ed. Roger Sharrock (Oxford: Clarendon Press, 1962).

—— *The Pilgrim's Progress* [1678, 1684], ed. James Blanton Wharey and Roger Sharrock, 2nd edn (Oxford: Clarendon Press, 1960).

Burnet, Thomas, *Sacred Theory of the Earth* or *Telluris Theoria Sacra* (London: 1681?–89?).

Burney, Fanny, *Cecilia, or Memoirs of an Heiress* [1782], ed. Peter Sabor and Margaret Anne Doody (Oxford: Oxford University Press, 1988).

Burton, Robert, *The Anatomy of Melancholy* [1621], ed. Thomas C. Faulkner, Nicolas K. Kiessling and Rhonda L. Blair; commentary J. B. Bamborough and Martin Dodsworth, 6 vols (Oxford: Clarendon Press, 1989–2000).

Calvin, John, *The Institutes of the Christian Religion*, I–II [1536], trans. Ford Lewis Battles (London: SCM Press, 1961).

Carroll, Lewis, *Alice's Adventures in Wonderland...* [1865] (London: Nonesuch Press, 1963).

Cervantes Saavedra, Miguel de [1605, 1615], *The Adventures of Don Quixote*, trans. Tobias Smollett, as *The History and Adventures of the Renowned Don Quixote* (London: A. Millar et al., 1715).

Chaucer, Geoffrey, *The Riverside Chaucer*, gen. ed. Larry D. Benson, 3rd edn (Oxford: Oxford University Press, 1987).

Cheyne, George, *The English Malady: or, A Treatise of Nervous Diseases of all Kinds* (London: G. Strahan and J. Leake, 1733).

Chudleigh, Lady Mary, *Essays upon Several Subjects in Prose and Verse* (London: R. Bonwicke et al., 1710).

Clifford, Samuel, *The Signs and Causes of Melancholy...Collected out of the Works of Mr. Richard Baxter* (London: S. Cruttenden and T. Cox, 1716).

Cowper, William, *Memoir of the Early Life of William Cowper, Esq.* [1816], in Dale Peterson (ed.), *A Mad People's History of Madness* (Pittsburgh: University of Pittsburgh Press, 1982), pp. 65–73.

—— *The Poems of William Cowper, 1748–1800*, 3 vols, ed. John D. Baird and Charles Ryskamp (Oxford: Clarendon Press, 1980–95).

Dart, John, 'Westminster Abbey: A Poem' [1721], *Westmonasterium or The History and Antiquities of The Abbey Church of St. Peter's Westminster* (London: Printed for T. Bowles and J. Bowles, 1742).

Defoe, Daniel, *The Fortunes and Misfortunes of the Famous Moll Flanders* [1722], ed. G. A. Starr (Oxford: Oxford University Press, 1981).

—— *The Life and Strange and Surprizing Adventures of Robinson Crusoe* [1719], ed. Thomas Keymer (Oxford: Oxford University Press, 1983, 2007).

—— *Roxana: Or, The Fortunate Mistress* [1724], ed. John Mullan (Oxford: Oxford University Press, 1996).

Derham, William, *Physico-Theology* (London: Printed for W. Innys, 1713; facs. edn, Hildesheim; New York: Georg Olms, 1976).

Dodsley, Robert, *Collections of Poems by several hands*, vol. 4 (London, 1755).

Dryden, John, *Of Dramatic Poesy and Other Critical Essays*, ed. George Watson, 2 vols (London: J. M. Dent, 1962).

Dutton, Anne, *A Brief Account of the Gracious Dealings of God, in Three Parts* (London: J. Hart, 1750).

Empson, William, *The Complete Poems of William Empson*, ed. John Haffenden (London: Allen Lane, 2000).

Fairer, David, and Christine Gerrard (eds), *Eighteenth-Century Poetry: An Annotated Anthology* (Oxford and Malden, Massachusetts: Blackwell, 1999).

Fenton, Richard, *Poems*, 2 vols (London: E. and T. Williams, 1790).

Fielding, Henry, *Amelia* (London: A. Millar, 1752).

—— *The History of Tom Jones: A Foundling* [1749], ed. Martin C. Battestin, Wesleyan Edition of the Works of Henry Fielding, 2 vols (Oxford: Clarendon Press, 1974).

—— *The History of Tom Jones, a Foundling* [1749], ed. John Bender and Simon Stern (Oxford: Oxford University Press, 1996).

—— *Joseph Andrews* [1742], ed. Martin C. Battestin, Wesleyan Edition of the Works of Henry Fielding (Oxford: Clarendon Press, 1967).

—— *Miscellanies*, ed. Henry Knight Miller, Wesleyan Edition of the Works of Henry Fielding, vol. 1 (Oxford: Clarendon Press, 1967–).

Fielding, Sarah, *The Adventures of David Simple* [1744, 1753], ed. Malcolm Kelsall (Oxford: Oxford University Press, 1969).

Finch, Anne Kingsmill (Countess of Winchilsea), *Miscellany Poems, On Several Occasions* (London: Printed for John Barber, 1713).

—— *The Poems of Anne Countess of Winchilsea*, ed. Myra Reynolds (Chicago: University of Chicago Press, 1903).

First Report. Minutes of Evidence Taken before The Select Committee appointed to consider of Provision being made for the better Regulation of Madhouses, in England (London: The House of Commons, 1815).

Freke, Elizabeth, *The Remembrances of Elizabeth Freke, 1671–1714*, ed. Raymond A. Anselment (Cambridge: Cambridge University Press, 2001).

Freud, Sigmund, 'Mourning and Melancholia' [1917], *On Metapsychology: The Theory of Psychoanalysis*, trans. James Strachey, Penguin Freud Library, vol. 11, gen. ed. Angela Richards (London: Penguin, 1984), pp. 245–68.

Godwin, William, *Caleb Williams* [1794], ed. David McCracken (Oxford: Oxford University Press, 1977).

Goldsmith, Oliver, *The Vicar of Wakefield* [1766], ed. Arthur Friedman, with an introduction and notes by Robert L. Mack, World's Classics (Oxford: Oxford University Press, 2006).

Gray, Thomas, *Elegy Written in a Country Churchyard* [1751], in Roger Lonsdale (ed.), *The Poems of Thomas Gray, William Collins, Oliver Goldsmith* (London: Longman, 1969).

—— *Letters*, ed. Paget Toynbee and Leonard Whibley (Oxford: Oxford University Press, 1935).

Green, Matthew, *The Spleen, and Other Poems* with a Prefatory Essay by J. Aikin, M.D. (London: Printed for T. Cadell, junr. and W. Davies, [1737] 1796).

Harrold, Edmund, *The Diary of Edmund Harrold, Wigmaker of Manchester 1712–1715*, ed. Craig Horner (Aldershot and Burlington, Vermont: Ashgate, 2008).

Hartley, David, *Observations on Man, His Frame, His Duty, and his Expectations*, 2 vols (London: James Leake and William Frederick, 1749).

Haslam, John, *Observations on Insanity* (London: Rivingtons, 1798).

Hays, Mary, *The Victim of Prejudice* [1799], ed. Eleanor Ty (Peterborough, Ontario: Broadview Press, 1994).

Hill, John, *Hypochondriasis: A Practical Treatise* [1766], ed. G. S. Rousseau (Los Angeles: Augustan Reprint Society, no. 135, 1966).

Hogg, James, *The Private Memoirs and Confessions of a Justified Sinner* [1824], ed. John Carey (Oxford: Oxford University Press, 1990).

Hume, David, *A Treatise of Human Nature* [1739–40], ed. David Fate Norton and Mary J. Norton (Oxford: Oxford University Press, 2001).

Ingram, Allan (ed.), *Voices of Madness: Four Pamphlets, 1683–1796* (Stroud: Sutton Publishing, 1997).

Johnson, Samuel, *The Complete English Poems*, ed. J. D. Fleeman (London: Penguin, 1971).

—— *A Dictionary of the English Language* (London: W. Strahan et al., 1755).

—— *The History of Rasselas, Prince of Abissinia* [1759], ed. Paul Goring (London: Penguin, 2007).

—— *Letters of Samuel Johnson*, ed. Bruce Redford, The Hyde Edition, 5 vols (Oxford: Oxford University Press, 1994).

—— *Lives of the English Poets* [1779–81], ed. George Birkbeck Hill, vol. 1 (Oxford: Clarendon Press, 1905).

—— *The Rambler, The Yale Edition of the Works of Samuel Johnson*, ed. W. J. Bate and Albrecht B. Strauss (New Haven: Yale University Press, 1958–).

—— *The works of Samuel Johnson, LL.D. A new edition, In twelve volumes. With an essay on his life and genius, by Arthur Murphy*, 12 vols (London: printed for T. Longman, B. White and Son, B. Law, J. Dodsley, H. Baldwin, 1792).

Jonson, Ben, *The Complete Plays*, ed. F. E. Schelling, 2 vols (London: Dent, 1964).

Keats, John, *John Keats: The Complete Poems*, ed. John Barnard, 2nd edn (Harmondsworth: Penguin, 1977).

Law, William, *A Serious Call to a Devout and Holy Life* (London: William Innys, 1729).

Lawlor, Clark, and Akihito Suzuki (eds), *Literature and Science, 1660–1834*, Part I, Vol. 2: *Sciences of Body and Mind* (London:Pickering & Chatto, 2003).

Locke, John, *Essays on the Law of Nature... together with Transcripts from Locke's Shorthand in his Journal for 1676*, ed. W. von Leydon (Oxford: Clarendon Press, 1970).

Lonsdale, Roger (ed.), *Eighteenth-Century Women Poets* (Oxford: Oxford University Press, 1990).

—— *The Poems of Thomas Gray, William Collins, Oliver Goldsmith*, Longmans' Annotated English Poets (London: Longman, 1969).

Mandeville, Bernard, *Fable of the Bees; or Private Vices Publick Benefits* (London: J. Roberts, 1714).

—— *Treatise of Hypochondriack and Hysterick Passions* (London: printed for the Author, 1711).

—— *A Treatise of the Hypochondriack and Hysterick Diseases* [1730], 2nd edn, intro. Stephen H. Good (New York: Scholars' Facsimiles and Reprints, 1976).

Milton, John, *Complete Shorter Poems*, ed. John Carey, Longman Annotated English Poets (London: Longman, 1978).

—— *Poems Upon Several Occasions, English, Italian, and Latin, With Translations, by John Milton*, with notes critical and explanatory, and other illustrations, by Thomas Warton (London: Printed for J. Dodsley, 1785).

Montaigne, Michel de, *The Essays of Michael Seigneur de Montaigne, Translated into English, 4 Volumes, 8th Edition* (Dublin: James Potts, 1760).

Norris, John, *A Collection of Miscellanies: Consisting of Poems, Essays, Discourses, and Letters, Occasionally Written* (Oxford, 1687); facs. edn (New York and London: Garland, 1978).

Parnell, Thomas, *Poems on Several Occasions*, ed. Alexander Pope (London: Printed for B. Lintot, 1722).

Peterson, Dale (ed.), *A Mad People's History of Madness* (Pittsburgh: University of Pittsburgh Press, 1982).

Pomfret, John, *Miscellany Poems, On Several Occasions* (London: Printed for John Place, 1702).

Pope, Alexander, *The Poems of Alexander Pope: A One-volume Edition of the Twickenham Text, with Selected Annotations*, ed. John Butt (London: Methuen, 1963).

—— *The Rape of the Lock and Other Poems* [1714], ed. Geoffrey Tillotson, Twickenham Edition, vol. 2 (London and New York: Routledge, 1993).

—— *The Twickenham Edition of the Poems of Alexander Pope*, ed. John Butt, 11 vols (London: Methuen, 1939–69).

Richardson, Samuel, *Clarissa: Or, The History of a Young Lady* [1747–48], ed. Angus Ross (London: Penguin, 1985).

—— *Pamela; Or, Virtue Rewarded* [1740], ed. Peter Sabor (Harmondsworth: Penguin, 1980).

Robinson, Nicholas, *A New System of the Spleen, Vapours, and Hypochondriack Melancholy* (London: A. Bettesworth, W. Innys and C. Rivington, 1729).

—— 'Of the Hypp', *Gentleman's Magazine*, 2 (November 1732), pp. 1062–4.

Rogers, Timothy, *A Discourse Concerning Trouble of Mind and the Disease of Melancholly* (London: Thomas Parkhurst and Thomas Cockerill, 1691).

Rowe, Elizabeth Singer, *The Works of Mrs. Elizabeth Rowe: including original poems and translations by Mr. T. Rowe. To which is added the life of the author*, 4 vols (London: John and Arthur Arch, 1796).

Shakespeare, William, *Hamlet* [1601?], ed. Harold Jenkins (London: Methuen, 1982).

Shaw, Peter, *The Juice of the Grape: or, Wine Preferable to Water* (London: W. Lewis, 1724).

—— *A New Practice of Physic* [1726] (London: Thomas Longman and Thomas Shewell, 6th edn, 1745), 2 vols.

—— *The Reflector: Representing Human Affairs, As they are; and may be improved* (London: T. Longman, 1750).

Smith, Charlotte Turner, *The Collected Letters of Charlotte Smith*, ed. Judith Phillips Stanton (Bloomington, Indiana: Indiana University Press, 2003).

Smith, David Nichol (ed.), *The Oxford Book of Eighteenth Century Verse* (Oxford: Clarendon Press, 1926).

Sterne, Laurence, *The Life and Opinions of Tristram Shandy, Gentleman* [1759–67], ed. Ian Campbell Ross (Oxford: Oxford University Press, 1983).

—— *The Life and Opinions of Tristram Shandy, Gentleman* [1759–67], ed. Melvyn New and Joan New, with an introductory essay by Christopher Ricks (London: Penguin Books, 2003).

—— *A Sentimental Journey Through France and Italy* [1768], ed. Ian Jack (London: Oxford University Press, 1968).

—— *A Sentimental Journey through France and Italy* [1768], ed. Graham Petrie (Harmondsworth: Penguin, 1967).

Stukeley, William, *Of the Spleen, Its Description and History, Uses and Diseases, Particularly the Vapors, With Their Remedy* (London: Printed for the Author, 1723).

Styron, William, *Darkness Visible: A Memoir of Madness* (London: Jonathan Cape, 1991; repr. London: Vintage, 2001).

Swift, Jonathan, *Gulliver's Travels* [1726], ed. Claude Rawson (Oxford: Oxford University Press, 2005).

—— *Prose Writings*, ed. Herbert Davis et al., 14 vols (Oxford: Blackwell, 1939–74).

Thomson, James, *James Thomson (1700–1748): Letters and Documents*, ed. Alan Dugald McKillop (Lawrence, Kansas: University of Kansas Press, 1958).

—— *Liberty, The Castle of Indolence and Other Poems*, ed. James Sambrook (Oxford: Clarendon Press, 1986).

—— *The Seasons* [1730], ed. James Sambrook (Oxford: Oxford University Press, 1981).

Tissot, Samuel A., *Three Essays: First, On the Disorders of People of Fashion, Second, On Diseases Incidental to Literary and Sedentary Persons, Third, On Onanism: Or, a Treatise upon the Disorders produced by Masturbation: or, the Effects of Secret and Excessive Venery*, trans. Francis Bacon Lee, M. Danes, A. Hume, M.D. (Dublin: James Williams, 1772).

Trosse, George, *The Life of the Reverend Mr. George Trosse* [1714], ed. A. W. Brink (Montreal: McGill-Queen's University Press, 1974).

Trotter, Thomas, *A View of the Nervous Temperament; being a practical enquiry into the increasing prevalence, prevention, and treatment of those diseases commonly called nervous, bilious, stomach and liver complaints; indigestion; low spirits; gout, etc*, 2nd edn (London: Printed by Edw. Walker, Newcastle, for Longman, Hurst, Rees, and Orme, 1807).

Tuke, Samuel, *Description of The Retreat, An Institution Near York* [1813], ed. Richard Hunter and Ida MacAlpine (London: Dawsons, 1964).

Walsh, R., 'The Life of Dr Cotton', in *The Works of the British Poets, with Lives of the Authors* (Boston, Massachusetts: Charles Ewer and Timothy Bedlington, 1822), vol. 35, pp. 313–17.

Warton, Joseph, *The Enthusiast or the Lover of Nature* (London: R. Dodsley, 1744).

—— *Odes on Various Subjects* (London: R. Dodsley, 1746).

Warton, Thomas, *The Pleasures of Melancholy. A Poem* (London: R. Dodsley, 1747).

—— *The Pleasures of Melancholy* [1747; 1755], in David Fairer and Christine Gerrard (eds), *Eighteenth-Century Poetry: An Annotated Anthology* (Oxford and Malden, Massachusetts: Blackwell, 1999), pp. 367–74.

Williams, Helen Maria, *Poems*, 2 vols (London: Thomas Cadell, 1786).

Willis, Thomas, *Two Discourses Concerning the Soul of Brutes*, ed. Samuel Pordage (London: Dring, Harper and Leight, 1683).

Wolpert, Lewis, *Malignant Sadness: The Anatomy of Depression*, 3rd edn (London: Faber and Faber, 2006).

Woodward, John, *Select Cases, and Consultations, in Physick* (London: The Royal Society, 1757).

Wordsworth, Dorothy, *The Grasmere and Alfoxden Journals*, ed. Pamela Woof (Oxford: Oxford University Press, 2002).

Wordsworth, William, *The Poetical Works of William Wordsworth*, ed. E. de Selincourt, 5 vols, 2nd edn (Oxford: Clarendon Press, 1952).

Wordsworth, William, and S. T. Coleridge, *Lyrical Ballads* [1798], 2nd edn, ed. R. L. Brett and A. R. Jones (London and New York: Routledge, 1991).

Young, Edward, *Cynthio: On the Death of John Brydges, Marquis of Carnarvon* (London: Printed for J. Roberts in Warwick-Lane, 1727).

—— *Edward Young: 'Night Thoughts'* [1742–46], ed. Stephen Cornford (Cambridge: Cambridge University Press, 1989).

—— *Edward Young's 'Conjectures on Original Composition'* [1759], ed. Edith J. Morley (Manchester: Manchester University Press, 1918).

Young, George, *A Treatise on Opium, Founded upon Practical Observations* (London: A. Millar, 1753).

Secondary sources

Alvarez, A., 'Introduction', in Laurence Sterne, *A Sentimental Journey through France and Italy* [1768], ed. Graham Petrie (Harmondsworth: Penguin, 1967), pp. 7–19.

Amend, Anne, 'Mélancolie', in Michel Delon (ed.), *Dictionnaire européen des Lumières* (Paris: Presses Universitaires de France, 1997), pp. 698–701.

Anderson, Linda, *Autobiography* (London: Routledge, 2001).

Anselment, Raymond A., 'Elizabeth Freke's Remembrances: Reconstructing a Self', *Tulsa Studies in Women's Literature*, 16:1 (1997), pp. 57–75.

Appleyard, Bryan, 'Have we lost all reason?', *Sunday Times* (5 July 2009), 'Culture', p. 45.

Babb, Lawrence, *The Elizabethan Malady. A Study of Melancholia in English Literature from 1580 to 1642* (East Lansing, Michigan: Michigan State College Press, 1951).

Barker, Hannah, 'Soul, Purse and Family: Middling and Lower-Class Masculinity in Eighteenth-Century Manchester', *Social History*, 33:1 (2008), pp. 12–35.

Barker-Benfield, G. J., *The Culture of Sensibility: Sex and Society in Eighteenth-Century Britain* (London: Routledge, 1992).

Barrell, John, 'The Uses of Dorothy: "The Language of the Sense" in "Tintern Abbey"', *Poetry, Language and Politics* (Manchester: Manchester University Press, 1988).

Barros, Carolyn A., *Autobiography: Narrative of Transformation* (Ann Arbor, Michigan: The University of Michigan Press, 1988).

Battestin, Martin C., with Ruthe R. Battestin, *Henry Fielding: A Life* (London: Routledge, 1989).

Bentall, Richard, *Doctoring the Mind: Why Psychiatric Treatments Fail* (London: Allen Lane, 2009).

Benveniste, Émile, 'Remarques sur la fonction du langage dans la découverte freudienne', *Problèmes de linguistique générale 1* (Paris: Gallimard, 1966).

Benwell, Bethan, and Elizabeth Stokoe, *Discourse and Identity* (Edinburgh: Edinburgh University Press, 2006).

Blodgett, Harriet, *Centuries of Female Days: Englishwomen's Private Diaries* (New Brunswick, New Jersey: Rutgers University Press, 1967).

Bonnefoy, Yves, 'La mélancolie, la folie, le génie – la poésie', in Jean Clair (ed.), *Mélancolie, génie et folie en Occident* (Paris: Réunion des musées nationaux/Gallimard, 2005), pp. 14–22.

Botonaki, Effie, 'Early Modern Women's Diaries and Closets', in Dan Doll and Jessica Munns (eds), *Recording and Reordering: Essays on the Seventeenth- and*

Eighteenth-Century Diary and Journal (Lewisberg, Pennsylvania: Bucknell University Press, 2006), pp. 43–64.

Bourdieu, Pierre, 'The Forms of Cultural Capital', in J. G. Richardson (ed.), *Handbook for Theory and Research for the Sociology of Education*, trans. R. Nice (New York: Greenwood Press, 1986), pp. 241–58.

Brady, Andrea, *English Funerary Elegy in the Seventeenth Century: Laws in Mourning* (Basingstoke: Palgrave, now Palgrave Macmillan, 2006).

Bree, Linda, *Sarah Fielding* (New York: Twayne, 1998).

Brennan, Tad, *The Stoic Life: Emotions, Duties and Fate* (Oxford: Clarendon Press, 2005).

Buie, Diane, 'Melancholy and the Idle Lifestyle in the Eighteenth Century', PhD thesis (University of Northumbria, 2010).

Byrd, Max, *Visits to Bedlam* (Columbia, South Carolina: University of South Carolina Press, 1974).

Camden, Vera J., 'Blasphemy and the Problem of Self in *Grace Abounding*', *Bunyan Studies*, 1:2 (1989), pp. 5–21.

Clemit, Pamela, *The Godwinian Novel: The Rational Fictions of Godwin, Brockden Brown, Mary Shelley* (Oxford: Clarendon Press, 1993).

Culler, Jonathan, *The Pursuit of Signs: Semiotics, Literature, Deconstruction* (London: Routledge & Kegan Paul, 1981).

Curtis, Laura A., *The Elusive Daniel Defoe* (London and Totowa, New Jersey: Vision Press and Barnes and Noble, 1984).

Dawson, Lesel, *Lovesickness and Gender in Early Modern English Literature* (Oxford: Oxford University Press, 2008).

Delaney, Paul, *British Autobiography in the Seventeenth Century* (London: Routledge & Kegan Paul, 1969).

Delon, Michel (ed.), *Dictionnaire européen des Lumières* (Paris: Presses Universitaires de France, 1997).

Essick, Robert N., and Morton D. Paley, 'Introduction: The Poet in the Graveyard', *Robert Blair's 'The Grave' Illustrated by William Blake: A Study with Facsimile* (London: Scolar Press, 1982).

Faubert, Michelle, *Rhyming Reason: The Poetry of Romantic-Era Psychologists* (London: Pickering and Chatto, 2009).

Ferguson, Harvie, *Religious Transformation in Western Society: The End of Happiness* (London: Routledge, 1992).

First, Michael B., Robert L. Spitzer, Miriam Gibbon and Janet B. W. Williams, *Structured Clinical Interview for DSM–IV Axis I Disorders – Clinician Version (SCID–CV)* (Washington DC: American Psychiatric Press, 1997).

Foucault, Michel, *The History of Sexuality, Vol. 1: An Introduction*, trans. Robert Hurley (New York: Vintage Books, 1980).

—— *Madness and Civilization* (Histoire de la folie, 1961), trans. Richard Howard (London: Routledge, 1967).

Freeman, Daniel, 'Health in Mind', *The Guardian* (25 July 2009), p. 6.

Gowland, Angus, 'The Problem of Early Modern Melancholy', *Past & Present*, 191:1 (2006), pp. 77–120.

Graham, Elspeth, ' "Oppression Makes a Wise Man Mad": The Suffering of the Self in Autobiographical Tradition', in Henk Dragstra, Sheila Ottway and Helen Wilcox (eds), *Betraying Our Selves: Forms of Self-Representation in Early Modern English Texts* (London and New York: Macmillan/St. Martins Press, 2000), pp. 197–214.

Green, Peter, ' "Job's Whole Stock of Asses": The Fiction of Laurence Sterne and the Theodicy Debate', PhD thesis (Open University, 2010).

Greenberg, Gary, *Manufacturing Depression: The Secret History of a Modern Disease* (London: Bloomsbury, 2010).

Griffin, Dustin, 'Collins, William (1721–1759)', in *Oxford Dictionary of National Biography* (Oxford: Oxford University Press, 2004), vol. 12, pp. 738–40.

Groom, Nick, 'Chatterton, Thomas (1752–1770)', in *Oxford Dictionary of National Biography* (Oxford: Oxford University Press, 2004), vol. 11, pp. 235–42.

Guerrini, Anita, *Obesity and Depression: The Life and Times of George Cheyne* (Norman, Oklahoma: University of Oklahoma Press, 2000).

Hall, Mary S., 'On Light in Young's *Night Thoughts*', *Philological Quarterly*, 48 (1969), pp. 452–63.

Hindmarsh, D. Bruce, *The Evangelical Conversion Narrative: Spiritual Autobiography in Early Modern England* (Oxford: Oxford University Press, 2007).

Hinnant, Charles H., *The Poetry of Anne Finch: An Essay in Interpretation* (Newark, Delaware: University of Delaware Press; London and Toronto: Associated University Presses, 1994).

Hodgkin, Katharine, *Madness in Seventeenth-Century Autobiography* (London: Palgrave, now: Basingstoke: Palgrave Macmillan, 2007).

Horwitz, Allan V., and Jerome C. Wakefield, *The Loss of Sadness: How Psychiatry Transformed Normal Sorrow into Depressive Disorder* (Oxford: Oxford University Press, 2007).

Hunter, J. Paul, *The Reluctant Pilgrim: Defoe's Emblematic Method and Quest for Form in Robinson Crusoe* (Baltimore: Johns Hopkins University Press, 1966).

Hunter, Richard, and Ida Macalpine (eds), *Three Hundred Years of Psychiatry 1535–1860* (Oxford: Oxford University Press, 1961).

Ingram, Allan, *The Madhouse of Language: Writing and Reading Madness in the Eighteenth Century* (London: Routledge, 1991).

Irlam, Shaun, *Elations: The Poetics of Enthusiasm in Eighteenth-Century Britain* (Stanford, California: Stanford University Press, 1999).

Jack, Ian, 'Gray's *Elegy* Reconsidered', in Frederick W. Hilles and Harold Bloom (eds), *From Sensibility to Romanticism: Essays Presented to Frederick A. Pottle* (New York: Oxford University Press, 1965), pp. 139–69.

Jackson, Stanley W., 'Acedia the Sin and Its Relationship to Sorrow and Melancholia', in Arthur Kleinman and Byron Good (eds), *Culture and Depression: Studies in the Anthropology and Cross-cultural Psychiatry of Affect and Disorder* (Los Angeles and London: University of California Press, 1985), pp. 43–62.

—— *Melancholia and Depression: From Hippocratic Times to Modern Times* (New Haven: Yale University Press, 1986).

Jamison, Kay Redfield, *Touched with Fire: Manic-depressive Illness and the Artistic Temperament* (New York: Free Press, 1993).

—— *An Unquiet Mind: A Memoir of Moods and Madness* (New York: Alfred A. Knopf, 1995).

Jewson, N. D., 'The Disappearance of the Sick-Man from Medical Cosmology, 1770–1870', *Sociology*, 10 (1976), pp. 225–44.

Kleinman, Arthur, *Social Origins of Distress and Disease: Depression, Neurasthenia, and Pain in Modern China* (New Haven, Connecticut: Yale University Press, 1968).

Klibansky, Raymond, Erwin Panofsky and Fritz Saxl, *Saturn and Melancholy: Studies in the History of Natural Philosophy, Religion, and Art* (New York: Basic Books, 1964).

Lawlor, Clark, *Consumption and Literature: The Making of the Romantic Disease* (London and New York, now Basingstoke: Palgrave Macmillan, 2006).

Long, A. A., and D. N. Sedley, *The Hellenistic Philosophers*, 2 vols (Cambridge: Cambridge University Press, 1987).

McGovern, Barbara, *Anne Finch and Her Poetry: A Critical Biography* (Athens, Georgia, and London: The University of Georgia Press, 1992).

May, James E., 'Young, Edward (*bap.* 1683, *d.* 1765)', in *Oxford Dictionary of National Biography* (Oxford: Oxford University Press, 2004), vol. 60, pp. 882–7.

Mazzeo, Tilar, *Plagiarism and Literary Property in the Romantic Period* (Philadelphia: University of Pennsylvania Press, 2007).

Meek, Heather, 'Creative Hysteria and the Intellectual Woman of Feeling', *Before Depression: The Representation and Culture of Depression in Britain and Europe, 1660–1800 (Figures et culture de la dépression en Grande-Bretagne et en Europe, 1660–1800), European Spectator*, vol. 11, forthcoming.

Michaux, Henri, *Plume précédé de Lointain intérieur* (Paris: Gallimard, [1938] 1963).

Miller, Henry Knight, *Essays on Fielding's Miscellanies: A Commentary on Volume One* (Princeton, New Jersey: Princeton University Press, 1961).

Morris, David B., *Illness and Culture in the Postmodern Age* (Berkeley, California: University of California Press, 1998).

—— 'A Poetry of Absence', in John Sitter (ed.), *The Cambridge Companion to Eighteenth-Century Poetry* (Cambridge: Cambridge University Press, 2001), pp. 225–48.

Mullan, John, *Sentiment and Sociability: The Language of Feeling in the Eighteenth Century* (Oxford: Clarendon Press, 1988).

Newey, Vincent, *Cowper's Poetry: A Critical Study and Reassessment* (Liverpool: Liverpool University Press, 1982).

Norton, David Fate (ed.), *The Cambridge Companion to Hume* (Cambridge: Cambridge University Press, 1993).

Nussbaum, Felicity A., *The Autobiographical Subject: Gender and Ideology in Eighteenth-Century England* (Baltimore, Maryland, and London: Johns Hopkins University Press, 1989).

Ober, William B., 'Madness and Poetry: A Note on Collins, Cowper, and Smart' [1970], *Boswell's Clap and Other Essays: Medical Analyses of Literary Men's Afflictions* (Carbondale and Edwardsville, Illinois: Southern Illinois University Press, 1979), pp. 137–92.

Parisot, Eric, 'The Paths of Glory: Authority, Agency and Aesthetics in Mid-Eighteenth-Century Graveyard Poetry', unpublished PhD thesis (University of Melbourne, 2008).

Porter, Dorothy, and Roy Porter, *Patient's Progress: Doctors and Doctoring in Eighteenth-Century England* (London: Polity Press, 1989).

Porter, Roy, 'Introduction', in Thomas Trotter, *An Essay, Medical, Philosophical, and Chemical, on Drunkenness, and Its Effects on the Human Body* (London: Routledge, 1988), pp. ix–xl.

—— *Madmen: A Social History of Madhouses, Mad-Doctors & Lunatics* (Stroud: Tempus, 2004).

—— *Mind-Forg'd Manacles: A History of Madness in England from the Restoration to the Regency* (London: Athlone Press, 1987).

Porter, Roy (ed.), *Rewriting the Self: Stories from the Renaissance to the Present* (London and New York: Routledge, 1997).

Price, Cecil, *Theatre in the Age of Garrick* (Oxford: Basil Blackwell, 1973).

Radden, Jennifer, 'Is This Dame Melancholy?: Equating Today's Depression and Past Melancholia', *Philosophy, Psychiatry, & Psychology*, 2003, 10:1, pp. 37–52.

—— *Moody Minds Distempered. Essays on Melancholy and Depression* (Oxford: Oxford University Press, 2009).

Radden, Jennifer (ed.), *The Nature of Melancholy from Aristotle to Kristeva* (Oxford: Oxford University Press, 2000).

Reed, Amy Louise, *The Background of Gray's Elegy: A Study in the Taste for Melancholy Poetry, 1700–1751* (New York: Columbia University Press, 1924; New York: Russell and Russell, 1962).

Risse, Guenter B., 'Medicine in the Age of the Enlightenment', in Andrew Wear (ed.), *Medicine in Society: Historical Essays* (Cambridge: Cambridge University Press, 1992), pp. 149–98.

Rousseau, G. S., 'Nerves, Spirits, and Fibres: Towards Defining the Origins of Sensibility', in R. F. Brissenden and J. C. Eade (eds), *Studies in the Eighteenth Century* (Toronto: University of Toronto Press, 1976), pp. 137–57.

—— *Nervous Acts: Essays on Literature, Culture and Sensibility* (Basingstoke: Palgrave Macmillan, 2004).

Sams, Henry W., 'Anti-Stoicism in Seventeenth- and Eighteenth-Century England', *Studies in Philology*, 41 1 (1944), pp. 65–78.

Sant, Ann Jessie van, *Eighteenth-Century Sensibility and the Novel: The Senses in Social Context* (Cambridge: Cambridge University Press, 1993).

Schmidt, Jeremy, *Melancholy and the Care of the Soul: Religion, Moral Philosophy and Madness in Early Modern England* (Aldershot and Burlington, Vermont: Ashgate, 2007).

Scull, Andrew, *Hysteria: The Biography* (Oxford: Oxford University Press, 2009).

Sena, John F., 'The English Malady: The Idea of Melancholy from 1700–1760', PhD thesis (Princeton University, 1967).

—— 'Melancholy in Anne Finch and Elizabeth Carter: The Ambivalence of an Idea', in *The Yearbook of English Studies* (1971), vol. 1, pp. 108–19.

Sherman, Stuart, 'Diary and Autobiography', in John Richetti (ed.), *The Cambridge History of Literature 1660–1780* (Cambridge: Cambridge University Press, 2005), pp. 649–72.

Showalter, Elaine, *The Female Malady* (New York: Pantheon, 1987).

Sickels, Eleanor M., *The Gloomy Egoist: Moods and Themes of Melancholy from Gray to Keats* (New York: Columbia University Press, 1932).

Sim, Stuart, *Negotiations with Paradox: Narrative Practice and Narrative Form in Bunyan and Defoe* (Hemel Hempstead: Harvester Wheatsheaf, 1990).

Sitter, John, *Literary Loneliness in Mid-Eighteenth-Century England* (Ithaca, New York: Cornell University Press, 1982).

Sitter, John (ed.), *The Cambridge Companion to Eighteenth-Century Poetry* (Cambridge: Cambridge University Press, 2001).

Solomon, Andrew, *The Noonday Demon: An Anatomy of Depression* (London: Vintage, 2002).

Spencer, Jane, *Literary Relations: Kinship and the Canon 1660–1830* (Oxford: Oxford University Press, 2005).

Stachniewski, John, *The Persecutory Imagination: English Puritanism and the Literature of Religious Despair* (Oxford: Clarendon Press, 1991).

Starr, G. A., *Defoe and Spiritual Autobiography* (Princeton, New Jersey: Princeton University Press, 1965).

Swearingen, James E., *Reflexivity in Tristram Shandy: An Essay in Phenomenological Criticism* (New Haven, Connecticut, and London: Yale University Press, 1977).

Tallis, Frank, *Love Sick: Love as a Mental Illness* (London: Century, 2004).

Terry, Richard, *Mock-Heroic from Butler to Cowper: An English Genre and Discourse* (Aldershot and Burlington, Vermont: Ashgate, 2005).

—— 'Thomson and the Druids', in Richard Terry (ed.), *James Thomson: Essays for the Tercentenary* (Liverpool: Liverpool University Press, 2000), pp. 141–63.

Todd, Janet, *Sensibility: An Introduction* (London: Methuen, 1986).

Traugott, John, *Tristram Shandy's World: Sterne's Philosophical Rhetoric* (Berkeley and Los Angeles: University of California Press, 1954).

Van Os, J., et al., 'A Comparison of the Utility of Dimensional and Categorical Representations of Psychosis', *Psychological Medicine*, 29 (1999), pp. 595–606.

Vickers, Sally, 'See a psychiatrist? Are you mad?, *The Observer* (21 June 2009), p. 19.

Vila, Anne C., *Enlightenment and Pathology: Sensibility in the Literature and Medicine of Eighteenth-Century France* (Baltimore: Johns Hopkins University Press, 1998).

Wenzel, Siegfried, *The Sin of Sloth: Acedia in Medieval Thought and Literature* (Chapel Hill, North Carolina: University of North Carolina Press, 1967).

Willey, Basil, *The Eighteenth Century Background: Studies on the Idea of Nature in the Thought of the Period* (London: Chatto and Windus, [1940] 1963).

Wilson, Eric G., *Against Happiness: In Praise of Melancholy* (New York: Sarah Crichton Books, 2008).

Wray, Ramona, 'Depressive Patterns and Textual Solutions in Seventeenth-Century Women's Autobiography', conference paper presented at *Before Depression: The Representation and Culture of Depression in Britain and Europe, 1660–1800*, 19–21 June 2008, Northumbria University.

Index